RED GRASS RIVER

A LEGEND

James Carlos Blake

Perennial

An Imprint of HarperCollinsPublishers

Author's Note

The Ashley Gang is a historical reality. Most of the characters in this novel did exist, and most of its major events did take place. Still, this is a work of fiction, and those familiar with the facts about the Ashleys and the Florida of their time will discern the liberties I've taken with the record.

A hardcover edition of this book was published in 1998 by Avon Books, Inc.

RED GRASS RIVER. Copyright © 1998 by James Carlos Blake. All rights reserved. Printed in the United States of America. No part of this book may be used or reproduced in any manner whatsoever without written permission except in the case of brief quotations embodied in critical articles and reviews. For information address HarperCollins Publishers, 195 Broadway, New York, NY, 10007.

HarperCollins books may be purchased for educational, business, or sales promotional use. For information, please e-mail the Special Markets Department at SPsales@harpercollins.com.

First Perennial edition published 2000.

Designed by Kellan Peck

The Library of Congress has catalogued the hardcover edition as follows:
Blake, James Carlos.
    Red grass river : a legend / by James Carlos Blake.—1st ed.
      p.   cm.
    I. Title.
PS3552.L3483R43   1998   98-18692
813'.54—dc21   CIP

ISBN 0-380-79242-7 (pbk.)

HB 12.09.2022

For
Len Richardson
a good old boy and damn fine man . . .

and
the coterie of my Bowling Green days:
Fare ye well, gents and ladies, each and all.

As for man, his days are as grass: as a flower of the field, so he flourisheth.

For the wind passeth over it, and it is gone; and the place thereof shall know it no more.
—Psalms, 103:15

—

The terrible thing is, everyone has his reasons.
—Jean Renoir

PROLOGUE

The Liars Club

If THE DEVIL EVER RAISED A GARDEN THE EVERGLADES WAS IT. THE
biggest and meanest swamp you're ever like to see—bigger than
some entire states of the Union—it's pineywoods and palmetto
scrubs and cypress heads and tangled vines but mostly it's a river, a
river like no other on this earth. It's sixty miles wide and half-a-foot
deep and runs from Lake Okeechobee to the south end of the state
over a layer of muck thats got no bottom. The whole thing covered
with sawgrass sharp as a skinning razor. Not a thing else in that sawgrass country but here and there some hammocks—highground islands
of hardwoods and palms—and most of them never been set foot on.
Out there the world looks a whole lot bigger and there's no end at all
to the sky. They say it's hardly another place in the world where you
can look farther and see less. And all of it green of one shade or
another except at sunrise and in the dying light of day when that great
grass river goes so red it looks like it's on fire or stained with blood.

Only the godawful desperate or the plain goddamned could ever
live out there. It's ever kind of thing in the Everglades to cut you or
burn you or itch you or sting you or poison you or eat you up whole.
It's quicksand and gators and panthers and snakes and mosquitoes and
ever sort of bug in hell to drive you insane. In summer the air's so
hot and wet it's like trying to breathe boiled cotton. Lord only knows
what-all's been swallowed up in that rotten ooze under the sawgrass
and won't never again see the light of day. It's bones in that muck a

million years old and bones aint been there a week. Animal bones. Bones of men. It's ten thousand stories buried out there aint nobody heard but the devil.

Yessir, the Devil's Garden was as right a name as was ever give to any place there is. Even on today's maps you'll see the name on a portion of wildland just east of Immokalee. It was the early crackers who come up with the name—and big as the Glades is now, in them days it was even bigger and took in most of the region to either side of Lake Okeechobee. A cracker is somebody who grows up in the swamp country and provided his daily bread mostly by hunting and trapping, though some did a little hardscrabble farming, some a little cattle ranching, some a little of it all. The first of them to show up in Florida come from all over the South but most of them from Georgia. They got their name on account of the sound their whips made as they drove their stock ahead of them. Some of them latigo whips was so big they had to hold them with both hands. They cracked loud as rifleshots and you could hear them from miles away.

No white people ever knew the ways of the Devil's Garden better than the crackers. And no crackers knew them better than the Ashleys.

It's only a few of us oldtime crackers left anymore who go back that far and knew the Ashleys in the living flesh. I mean we're old, the bunch of us, old and aching ever kind of way and all of us needing a cane at the least and a couple of us a damn walker. Hardly a man among us dont wear specs as thick as bottle glass, or says "What?" ever time somebody says something to him, or can sleep through the night without having to get up a time or two to piss. But near all of us knew the Ashleys when we was kids, leastways knew them well enough to say "How-do" to and get a "Hey" in return, which was about as well as anybody who wasnt kin ever got to know an Ashley. They was a clannish family and hard to get to know personal, but we all of us saw one or another of them ever now and then, and we heard talk about them all the time.

We grew up hearing a hundred stories about the Ashleys and about John Ashley's gang and the crimes they did. We heard all about the bad blood between John Ashley and Bobby Baker and about the war the Ashleys had with Yankee bootleggers who tried to cut in on their territory. We heard a dozen versions of what happened at the Sebastian River Bridge when the gang was finally put to an end. We *still* tell them stories ever time we get together in the park to sun our old bones and pass the time and talk about something other than whether there's a Democrat alive who can win the next election.

The thing is, so many stories about the Ashley Gang have been told for so long by so many who have bent the facts so many ways that there's hardly no way of knowing anymore what's the true facts and what aint. It probly dont really matter all that much. Everybody knows that the plain and simple facts about something dont necessarily tell the truth of it. Some people can lie all day long with nothing but the facts, and what goes on in most courtrooms is proof enough of that. On the other hand, sometimes a story that stretches a fact here and there can tell more of the real truth of a thing as you're ever like to get. Leastways thats what the bunch of us think.

Our growed-up children tend to smile and wink at each other and shake their heads at the tales we tell, but there's been a bunch of old farts like us in barbershops and cafes and courthouse squares in ever town there ever was. That's for damn sure the way of it down South. Back when we was pups a bunch of graybeards used to sit around in the town square and tell stories about the War Between the States and the bad old days of Reconstruction and the doings of the Klan and such. Everybody used to call those oldtimers the Liars Club. And it's what everybody calls us too. . . .

ONE

December 1911

THE BOY POLED THE SKIFF ALONG THE WINDING SAWGRASS CHAN-
nel and heard now a faint chanting through the bird cries from
the hardwood hammock just ahead. He knew it was the Indian
come to meet him and that he was drunk and not alone. He let the
pushpole trail alongside the skiff and considered his circumstance as
the boat glided slowly through the sawgrass that stood higher than his
head. His father always said a drunk Indian could be the easiest delivery in a day's work or the most troublesome, depending on the Indian.
The boy knew this Indian for the troublesome sort. But if he shied
from making the delivery just because you never knew what a drunk
Indian might do his father would mock him for a nancy forever. He
spat into the sawgrass and leaned into the pole and pushed the skiff
ahead, feeling the comforting press of the revolver at his back where
it was tucked in his waistband under his loose shirt.

His name was John Ashley and he was eighteen years old.

In the west the high enpurpling sky showed streaks of orange and
reefs of red clouds flanking the lowering sun. To southeastward rose
a high black column of boiler smoke where a dredge was digging a
canal. This earlywinter's day had begun dry and almost cool but had
since assumed a hint of unseasonable rain. The air was sweet with
the smell of swampwater and vegetation, with the redolence of the
approaching hammock's ripe earth under the canopy of magnolia and
gumbo limbo trees. Even if there had been some elevated vantage point

as near as fifty yards of him from which an observer might scan the vast encircling vista of sawgrass and scattered hardwood hammocks and pine islands (and the only such vantage points were the tops of the hammock trees where at this hour the birds were coming to clamorous roost), the observer would not have spied either the channel or his movement through it, so high was the grass and so narrow the waterway and so smoothly did he navigate it. Only a circling fish hawk high overhead bore witness to his progress.

The Indians' chanting ceased as he poled into the shadowed green light under the heavy hardwood overhang and the sawgrass fell away and the canoe carried into the natural moat of copper-colored water that girt the hammock. The roosting birds were quieting now. Their droppings shook leaves on the lower branches, flashed whitely to the ground, poked ripples in the pool. The hammock rang with the croaking of frog colonies. He made toward a rough-sloped mudbank where the root vegetation had been hacked away to shape a landing for canoes.

He smelled the Indians before he caught sight of them in their baggy white shirts and black bowler hats on the higher ground in the darkness of the trees. Two of them. Sitting crosslegged and watching him and passing a jug between them. At the edge of the landing a single long dugout was tethered to a jutting root and now the scent of the otter skins piled within carried to him under the smell of the Indians. The water surface shattered lightly as a school of fingerlings broke away from a rushing bass.

He pulled hard on the pole and the prow bumped up onto the muddy landing and the skiff's abrupt halt shook the wooden cases nestled toward the bow and there was a clinking of jug on jug. The smaller of the Indians grinned whitely. Mosquitoes raged at the boy's ears. A gray haze of them quivered about the Indians' heads without settling on their skins. He spotted a shotgun propped against a tree behind the Indians but saw only knives on their belts.

"We been hearin you from a mile off," the bigger Indian said. His voice was wetly raw. "Been hearin you comin like a fucken steamboat."

John Ashley doubted that. This big one—whose name was DeSoto Tiger and who resold to other Indians in the deeper Glades most of the moonshine he bought from the boy's father—was said by some to be a good man who took after his daddy and his uncle, both of whom were chiefs in local Seminole tribes. But John Ashley knew him for a mean drunk and had for years heard terrible stories about him. He was said to have beaten a wife to death for infidelity and to have cut the dick off the man who put the horns on him. He was said to have drowned a Negro in a creek for trying to steal his traps. The boy's father had told him that most of those stories were lies DeSoto Tiger had himself concocted to keep other Indians in fear of him. But other white men believed the big Indian was every bit the bad actor his reputation held.

John Ashley had known him only to nod to until almost a year ago when he and his daddy had come on him one day at Blue's store on Lake Towhee and the Indian asked the boy if he wanted to go for alligator hides in the Okaloosa sloughs with him on shares. He said he wanted a white partner so he could get a better price for the hides on the New River trading dock and he'd heard the boy was a good enough skinner to go shares with. John Ashley had turned to his father who affected to study the clouds in the distance. He did not really want to work shares with the Indian but he wanted to show his father he was not afraid of DeSoto Tiger. He told the Indian he'd do it if he would agree to take no whiskey on the hunt. His daddy had smiled without looking their way and DeSoto Tiger laughed and said that was fine, he anyway never drank when he was working.

They'd gone south with a string of four empty dugouts and over the next fortnight killed gators through the nights and skinned the carcasses through the mornings and slept through the afternoons and did not talk much the whole time. They piled three of the dugouts high with hides and another with the tailmeat, which they could readily sell in the Negro parts of town. En route to the trading docks they came upon a whiskey peddler and the Indian bought a quart bottle. John Ashley gave him a look and the Indian said, "Hell, boy, the work's done."

When they arrived at the New River trading post DeSoto Tiger was drunk. Their boat no sooner bumped up to the dock than the Indian spied a tribesman named Henry Little Bear who he believed had been trying to steal his sweetheart's affections. A loud row ensued and knives came into play and it required several dockhands to subdue the big Indian and hold him until the police arrived and took him away to jail. Henry Little Bear was sopping with blood as he was borne to the nearest doctor with his belly gashed and most of his nose missing and half his face flensed to the skull. Like the other witnesses John Ashley had been impressed by DeSoto Tiger's spectacular proficiency with a knife. For the next few days the talk on the docks was of little else but the Indian fight. The boy sold the hides and put aside the Indian's half of the proceeds.

Because Henry Little Bear didnt die but had only been mutilated—and because DeSoto Tiger's father and uncle were chiefs in the regional Seminole confederation and often proved of assistance to the white authorities in their Indian dealings—and because the law didnt much care what Indians did to each other anyway as long as they didnt disturb decent white folk by it, DeSoto Tiger was obliged to serve but ten days in the county lockup. When the Indian got out of jail John Ashley retrieved his share of the gatorhide money and met him at Blue's store and turned it over to him. DeSoto Tiger stared at the money and then at the boy, his eyes hard with accusation. John Ashley took insult and told him he could check the price he'd got with Mister Williams, the hide buyer. The Indian said he knew better than to ask any white man for the truth. He spat on the ground between them and stuffed the money in his pocket and stalked away.

They did not see each other again until three months ago when the boy's father sent him to make delivery to this hammock in the sawgrass country southeast of Lake Okeechobee, one of several way-camps DeSoto Tiger was reputed to have in the region. Although John Ashley had told none but his brother Bob of the Indian's accusation that he'd cheated him, his father seemed aware that his brief partnership with DeSoto Tiger had not concluded well, and yet sent him to deliver to the Indian anyway, maybe for that reason. His father wasn't one to explain his actions but he'd always told John Ashley and his brothers that the only way to deal with bulls of any sort was to take them by the horns. The boy had been apprehensive on that first delivery but the big Indian had affected remoteness and made no mention of the last time they'd seen each other and their transaction was brief and without incident. Thus had they carried on in every meeting since and the boy was content to have it that way.

This was the first time the Indian had shown up drunk. John Ashley saw that the jug the Indians were hefting was not one of his father's. He stepped out of the skiff and nodded at the jug in DeSoto Tiger's crooked finger and said, "Hope you boys aint switchin to another supplier. We'd hate to lose you all's business."

DeSoto Tiger stared at the jug as if he'd only just noticed it. The other Indian laughed and said hell no, they weren't switching, they'd found the jug just laying there in the scrub. The Indians looked at each other and laughed. Shit, John Ashley thought, one drunk Indian's bad enough and here I got two.

"Hell, boy, we dont drink nothin but your daddy's wyome," the smaller Indian said, using the Indian word for whiskey. "Everbody knows Old Joe's stuff is the goodest." This one's name was Jimmy Gopher and he was a halfbreed as much scorned by Indians as by whites. John Ashley knew him for a mediocre trapper and truckling friend to DeSoto Tiger. "We don't buy no shine cept your daddy's," Jimmy Gopher said. He stood up and came to the skiff and peered at the two cases inside and grinned.

John Ashley hefted each case in turn and set it on the ground and looked at DeSoto Tiger who still sat crosslegged. The Indian looked back at him for a long moment and then withdrew a clump of bills from inside his shirt and handed it up to Jimmy Gopher who passed it to the boy. The money was damp and pungent with the smell of Indian. John Ashley counted it carefully and then folded it neatly and put it in his pocket. "Well," he said, turning to the skiff, "see you next month."

"Have a drink fore you go," DeSoto Tiger said, and got to his feet as lightly as rising smoke. He stood a head taller than the boy who was himself nearly six feet. He wore his bowler tilted forward so the narrow brim shadowed his eyes.

"Sorry," John Ashley said, "but I got to get."

"Heard you sold a bunch a egret feathers to Burris' Store in Palm Beach," the big Indian said. "For good money."

John Ashley looked at him, then at Jimmy Gopher and then back at DeSoto Tiger. "I sell plumes sometimes," he said. "Everybody knows that."

"Heard you took them birds over by Pahokee Slough," DeSoto Tiger said. His face held no hint of fellowship. "Everybody knows Pahokee Slough's my bird ground. *That's* what everybody knows."

Only now did John Ashley perceive that the Indian was drunker than he'd thought. He wished his brother Bob was with him. Bob always offered to come along on the deliveries to the Indians and John Ashley always said no, he could make the drops himself. And his daddy always looked at him from the head of the supper table and smiled.

"Aint nobody got a deed to no rookery," he said, showing a grin and instantly chiding himself for it. You aint scared of this sonofabitch, he told himself, dont even wonder if you are.

The big Indian took a step toward him. "I wonder did you go shares with anybody in them feathers," he said, "and I wonder how much did you cheat him on them."

Jimmy Gopher leaned on a tree, grinning, watching with bright eyes. He'd opened one of the shine jugs and was sipping from it off his elbow.

DeSoto Tiger drew his knife from its belt sheath and affected to strop it on his shirtsleeve as he smiled thinly at John Ashley. The boy had a fleeting vision of Henry Little Bear weighted with his own bloody clothes as he was carried off the New River dock. He put his hand behind him and under his shirt and around the pistol grips.

The Indian grinned and stepped nearer to the boy. "What you got there, whitedove? A bible? A *weapon*?" He took another step toward him and John Ashley pulled out the pistol, a single-action Colt .44, and cocked it and pointed it outstretched at DeSoto Tiger's chest. "Quit right there," he said.

He'd never before pointed a loaded firearm at anyone but he had several times seen it done. He'd seen his first mankilling at age seven when Porter Longtree shot Morris Jones through the eye on the front steps of Kennison's Store. There had long been bad blood between the two men and the general opinion of the killing was fairly summed up by John Ashley's daddy when he said it couldnt have ended any other way and whichever of them got killed for sure had it coming. John Ashley had since witnessed other acts of bloodletting and seen other men killed and could not have named an acquaintance who had not. And now, pointing the .44 at DeSoto Tiger, he was pleased to feel no tremor in his gunhand even as he felt his pulse thumping in his dry throat.

DeSoto Tiger raised his hands and said, "*Whoa* now, boy." He laughed and said, "Dont you know when you being *wolfed*?" He lowered his hands and shook his head, still grinning. He looked at Jimmy Gopher whose smile had gone weak. "Boy thought we was *serious*."

Jimmy Gopher's laugh was hollow. His eyes had gone skittish.

John Ashley lowered the gun, still unsure of the moment.

"We had you goin, huh?" the big Indian said. "Should see your face. Hell, I bet you'd jump five feet if I did *this*." The Indian feinted with the knife and the boy jumped back and lost his footing on the slick landing and staggered into the water up to his knees and regained his balance and again pointed the gun at DeSoto Tiger.

"*Easy* now," DeSoto Tiger said, laughing and raising a placatory palm. "See how we got you goin? Hell, boy, we just funnin. You dont want to shoot somebody's just *funnin*." He stepped forward and put his hand out to John Ashley and said, "Come on out the water."

He gave his free hand to the Indian and DeSoto Tiger's fingers locked around his wrist. Jimmy Gopher called "Hey Johnny" and as he turned to look at him the big one yanked him off-balance and he knew the knife was coming and he lunged sideways and felt the blade nick his neck. The big Indian's hold was iron and the blade was on its backswing and all in the same instant the boy turned his head aside and shoved the pistol against the Indian and the knife cut through his cheek as he pulled the trigger. DeSoto Tiger grunted and fell away.

The pistol blast raised a great wingbeating cloud of shrilling white egrets off the trees. John Ashley swung the pistol toward the tree where he'd seen the shotgun and saw that the gun was still there and he caught a flash of Jimmy Gopher's white shirt as the Indian vanished into the deeper hardwoods.

DeSoto Tiger was sitting in water to his chest with his hands clasped to his stomach, staring down at the blood rising darkly to the surface.

John Ashley slogged up onto the bank and retrieved the Indians' shotgun and took it to his skiff and laid it inside. Then heard an agitation of water behind him and turned to see DeSoto Tiger looming huge and brightly bloodstained at his belly, his face contorted with malice as he came with one hand clawing for him and the other brandishing the knife. John Ashley shot him in the chest and the Indian stopped short and took a step back and then started for him again and the boy fired into his face and the Indian's head jerked and his bowler tumbled from his head and he did a wobbly sidestep and fell on the sloping bank and slid in the mud to the edge of the water and under the dark hole in his forehead his open eyes held no light at all.

John Ashley felt of the cuts on his neck and cheek and neither was severe. He packed mud in the wounds to stanch the bleeding. A riot of sensations churned in his chest. He looked on the dead man and felt a confusing tangle of regret and exultation. Then said aloud: "Try to cut *my* head off. You damn well had it comin."

It took a while for his pounding heart to slow, his breathing to ease.

He set the two cases of whiskey back in the skiff—and then paused to consider. He went to the Indians' dugout and in the last light of day saw that the pelts were prime quality. They could not belong to a dead man nor to any who abandoned them. He brought the bow of the Indian dugout around and tied it to a stern ring on his skiff with a short length of line. He thought of going through DeSoto Tiger's pockets but could not bring himself to touch the body.

Then he was poling hard in the sawgrass channel and making away into a moonless night black as ink but for a blazing spangle of stars.

*　　*　　*

Later that night the stars dimmed and then disappeared altogether behind a massing of clouds in which lightning at first shimmered soundlessly and then began to be trailed closely by low rumblings. The wind roused, gained force and began pushing hard against the sawgrass. The hammock palms tossed and clattered. The susurrous hardwoods swayed. An incandescent flash of lightning made a ghostly blue noon of the night and illuminated the shadowed corpse of DeSoto Tiger sprawled on the bank of the hammock with face up to the first sprinkles of rain, eyesockets freshly hollowed by a possum and teeming with ants at their ancient industry.

Now lightning jagged across the sky and thunder blasted close behind and the rain came crashing down, shaking the sawgrass, pocking the water. Lightning branched blue-white across the black sky. The sawgrass quivered under the explosive thunder as the storm rolled hard into the Everglades. Rain fell in a steady torrent and the water rose on the bank and after a time the dead man bobbed off the ground and was borne slowly from the hammock and out into the sawgrass channel. The body carried on the winding current all through the night and all the next day and then for two days more until it debouched onto the Okeechobee Slough and in another two days arrived at a canal being dredged to Fort Lauderdale. The corpse bloated now, blackened and malodorous, faceless for having been fed upon by birds, its ears and fingers gone to garfish.

Near noon of that day it was scooped up with a load of muck and the dredge operator saw the legs overhanging the crane bucket and he deposited the load on the bank and called to his fellows to come see what he found.

TWO

February 1912

SHE WAS A BOBHAIRED SEVENTEEN-YEAR-OLD BLONDE WITH FULL
breasts and smoothly round hips and a wide sensual mouth. And
she was blind. She'd shown up at Miss Lillian's house in the
tenderloin district of West Palm Beach eight months ago in the company of a stranger named Benson who drove a brand new Model T.
This Benson raised eyebrows by leaving her to sit in the parlor and be
leered at by other patrons who jutted their chins at her and grinned
and winked at each other while he took his pleasure with one of the
girls upstairs. When he was done with his business he raised brows
higher still by getting his hat and slipping out the side door and aban-
doning her. The girl cried less about it than one might have expected.
She told Miss Lillian her name was Loretta May and that Benson had
proved himself a son of a bitch in so many ways already that this
further proof came as no surprise. But she said she'd rather starve out
in the road than return to Atlanta and the only living kin she had, a
sister she hated who'd grudgingly taken care of her for all seven years
she'd been blind due to a swiftly degenerative disease of the retina.
"Only reason I run off with the likes of Benson is I couldn't stand
another day more with Berniece," she said.

Miss Lillian felt sorry for her and offered to let her stay in a small
room off the kitchen in exchange for whatever light housekeeping she
might manage in her handicap. The girl said she never was much of
one for housekeeping even when she could see what she was doing

but she'd never been much of a shrinking violet either and one thing she knew she could do real well even blind was what she'd been doing with Benson in hotels every night since leaving Atlanta. She reasoned that from now on she might as well get paid for it and asked outright and with blushing cheeks if Miss Lillian was of a mind to hire her to work upstairs. Miss Lillian had already favorably appraised the girl's pretty face and fine figure but she'd never worked with a blind girl before. She was sure some men wouldn't care at all for a girl who couldn't see what they were made of. Still, she liked this girl and was impressed with her grit, so she said, "Loretta May, honey, welcome to the house." And although the madam been right that some of her patrons wouldn't even consider humping the blind newcomer, others did it at least once just to see what it was like, and some of them liked it so much they wanted her every time thereafter. The girl more than earned her keep.

Among those who favored her was John Ashley. He'd been patronizing Miss Lillian's since turning sixteen some two yeas before and the madam was fond of him and thought him handsome with his mop of black hair and wide amused mouth, his quick lively eyes that seemed to miss nothing. His visits were irregular but whenever he presented himself early in the week when the house's business was at its slowest, Miss Lillian would let him have the whole night with Loretta May for the bargain rate of five dollars.

He liked that Loretta May's skin smelled naturally of peaches and her short yellow hair was always freshly washed. She was the cleanest woman he'd ever put hand to, by far the best natured, the most ardent in the practice of her trade. He mentioned this last to her one time and she'd giggled and told him she was not so enthusiastic with others as with him. He thought she was lying but he could not deny the pleasure he took in the lie. Nor could he deny to himself how much he liked that she could not see him looking on her nakedness. He would often caress one part of her even as he secretly gawped upon another. Because she could not know where his gaze was set or see his face and whatever unguarded yearnings might show there, he felt possessed of a strange and keenly exciting power. But her defenselessness against his eyes also made him feel vaguely ashamed, and the way she sometimes smiled as he caressed her made him suspect she sensed his shame and that her knowledge of it gave her a kind of power too. His times with her were the best he'd had with a woman.

One cool Monday evening he arrived at Miss Lillian's in the company of his brother Bob, who never tired of chiding him for sporting with the same girl on every visit. "Might's well get married, you gone do *that*," Bob had said to him more than once. He himself insisted on a different whore every time and sometimes would enjoy two of them on a single visit, sometimes in the same bed, sometimes by turn, but in any case he kept strict account of his rotation among girls of the house. The only girl he did not include in the rotation was Loretta May, whom he'd tried once and then no more. "She's a fine-lookin thing, but it aint no real fun in it if the woman cant see Captain Kidd standin tall," he said, referring to his member by the name he'd given it when he was twelve years old.

As John rapped on the door with the horseshoe knocker that hung there, Bob said it was feeling like a two-time night to him. They were admitted to the plush red-satined parlor by a husky and jovial moon-faced man named Easton whose duty it was to defend the house tranquillity against troublesome patrons. Miss Lillian greeted the brothers affectionately and they nodded hello to Sherman the Negro piano player and to a derbied man they knew who worked at the train depot. The only others in the parlor were a pair of strangers in suits and ties—one burly, one lean—who sat on a sofa with a couple of girls and looked with urban disdain at the brothers in their faded denim and worn brogans. In their eagerness to get upstairs the Ashleys paid them no heed. A minute later Bob was ensconced in a room with a greeneyed girl named Sheryl Ann and John Ashley was rapping lightly on Loretta May's door and hearing her call, "Get on *in* here, you bad old gatorskinner, you."

As always she first bathed him in the large clawfoot tub Miss Lillian had placed in her room so that she would not have to use the common bath room the other girls shared—and so popular was she with the others that none but redhaired Quentin, who was quarrelsome by nature, had carped about her special privilege. After the bath she dried him and then dusted him with rose powder despite his usual happy protests. And then, because the moon was nearly full and its blue-silver blaze suffused the room, he extinguished the lantern and described to her the moonlight's play in her bright hair and on her pale flesh stretched on the bed under the tall open window. She drew him to her and they entwined limbs and tongues and he entered her. They rocked together smoothly and when she emitted a small gasp deep in her throat that signaled her readiness he groaned in satisfaction and permitted himself to climax. He did not know if she truly came at such times or if she was simply putting on an act. He asked her one time, saying that he didn't need any such pretense to enjoy himself, and she'd smiled and said, "Well, if you dont know, I aint gonna tell you."

Then lay in the moonlight and smoked cigarettes and she put her fingers to his cheek and then his neck and said it felt like his cuts were almost completely healed. "Feels like there wont be hardly no scar at all," she said. The first time he'd come to her she'd felt the freshly scabbed wounds he'd received in the fight with the Indian and when she asked where he got them he'd told her an alligator bit him. She laughed and said he was lying, that a gator bite would have done him a lot more damage, even she knew that. He said it was an old gator with only two teeth left in its head and thats why he only had the two scabs. She'd laughed even louder and kissed him hard on the mouth.

He'd only just fallen asleep with his face in her hair when he was awakened by a heavy crash from downstairs followed by shouts and curses and in the tumult he heard his brother's angry voice. He sat up and Loretta May grabbed his arm and said, "What?" He shook her off and scrambled from the bed and put on his pants and snatched up the pistol he'd sneaked in under his shirt. Miss Lillian expressly forbade guns in her house and he knew she would give him hell for it. He hurried shirtless and barefoot down the hallway and every head that appeared in other doorways as quickly withdrew at the sight of the pistol.

Down in the parlor Bob—wearing but his trousers—was trading kicks with the leaner of the suited men even as he tried to shake off the burly suit who held him fast in a bear hug from behind so that his arms were pinned at his sides. The three of them reeled in an awkward cursing dance, banging into walls and furniture and upsetting chairs and tea tables and breaking various things of glass. Easton the bouncer lay on the floor as though listening for activity in the crawlspace below and Sherman stood bigeyed before his piano with his palms out as if he would deflect the fight from it. A trio of swearing girls in states of undress were delivering kicks of their own at the suited men and shrilling and jumping aside each time the fight lurched their way. The stairway behind John Ashley was bunched with clamoring spectating whores and from the foot of the stairway his cry of "Hey!" was lost in the uproar.

All he could think to do was shoot. Without aiming he fired at the wall over the combatants' heads and hit a framed photograph of former president Theodore Roosevelt whom Miss Lillian worshipped and the gunshot shook the air and rained shards of glass on them. The room fell silent but for the ragged gasping of the principals who were seized in a tableau of contention—clothes awry, hair amuss, faces florid and wild and turned toward John Ashley as he pointed the pistol from one to the other of the two suits and said, "Hands up both you boys." As the suits put up their hands Bob Ashley drove a knee into the crotch of the burly one who'd held him and the girls cheered to see the man go bug-eyed and fall gagging to all fours. They cheered again when Bob struck the other suit a terrific roundhouse that spun the man three-quarters around and dropped him to his knees with blood running through the fingers of the hand he clasped to his broken mouth.

And then a handful of police came through the front door and the donnybrook was done.

The sergeant in charge was named Abel Watkins and when he saw that the Ashleys were on the scene he wasn't surprised. He'd known them for hellions since their boyhood. The brothers' clothes were retrieved from upstairs and while they got dressed and some of the girls helped Easton up onto a sofa and tended to him, Bob Ashley gave Sergeant Watkins an account of events.

After having his sport with Sheryl Ann, he had come downstairs to see what other girls might be available for his second go-round and found three of them sitting with the two men in suits. "You city boys sure take your time about pickin your pleasure," Bob said, and beckoned Jenny the Horse to him. But the burly one of the suits caught Jenny by the wrist and said in a Yankee accent, "Hold on there, sugar. I haven't decided who I want and it might be you." Bob said that if the suit was going to pick Jenny, then pick her, and if not, he was taking her upstairs himself. The suit responded that he'd take all the damn time he wanted to make his choice and no white trash son of a bitch was going to tell him different. Bob's response to that had been to kick the man in the face with the heel of his bare foot and send him over backward together with the sofa. Easton came on the run from the kitchen and grabbed Bob by the arm and Bob punched him backwards toward the other suit who bonked him on the crown with a half-full bottle and took him out of the fight. Then the first suit was up again and grabbed Bob tightly from behind and the other one commenced kicking him and hitting at him with the bottle. "Sonofa-bitches mighta put a hurt on me if Johnny didnt get their attention like he did," Bob told Watkins. He was sporting a swollen purple eye and Sheryl Ann pressed a wet cloth to his scalp to stem the blood running from his hair.

The city men looked even worse. The burly one had a broken

cheekbone and half of his face was grotesquely engorged. His gait was that of an old man, so bruised were his testicles. The lean one showed an upper lip like a large wedge of peeled plum and the fresh lack of a top front tooth. As Bob gave Sergeant Watkins his account of the fight, John Ashley heard the lean suit mutter to the other, "I *told* you we oughta come packing. But *nooo,* you said, whatta we need to *pack* for, you said. The fuck can happen in a damn cracker whorehouse, you said."

They told Sergeant Watkins they were from Chicago and en route to Miami for a fishing vacation. The burly one gave his name as Johnson, the lean one said he was Bode. They insisted that Bob had started the fight for no reason except jealousy over one of the girls who'd been keeping them company. But the three girls said that wasn't so, that the Johnson one started it by calling Bob trash.

"Christ," the Bode one said. "*thats* no reason to kick a man in the face."

Sergeant Watkins glowered and said, "You sure's *hell* from up north, aint you?"

He charged the Chicagoans with felonious battery and disorderly conduct but was willing to close the case on payment from each of a twenty-five-dollar fine if they also paid Miss Lillian one hundred cash dollars apiece to cover the damages to her parlor.

"Money wont patch up the insult to Teddy's eye," Miss Lillian said, looking at the skewed photograph dangling on the wall and at the bullet hole in Roosevelt's spectacles. "But thats somebody else's doing anyhow"—and here she gave John Ashley a tight-lipped look.

The suits muttered about it but they paid up. Everyone gaped at the roll of bills the Johnson one produced from his coat to peel off the requisite 250 dollars. Watkins then ordered the two men escorted to the depot to await the Miami train.

Sergeant Watkins concluded that Bob had acted in self-defense and so filed no charge against him. But he had to charge John Ashley. "It's too many people heard that gunshot, Johnny," he said. "The captain's gonna hear about it in the mornin and ask me where's the report. I dont charge you on it he'll sure-God skin me good." The captain was new to West Palm Beach, a hardliner from Jacksonville with a reputation for doing things by the book.

John Ashley said he understood. He agreed to a charge of reckless discharge of a firearm in the city limit and gave Watkins a bond of $25 which, rather than go to court, he would be able to forfeit as a fine. Watkins gave him back his pistol and the matter was closed. At the front door the sergeant exchanged winks with Miss Lillian and she waggled her fingers after him and said "Come back soon, Abel—but not in that uniform, you hear?"

Ten minutes later the Ashley brothers were having a drink and laughing along with a clutch of fawning girls who persisted in their excited babble about the fight when Miss Lillian's Negro cook Jewel came into the parlor and quietly informed John Ashley that there was someone at the kitchen door who wanted to talk to him. He asked who but she couldn't say—the man was holding back in the shadows like he didnt want to be recognized. John Ashley thanked her and stepped into the hallway to check the revolver and ensure it carried five ready cartridges, and then he went to the kitchen but saw no one at the door. He held the gun low against his leg and slipped out the screen door and stood fast in the shadow of the overhang and studied the moonlit sideyard.

A voice in the dark said, "Over here, Johnny."

He made out the figure of a man standing in the moon-dappled shadows of an umbrella tree beside the pump shed and then saw that the man wore a uniform and then recognized Buford Moore, a Palm Beach County deputy sheriff whose family were longtime acquaintances with the Ashleys. John Ashley's father had once carried Buford's daddy on his back for more than five miles after coming on him in the Glades where he'd broken his knee on a limerock outcropping and had been struggling along on a makeshift crutch for almost a day.

Buford Moore looked around nervously as John Ashley came up and said, "Hey, Buford, what you doin out here in the dark?"

"Get out of the light, Johnny," Buford whispered. "It won't do to have nobody see us talkin."

John Ashley stepped into the shadow of the umbrella tree and slipped the pistol into the waistband at the small of his back. "Damn, bubba, what's all the mystery about?"

"Listen, Johnny," said Buford Moore, "I got somethin to tell you." He asked if he remembered the dead Indian that was dredged out of the Lauderdale canal about six weeks ago. "His face was pretty bad but his daddy knew him right off. He anyway had a panther head tattoo on his shoulder made it certain who he was. Name's DeSoto Tiger. His daddy and uncle both some kind of high-muckety chiefs. Made a lot of noise about wantin justice for his nephew and yackety-yack-yack. Remember?"

John Ashley said he had a vague recollection of all that. He took out his fixings and began to roll a cigarette.

Well, Moore told him, just last week a couple of sheriff's deputies arrested an Indian breed trying to break into Willis' Grocery over near Delray. It was about the fifth or sixth time they'd caught this son of a bitch thieving and this time Sheriff George meant to put him away for a good while. But the breed said he knew something the sheriff might like to know and he'd tell it to him if he let him go. The sheriff asked what and the breed said he knew who killed DeSoto Tiger. Sheriff George said who and the breed told him. The sheriff asked how did he know and the breed said because he saw him do it. Sheriff George said the breed's say-so wasn't hardly good enough and asked could he prove it and the breed says it shouldn't be too hard since the fella stole about a thousand dollars' worth of DeSoto Tiger's otter furs and all the sheriff's got to do is find out if this same fella's sold about that much worth of otter furs to anybody lately.

John Ashley ran his tongue along the edge of the paper and sealed the cigarette and asked Deputy Moore if he had a match. The deputy dug one out and struck it and held it cupped to him. John Ashley took a deep drag and said, "And so?"

And so, deputy Moore said, Sheriff George had sent people out to check with all the fur buyers along the coast. They checked all the way down to Miami and bedamn if the Girtman Brothers hadn't paid twelve hundred cash money for a load of otter skins brung to them by the very same fella the breed had told Sheriff George about. Sheriff George had got up a murder warrant last night and was sending it all over.

"Well now, Buford," John Ashley said, "let's be real clear about this. Exactly who's the warrant for?"

"Well, John," Buford Moore said, "exactly, the warrant's for you."

John Ashley nodded and took a deep drag on his cigarette. "Yeah," he said. "Figured it might be. Where's that breed now? All safe and sound in a jail cell?"

"Nuh-uh. Sheriff George did like he promised and let him go this afternoon. You know Sheriff George—trusts everybody to keep his word till they give him reason not to. But he made the breed promise to report to him once a week and told him if he broke his word he'd see to it he got sent to a turpentine camp for the rest of his days. That might could be enough reason to make the breed hold to his promise."

John Ashley spat. "Goddamn breed."

"I thought you oughta know," Buford Moore said. "I been scoutin for you all day. I finally come here and seen the police wagon out front and I figured they'd maybe already got the word somehow, but when they come out you wasnt with them." The deputy licked his lips. "Listen Johnny, I *got* to give the city cops this warrant"—he tapped a long folded paper in his shirt pocket. "Sheriff George'll have my hide if they dont get it tonight. I been carrying it since this mornin. You understand, dont you?"

John Ashley said he surely did and he thanked Buford Moore for the information. The deputy took a nervous look around and said, "Listen Johnny, the last time you and me saw each other was over a week ago, all right?"

"Sure enough, Buford," John Ashley said. The deputy smiled and shifted his weight awkwardly and said, "All right, well, you take care, hear?" He raised his hand in farewell and hastened away around the corner of the house.

John Ashley went back into Miss Lillian's parlor and took his brother aside and whispered to him what Buford Moore had said. He then went upstairs and told Loretta May something had come up and he had to go take care of it. He kissed her goodbye and said he'd see her soon. As he went out the door she stared after him with her sightless eyes.

They bid Miss Lillian and the girls goodbye and exited by the back door and made away into the shadows of the pine forest.

They jogged over a vague trail through the pineywoods, navigating the darkness with the sureness of bats. After a time they came out from the trees onto a grass prairie illuminated pale blue under a bone-pale gibbous moon and in another quarter mile came to the Loxa-hatchee Canal. From the thick palmettos along the bank they withdrew a canoe they'd hidden there and slipped it into the moon-silvered water and began paddling north at a strong steady pace. Before they'd gone half a mile the palmettos fell away and ghostly bluegreen vistas of moonlit sawgrass opened to all points of the compass.

As they bent to their paddles Bob cursed once again Jimmy Gopher for a loose-lipped son of a bitch and swore he was going to track down that red nigger and put a slug in his brainpan. At his knees lay the .30 caliber Winchester carbine with which he intended to do it. John Ashley told him to do no such thing, that they had enough trouble as it was. "We'll let Daddy say what to do."

"I already know what Daddy's gonna say," Bob said, "and so do you. He aint never been abidin of them who tells tales to police."

"Well, we'll just let him *say* what to do," John Ashley said. He looked at his brother over his shoulder. "Dont be goin off half-cocked like you prone."

Bob Ashley snorted and spat in the passing water. A moment later his conversation turned to the fine time he'd had with Sheryl Ann and he told his brother of a new technique she'd taught him. "That gal's *always* got some new trick to show," he said. "Wonder where-all she gets them?"

"Where you think?" John Ashley said and turned to his brother with a white grin. "It's some men just natural-born good teachers."

Bob Ashley splashed him with his paddle and said, "You lying sack!"

As they stroked their way upstream and Bob talked on about Sheryl Ann, John Ashley tried to anticipate what their father might say about all this, but his thoughts kept drifting to Loretta May, to images of being spooned against her fine ass with his face in her sweet-smelling hair.

Bob at last fell silent and the only sounds were of their paddles cutting through the water and of animals rustling into the shorebrush at the canoe's approach. At one point as they passed through the closing blackness of a hardwood overhang a huge bull gator let a resonant grunt so close to the boat that both brothers flinched and yanked their paddles from the water and then giggled at their start.

"We ought take that hide," Bob Ashley whispered, straining his eyes into the passing darkness to try to make out the gator. "I bet that grandaddy sumbuck goes sixteen feet if he goes a inch."

"Aint got the time and you know it," John Ashley said, resuming his stroking. "From the sound of him we're lucky he didnt want *our* hides, you ask me." They chuckled softly as they emerged from the hollow and into the brightness of the moon and the clustered stars.

They paddled in silence for a time and then Bob said softly: "Hey? You ever think about the future?"

"What?" John Ashley said, stroking easily.

"The future," Bob said. "You ever think about what you want in the days to come."

John Ashley let off paddling and looked at him over his shoulder. "In the days to come?" He could not see Bob's eyes under the shadow of his hat brim.

Bob spat into the passing water. "Yeah," he said. He looked about at the measureless compass of starry sky and the dark surrounding wilderness and said, "You know what *I* want?" He swept his arm before him and said, *"This."*

John Ashley looked around as though Bob might have indicated something he had not seen before. Then turned back to his brother and said, "This *place*? Hell boy, you got it."

Bob laughed softly. "I know. Jesus Johnny, look at it! *Smell* of it! Of all the damn places in the world we might of got born in, we're some lucky sumbucks to get borned here."

John Ashley regarded the immense expanse of shadowed sawgrass and the near and distant hammocks silhouetted under the moon and he thought of the shallow bankless river that flowed through it all and was the lifeblood of this great wilderness. He breathed deeply of the night air pungent with the smells of ripe vegetations and raw earth and water richly seasoned with matter living and dead. We are, he thought. We are.

Bob spread his arms as if he would embrace all the starry night and all the world both visible and enshadowed. "Just *look* at it, man! Aint it *beautiful*?" He laughed with a low vehemence, like one near to madness with a secret joy. And John Ashley laughed with him.

Two hours later the trees drew in close on both banks of the canal. Against the moonbright sky they spotted the high black silhouette of a lightning-charred oak that served as their landmark. They put in against the bank and pulled the canoe out of the water and Bob Ashley removed the carbine and they hid the boat in the brush. They pressed ahead on foot and followed narrow winding trails through hardwood forest and underbrush. As they went they listened intently for anything that sounded out of place but heard only the calls of owls and night-hawks, the scuttling of creatures in the brush, the rantings of frogs, the keening mosquitoes at their ears. Their plan was to gather the gator hides they'd left to dry at their waycamp by the north bend of the Loxahatchee River and then make for home and tell their father the news about the Indian.

The eastern sky was showing a pale band of pink light as they drew close to their camp. When they werent slogging through mud they had to step carefully over vinecovered ground. Up ahead the trees abruptly fell away. They paused at the edge of the woods to listen hard and survey the open ground to the east where it came up against a dense palmetto thicket and the pinewoods beyond. Their waycamp lay in a natural clearing a hundred yards into those pines. In addition to the gator hides, they had a wagon in there and a tethered mule. On the far side of the camp was a corduroy track of pine timbers they'd laid over the mucky ground for a distance of a quarter-mile to where the ground was higher and the track became a solid limestone trail.

From there the going in the wagon was easier the rest of the way to their father's whiskey camp at the edge of the deeper swamp and but a few miles from Twin Oaks.

But now they heard the chugging of a motorcar and made out dim headlamps coming along the open ground. The lights progressed on a narrow raised-rock road a timber company had once used to take out pine logs. After clearing the trees for twenty yards on both sides of the road the company went broke and abandoned the site and the Ashleys had since used the road for their own purposes. It originated at the Dixie Highway about a mile to the east and terminated at the palmetto thicket.

"Who you reckon?" Bob asked, looking off at the coming lights.

"Nobody we call friend, I'll wager," John Ashley said.

They made for a better vantage point closer to the road as the motorcar came on. They were hiding in the high shrubs near the end of the road when a Model T sedan came clattering into view in the dawn gloam and halted. The motor shut off and the headlamps extinguished and two uniformed county deputies got out of the car and stood staring at the seemingly impenetrable palmetto thicket before them. One of the men said something the brothers couldn't hear clearly and the other said, "Maybe so but Daddy said check it and thats what we going to do."

"Bobby Baker," Bob whispered. "And Sammy Barfield with him. How you reckon they know about this camp?"

"No tellin who's seen us comin and goin on that road," John Ashley said. "It's too open. I told Daddy we ought of quit this camp."

The deputies now found the narrow path the Ashleys had cut through the palmettos and they trudged into the thicket in the direction of the camp. The Ashleys set out after them, following at a short distance and moving easily as shadows. Halfway to the camp the path abruptly opened into a small clearing where the Ashleys had felled most of the pines they'd used to make the corduroy track—and now John Ashley raised his fist in signal to Bob and they quickly closed in on the lawmen.

The deputies heard them too late. They turned and saw the brothers emerging from the brush not fifteen feet behind them, saw Bob Ashley holding the carbine at his hip like a long-barreled pistol and John Ashley pointing the .44 Colt as he came.

"Oh shit," the one called Sammy Barfield said, and he quick put up his hands.

The other kept his hands at his sides as Bob Ashley hastened to

Sammy and snatched his service revolver from its holster and lowered the carbine and pointed the pistol squarely at Sammy's chest. Sammy's arms were up as high as they could go and he said, "Oh shit, Bob, dont shoot me."

"You're under arrest, Johnny," the other deputy said.

John Ashley was smiling widely as he came up to this deputy and said "Hello to you too, Bobby. How's daddy's little deputy?" Bob Baker's father George was the high sheriff of Palm Beach County and had been since the county's inception three years earlier.

John Ashley relieved him of his revolver and gave the piece cursory examination and stuck it in his waistband. Then said: "Under arrest, you say?" He laughed. "Hell, Bobby, do I *look* under arrest?"

"For murder, John."

"That right? Who'm I sposed to killed?"

"DeSoto Tiger."

"*Who?*"

"Quit the bullshit. We know you shot that Indian. We got a witness.'

John Ashley grinned hugely. "Well if I did, I guess it wouldn't mean nothin to shoot the both you too. I mean, they can only hang me once, aint that right?"

"Even you aint that damn dumb," Bobby Baker said.

John Ashley laughed. He spun the .44 on his finger like a storybook cowboy and then affected to aim very carefully between the deputy's eyes from a distance of four feet.

"You dont scare me a goddamn bit and you never have. You shoot me, every police officer for three counties around will come huntin you."

John Ashley moved the gunsights down to Bobby Baker's heart and stroked his chin in affected contemplation for a moment, then shook his head and raised the sights to Bobby's forehead once again. "Bang!" he said and lowered the pistol and grinned. "You that important now, hey Bobby? All them police would be lookin to even the score for you?"

"I aint no Indian, Johnny."

Bob Ashley said "You sure aint, bubba. You got to be near deaf not to heard us comin up behind you."

"You're under arrest too," Bobby Baker said to him. "As an accomplice."

Bob Ashley hooted and shook his head. "I guess we *best* shoot these boys, Johnny, before this hardcase decides to tote the whole damn family off to jail."

"Oh lord, boys," the deputy called Sammy said, "dont shoot us, boys."

"Shut up, Sammy," Bobby Baker said. "They aint about to shoot anybody."

"Maybe yes and maybe no," John Ashley said. He gestured at Bob Baker's leg and said, "Take that thing off and hand it here."

Two years earlier Bob Baker had tracked down a Negro fugitive wanted for the murder of his wife and brother and in the ensuing confrontation he had shot the Negro dead at the same moment that the man blew off most of his lower leg with a twelve-gauge buckshot load. The doctors amputated just below the knee and he had since worn a wooden prosthetic. He had become so proficient with it that his walk showed only a hint of awkwardness. None who knew him considered him handicapped. It was a point of pride with him never to mention the leg and his friends knew better than to refer to it in his presence.

"Well dont just stand there gawkin," John Ashley said. "Take it off and hand it over." Bob Ashley guffawed.

Bob Baker stood fast and glared at him. John Ashley cocked the .44 and aimed it at Bob Baker's good foot. "You tirin my patience, peckerwood," he said. "You dont take that thing off right now, I'm gonna shoot you in the other foot is what I'm gonna do." The early dawnlight had not yet dispersed the ground darkness and everyone's feet were but vague entities.

"You aint gonna shoot any part of me, John, and you damn well know it."

John Ashley fired. The round tore a chunk off the heel of Bob Baker's boot and the deputy yipped and flinched sidewise and the loud crack of the gunshot was swallowed almost instantly by the breadth of the surrounding country.

"Goddamn me if I aint a piss-poor shot," John Ashley said. Bob Ashley laughed so hard he had a coughing fit.

John Ashley cocked the piece and this time held it with both hands and aimed at Bob Baker's foot again and the deputy said, "*Hold* it! *Hold* it, you crazy son of a bitch!" He sat on the ground and tugged up his pants leg and unbuckled the straps holding the prosthetic in place. He handed it up to John Ashley. "You aint right in the head, you know that? You never been."

John Ashley was enjoying himself immensely. He hefted the prosthetic leg with its boot still attached and said, "Do much dancin with this thing, Bobby? I guess you lost your taste for dancin since before you got crippled, huh? You know, I dont recall seein you at one single dance after that one you took what's-her-name to. Judy? Junie? *Julie*—thats it. Say, whatever become of her, anyhow?"

Bob Ashley whooped and had another spasm of coughing laughter. Bob Baker sat in place and said nothing but glared at John Ashley who could almost smell the anger rising off him like a malefic vapor. He smiled at how easy it was to rile him with just mention of a girl from their past. "Ah well, enough of relivin the good old days, eh Bobby? You, Sammy, help this poor crippled man to his feet—his foot, I mean."

Deputy Barfield pulled Bob Baker up onto his good leg and Bobby braced himself on Sammy's shoulder. Still chuckling, Bob Ashley went to the deputies' car and punctured all four tires with his buck knife, then opened one of the hood panels and reached in and yanked several wires off the engine and flung them far into the brush.

"Now you boys get goin," John Ashley ordered. "And tell your daddy, Bobby, the next time he sends someone after me he best send a whole man."

The two lawmen started off for the highway with their arms around each other's shoulders, their three-legged gait awkward and shambling and the Ashley brothers' laughter in their ears. The brothers watched them at their slow progress until they were distant figures nearly a half-mile away against the redly rising sun. Then John Ashley went to the disabled Model T and tossed the wooden leg onto the backseat and he and Bob went on to their camp.

An hour later the brothers had the hides on the wagon and had retrieved and hitched the mule and were on the corduroy track for home.

THREE

March 1912

FOLLOWING HIS RELEASE FROM THE PALM BEACH COUNTY JAIL
he'd made directly for the deeper reaches of the Everglades,
avoiding all the various waycamps he and DeSoto Tiger had ever
used, bypassing widely all Indian villages and the possibility of inform-
ers who would point out his direction to some who might come inquir-
ing. For five days he poled his dugout through the maze of waterways
winding through sawgrass and around hardwood hammocks and palm
islands and pine stands and along sloughs wide and narrow until he
arrived in a region unfamiliar even to him, who had lived in the Everglades all his life and hunted and trapped and ranged over a consider-
able portion of it. For five nights he slept in the dugout or on the
raised ground of hammocks, face and hands coated heavy with muck
against the mosquitoes. Quick rain showers came and went, drumming
on the hard crown of his bowler. And when he was at last so deep in
the wilderness he could not except in the vaguest sense have said where
he was, he beached the dugout in the high dark shade of a cypress-
and-palm hammock and there made a camp of sorts and settled in to
let time pass and to ponder the possibilities of his future.

He'd heard that John Ashley had been warned about the murder
warrant and had left the state to avoid prosecution, but he put little
stock in the rumor. No telling where the man might be. He could be
hid out somewhere in the Glades just as he himself was and who'd
know it but them who'd never tell. Besides, there were other Ashleys

who might come looking for him and any of them capable of settling accounts for brother John. Lay low was the thing to do. Way out here where none but the wildest ever ventured.

He subsisted on fish and turtles, on eggs pilfered from bird nests. He built small cookfires of lighterwood only in the brightest hours of the day the better to hide against the sunlight and clouds whatever smoke might ascend through the thick cover of the cypress branches. He napped often but never deeply and always with an ear cocked for anomalous sound. At various times every day he climbed high in a tree and scanned the horizon for signs of encroaching others but saw none.

A week went by and then another and with the passing of each day he grew more confident that his hideout was a good one. He constructed a solid lean-to of saplings and palm fans against the occasional rain shower and the nightly dew. He built a bed of palm fronds. On the far side of the hammock he discovered a wide shallow creek just beyond the reach of the tree overhang, its current clear and smooth and thronged with turtles and bream and bass as long as his forearm. His immediate thought was of a trotline, a line with baited hooks affixed to it at intervals and let to hang into the water from one bank to the other overnight and retrieved the next day with its catches. In the dugout he had a sufficient length of line and plenty of hooks, and about ten yards onto the grassy bank on the other side of the creek stood a small cypress to which he could attach the other end of the line. But the range from the edge of the hammock and across the creek to the dwarf cypress was perhaps forty feet and all of it out in the open and his wariness would not easily abate. He was loathe to expose himself for even so short a distance and for as brief a time as it would take to tie the line.

Another week passed and each day found him squatting in the shadows of the hammock bank and considering the creek. The trotline he'd fashioned days before and then lain aside was unnecessary to feed himself—he every day on his handline caught more fish than he could eat. But he was angry at himself for being too fearful to string the trotline. He had been fearful his entire life and knew it. And knew too that others knew it. Neither white man nor Indian had ever shown him a measure of respect and he could not fault them for that. Why should anyone respect him, who could not respect himself for his cowardice?

He determined to do it. He would wait for dark and then cross the creek and attach the line. The resolution was heady. Yes, he would do it and be done with being afraid. And now asked himself why he should wait until dark. Who but he and the beasts inhabited this portion of wildland for miles around? Now—now in the clarity of full daylight—was the time to prove to himself he could do it. He retrieved the ready trotline and baited the hooks with chunks off the several largemouth he'd caught earlier that morning and he fastened one end of the line to a ground root and fed out the line behind him as he walked backward out of the cover of the trees. He eased into the creekwater and it rose to his chest as he sidestepped his way across, playing out the trotline as he went. As he clambered up the other bank he almost laughed out loud in his exultation at being unafraid. And now he reached the little cypress and checked the lay of the line behind him and then tied this end to the cypress and the job was complete.

He went to the creek bank and admired the hang of the line in the water and already a fat turtle took the bait on one of the hooks and was caught. He looked all around and smiled at the infinite depth of dizzying blue sky carrying a few thin clouds above a scattering of hammocks in a vista of sawgrass to the horizons. And never heard the carbine crack from the cluster of cabbage palms some one hundred and fifty yards distant that sent up a fluttering flock of roseate spoonbills from its feed in the grass shallows and sped before it a .30 caliber bullet to enter his skull in front of his right ear and spin him about completely before he pitched into the creek with a huge splash. He bobbed to the surface facedown and floated there as the water again stilled and the blood issuing from his head drifted away on the slow current in wispy red rivulets as vague and elusive as dreams of courage.

FOUR

—

The Liars Club

OLD JOE ASHLEY'S DADDY COME TO FLORIDA AS A YOUNG MAN
after the War Between the States. Him and his wife. They come
from Tennessee by way of more than a dozen years in Georgia
and then settled in Lee County, on the Gulf side nearabouts Fort
Myers. The story has it he was killed in a timber camp one winter by
a rattlesnake bit him in the chin when he woke up from a dinnertime
nap under a tree. They say he died with his face all swole up just ugly
as sin. Old Joe used to tell folk the only three things his daddy left to
him was a scarred-up fiddle, the know-how for making good moonshine, and a damn good reason never to sleep on the ground unless
he absolutely had to.

Old Joe moved his family to this side of the state in ought-four,
some seven years before John killed that Indian and all his bad troubles
began. Besides Joe and Ma Ashley, there were five boys and two
girls—and two more daughters would be born some years later. It was
no more than a fair-sized family, as cracker families go. They come
across in a pair of wagons pulled by mules wearing muck shoes, come
all the way through what was still awful wild country along the Caloosahatchee River and over to Lake Okeechobee and on down through
the sawgrass glades to Pompano on the coast. In them days only a
Indian or a hardshell cracker could make a trip like that across the
Devil's Garden.

Those who first saw them come out on this side of the glades with

Old Joe driving the mules along with his whip popping like gunshots said both the family's wagons was near covered with the hides of all the diamondbacks they'd killed along the way and not a hide under six feet. Old Joe always wore a rattlesnake hatband and a rattlesnake belt. Carried a rattle in his pocket about the size of a kazoo and liked to come up quiet behind an ole boy and shake it hard and laugh like hell to see the fella jump five feet in the air and whirl around all bigeyed. Some called him Rattler Joe and said he never did seem to mind the name a bit.

He told folks he'd made the move because he was tired of trading in hides and furs for a living and wanted some of the steady wages Henry Flagler was paying his railroad workers. Maybe so. But there was a bunch of stories that followed right behind him when he come over from the west side and one of them was that he'd started cutting in on the wrong people's whiskey business in Lee County. When he didnt take their warnings to quit they busted up his operation and whipped his nigger helper near to death and threatened to burn down his house with everybody in it if he didnt clear out. According to this story Joe and the family was in the wagons and on their way east by the next sunup. That story'd been whispered around for a couple of years when some fella named Witliff in Pompano made the mistake of telling it out loud to a bunch of old boys that included a friend of Joe's who took it back to him. Joe went to Witliff's house and called him out and beat him senseless right there in his yard and in front of his family. Told him if he ever told tales about him again he'd cut out his tongue.

Another story said he'd left Lee County after clubbing a young fella near to death with a grub hoe handle for getting improper with one of his daughters. They say he gave that boy a stutter and a useless left arm and a droop-eye the rest of his life. Trouble was, one of the boy's best uncles was a rich Fort Myers cattleman who was related by marriage to the high sheriff and was friends with all the local judges. Joe didnt much care for the odds, so he packed up the family and headed out on the Caloosahatchee trace. Story has it that the cattleman sent a couple of roughs after him but they never come back. Could be they simply made off with the money they was paid to deal with Joe. Or could be they had the bad luck to catch up to him.

Joe Ashley paid bottom dollar for an abandoned half-burned-down house in the deep pineywoods just west of Pompano and pretty soon him and his boys fixed it up good. They were a tight family that mostly kept to itself but they were friendly enough whenever they came into town or met with a neighbor out on the Old Dixie Highway, which at that time wasnt much more than a bunch of ruts packed with rock in some stretches and with shell in others and hardly wide enough for a pair of wagons to pass each other by. Most who got to know the Ashleys liked them fairly well. But there were some who were quick to believe every mean story ever told about them and thought the whole family was a bunch of naturalborn outlaws. Such folk were just too flat afraid of them not to hate them. The Ashleys always would have admirers, bunches of them, but they'd always have bad enemies too. Everybody who knew them was pretty much one or the other.

For a time after they first got to Pompano, Joe and two of his boys—Frank and Ed—worked as woodchoppers for Flager's railroad. The eldest boy Bill worked as a chopper a few months too but pretty soon gave up axing to go work in a general store. Not long after the Ashleys moved to Pompano he took Bertha Rodgers to wife. He was the brainy one, Bill, the most serious, though they say he could play the banjo like he'd been born to it and he'd sometimes take a turn with a string band at a local dance. You'd see him around town more often than his brothers, reading magazines or the newspaper in the cafes, coming and going from banks and lawyer offices, taking care of Old Joe's business matters. He never did get in such bad trouble as his daddy and his little brothers did, but some say it's only because he did all his crimes with a pen instead of a gun.

All five of the Ashley brothers were close, but Frank and Ed were said to be fraternal twins and so naturally they was extra tight. And John and Bob were special-close because they were the youngest and grew up together hunting and trapping in the Everglades from the time they were big enough to shoot a rifle. John wasnt but eleven at the time the family moved to Pompano and Bob about a year older, and while Frank and Ed were cutting railroad ties with their daddy the two pups were bringing home meat for the table and gator and rattler hides to sell at the trading posts. Trapping and hunting was what they liked best but they could do lots of other things real well. Old Joe always could do damn near anything with his hands and he taught his boys the same. John was fourteen when a doctor down in Miami hired him and Bob to roof his house and over the next thirty years that roof never lost a shingle, not even in a hurricane. They worked in a Pompano packinghouse for a time and were said to handle a butchering knife as good as anybody in the place. But they didnt much like working for wages and went back to trapping for their daily bread. They got to know their way all over the Glades even better than their daddy—and Old Joe was as much at home in the Devil's Garden as a cottonmouth. John and Bob were the wildest of the Ashleys, everbody pretty much agreed on that, though John wasnt nearly the hothead Bob was. They say John was generally one to think a thing through before acting on it, leastways if he had the chance. Bob, he was always quick as a struck match to flare and burn. Which is exactly why he died the way he did.

They were the best shooters in the family too, John and Bob—not counting their daddy. They said Bob could shoot the whiskers off a rabbit at over a hundred yards with his old lever-action Winchester, but John was even more of a deadeye. At a traveling show in West Palm one time there was a .22 rifle shooting gallery with a line of little tin ducks steady moving across the far end of the tent on a conveyor belt in front of a backboard. The five brothers had a contest and by the time John and Bob were the last two left they were shooting at the ducks from forty feet outside the tent. They'd drawn a crowd by then and Old Joe was looking on too. When John finally won from some fifty feet out, the onlookers gave him a big hand and he bowed like an actor on a stage. He wasnt but fifteen at the time and loved to show off. Then Old Joe took the little .22 from him and backed up another ten feet and bang-bang-bang he knocked down a line of twelve ducks without a miss. Then he gives the rifle back to John and the boy didnt hit but nine of his twelve. The crowd gave Joe a bigger hand than they had John. When it came to showing off, Old Joe never was one to be outdone by his boys.

They'd been in Pompano about six years when word got around that Joe had set up a still somewhere in the pines and gone in the whiskey business. Gone *back* in the whiskey business is what most said. And because Bill had such a good head for account books and such, Ole Joe made him his business manager. The Ashleys didnt have any local rivals in the trade except for a couple of swamp-rat shiners named Runyon and Aho who'd been around for years and years although hardly anybody ever saw them because they never come into town but once in a blue moon. They had a cabin somewhere in the Devil's Garden and shared an Indian woman who lived with them. She never come to town. After Joe started making and selling whiskey on this side of the state neither Runyon nor Aho ever come to town again and nobody ever saw them anywhere else either. And somewhere along the way Joe took over their stills as abandoned property. There were some mean stories told about what might of happened to the swamp rats, but the plain and simple of it was that nobody knew if the Ashleys had anything to do with their disappearances and nobody cared a tinker's damn anyhow. The only thing for sure was that Old Joe's product was way better than what the swamp rats had been peddling. Everybody who ever tasted the stuff will tell you that Joe Ashley's shine was the finest ever made in the south of Florida. He soon had a steady line of customers from Stuart to Lauderdale and was using his boys to deliver the loads. And it wasnt much of a secret that he was selling to the Indians.

There's something more to tell about Runyon and Aho. It was a common story that one or the other of them sired a child by the Indian woman who lived with them, a boy they named Hector. When the kid grew up he used the name Runyon but that dont mean Runyon was his daddy. Some say he just ruther have that name than Aho, and who could blame him. You'd see him roundabout the Indian River towns a lot more than either of the two men because he was the one they sent in to get whatever supplies they needed. Like most breeds he looked more Indian than white. He was brownskinned and his hair was as black as ink and he wore it long from the time he was a child. But he had blue eyes and the inside of his forearms was pale as any white man's.

He was bad-dog mean, that boy, everybody said so. Sometimes he'd come into a town for no reason but to pick a fight with another boy and then just tear him up. He'd as soon gouge out your eye in a fight as not, as soon bite off your ear, your damn nose. The only boy who wasnt afraid of him was Bobby Baker, who was a few years older and some bigger, and for some reason they got along. Far as anybody knows, Bobby was the closest thing to a friend Heck Runyon ever had.

When he was about fourteen he was accused of stealing a farmer's horse off a farm and the man wanted him throwed in jail. Sheriff George went out in the Glades to look for him and came back saying he couldnt find hide nor hair of him anywhere. But there was some who said he'd found him all right—and then helped him to get away to DeSoto County where he got work as a cowhunter, which is what they called a cowboy in Florida in them days. That all happened around ought-eight, a couple of years before Joe Ashley started up his whiskey business and Runyon and Aho vanished.

It wasnt till seven years later that Heck Runyon showed up again on this side of the state. At the time he come back he was still wanted for stealing the horse but the farmer dropped the charge a few days after Heck went to live in a hut out behind the Baker place. Some said

Sheriff George made a deal with the farmer. A story went around that Heck had been working the last couple of years as a regulator for a rich DeSoto County rancher. A regulator was somebody paid to stop rustlers, and they say Heck Runyon stopped a bunch of them as stopped as they could get by shooting them graveyard dead. Then he got in a saloon fight with a cowhunter and cut the fella up pretty bad. Ruther than stick around and see what the law might say about it, he'd come back to his old stomping grounds. He'd been back about six months when Sheriff George made him a Palm Beach County deputy.

Not too long later he killed a prisoner. He was bringing the man back to the county jail in West Palm Beach after the fella was convicted in a trial in Stuart and they were sitting in the coach while the train made a whistle stop in Jupiter. Witnesses said the prisoner called him a mongrel dog and spit in his face and Heck Runyon clubbed him to death with his revolver right then and there. Women and children saw it and was screaming and running off the train. They say it was a bloody mess. There was talk that Heck Runyon ought be charged with murder since the prisoner had his hands cuffed at the time. The news-paper said he ought for sure at least be fired, that the county didnt need any deputies who thought they were judge, jury and executioner. Sheriff George argued that Deputy Runyon had been strongly provoked and had just cause, but he was enough of a politician to know when to give in to popular opinion and so he fired him.

Heck Runyon hardly ever showed himself in town after that but it was said he was still living out on the Baker property and that Sheriff George was still using him to track down fugitives who made off into the Devil's Garden.

The bad blood between John Ashley and Bobby Baker started over a girl, which aint such an uncommon story. Leastways thats how most tell it. John Ashley was fifteen at the time and Bobby about nineteen. They'd knowed each other since the Ashleys moved to Pompano. They werent never exactly friends, but during those first few years they'd been friendly enough. They say Bobby Baker was the one showed John Ashley all the best fishing spots in the Indian River and John taught Bobby plenty about tracking game in the Glades. Their daddies got along all right too—at least in the years before John's trouble over the Indian. Old Joe and Sheriff George would take a cup of coffee together in Lucy's Cafe in West Palm sometimes or buy each other a drink at Blue's store at Lake Towhee and talk about mules and dogs and fish-ing. Like with their boys, nobody'd go so far as to say they were friends, but Old Joe made it plain he appreciated that the high sheriff was one to live and let live when it came to whiskeymaking. The way Sheriff George saw it, if the federal government wanted to tax the whiskey a man made, it could damn well send its own men to collect it. Sheriff George was anyway known to take a drink ever now and then and was said to be pretty fond of Joe Ashley's product his ownself.

Anyhow, there used to be a dance every Saturday night in a big auction barn a few miles south of West Palm and the Ashley boys would usually come up from Pompano to dance and meet girls. Even Bill Ashley would come up sometimes just to play his banjo with the band and have a dance or two with his wife Bertha, who everybody liked. They were lively affairs with good string bands and plenty of food and punch and of course every man brought his own jug. One Saturday evening Bobby Baker showed up with a girl named Julie Morrell, a pretty sixteen-year-old who had long honey-colored hair and freckles and a smile to melt a grown man's heart. Bobby was crazy in love with her and didnt make any secret of it. He'd met her just a few weeks earlier and was telling people he was by God going to marry her one day or know the reason why. The Ashleys were there that night as usual and the brothers took turns dancing with every girl in the place. Frank and Ed and Bob cut in on Bobby one after another but he didnt seem to mind all that much. He was proud of his pretty sweetheart and they say he liked being envied by the other fellas. Then John Ashley cut in on him, and while Julie was spinning around in John Ashley's arms Bob Ashley sidled up to Bobby and started up a conversation and the next time Bobby looked out to the dance floor neither Julie Morrell nor John Ashley was anywhere in sight.

Everybody knows John Ashley always did have a way with the ladies—with proper ones as well as them not so proper. Just exactly how much of a way he had with Julie Morrell in the darkness of the pines beyond the barn that evening is something nobody but him and her would ever know for certain. But it aint hard to imagine what Bobby Baker thought when he saw they were gone from the barn.

He went running out to look for her and the Ashley boys followed him outside and watched him run around yelling Julie's name to make himself heard over the music from the barn. When they started laughing at him, Bobby went at Bob Ashley with both fists swinging. Maybe he picked out Bob because he was the one who'd distracted him long enough for John to make off with Julie, or maybe just because Bob was the Ashley standing closest to him at the moment. He was older and bigger than Bob, but Bob had a reputation as a vicious scrapper who even a lot of the older fellas were afraid of. They punched and kicked and bit and scratched and gouged and pulled each other's hair and rolled around on the ground all locked up like a couple of pit dogs. A small bunch of spectators gathered round to root for one or the other but most people at the dance never even knew the fight took place. It was fairly even going for about five minutes and then Bobby got astraddle of Bob Ashley and got both hands on his throat and try as he might Bob Ashley couldnt buck him off. When it was pretty clear that Bobby was going to kill him if somebody didnt stop him, Frank and Ed finally stepped in and pulled them apart. They say Bob Ashley was black in the face by then and likely wouldnt of lasted another half-minute. They said his eyes were bloodshot for a week after. They said both them boys looked like they'd been hit by a train.

A deputy sheriff showed up about then and Frank and Ed were explaining things to him when here comes John Ashley and Julie Morrell out of the pines. Julie was blushing and her hair was all messy and with leaves in it and she never said a word nor looked anybody in the eye but just went right on by them all and into the barn. They say John Ashley was grinning like a keyboard and said, "What's goin on, boys?" Bobby Baker was so beat up and wore out he couldnt hardly stand by himself but he tried to go at John anyway and had to be held back by the deputy. They say if looks could kill, Bobby Baker would've put John Ashley in his grave right then and there.

The way the story goes, when Julie Morrell's daddy who was a grocer heard what happened he wanted to charge John Ashley with rape, only Julie insisted to him it had been no such a thing and swore she'd never lie to the contrary in court. They say he whipped her bare ass bloody with a razor strap. Supposedly he made threats against John Ashley and against Bobby Baker too because he was the one he'd entrusted with his daughter's safekeeping that night—but it's probly not true. Like most folk he was too afraid of the Ashleys and the Bakers both to of said anything so reckless. Nobody was surprised when he finally never did anything except pack up his family and move away. Some said they went to the panhandle, some said out to Arkansas where he had kin. Nobody knew for sure. A few years later during the war, one of the boys come home on leave from an army aviation school in Alabama and swore up and down he'd had the pleasure of sweet Julie Morrell in a Birmingham whorehouse. Whether it was true or not, it's what most people come to believe became of her.

As for the Ashleys and Bakers, well, Old Joe and Sheriff George were seen having a drink together in a Pompano saloon not a week after the fight and joking about how a pretty girl could sure make the bucks lock horns. And about a month later a dozen witnesses saw John Ashley meet up with Bobby Baker on the New River trading docks. John poled up in a skiff and was pulling a second one loaded with plumes. Bobby was there helping his cousin Freddie to patch the bottom of his fishing boat and was still carrying scars from the fight with Bob Ashley. They say John Ashley greeted him as friendly as you please although nobody made to shake hands. John had a round of beers brought out to the dock from the trading store and told about his plume hunt in the rookeries southwest of Okeechobee. He told Bobby they ought to go fishing together in the Indian River again sometime like they used to. If anybody had Julie Morrell on his mind nobody said so. Neither Bobby nor Freddie hardly said a word the whole time. Then John Ashley said so long and got in his skiff and poled away. They say the Baker boys watched him go and then poured out the bottles of beer they neither one had taken the first sip of. Far as anybody knows, Bobby Baker and John Ashley never did go fishing together again.

In nineteen and eleven the Ashleys made theirselfs a new homestead in the piney swamps a few miles southwest of Gomez. Old Joe bought sixty acres set about midway between Peck's Lake and the south fork of the St. Lucie River. Not a neighbor for miles around. About three-quarters of the place was nothing but pine swamp, but there was a wide high clearing in the middle of the property and him and his boys built a good-sized house on it. It was a dogtrot—had a breezeway between the two halfs of the house—with a full wide porch both front and back and a steep-pitched roof and a chimney at either one of the gable sides. Had a big kitchen out back. They built the thing of Dade County pine and shingled it with cypress to let the heat out through the roof. That Dade pine's about the best lumber in the world but it's mostly all been cleared away and you cant hardly find a stick of it anymore. It's so fulla resin you can work it real easy while it's green but once it ages and that resin dries up you cant drive a nail in it with a sledgehammer. Termite'll bust its teeth on it is how hard it gets. The bad news is, a house made of Dade pine ever catches fire it'll burn down quick as a kitchen match on account of all that resin. They call it lighterwood out in the Devil's Garden because it's so easy to start a campfire with it.

The house was shaded by a big live oak to either side and had a

clear view for forty yards in all directions right up to the edge of the
pine swamps all around. The two shade trees were pretty near the
same size and the reason Old Joe named the place Twin Oaks. There
was dozens of creeks and waterways all around the property connecting
it east and west to ever part of that region between Lake Okeechobee
and the Indian River lagoon and south to the sawgrass country. But
there was only one road into the property—a narrow roundabout trail
they'd cut through all that swampy pineland between the house and
the Dixie Highway. It was awful rough going for a motor vehicle, but
that was the idea, to make it damn hard for anybody to drive up to
their place, especially at night. That trail was hardly wide enough for
a wagon except at a couple of points where they'd broadened it enough
so a car could make a turnaround—just in case it ever had to.

Joe pretty soon had him a whiskey camp about three miles southwest of the Twin Oaks house—out at the Crossbone Creek at the edge
of the Devil's Garden. Even after he built his other camps this one
was said to be his favorite. It was the biggest and about the best hid.
His next one was set a few miles farther south in the Hungryland
Slough. By then he was making deliveries as far north as Fort Pierce
and as far south as Miami and his business was better than ever. Then
that Indian turned up dead in the Lauderdale canal and Palm Beach
County Sheriff George Baker charged John Ashley with murder.

A lot of people couldnt understand why all the to-do about a damn
dead Indian. But Sheriff George said he had to do something about it
because there was a witness who'd seen John Ashley do the deed and
there was other evidence besides. The "evidence," as he called it, was
a bunch of otter furs John Ashley'd sold down in Miami. That struck
lots of people as pretty damn slim evidence because one bunch of otter
furs looks just like every other bunch and how was anybody gonna
tell em apart? As for the witness, he was a low breed named Jimmy
Gopher and such a naturalborn liar that if he told you water ran
downhill you'd have your doubts. He was lying if he said hello. He'd
vanished into the Everglades just as soon as he was set loose from jail
and didnt nobody ever see him again. There was talk Bob Ashley
hunted him down deep in the Devil's Garden and killed him so he
couldnt never testify against John Ashley but there never was any proof
of it. It might of been just talk from those who hated the Ashleys and
would tell any sort of lie to try to put them in a worse light with
the law.

We no sooner heard about the warrant for John Ashley than we
heard Bobby Baker and Sammy Barfield had caught up to him and

his brother Bob in one of their waycamps—but the Ashleys had somehow got the drop on them and took away their pistols and disabled their car and made them to walk home. A Palm Beach deputy found them sitting by the side of the Dixie Highway the next morning. What made it even more embarrassing for Bobby was he'd lost his artificial leg. He said he somehow got it caught in a hole in the limerock trail they'd been walking on and it was stuck so fast he didnt have no choice but to unstrap it and leave it there. Sammy Barfield didnt have much to add to the story except to say it was just the way Bobby told it. Poor Sammy looked pretty shook up for a time afterwards. He always was strung too tight for police work and he got out of it before much longer.

When Sheriff George sent some men out into that piney swamp to fix the car and bring it back they found Bobby's leg in it. All anybody could figure was that somebody had come along and found it and knew damn well who it belonged to, especially with the county police car just down the trail. Whoever it was had got it unstuck and throwed it in there.

Nobody roundabouts saw hide nor hair of John Ashley for the next two years. Some said he'd gone to Alabama, some said out to Oregon. Others said he hid out someplace in Texas where he had kin who ran a hotel. Wherever it was he went, two years later he came back. Just walked into Sheriff George's office one day in the company of his daddy and a lawyer and give himself up.

FIVE

April 1912–June 1914

THE GALVESTON SUMMERS WERE HOT AND WET AND LITTLE DIFFER-
ent from those he'd known in Florida. The fitful breezes off the
Gulf moistly warm as dogbreath. Hordes of mosquitoes. Regular
evening rainstorms that flared whitely at the windows and rattled the
glassware with their thunder and sometimes became downpours that
lasted for days. All such was familiar to him. But winter's occasional
blue northers were an alien brutality that made his teeth ache and
burned his face raw and made him think his feet would never again
be warm.

He'd arrived on a boat from New Orleans, where he'd steamed to
out of Tampa. His father had sent word ahead to his sister July of
John's troubles with the Florida laws and asked her to take him in for
a time. When he showed up one early afternoon at the front door of
her pink two-story clapboard on Post Office Street in a part of town
long known as Fat Alley, Aunt July welcomed him warmly. She was
a lean darkhaired woman who looked younger than her forty-four years
except in the eyes which looked to him to have seen everything. While
they took lunch on the back porch off the kitchen she said she had
friends who could get him work on the Galveston docks if he was
interested. John Ashley said he had given the matter of a job some
thought on the voyage from Florida and believed he was well-suited
to work for her as what was commonly called a bouncer.

"Houseman, we call them," Aunt July had said, looking surprised, "or mostly just the man." Her gaze turned appraising. "Well, you're certainly of size for the job," she said, "but you *are* awfully young. Besides, the house already has a man." She turned toward the kitchen and called out, "Hauptmann!"

A beefy balding man in a collarless striped shirt and suspenders came to the screen door and looked out at them without expression as he noisily ate an apple.

She looked at John Ashley and arched her brow. John Ashley smiled at her and then turned to the man at the door and said, "Hey, Hauptmann, why dont you just get your hat and go? Or if you ruther, you can step out here and we'll settle who's man of the house."

Hauptmann's forehead furrowed and he stopped chewing. Then he snorted and said, "There aint but one man of the house here, sonny, and you lookin at him."

John Ashley stood up and took off his coat and draped it over the porch railing and said, "Come show me."

Aunt July looked from one to the other and said, "Now boys, I wont stand for you either one getting bad hurt. No knives, you hear me?"

They stepped down to the weedy courtyard shaded by white-blossomed oleander trees and stripped off their shirts. Girls flocked to the rear windows of both floors to witness the job competition. Hauptmann was the bigger man but he'd grown soft and slow with whorehouse life and in minutes his nose was broken and one of his ears was a ruination and one eye was swelling and closing fast and he told John Ashley he'd had enough. Ten minutes later Aunt July had paid him his wages and he was gone. And John Ashley sat in the kitchen and smiled and had his skinned knuckles tended by a pair of girls as Aunt July explained his duties to him.

He rarely had to use force to put anyone off the premises and even then most of the rowdies were too drunk to put up much of a fight and he easily enough muscled them to the side door and pitched them into the alley and their hats after them. When he did have to get tougher a hard hook to the belly or a punch to the neck was usually sufficient to quell all dispute. He had expected a rougher patronage but Aunt July's regulars were mostly a tame bunch and he now and then found himself wishing some old boy who could scrap would start trouble simply to relieve the boredom. To exercise himself to a sweat he'd several times a week set loose all the chickens in the little coop in the courtyard and then chase them down again to the delight of the spectating girls.

The girls were the job's grand compensation. Eight inmates as they called themselves resided in the house and only a couple were older than he and none were less than pretty and nearly all freely available to him when the business hours were done. Besides deferring to his status as the man of the house and as their employer's favored nephew the girls were anyway attracted to him for his youth and good looks and pleasant Deep South manners—and for the mystery of his past which included the rumor that he'd killed a man. They admired and took comfort in his adeptness at dealing with trouble. He made joyful daily claim on this sexual perquisite during the whole of his first year in Galveston. Only two of the girls would not permit him in their beds—Laraine who was married and truly loved her husband and would not cheat on him by having congress with any other man but a paying customer, and Cindy Jean who said he so much reminded her of her brother Royal back home in Fort Worth that it would feel like the awfulest sin. He took the other six in turn, a different one every night, and so each week had one of them twice—once on Sunday and again the following Saturday.

At the dinner table one afternoon Aunt July mock-admonished him for his unflagging concupiscence. "It's a scientific fact that a man can go crazy doing it as much as you do," she said. "It's all that constant friction. Sends way too much heat up your tallywhacker just like a fuse and on up your spinebone and when it reaches your brain, why, it just cooks it like an egg. Too much hokey-pokey has been known to turn a man into a drooling fool fit for nothing but a freak tent."

To which John Ashley raised his face to the dining room ceiling and bayed like a moonstruck hound and his aunt couldn't help but join in the girls' laughter.

Wiser heads might have warned him that ever-ready pleasures cannot long endure, that sexual indulgence requires respite and even occasional lack in order that its enjoyment not jade. He was young and did not know these things and would anyway not have believed them had he been told and so was obliged to discover their truth for himself. By the end of his first year in Galveston he was beyond surfeit with pleasures of the flesh. He took to waking in the forenoon before the girls arose and slipping out of the house and staying away until early evening and the hour of his employ. At supper the girls began to look at him askance but they held their tongues. Not until he'd kept his distance from them for more than two weeks did a roanhaired inmate named Sally make bold to inquire: "Dont you like us no more, Johnny?"

He heard the injury in her voice and saw in her face and in the faces of the others that a man's failure of desire for them was the harshest of rebuffs. He felt mean for making them feel unwanted.

"*Hey* now, girls," he said, turning up his palms, "I just need a little rest from you all or like Aunt July says I'll sure enough go loony from way too much of a good thing."

They smiled with ready acceptance of this explanation and winked at each other with relief and fell to their suppers with a happy clatter of dishware.

He did resume his visits with the girls but now dallied only twice or thrice a week—often enough to avoid giving further offense but not so often as to glut himself again. He spent the larger portion of his days walking the city and at last acquainting himself with it. He bought a white suit and wore it everywhere against a light blue shirt and black tie and all under a widebrimmed white Panama. He went to the bayside docks and watched the loading and unloading of cargoes of every sort and heard seamen speaking in the tongues of nations whose names he did not know. He daily joined the crowd that gathered every afternoon to see what the fishing boats brought in and one day marveled with them all at a fourteen-foot tiger shark with a girth twice his own as the beast was hung up by its tail and the captain dissected its belly and among the contents to issue onto the dock were a rum bottle and a horseshoe and most of a woman's bare arm as yet hardly digested and whose finger bore a gold wedding band. The sight reminded him of a time he'd cut open the stomach of a bull gator he'd shot at the south rim of Lake Okeechobee and therein found a boot containing a pale hairy foot.

He ambled along the Strand and admired its ornate Victorian architecture and several times attended matinee theater performances and once and only once a matinee at the opera house. He liked walking in the drizzling rain after dark in the misty glow of the streetlamps. He took long noonday strolls along the seawall so recently completed after the hurricane of 1900 that killed 6,000. In the saloons they yet told stories of workgangs impressed at gunpoint and given whiskey rations through the day and night that they might stay halfdrunk and abide the labor of heaving corpses into the towering bonefires on the beach. The fires blazed for weeks and hung the island with a dread and hazy stench. Now the city streets rattled and honked with more than 200 motorcars and pedestrians scurried aside with hardly a glance at them and only the most nervous horses still stamped and kicked at their passing. The speed limit in town was ten miles per hour but there were daring motorists who raced each other on the beach all the way to San Luis at the west end of the island. In the parks he watched baseball games and boxing matches and bicyclists and schoolchildren at their gymnastics. He put on a bathing suit in a beach bathhouse and went for long swims in the mirrorsmooth morning sea. And yet, in this his second year of exile in a modern city whose pleasures he could not refute, he could not deny either his increasing yearning for home.

He often went fishing from the beach in the afternoons and sometimes thought of Bobby Baker who'd shown him the best places in the Indian River for trout and how to read the weather—taught him that when you saw sand sharks jumping between dawn and sunrise you could look for sporadic southwest winds in about five or six hours, that when the whip rays jumped in the morning you knew a northwester would soon hit and rough up and silt the water, but when the morning cobwebs were thicker than usual you could bet on good weather for fishing out on the salt.

John Ashley felt almost friendly toward Bobby Baker in his recollections. He had always considered him a good old boy who seemed to have no lack of grit—as he'd proved on such occasions as the fistfight with his brother Bob and the attempt to arrest them that night at the waycamp, the night he'd sent him home on one leg.

But as he cast into the gentle surf one afternoon it occurred to him that Bobby Baker wasn't likely to forget the humiliations of Julie Morrell and being stripped of his gun and leg. It struck him that Bobby might evermore seek to get even for those public humblings. The notion that Bobby might even be pleased to see him dead came quite suddenly and made him at once melancholic and angry.

These feelings confused him and would not dismiss. They persisted for the next several weeks and because he could not say why he felt as he did he became even more nervous and irritable. He twice in one week badly battered troublesome patrons he could easily have handled without letting blood. Aunt July gave him a reprimanding look in the first instance and a severe rebuke after the second, reminding him that she needed no additional difficulties with the police or from some young muckraker's righteous journalistic denunciations of the whoring trade. He had thought that the fights might soothe his gloomy agitations but they did not. He ached for an action he could not name.

One morning just a few days after Aunt July's scolding he was walking by a bank a block removed from the Strand and chanced to look into the lobby just as a customer was receiving money at a teller's window. He paused and watched the man tally the bills and then smile and say something to the teller who seemed a sulky young man and who showed not a hint of smile in return but simply nodded. The customer folded the money and put it in his coat and came out and gave John Ashley a polite smile in passing. John Ashley glanced at the bulge in the man's coat pocket and then watched him cross the street and go into a restaurant. Then he looked back into the bank for a long moment, at the polished wood floor gleaming against the yellow sunlight slanting through the windows. He made his way back to the house by a slow roundabout route, noting carefully the lay of every street and alley as he went, stopping in at a pharmacy to buy a small package of gauze and a roll of adhesive tape. By the time he was back at the house his melancholy had lifted, his nervousness dissipated like blown smoke.

Early the next morning after the house had turned out its last patron of the night and everyone had gone to bed and only the domestics were moving about at their housekeeping and cooking duties, he cleaned his pistol at the small table by his bedside window and then loaded it. He dressed in his white suit and from his suitcase withdrew a floppy-brimmed black felt hat and pair of overalls no one in the house had ever seen and he put them in a large paper sack together with the pistol and the gauze and the roll of tape. He descended the stairs quietly and slipped out the back door and went to the tool shed at the rear of the property. The day was cold enough to show his breath. In the shed he emptied the sack and changed from his white suit into the overalls and tucked his long hair up into the hat. He had let his hair grow nearly to his shoulders because several of the girls had dared him to do so and then all of them had said they preferred it like that. He neatly folded his white suit and put it in the bag and cached it in a corner. He slipped the pistol into the bib pocket of the overalls and then carefully set a wide strip of gauze over his nose and cheekbones and taped it in place.

Five minutes after the bank opened for business he walked in and stood at the central counter and on a withdrawal slip wrote "Give me all your paper money." The guard was a uniformed big-bellied fellow engaged in conversation with a young female clerk at her desk in a corner and the only other customer of the moment was in discussion with the bank manager at his desk at the far end of the room. There was but one other teller on duty and he was busy with a ledger.

John Ashley went to the sulky teller's window and pushed the slip of paper at him. The teller read it and looked up at him and John Ashley leaned close against the counter and exposed enough of the revolver in his bib for the teller to see what it was.

Even as the teller's eyes widened and his mouth came open John

Ashley smiled and said softly, "Everything's just fine, bubba, you do like I say. Act natural and don't holler. Make me any trouble I'll shoot you graveyard dead. Now gimme it."

The teller did it. He handed over a banded pad of twenty-dollar bills with "$400" imprinted on the band and then several handfuls of loose paper currency of various denominations. John Ashley casually put it all into his overall pockets with the insouciance of a man reaping his just desserts. The teller handed him yet another small stack of bills and said in a quavering whisper, "That's all I have in my cash drawers, sir, really it is."

John Ashley grinned under his bandaged nose and said, "Well, then, bubba, thats all I'll take." The teller looked dazed and for a moment John Ashley thought the man might faint. "Sit down at that desk back of you and just stay there and don't say nothin to nobody for five minutes, you hear?" He said all this in a low conversational tone and with a broad smile and anyone looking their way would have seen a friendly farmer with an injured nose chatting with a teller who looked but a little more out of sorts than usual.

As the teller turned and went to the desk John Ashley left the bank, whistling lowly and waving so long at the guard and feeling his heart banging against his ribs as if trying to make its own wild escape ahead of him. He steeled himself to walk at a normal pace as he made his way along the serpentine route he'd laid out through the alleys. At every step of the way he expected to hear police whistles suddenly shrilling behind him and shouted commands to stand fast and put up his hands.

And then he was back in the shed and the gauze was off his face and he quickly changed into his white suit and stuffed the overalls and the hat in the paper sack and hid it behind a nail barrel in the corner. He put the money in his coat pockets and then went into the house and up to his room. In response to the look of curiosity he received from the cleaning women on the stairs he said, "Forgot my pipe."

He counted the money out on the bed—one thousand two hundred and seventy-two dollars, most of it in twenties and tens and no bill larger than a fifty, of which there five. He counted all of it again and laughed out loud. He felt better than he had in weeks—even as his heart yet pounded and he tasted now the brassy flavor of the apprehension he'd been holding in tight check all morning. He wanted to howl his elation. He divided the money into four even piles and rolled them tightly and stuffed them into a spare pair of boots and then went for a long walk on the seawall. He could not stop grinning.

By the time the house sat down to dinner that afternoon the news of the robbery was all over town. The talk at the table was all about it and the bold broken-nosed farmer who'd done it and got away. The most popular sentiment among the girls was the hope that the hayseed would come to the house to spend some of his loot.

"I'll show him how to do a damn *stick-up* like he aint never done," Cindy Jean said, and all the girls laughed.

John Ashley laughed with them. The girls had several times remarked on his high spirit all afternoon and some now wondered aloud as to its cause. He told them he just felt good being in their company, that was all, and they grinned and blew kisses at him. It was all he could do to keep from bragging to them that he'd committed the crime. But he knew too well the whores' love of gossip and knew that if he confided in even one of them about the holdup they would all soon know the story and so would others outside the house. He felt cheated that he could not crow about it to anybody.

Two months later his euphoria from the robbery had ebbed and he found himself standing across the street from a Broadway Avenue bank and considering the possibilities. He decided that yes, he could take this one too. He thought about it for the next few days and was almost decided on doing it when a telegram arrived from his father: "Get home. Gordy says all will be well." Gordy was Gordon Blue, attorney-at-law with offices in Palm Beach and Chicago and an occasional partner of Joe Ashley dating back to their days in Lee County.

The girls were sorry to see him go. The night before his departure Aunt July threw a party and hired a dance band to play in the crowded parlor and each girl in turn took him aside and kissed him goodbye and petted him and whispered endearments. He three times went upstairs with a different girl each time including Cindy Jean who said she didnt care anymore how much he looked like her brother.

When he boarded the steamer next morning he was redeyed with hangover and exhausted to the marrow and his flayed peeter pained him in his pants. Yet he grinned wide as he stood at the rail in the cold wind and returned the goodbye waves of the girls on the dock. Then the ship cleared the channel and entered the silver-green Gulf and he watched Galveston recede in the wake and he told himself that if he should ever have to live someplace other than Florida he would come back to this old island. Under a sunwashed sky laced with white clouds a school of dolphin rolled up beside the ship like old friends attending him home.

SIX

July 1914

ON A CLEAR HOT SUMMER SUNDAY JUST DAYS AFTER JOHN ASHLEY debarked at Tampa and was driven home to Twin Oaks by his brother Bob, the family celebrated his return with a great feast and invited every friendly acquaintance in the county. In the shade of the wide live oaks whole pigs crackled and dripped from their spits above open fires tended by Old Joe's Negro help. Huge racks of beef ribs sizzled on thick iron grills over firepits. Puncheon tables held heaping platters of smoked mullet, roast backstrips of venison, fried catfish, skin-crisped sweet potatoes. There were huge steaming kettles of clams, of oysters, of corn on the cob, of seasoned swamp cabbage which is the heart of palm. There were pots of grits and of greens of several kinds, bowls of hush puppies, baskets of boiled turtle eggs. There was cornbread, flour biscuits, Seminole bread made of coontie starch. There were jars of molasses, jellies of guava and strawberry and seagrape. There were barrels of mangoes and limes. Several tables held kegs of beer and Old Joe had brought in a wagonload of his best jugged whiskey.

The huge party ate and drank, talked and laughed and told tales of every sort. It danced to the music of a string band out of Stuart and Old Joe took a turn with them on his fiddle and Bill Ashley plunked his banjo for several sets. Children ran about in shrieking play or danced at the periphery of the packed-dirt clearing where the adults reeled and waltzed and square-danced and dogs ran yapping through the crowd. A dozen smoking smudge pots stood at intervals between the house and the surrounding swamp to keep down the mosquitoes.

John Ashley sat at one end of the family table and Old Joe at the other. Bob Ashley sat by John and told him about Bob Baker's recent marriage. "She's a Georgia girl," he said. "They say she's real nice. I saw her in West Palm one time. Goodlookin thing—way too goodlookin for the likes of him. I figure she musta took pity on him is why she married him. Maybe she figured a one-legged man wouldnt never get nobody to marry him and she just felt good and sorry for him."

"Maybe she was just good and drunk," John Ashley said.

"Maybe she's just good and *dumb*," Bob said. He leaned closer and lowered his voice and said, "But look here, Johnny, tell me more about Aunt July's."

With them sat their twelve-year-old nephew Hanford Mobley who idolized both these uncles who treated him like the young man he believed he already was. Earlier that day they had let him go with them into the pineywoods to watch them have a shooting contest. They had fired twelve shots each at pine cones they lined up on a fallen trunk and John had won by a score of twelve cones to eleven and laughingly claimed that all the pussy he'd had these past two years had made his shooting eye even sharper than it always was. John then let Hanford Mobley have a turn with his pistol and the brothers stood astonished to discover that their slight small-boned nephew who had to use both hands to aim the big .44 was a natural-born deadeye. The boy hit all twelve cones he shot at and didnt stop beaming the rest of the day. When they told old Joe about it he said of his grandson, "Hell yeah that sprout can shoot. Been thataway since he was eight or so. He's a good one, that little fella. Aint afraid a the devil hisself neither. You ought see how he can use a knife."

Now John Ashley grinned at his brother's insistence on hearing more about his lickerish life at their aunt's house in Galveston. "Hell, brother," he said, "I done told you all there is to tell." He ran a hand over the unfamiliar feel of the exposed back of his neck, which showed as pale as the narrow strip of shaved skin above each ear. The first thing Old Joe had said on seeing him after his absence of nearly two years was, "Boy, I dont what-all they think of hair like that on a man in Texas, but round here they wont know whether to kick your ass or kiss you. Ma! Get me the shears and razor!"

John Ashley had also told Bob earlier about the Galveston bank robbery. His brother had whooped and clapped him on the shoulder and called him a lying sack. John then took him into his room at the rear of the house and pulled a suitcase from under the bed and opened it and showed his brother the more than one thousand dollars that yet remained of the take. Bob's big-eyed flabbergast struck him as comic and he laughed and said, "Lying sack, hey?"

Bob asked what in purple hell had possessed him to rob a damn *bank*, and John tried to explain about the mixed-up feelings he'd had when he was fishing on the beach one day and thought about Bobby Baker holding a lifetime grudge and maybe even wanting him dead. Tried to explain his frustration over not knowing what to do about it but that he felt he had to do *something*, something *daring*, even though he couldn't say why. "Hell, I dont know," John Ashley said. "I dont know *why* I did it. All I know is I felt pretty damn good after."

"You just up and decided that robbin a bank was a way to make yourself feel better, hey?" Bob said, grinning. "Shitfire, I guess it's lots of fellas'd feel better about things if they got away with robbin a bank."

John Ashley said, "Well . . . yeah." He was not sure he could ever explain the thing clearly even to himself. And so he changed the subject: "Let me tell you about somethin that damn sure makes any man feel a whole lot better, bubba. I mean, it's some nice little business Aunt July's got there. . . ."

And now Bob still had not heard enough about their aunt's establishment in Texas and his brother's time in it. "Was you tellin me true?" he said in low voice, glancing down the table to ensure no ear other than young Hanford Mobley's was listening in. "About havin run of the place? You really and truly could have *any* them girls you wanted?"

"Any damn time they wasnt workin on the house clock," John Ashley said.

"You *lyin* sack," Bob Ashley said, grinning hugely.

"I had me my first piece last month," young Hanford Mobley said. "Wasnt nothin so dang special."

His uncles turned to him and said together, "*You* lyin sack!" and the boy reddened with his lie and he shrugged and could not restrain his grin.

At the other end of the table Old Joe as holding forth about the stupidities of the legal system. He had over the past two years grown steadily angrier that his son was being forced to live apart from his family for no reason but having killed some Indian. "The law," Old Joe said, "is a goddamned horse's ass."

"Hear, hear," said Gordon Blue, raising his glass in a toast. The dapper goateed lawyer was the only person present wearing a suit and

tie. The day before, he and Old Joe had explained to John Ashley
how they intended to get him out from under the law's deep shadow.

"If your daddy here hadnt kept it from me for so long that he
knew where you were and how much he wanted to have you back
home," Gordon Blue had said, "we wouldve had you back long before
now." He gave Old Joe a sidewise look. "But *nooo.* Joe couldnt bring
himself to trust *anyone,* not even Old Gordy, no matter that I've helped
him a time or two in worse trouble than this. Couldnt tell me about
it till a few weeks ago, could you Joseph?"

Old Joe's smile was small. "I dont know why the whole thing
wasnt plain to me as the nose on my face till I talked to Gordy about
it," he said to John Ashley. "The simple fact is, they got to give you
a jury trial—and what jury's gonna convict you in Palm Beach County?
Besides, the state's havin trouble findin their main witness, aint they?
The only ones to testify against you will be Sheriff George and them
who heard that breed accuse you. But aint nobody seen that breed
since you been gone—or goin to, neither."

Bob Ashley chuckled and said, "I dont guess *he's* gonna do any
testifyin, no sir." On the drive home from Tampa, he had proudly
recounted to John Ashley how he'd tracked down Jimmy Gopher in
the Everglades and put a round through his head at nearly two hundred
yards. John Ashley had looked at him partly in surprise that he could
speak so easily of having killed a man and partly in admiration of the
same thing—and of his utter confidence in having done the right thing.
Bob said, "Hell man, he'd of spoke against you in court. It wasnt
nothin else to do. What the hell, man, he anyway had it comin."

"The point is," Old Joe now said, "most ever man in the county's
on our side in this thing and thats a fact. Aint none of em gonna say
you guilty if they get on the jury."

John Ashley looked at his brothers gathered by the door and listening and all of them grinning except Bill the elder who never was
one to smile except sometimes when playing his banjo. He turned to
his father and said, "Not *everybody* in the county's our friend, Daddy.
What if some of them get on the jury?"

"I wouldn't be too concerned about that," Gordon Blue said.
"There's a story been going around for months that this Gopher fellow
who accused you to the police was set upon in the Everglades by
persons unknown who were sympathetic to your cause. Supposedly he
was dismembered with an ax and his remains fed to the alligators."
Gordon Blue made a face of distaste and gave a little theatrical shiver
and then smiled widely. "Although the story isnt true, it *is* true that

this person seems to have fallen off the earth, and I suspect that no potential juror will be able to completely ignore the possible implications of the tale."

The Ashley men all looked at one another and grinned. Gordon Blue smiled and poured a touch of bourbon from his gilded flask into his cup and then took a small sip. He cleared his throat and said to John Ashley: "It's all arranged. Tomorrow your father and I deliver you to Sheriff George Baker at the county jail in West Palm. The trial opens on Tuesday, so you'll be there only one day before it starts and then for only as long as it lasts, which I dont believe will be very long. Sheriff George has also agreed that you wont be handcuffed on your promise not to attempt escape."

He paused to light a cigarette, one of the tailormade Chesterfields he bought by the case in Chicago. He exhaled a blue plume of smoke and smiled at John Ashley. "In a week, two at the most, you'll be free and clear."

And so Old Joe had laid out that Sunday's repast at Twin Oaks for all local friends of the family, all of whom were in John Ashley's jury pool. And on that Sunday afternoon John Ashley ate and drank and danced and swapped stories with his brothers. And after sundown he and Bob drove to West Palm Beach and went to Miss Lillian's.

The madam was surprised to tears to see him again and greeted him like the Prodigal returned. Then he went upstairs and tiptoed to Loretta May's room and looked in the open door and saw the tub of steaming water before he saw her sitting in a yellow shimmy at the window and facing out into the darkness. Her blonde hair had grown to below her shoulder blades but the breeze through the window carried to him her familiar smell of peaches. He thought her more beautiful than ever and was content to stand there in silence and look upon her.

Without turning she said, "About time you got here, you bad ole gator-skinner you."

He grinned and felt himself flush, as though she'd caught him at something sneaky. "How'd you know I was standin here? How'd you know it was *me*?"

She laughed like a small bell and stood and turned smiling and opened her arms to him.

After the bath and the powdering and after they'd made love twice they lay entwined and smoked cigarettes and spoke very little. When they'd first met he'd asked her what pleasure she got out of smoking since she couldn't see the smoke and she'd said, "I cant?"—a response that so confused him he let the question go. Now he was surprised that she did not ask where he'd been these past two years. And yet, somehow, he felt she knew.

"I done somethin while I was away," he whispered, feeling strangely as if he were asking a question of her as much as telling her something. "Somethin I hadnt ever done before."

She nuzzled his neck and murmured, "I know. Made the world spin a little faster for a while, huh? Made everything a little more *excitin*."

He drew back so he could look into her face in the weak reflected light of the torches in the courtyard below the window. Her eyes were shut. "You know what I done?" he said. "You dont know what I done."

She opened her eyes and turned her face toward him. "Yes I do—and I know more than that, boy. I even know what you're *gonna* do. Bet you a dollar I know what you gonna do."

"Cant nobody shine the future. That ain't but swamp nigger hoo-doo."

She felt for his face and put her fingers to his lips and said, "You're gonna have a real good time with a blind girl *real* soon is what you're gonna do. Now, you think I'm wrong?" He grinned under her fingers and then she grinned too.

She sat up and straddled his thighs and her hands stroked him and in an instant he was ready. She moved up and fit herself onto him and brought his hands up to her breasts as she slowly rolled her hips. He groaned with pleasure.

"I guess," she said, "I won me a bet."

"Lord girl," he gasped, "I believe you sure enough got what they call the sight."

She giggled and worked herself hard against him. They laughed and made love deep into the night.

And in the morning he went to jail.

The jailhouse was a single-story stone-and-concrete structure surrounded by a fence of chickenwire eight feet high and set thirty yards from the building all the way around. Sheriff George Baker met them at the gate. He and Gordon Blue exchanged a few official words and each man signed a paper and then the sheriff smiled at John Ashley and said, "How do, John. Been a while. You lookin fit."

"What say, Sheriff George," John Ashley said. He reached into the motorcar and withdrew the freshly cleaned white suit he would wear in court. Then he stood before his father and they looked at each other for a moment and then Old Joe turned to Sheriff George and said, "You wont be takin him to court in handcuffs you said. It's the deal."

"Not as long as he gives me his word he wont try and escape," Sheriff George said.

"You got it, sir," John Ashley said.

Sheriff George nodded and said, "Well then, let's get inside."

John Ashley looked at his father and Old Joe said, "Go on now. You'll be out quick enough and we'll be done with this horseshit." John Ashley nodded and then followed the sheriff up the walk to the jail. Sheriff George rapped on the heavy front door with its iron knocker and there came the sound of metal sliding on metal and a loud clack and the door swung open.

They entered into an administration room containing a few scattered desks and filing cabinets. There were two uniformed policemen in the room. One was a clerk working at a typewriter, and the other, sitting in a swivel chair with his booted feet crossed on the desk, was Bobby Baker. He was smoking a cigar and grinning at John Ashley.

"That's Norman," Sheriff George said, indicating the clerk. "Hang your suit on that wallhook yonder and empty your pockets on Norman's desk. We'll give you the suit in the morning for court." He saw John Ashley staring at Bob Baker and said, "Bobby's jailer now."

"Hello, John," Bob Baker said. "How you keepin?"

"Just fine, Bobby. How about youself?"

"Well hell, never better," Bob Baker said.

He saw that Bob Baker's brown boots were new and low-cut in the style that civil engineers favored and each was embossed with a white star on the instep. A portion of wooden ankle was visible under the real ankle crossed over it. He seemed to have grown larger since John Ashley had last seen him—not fatter but thicker through the chest and arms. His face looked harder, his eyes. His hair was thick as ever. He held the cigar in his right hand and the knuckles were freshly skinned. He laughed at John Ashley's scrutiny of him. "By the way, John," he said through a blue billow of smoke, "you owe me a gun."

"Any man loses his gun to another aint never owed it back," John Ashley said.

Bob Baker's smile held but his face assumed a rosy tint. Norman the clerk looked over and saw their eyes and quickly looked away.

Sheriff George glanced at them with his brows raised. "Do like I said, John."

John Ashley hung up his suit and then emptied his pockets on the desktop—some coins, seven dollars in bills, a sack of tobacco and cigarette papers, a box of matches, and a pocket knife. Norman pushed the tobacco and papers and matches back to John Ashley and carefully counted the money and entered the total amount on a property slip and made notation too of the pocket knife. Then he took a large brown envelope from a desk drawer and wrote John Ashley's name on it in tall letters with a fountain pen and put the money and the knife in it and sealed it and put it back in the drawer.

Sheriff George headed for a door on the other side of the room and said, "Come along here, Johnny." John Ashley followed and Bob Baker got up from the desk and came behind.

The door opened to the jail's cell block in the center of which was a single steel-barred cell that looked exactly like a cage about the size and shape of a railroad car. It was illuminated from above by three dangling electric light bulbs and contained a row of double-tiered bunk beds and a two-hole board over low rough-hewn cabinets in which the shitcans were set. In addition there were a half-dozen smaller cells built into the rear stone wall, the door to each one open wide and showing them to be empty. The room smelled of waste and disinfectant and was ventilated only by whatever fitful breezes might come through the small barred windows set high in the walls. At the moment only two other prisoners were in the main cell. The sheriff unlocked the door and John Ashley entered the cage and the sheriff locked the door behind him.

"Breakfast six o'clock, Johnny," she sheriff said as he started for the door. He paused and looked back at Bob Baker, who was lingering near the cage.

"I'll be along, Daddy," Bob Baker said.

"Dont devil the boy, son," Sheriff George said, and then went out into the front room.

John Ashley stood near the bars with his hands in his pockets and watched Bobby Baker roll a cigarette and light it. One of the other prisoners was standing against the far wall of bars, smoking and gazing at his hand closed around a bar and paying them no attention. The other inmate lay in an upper bunk with an arm over his eyes.

Now Bobby leaned on one elbow against the cell bars and smiled at John Ashley. "Tell me somethin, Johnny: you ever see a man hung?" he asked.

"Yeah I have," John Ashley said. "Just after, anyway."

"A nigger, right?"

"Hard to say. By the time I saw him he'd been burned up so bad he didnt look like much of anything but a big chunk of charcoal."

"That's a nigger lynchin sure," Bob Baker said. "I mean you ever seen a white man hung?"

"Guess not."

Bob Baker smiled and took a drag on his cigarette. "I have," he said. "Up in Saint Lucie County Jail, about a year ago. They hung a old boy for murder. Killed his partner in a moonshine business—cut his head off with a cane knife—and they gave him the rope. They built a gallows back of the jailhouse and before dawn they stood the fella up there and asked him did he have any last words and he just shook his head. I'd been told he was a rough old boy but up on that gallows he didnt seem all that tough. Looked too scared to open his mouth—like he might of started cryin if he did. They put hood over his head and you could see the cloth suckin in and out against his mouth he was breathin so hard. His neck was sposed to break when they dropped him through the door but it didnt. They say thats what happens more than half the time, the neck dont break like it ought, and what happens then is the fella chokes to death. You shoulda seen the way he was jerkin and kickin ever which way, just like a damn fish on a hook. Makin sounds all wet and choky like water going down a mostly clogged drain. I bet he was gaggin and kicking for five minutes before he finally give up the ghost. And the *smell*! Lord Jesus! He couldnt help but shit his pants—I'm told they all do. But that aint the half of it, listen to this: the sumbuck got a *hard-on*! I aint lyin. He got this boner in his pants you could see from all the way cross the room. They say some of em even shoot off and you can see the stain on their pants. Aint that a hoot? I mean to tell you, Johnny, hanging is just about the most godawful humiliatin way in the world for a man to die."

Bob Baker leaned closer against the bars and said softly: "When they find you guilty, John, that's what's gonna happen to *you*." He smiled genially, his aspect all bonhomie, then took a deep pull on his cigarette and dropped the butt on the floor and ground it under his heel. "Thought you might wanna have somethin to think about between now and then," he said through an exhalation of smoke.

"Well dont get too way ahead of youself, Bobby," John Ashley said, forcing a grin. "I aint hung yet. But I tell you what—even if they did hang me, leastways I'd still be able to stand up there on my own two legs, which is more than I can say for some."

Bob Baker's smile twitched and he blinked quickly several times. He stepped back from the bars—and then suddenly laughed like he'd been told a good joke. He put a fist to the side of his neck and then jerked the fist straight up as though yanking on a noose and he crooked his head and struck out his tongue and crossed his eyes. He was still laughing as he went out the door.

The morning dawned hot and humid. To either side of the rising sun low heavy clouds looked streaked with fire. The courtroom filled early and the small room was murmurous with excitement as spectators fanned themselves against the heat. A weakling breeze sagged through the courtroom's tall windows. A growing line of prospective jurors was already crowding the hallways and many of the veniremen were forced to wait outside in the shade of trees. Now the bailiff announced that court was in session, the Honorable H. P. Branning presiding.

Gordon Blue had informed the Ashleys that Circuit Court Judge Branning had a reputation for no-nonsense legal proceeding, a factor in their own favor. "Gramling's going to challenge so many of the jury candidates," Blue had told Joe Ashley, referring to John Gramling, the state prosecutor, "that he'll use up all his peremptories by tomorrow. In the meantime Branning will get his fill of him for slowing things down so much. By the time the jury's seated we'll have them *and* the judge on our side."

And so did the first day of the trial go. Of the twenty juror candidates questioned, Gramling challenged seventeen and did not seem happy with the other three. Gordon Blue challenged none. Near the end of the day Judge Branning called both lawyers to the bench and asked the state's attorney whether he intended to continue to weigh down the proceedings with still more challenges tomorrow. "The peremptory is not an infinite privilege, Mr. Gramling," the judge said. Gramling said he was fully aware of that—and aware as well that every potential juror so far, with a single exception, was a friend of the Ashleys, and the one exception was so clearly intimidated by the family he couldnt even look the defendant in the eye and could hardly be relied on to be impartial. The judge looked at Gordon Blue who shrugged in the manner of one baffled utterly by the state's argument. After warning Gramling not to test his patience the judge adjourned court for the day.

As Bob Baker led John Ashley by an arm toward a side exit, John

Ashley looked over at his family seated behind the defense table. His father nodded to him and his mother and sisters blew kisses and the twin brothers Frank and Ed each showed him a fist of encouragement. Bill was scribbling in a notebook—having been recruited as a secretarial assistant by Gordon Blue. Bob Ashley shouted, "We gone beat em, Johnny!"

Then he was outside and in Bob Baker's Model T and they were clattering down the road on the short drive back to jail. As when they'd come to court in the car that morning—he in his fresh white suit and Bob Baker in a starched uniform and wearing his holstered and strapped-down pistol on the side away from John Ashley—they made the ride in silence.

The following day was mostly a repetition of the first—one venireman after another was eliminated from the jury pool by Gramling's peremptories. Judge Branning's irritation grew. When he recessed for lunch he brought the gavel down like he was trying to break it. The early afternoon saw still more candidates dismissed by Gramling's challenges. The judge drummed his fingers.

The sky framed in the windows began to darken with gathering clouds. The wind kicked up and carried on it the smell of the coming storm and brought to the courtroom some relief from the stifling heat. Thunder rolled in the distance. The first scattered raindrops were smacking the roof and the raised shutters when Gramling at last used up the last of his peremptory challenges. The judge heaved a theatrical sigh and said perhaps they could now proceed at quicker pace.

But Gramling then filed a motion for change of venue, citing the pertinent statutes permitting the action. He wanted the trial moved to Dade County, where, he argued, there was much better chance for the state to seat an impartial jury.

Judge Branning rubbed his face with his hands and said he'd take the motion under advisement and rule on it first thing in the morning. Gordon Blue muttered, "Damn!" and the look on his face made John Ashley's chest go tight. The judge motioned the bailiff to the bench for a private word with him. John Ashley wondered if Blue had considered that the judge might get *so* fed up with Gramling he'd let the trial go elsewhere.

His father was whispering to Bill in obvious agitation as his other three sons leaned in to listen. Blue patted John Ashley's shoulder and said, "Don't worry, they cant do this." He began gathering his papers.

"I'm going to talk with your daddy. I'll see you in the lockup later." The judge banged his gavel and adjourned for the day.

In the clamor of voices that rose behind the judge's exit from the room, John Ashley was suddenly certain the trial was going to go to Dade County—to Miami—to a jury of complete strangers. His mother scowled at John Gramling who took no notice as he gathered his papers. Old Joe was listening to Bill. Bob waved to catch John Ashley's attention and pointed at Bob Baker who was talking to the bailiff. John Ashley did not understand what Bob was signifying but Bob and Frank and Ed were already hastening from the courtroom.

Bob Baker came over and took him by the arm and said, "Let's go."

The rain was coming down hard now and they were sodden by the time they reached the open-sided Ford. John got in and Bob Baker cranked the motor and then got in and adjusted the spark lever and they started back to the jail. The air shook with thunder and the sky was rent bright with lightning. The trees whipped in the wind. They drove along in the jouncing car with mud slapping up under the floorboards. John Ashley stared glumly at the gray world passing and felt that all matters of import to him had already been decided and none of them in his favor.

With the storm had come an early twilight. Sheets of water swept across the narrow road and soaked them all the more in the open car. The jailhouse came into view, the light above the door already on and glowing hazy yellow in the gloom. John Ashley cut his eyes everywhere but saw no sign of deliverance.

Bob Baker parked the car alongside the fence gate and cut off the motor which chugged for several more revolutions before shutting down. Wisps of steam issued from under the hood covers. John Ashley slid out of the car and scanned the area as Bobby worked a key into the gate lock.

"Come on!" Bob Baker hollered through a crash and roll of thunder, beckoning irritably as he swung open the gate. John Ashley entered the compound and Bobby re-locked the gate and they slogged through the mud up to the jailhouse which loomed now in John Ashley's eyes like an enormous crypt.

As Bob Baker reached for the iron knocker to summon Norman to unlock the door John Ashley acted on his impulse of the moment and grabbed him from behind in a headlock and wrestled him away from the entry.

Bob Baker snarled a muffled curse under John Ashley's arm and became a bucking writhing frenzy trying with both hands to break free. But John Ashley held the arm clamped round his head as hard as he could and they reeled and staggered and splashed about like mad dancers in the muddy rain. And now Bob Baker was clawing at John Ashley's binding arm with one hand and trying to unholster his pistol with the other and John Ashley got the leverage and purchase he was struggling for and lunged toward the jail wall and rammed the crown of Bob Baker's head against it. Bobby went slack and sagged full weight in the vise of his arm and John Ashley feared he might have killed him. So tightly was his arm locked that he had to force it open with his other hand before he could let Bob Baker fall.

He stood gasping, massaging his aching arm, watching the jailhouse door in expectation of Norman's appearance, but the door remained shut. The wind had died of a sudden and the rain was falling straight down and spattering high and loud. He saw now that Bobby's face was in the mud and if he was not already dead he was going to drown. He knelt and pushed him onto his side and Bob Baker sucked a huge muddy mouthful of air. He was yet unconscious and blood ran from his hair and rubied the mud under his head. The hold-down strap of his holster was unfastened and John Ashley for the second time in their lives relieved him of his gun, once again a .38 caliber Smith & Wesson. He checked the loads and then stuck the pistol in his waistband.

"Johnny!"

He looked to the yard gate and saw his brothers Bob and Ed coming on the run, each with pistol in hand, and behind them, in the driving rain, a shimmying Model T emitted vague smoke from its exhaust pipe and Frank was behind the wheel and was looking out for anyone coming from either direction in the road.

Bob kicked and kicked at the gate lock and John Ashley was about to yell out for him to hold on, he'd get the gate key out of Bobby's pocket, but Ed was already backing up a dozen feet and now running at the fence and throwing his full weight against it and a fifteen-foot portion of chickenwire ripped off its support posts and scooped down into the mud as Ed sprawled on the fallen fence and regained his feet and here came Bob behind him laughing raucously and yelling, "Whooo! Some damn jail, aint it? Fucken *chickenwire*!"

They clapped him on the shoulder and grinned hugely and he felt himself grinning back. "We'd been here waitin to jump the sonofabitch," Ed said, "but Frankie run off the road about a quarter-mile back and it took a while to get the machine out the damn ditch."

"He *dead?*" Bob asked, nudging Bobby Baker with his toe. Bob Baker groaned but his eyes were still closed.

"You all get back to the car," John Ashley said. "Best he dont see you here. Go on now."

"Hell, I aint scared of this mullethead," Bob said. "Let him see me all he wants."

"It's got nothin to do with bein scared of him, Bob," John Ashley said. "Right now he aint got a thing on any you, only me. Let's keep it that way. Get on to the car and I be right there. I want a word with this sumbitch."

"He's right," Ed said, tugging on Bob's sleeve. "C'mon, let's get." Bob spat and hustled his balls and looked from one to the other of them and said, "Well all right, hell," and went off with Ed through the rain and over the downed portion of fence and got in the car with Frank.

John Ashley knelt and turned Bobby Baker on his back and shook him by the shoulder and patted his face and tugged repeatedly on his ears and in a moment Bobby coughed wetly and choked and rolled toward John Ashley who jumped up and away to avoid the gush of vomit he heaved up.

Bobby gasped and opened his eyes and saw John Ashley grinning down at him. He started to sit up but John Ashley put his foot against his shoulder and pushed him onto his back again. "Just you stay there."

"Son . . . bitch," Bobby muttered. He managed to get up on all fours before John Ashley kicked him in the ribs and the air whooshed out of him and he fell on his side with eyes wide and blood running from his hair and down the side of his face and his mouth working for breath. John Ashley squatted and grabbed a fistful of his hair and turned his face up into the rain.

"So I'm gonna hang, hey?" John Ashley said. "Gonna shit my pants? I told you not to get so ahead of yourself, didnt I?" He yanked Bob Baker over onto his stomach and pushed his face into the mud for several seconds and then yanked his head up again by the hair. Bob Baker snorted and spat mud and tried weakly to wrest free and John Ashley punched him in the back of the neck. "I wouldn't try and make a fight of it just now, I was you," he said.

A piercing whistle he recognized as Bob's cut through the rain and he looked at the idling Ford. The rain was falling harder now and he could see his brothers as only vague forms within the car and he knew Bobby would not recognize them if he should look their way. Bob

Baker cursed lowly and tried to pull John's hand off his hair and roll over. John Ashley released him and got to his feet and thought to kick him again but the sight of his bloody head and the sound of his gasping decided him against it. The man was beat, so let him lay. He turned and ran for the fence and clambered over the skewed chickenwire and loped to the car and the open door waiting for him.

And Bob Baker, bleeding and breathless in the mud, heard him laughing and laughing as he made away.

He confided the details of the escape to no one but his father, and in addition to the warrants on John Ashley for murder and escape from custody, Sheriff George Baker had also wanted one for assault on a police officer. But Bob Baker did not want the assault known publicly and his father had deferred to his wish that they keep it to themselves. In his official report Bob Baker asserted that John Ashley had broken his word not to escape and bolted away into the rainy darkness when they got back to the jailyard from the courthouse. He said he could have shot him down but he was not one to shoot an unarmed man, not even a fleeing prisoner, not if he had not yet been convicted of a crime. Because he did not remove his hat in public during the entire time he wore a bandage on his crown, no one but his father and his wife Annie—who'd been the one to tend his wound—ever saw evidence of the beating he'd taken.

As she ministered to his bloody scalp Annie had asked what happened but he'd only looked at her and she'd questioned him no further. She'd come to know him for a moody man best left alone when withdrawn into himself.

That night he made love to her despite the pain of his throbbing head—made love with a passion near to ferocity and the woman in his mind was not his wife but a girl long gone. Two months later Annie happily informed him that she was carrying a child. He was delighted and said they would name it after his father. Annie made a mock face of distaste but said all right, but if it was a girl she wanted to name it after her favorite aunt. Bob Baker said fine, whatever the name it was fine with him. Annie's smile at him then had been wide and warm and full of love. "Good," she said. "I just love the name Julie."

Seven months later she gave birth to the girl. Bob Baker smiled on his wife in the hospital room and gingerly cuddled the infant in his arms and cooed to her and called her his pretty little bird and evermore called her by that nickname rather than her Christian name. If his wife or the girl herself were ever curious about that, they neither one ever said.

Although John Ashley remained in the region, the Palm Beach sheriff was hard-pressed to arrest him. When Dade County went dry the year before, Joe Ashley's moonshine business boomed, and now John Ashley was making regular runs to Miami to deliver his daddy's hooch. Sheriff George knew that. But he was not on friendly terms with the Dade County sheriff and the Ashley family was. And he'd heard enough tales about the corruption in the Miami Police Department to know it would be useless to ask for its help.

There were steady reports of John Ashley sightings in the local region too—mostly in its portion of the Everglades. He was seen at Indian villages and at fishing and hunting camps from the north shore of Lake Okeechobee to the south end of the Loxahatchee Slough. But Sheriff George knew there was as much chance of catching John Ashley in the Devil's Garden as there was of catching a hawk on the wing. He figured his best chance for an arrest would at the Ashley homestead, and so he posted a continuous surveillance on the Twin Oaks house. His deputies made their way to the Ashley property on foot through the piney swamp and took up positions among the trees from which they had a good view of the front of the house some forty yards distant. They reported seeing all the other Ashleys come and go at irregular intervals but never spied John among them.

One late evening a pair of motorcar headlamps came waggling along the trail leading from the highway to the Twin Oaks property and the two mosquito-plagued policemen watching from their post in the pines nudged each other excitedly and jacked rounds into their rifles. Then the front door of the house swung open and laid out a shaft of yellow lamplight bearing the elongated shadow of Ma Ashley as she came out to the top of the porch steps. She raised a shotgun and discharged both flaring barrels into the sky as if bent on felling the bright crescent moon. The carlights halted and swung about through the trees as the car wheeled tightly in reverse and then the lights extinguished and the two cops stood in the darkness and listened to the motor fade into the distance. And they heard too Ma Ashley's laughter as she went back into the house with her shadow following behind and the length of jaundiced lamplight scooted after her just ahead of the shutting door.

SEVEN

The Liars Club

MIAMI WASNT BUT ABOUT FIFTEEN, SIXTEEN YEARS OLD WHEN THE
Ashleys started running whiskey down there. The damn town was
a flat crazy place right from the start and never did lack for grifters
and gamblers and highrollers and bad actors of all sorts. It wasnt many
crackers liked Miami and its ways but the Ashley boys was among
them that did.

Since the turn of the century somebody or other had been dredging
canals between Lake Okeechobee and the Atlantic with the idea of
draining the Everglades and creating a lot more acreage to sell. Before
you could say "Sign right here on the dotted line," Miami was full of
sharpies making money off that scheme. The first dredge boilers were
just getting fired up when the sharpies started advertising virgin farm-
land for sale in the northern newspapers and a bunch of fool Yankees
started buying it through the mail, sight unseen. Hell, they couldnt of
seen it if they wanted to—most of what was being sold was still under
water, and a lot of it would stay that way. The dumbshits were paying
for it by the acre but really buying it by the quart. This sort of conniv-
ing was routine stuff up through the boom of the 1920s when it got
worse than ever—and then a hellacious hurricane blew away a lot of
the enthusiasm for Miami and South Florida for a while.

When they started digging the Miami Canal the engineers built a
dam to hold the water back until the job was done. Once the canal
was dug out to the Glades, they dynamited the dam to let the water

run out and, Lord amighty, did it ever! Water come pouring out of the Glades like some terrible punishment from the Bible. It rushed on down the canal to the Miami River and overran the banks in some places and knocked down sheds and shacks and boat stands and it grabbed up dogs and pigs and anybody who didnt get out the way quick enough and just carried everything it picked up right on down to the bay and dumped it in there and turned that pure blue baywater the ugliest shit-brown you ever saw. The water kept pouring down that canal for *weeks*. Made a godawful mess. Then come the dry season and way out where the swamp had been drained the muck got drier than it was ever meant to be and just any old spark would set it afire. The grass for miles around would catch fire too and the trees would get burnt to black skeletons and the muck would just go on burning and burning and at night you could see the sky glowing orange way out in the Devil's Garden. The smoke would drift in on the wind and turn the high noon sun red as blood and sometimes got so thick you couldnt hardly tell high noon from dawn or dusk. For weeks at a time everybody in town went around with their eyes watering and their throats sore and scratchy from breathing that muck smoke. To make things worse the fires would drive all kinds of critters out of the swamp and there was times when Miami was just overrun with animals getting away from the flames—possums and coons, rats big as cats. You'd see a dozen rattlesnakes a day right in the damn streets. If a little baby in a stroller so much as gave his rattle a shake people would jump a foot in the air and look all wild-about for snakes at their feet. Alligators would come downriver in bunches like timber logs. But hell, the gators was even worse in the wet season, the cottonmouths too. That's when the streets would flood with the rain running off the burnt-up Glades like water off a bare table.

As for them who bought land that actually *did* get drained, well, they set to farming on it and at first they was all excited to see how high the sugarcane grew in the dried-out muck, how the cabbages was big as a man's head and the tomatoes twice the size of a fist. Them farmers figured they'd sure enough done the right thing and it was worth getting a little burnt up in winter and regular flooded in the summertime. Then just as quick as all that growth come out the ground, it shriveled up and died. Turned out the drained muck didnt have the minerals necessary to sustain the crops. Couldnt none of them farmers get anybody to take their land off their hands for as low as ten cents on every dollar they'd paid for it. A lot of them said the hell with it and packed up and left it to whoever was fool enough to claim it.

They'd started clearing the mangroves out of Miami Beach around that time and the rank smell of all that dug-up seabottom was on every ocean breeze carrying into the city. Beginning in 1913 you could drive into the heart of that stink in Miami Beach by way of the Collins Bridge, back then the longest wooden bridge in the world. Most folk today who tell about Old Miami never bother to mention the smell that used to hang over the town. Well, take it for a fact, the stink of Miami was damn near constant and something to reckon with till you got used to it.

But Lord, that crazy place was growing fast! Wasnt ten thousand people there in 1910 and by 1920 it had more than thirty thousand souls. In 1913 a fella named Deering started building himself a humongous old-fashioned Italian-style mansion he called Vizcaya. Built right on the edge of the bay in the Brickell Hammock between Miami and Coconut Grove. Spent millions of it—back when a million dollars was a sum you couldnt imagine. Up till the time Deering built his dream house, the town pretty much depended on a small but regular tourist business in the winter and on Mister Flagler's railroad. But Deering imported hundreds of European craftsmen to do all the fancy masonry and scrollwork and tile-setting and so forth, and he hired about half the men in town to do everything else. In the two years it took to build the place, Miami grew to almost twice the size it'd been and you couldnt hardly go anyplace in town without hearing all kinds of funny foreigner languages being spoke.

In those days Biscayne Bay came right up to the Boulevard and was so clear you could see the stingrays gliding through the grass on the bottom twenty feet down. At the north end of town the bay formed a pretty little cove that tailed in at the Florida East Coast Railroad depot—and down at the south end Flagler's Royal Palm Hotel was set at the mouth of the Miami River. In between was the rest of the town. The center of business was along Flagler Street between the railroad tracks and the Boulevard. The rowdiest area of all—which included the red-light district—was over along 11th Street and a tad west of Miami Avenue, just outside the city limits. That area was called Hardieville in honor of Sheriff Dan Hardie who'd run the whores out of town. There was a story that Ed Ashley had got in a bad fight in a Hardieville cathouse over some girl the very first time he was in there and thats how he got the scar acrost his mouth that for the rest of his life left him looking like he was about to smile or cry and you never knew which one.

The city streets were paved with pulverized limestone back then and the glare of them under the sun would about knock you blind.

When it rained, the limestone went muddy and got tracked into every house and office. In dry weather the lime dust rose in a thin pale haze and blew in through the windows and doors and got on everything. It wasnt until after the War that the city commission decided to improve on those streets and got the bright idea to pave them over with eight-by-four-inch wooden blocks. They were cut from cypress and boiled in creosote and would last till Judgment Day. The workmen laid a layer of white sand over the limestone base and then snugged the blocks in place—and bedamn if the ride over them blocked streets wasnt the smoothest you'd ever know. Then came a frog-strangler of a rainstorm and huge puddles formed in the street and water seeped into the wooden blocks and they started to swell up. Little mounds began forming all over the streets and the rain kept falling and next thing you know—*pop! pop! pop!*—those blocks started flying up off the streets with a sound like gunshots, just whizzing in every direction and ricocheting off the storefronts and busting windows and scaring the bejesus out of the dogs and the draft animals and anybody standing out there at the time. It kept on like that even after the rain stopped, and halfway into the night you'd still hear an occasional pop out in the street and hear a block crack off a wall or pang against an ashcan. The city commissioners didnt want to give up the smoothness of those wooden-block streets, but they didnt want the blocks flying through the air every time there came a downpour neither. They thunk it over for a while and then decided to put the wooden blocks back in the street, only this time with plenty of play between them to allow for swelling the next time it rained. Everybody thought that was a real smart idea. But now the blocks were so loose they clattered when motorcars and wagons rolled over them. When traffic was heavy the clattering was so loud people on the sidewalks had to shout at each other to make theirselves heard. Even those of us who wasnt but squirts back then can recall the godawful racket of them loose wooden blocks. The first rain to come along after the blocks had been reset swelled them up just enough to fit together real nice and for the next day or two they didnt clatter hardly at all and they gave a real smooth ride and everybody smiled and said the commissioners had done a heck of a smart job of it. A few days later it rained again, only harder, and the blocks swelled up a little snugger against each other. But this time the rain kept falling all through the day and the blocks kept swelling and swelling and suddenly *pop! pop! pop!* they started shooting out all over the place just like before.

One fella was running across the street in the rain to get to the

barber shop when a block exploded off the street and hit him between
the legs and he let out a yelp they probably heard up in Fort Lauderdale. The way the story went, he wasnt much good to his wife in bed
after that and she was a high-spirited gal who liked her fun, so she
left him a few months later for a Hardieville piano player she'd met
in the lobby of a movie house. The abandoned husband was so full of
grief he tried to kill himself by jumping in front of a train as it rolled
out of the depot but all he managed to do was get both legs cut off a
little below the hips. After that he had to push himself along on one
of them little platforms on rollers. He begged money on the streets
with a tin cup all day and got drunkern hell every night. But he was
a mean drunk and one night he got into it with a fella in a Hardieville
bar and bit into his shin just as tight as a bulldog and wouldnt let
loose for love nor money. The fella was screaming and smacking him
with a beer mug and the barkeep came around and started hitting the
cripple over the head with a billy like he was driving nails and between
them they beat that poor legless fella to death, sure enough. But even
then he didnt let go his bite. They finally had to break his teeth with
a hammer to get him loose of that shinbone. The cops figured a man
being bit had every right to hit whoever was biting him but they knew
the bartender for a bully and thought he'd beat on the fella as much
for fun as anything else and they charged him with manslaughter. He
went to trial and was acquitted real quick because all the jurors were
businessmen and understood how it'd be real bad for business if a man
let some fella bite on one of his customers without doing something
about it. The legless man was buried in a box not four feet long—
looked more like a fat child's coffin than a man's The whole thing
was a terrible true story but a hard one for most folk back then to tell
or listen to without grinning by the time they got to the end of it.
Oh, that Hardieville was a rough place. Whole damn town was, truth
be told.

Across the street from the Royal Palm Hotel was a park with a
bandshell, and across from the park was the Biscayne Yacht Club,
where the rich people kept their boats. The club had a cannon they
fired every day at eight in the morning when they raised the Stars and
Stripes and again at sunset when the flag came down. They say that
many a visitor to the city who didnt know about that cannon and
happened to be near the yacht club at eight A.M. or sundown when
the fuse was touched off soiled himself. Anybody who ever heard it
can tell you how the blasts rattled windows all down the Boulevard
and sometimes shook coconuts off the trees.

Most visitors to Miami were still coming by train or boat but more and more were now driving down on the Dixie Highway which was already a pretty fair whiterock road by then. And starting in 1913 when Dade County went dry—like most Florida counties already were—the Ashleys had good reason to ride that road to Miami fairly often. This was just a few years after that loony bitch Carry Nation showed up in town with her damn hatchet and made a mess of some of the finest polished-mahogany bars in town. They say she could of used her *face* for a hatchet. Most waterholes had a sign over the backbar saying "Every Nation Welcome But Carry."

Of course, the county law against booze didnt stop Miamians from drinking anymore than a law against breathing would make anybody but a fool go blue in the face. What the law *did* was help boost Old Joe's moonshine profits by removing all his legal competition. After John Ashley escaped from Bobby Baker's custody right there in the yard of the Palm Beach County Jail he became his daddy's main whiskey runner to Miami. The time was fast approaching when Old Joe would have some mean competition for the whiskey market in Miami—some of the toughest coming from Chicago, if what we heard was right—but for a fact Old Joe was selling more whiskey to the Indians than he ever had, and nobody could cut into his business with them because nobody else knew the Devil's Garden as well as him and his boys did.

No question about it, the Ashleys were making money hand over fist. You'd see Old Joe and his boys driving along the Dixie Highway in Palm Beach County and each one in his own brandnew car. John Ashley had him a spanking new Oakland for a while but we heard he lost it in a poker game in Miami. In Daytona Frank and Ed bought theirselves one of the first Dusenbergs sold in Florida. We heard they took it out on the beach and run it up to over ninety miles an hour but nobody really believed that story. Mind you, this was at a time when *forty* miles an hour was just *flying*. People used to say that at ten miles an hour in a Model T the fenders rattled, at twenty the headlamps rattled, at thirty the windshield rattled, and any faster than that your bones rattled. Frank and Ed brung that Dusenberg down to West Palm Beach but the roads around here wasn't yet ready for any such car and next thing we heard Frank had run it through palmetto pasture and into a live oak and nearly kilt himself. After that the car didnt run no more, so they took the seats out of it and put wire in the windows and used it for a dog pen.

EIGHT

August 1914–January 1915

FOLLOWING HIS ESCAPE FROM BOBBY BAKER HE SENT MOST OF HIS days in the Everglades for months thereafter where none of any race or purpose could close on him without warning. He moved from one to another of his father's whiskey camps and carried skiffloads of Old Joe Ashley's hooch to Indian villages in the depths of the Devil's Garden. He hunted and took hides and feathers and his brothers carried them to sell in Stuart or Pompano or on the New River or Miami docks.

Every few weeks he drove a load of his daddy's whiskey down to Miami, going to restaurants and pool halls and hotel kitchens and pleasure houses to make the deliveries and collect the money. Now and then his brothers sojourned to Miami with him to have a high time—always less Bill, whose sense of adventure seemed bounded by account ledgers and whose lust knew no object but his wife. As the town had grown, its pleasures had become plentiful and ever more varied, and the Ashleys found the local attitude toward law enforcement far more amenable than that of Palm Beach County. Both the chief of police and the county sheriff were good old boys largely indifferent to victimless and bloodless violations of the criminal statutes—so long as they received their respectful portion of the profits from all such enterprises. Both men had come to be on first-name acquaintance with the Ashley boys.

In Miami the Ashleys would check into a hotel and bathe in porcelain tubs and dress in new suits and sport with the prettiest whores in town and gamble with the sharps and dine on restaurant glassware and sleep on soft beds with fresh linen. These periodic Miami visits both sated their yen for city wickedness and renewed their appreciation of their natural wildland life. They each time asked Old Joe if he would accompany them and he each time fulminated anew against the failings and follies of all cities and loudly lamented the sins of his youth for which God was punishing him by way of sons too ignorant to recognize a city for the shithole it was.

Gordon Blue had by now opened an office in the Biscayne Hotel on Flagler Street, the city's main thoroughfare, routinely thick with motor vehicle traffic and flanked by a multistoried architectural motley of gables and oriels and turrets and verandahs and balconies, lined with arcades and awninged sidewalks heavily overhung with black electric and telephone lines depending from tall cross-beamed poles smelling of creosote. Crooning pigeons nestled on Blue's windowsills. From those widows he would watch pelicans gliding in V-formations over the bay where tall-masted ships lay at anchor. Seagulls wheeling and shrilling over the city. Turkey buzzards roosting on the roof ledges, nodding their ugly red-naked heads and chuckling as though at dirty jokes, putting him in mind of judges he had known and done business with.

Blue had not approved of John Ashley's escape from Bobby Baker's custody, not after they had promised Sheriff George Baker that John would not try to get away. "Your promise not to try a break was why he left the cuffs off you when you went to court," he said to John Ashley. They were in his office and it was the first time they'd seen each other since John's escape. "They catch you again, Johnny, they'll lock fifty pounds of chain on you and throw away the key."

John Ashley had to laugh. "They didn't *catch* me the first time. I gave myself up, and thats some different. And I did it because they said the trial would be in Palm Beach County. Then those bastards tried to get it moved to Dade. Only a sonofabitch tries to change a deal after it's been agreed on, and only a damn fool thinks he ought keep his word to a sonofabitch. Hell, it aint givin your word that counts, Gordy, it's *who* you give it to. If George Baker was fool enough to leave the chains off me while they were tryin to crawfish on our deal, thats his damn fault and nobody else's."

"The judge hadn't decided yet that the trial was going to Miami," Gordon Blue said. He heard the defensiveness in his own voice. "I think I could have kept that from happening."

John Ashley narrowed his eyes at Gordon Blue and smiled.

Gordon Blue let the matter drop, partly because it would have been fruitless to argue the point—what was done was done and could not be undone—and partly because he believed John Ashley could be right.

It was Blue who introduced the Ashley boys to Miami's backroom gambling spots and hotel poker games frequented by some of the highest rollers in town. Rather than the four of them competing directly against each other, the brothers would split up into paired teams and gamble in different locales—Frank and Ed going to one place, John and Bob playing at another. At the end of the night they would pool whatever winnings they'd pulled in and divide them into equal shares. As far as Gordon Blue knew none of them ever held out on the other, a circumstance that flew in the face of his experience with human nature where money was concerned.

At one of these poker sessions in the Biscayne Hotel on a late fall Friday evening Gordon Blue introduced John and Bob Ashley to someone he called the nephew of an old friend, a freckled young man named Kid Lowe, just arrived on the train from Chicago. The fellow seemed to the Ashleys aptly named: in both stature and visage—and in his white boater and red bowtie—he looked about fourteen years old, even though he chainsmoked cigarettes and played a good game of poker. Only his eyes were parcel of a grown man—wary and quick and mistrustful. But as soon as he spoke and they heard his accent they knew him for one of their own. He was not shy in telling of himself and over the course of the next few hours they learned he'd been born in Tallahassee to a footloose mother, herself a native of Tally Town, but he'd been reared from infancy by maiden aunts in Leesburg till he was eighteen. Then he went to Chicago to work for an uncle in the stockyards and eventually became a bodyguard for a man named Silver Jack O'Keefe, whose trade consisted of acquiring high-interest loans from private sources and then lending the money to somebody else at higher interest yet.

"Bodyguard?" John Ashley echoed. He gave the diminutive Kid Lowe a pointedly appraising look.

Kid Lowe scowled and said, "It aint the size of the dog in the fight, it's the size of the fight in the dog. I'da figured you all to know that."

Bob Ashley grinned. "That's sure enough true about dogs, cousin, it sure enough is."

At the game's conclusion John and Bob Ashley accepted Gordon Blue's invitation to join him and Kid Lowe at a brightly-lighted cafe on Miami Avenue for pork chop sandwiches and beer. There Gordon

Blue informed the brothers that Kid Lowe was in difficult circumstances with business associates in Chicago. He did not get specific beyond saying that the matter concerned Silver Jack O'Keefe's failure to meet a certain financial obligation and that Silver Jack was now said to be at the bottom of Lake Michigan with one end of a rope around his neck and the other tied to a hundred-pound bag of bricks.

"What's that got to do with young Lowe here?" John Ashley said.

"I paid a visit to the sumbitch responsible for that sack a bricks," Kid Lowe said. "I mean, hell, it made me look bad, them snatching him out of the restaurant like they did while I was taking a piss. Made me look like I didnt know how to do my job."

John Ashley nodded and studied the Kid more closely. "That sumbitch in the lake now too?"

"Ask me no questions," Kid Lowe said, "I'll tell you no lies."

John Ashley laughed and said that was fine by him.

Gordon Blue was sure the matter would be cleared up in a week or two, but until then Kid Lowe needed a safe place to lie low. The Ashley boys grinned at the little fugitive and said any friend of Gordon's was a friend of theirs and they'd be happy to put the boy up for a time, so long as he kept to himself all complaints about mosquitoes or the lack of city amenities he might be used to—such as running water or electricity. Kid Lowe smiled shyly and thanked them and said he'd be proud to get back to country living after three years of the big city life, which he had lately come to lose all fondness for.

They returned to the hotel to meet with Ed and Frank Ashley and then at Gordon Blue's suggestion they all packed into a taxi and headed for the city limits and Hardieville. One side of Frank Ashley's face was yet puffed and patched with purple from its impact with the windshield when he ran the Dusenberg squarely into an oak. A drizzling rain had fallen through most of the early evening and the limestone streets shone pale under the rattling taxi's headlamps and in the cast of the infrequent streetlights. A cat's-eye amber moon rose out of the Atlantic. The air had cooled and the wind was to seaward and carried on it the scent of wet earth and ripe foliage and was free of the usual stink of dredged bay bottom.

At this late hour of a Friday night the Hardieville sidewalks were raucous with revelers and with drunks doing the hurricane walk. From its brightly blazing doors and windows came the smells of whiskey and cooking grease, sweat and perfume, the sounds of laughter and shouting and badly sung songs, the plinking of ragtime pianos and the blatting of brass bands. They went into The Purple Duck, a supperplace offering three musical floorshows per evening, one of which was in progress before a sparse crowd as they made their way past the dining room—a trio of boaters and peppermint jackets softstepping on a tiny stage and singing "On Moonlight Bay." A woman in a green satin dress came forth to greet Gordon Blue with a kiss that left its cheerful lipsticked imprint on his cheek. Her smile was warm but her eyes quick and assessing and John Ashley figured her for nobody's fool. Gordon Blue introduced her as Miss Catherine, the proprietress, and she smiled around at them all and bade them have a swell time.

Gordon Blue led the way through a curtained doorway in the rear of the room and down a narrow hall to yet another door. He grinned at his friends and delivered three sharp raps and then two lesser ones. A small peephole opened in the door for a moment and then closed and there was the sound of a latch working and the door opened and a short broad man in a red bowtie and black vest nodded at Gordon Blue and permitted them to pass into a room hazy with dim yellow light and cigarette smoke and loud with ragtime music and laughter and talk. There were crowded tables all about and a small dance floor at one end of the room and beside it a bandstand and on it a Negro pianist playing his rag tunes in a sweat. A brass-railed bar ran the length of the room and the backbar was resplendent with a tiered array of every variety of bottled spirits. Whores everywhere—in shimmies and in filmy Arabian pantalettes and vests and in white cotton bloomers and beribboned lace bodices cut low on their milky breasts—whores plying the tables and bantering with the patrons at the bar and here and there twining arms with a grinning man and the pair making for the stairway leading to the rooms above.

They wended their way to the bar and each man called for bourbon. As the bartender set them up John Ashley scanned the crowd and marveled happily at the great allure of vice. He turned to Gordon Blue and said, "I've heard tell it aint no fruit so sweet as that which is forbidden, and ever time I come in a place like this I do believe I heard tell correctly."

Gordon Blue grinned and said, "Spoken like a true philosopher, Johnny."

John Ashley smiled. "I do hope and pray the damn Saloon League gets the federals to outlaw spirits. Hellfire, Gordy, we'll all be rich in no time."

Gordon Blue raised his glass high and said, "To the Saloon League! May its high moral principles enrich us all!"

Four hours later they'd each of them made a trip upstairs with a girl and Frank and Ed told their brothers they would see them back at the hotel and then departed for The Pair-'O-Dice down the street to see what it was like. John and Bob Ashley, Kid Lowe and Gordon Blue then posted themselves at the bar of The Purple Duck's backroom and were shortly joined by Miss Catherine who clearly had a special fondness for Gordon Blue. Each man bought a round in his turn and they talked and told jokes and finally agreed to call it a night.

The crowd had grown larger now and the air was thick and warm with body heat and gauzed with cigarette smoke and the front door seemed very far away at the other end of the room. Gordon Blue asked Miss Catherine if they might use her special side door and she led them to her office and shut the door behind them and pulled back a heavy set of curtains against the wall to reveal her private door. It opened into a dark alley thick with mud on which a walkway of planks had been laid end to end from Miss Catherine's door to the street some forty yards distant to their right. Immediately to their left was a cul-de-sac. A light drizzle yet fell in a mist and the alley reeked of rot and human waste and the only light in the alleyway was the dim glow from the streetlamps.

While Gordon Blue said his private goodnights to Miss Catherine, John Ashley stepped out onto the plank walkway and the others followed behind. Now Gordon Blue came out and Miss Catherine waved from the brightly lighted doorway and said, "You boys take care now, you hear?" and closed the door behind them.

They began to file along the boards, one behind the other, just as a trio of men in derbies came round the corner at the far end of the alley and started toward them on the planks, stark black silhouettes against the yellow backlight of the street, their shadows stretching before them like shades loosed of the graveyard.

"This might could get interestin," Bob Ashley said.

Near the midpoint of the walkway, John Ashley and the other point man halted with three feet between them and regarded each other. John Ashley felt himself clearly illumined in the glow of the streetlights, but the other man remained indistinct, a backlighted silhouette. One of the other men raised a bottle to his mouth and it gleamed brightly against the light and John Ashley caught the redolence of rum.

"Well now, I guess you lads will be getting a bit of mud on your shoes now, wont ye?" the front man said, and John Ashley felt rather than saw the man's grin.

"We was on this walk before you boys," John Ashley said. "Anybody gone get their shoes muddy it's you."

"You were on these boards *first*?" the point man said sardonically. He laughed. "Well hell, I guess that fucken well settles *everything*, now dont it?"

"What the hell you doin *arguin* with these sonsofbitches?" said one of the other derbied men as he stepped off the plank and came around from behind the point man, his shoes sucking through the mud. The point man grabbed him by the arm and said, "Goddammit, Logan, I know how to deal with these hicks."

Logan shook off the man's grip and turned to John Ashley and brought a snapblade knife out of his pocket so fast and smoothly it was as if the weapon had been in his hand all along. The small *snick* of the blade snapping open seemed to John Ashley to make the air go thinner.

"Fucken hillbillies," Logan said and took a step toward John Ashley just as Kid Lowe came slogging up alongside the planks and delivered a grunting kick to the knifer's balls that raised the man to his toes. John Ashley heard the hiss of Logan's sharp suck of air and even as the man started to sag Bob Ashley stepped forward and struck him with a huge roundhouse that sent him sprawling back into the mud and Kid Lowe set to kicking the man in the head.

The point man caught John Ashley by the throat with both hands and they staggered off the planks and into the mud and John Ashley could not breathe. He grabbed the man's arms tight at the elbows and planted his feet and swung him around hard into the wall and the man's breath blew out of him. John Ashley broke free and grabbed him by the neck with one hand and by the hair with the other and rammed the back of the man's head into the wall a hard half-dozen times and then let him fall to a sitting position and drove his knee into his face and felt the man's front teeth give way as the man's head snapped back to strike the wall yet again with a hollow thunk. The man fell over sideways and lay still.

Kid Lowe and Bob Ashley were facing off warily against the third man who was armed with the jagged rum bottle he'd broken against the wall. He was feinting first at Bob and then at the Kid, making one and then the other jump back as from a striking snake. Now Kid Lowe said, "Fuck this," and pressed forward and the man slashed at him several quick times and the Kid fended with his hands but kept advancing and he backed the man against the wall and then charged into him with fists flailing. Bob leaped in and grabbed the man in a headlock and wrestled the bottle from him and drove it into his face and the man screamed. Now the Kid had the man by the hair and was biting into his ear and the man screamed again as his ear came away in the Kid's teeth. Bob and the man fell together in the mud and the kid kicked the man in his gashed face again and again and the man stopped screaming now and Bob was cursing and yelling "You kicking *me*, goddammit!" and turned loose of the man and rolled away from the Kid's frenzy.

John Ashley was laughing as he grabbed Kid Lowe by the collar and yanked him back and caught him in a bear hug from behind and said, "All right there, killer, all right, I believe you done made your point on the fella." Kid Lowe's breath was heaving, his lean muscles twitching under John Ashley's grasp.

Now Gordon Blue came forward from the shadows where he'd sought refuge and said, "Jesus Christ Almighty! Are they dead, any of them?"

Bob Ashley made a quick examination of the fallen and verified that all were alive, though none was conscious and the one whose face he and the Kid had mutilated was bleeding badly from a gash in his neck and breathing erratically. "This one aint like to make it," he said.

"Oh *Christ*," Gordon Blue said, and took a look around to see if there might be witnesses. "Let's get the hell out of here—*now*."

The Kids fury had abated and he said, "You can let go me now." He put his hands to John Ashley's arms to free himself of his embrace and John Ashley felt their touch slicked with blood.

"Damn, Kid, let's see them hands." He pulled the Kid over closer to the street where the light was better. "I need some kinda bandage here," he said.

Bob Ashley stripped the shirt off the Logan fellow and tore it in two and John Ashley held the Kid's dripping hands out while Bob bandaged them tightly each in turn. He told the Kid the niggerwrap job would have to do till they got him home and Ma could tend to his wounds proper. Both brothers were grinning as Bob finished tying off the bandages and remarked how damned glad he was that Kid Lowe was on their side because he sure didnt fancy fighting somebody who was half-crazy and half-cannibal besides. Kid Lowe was grinning with them now and saying the ear didn't taste half bad and maybe he ought to have cut the other one off him to have for breakfast in the morning. They all three laughed.

And now Gordon Blue was tugging at John Ashley's arm with one hand and at Bob Ashley's with the other and saying, "Let's *go*, let's *go*!" and the look on his face made them all three laugh the harder. And then they cleared out of there fast.

*   *   *

Two days later Kid Lowe was living in a small pinewood cabin behind the outside kitchen of the Ashley home. And three weeks after that, Ma Ashley's good stitches now removed from his hands and his hands almost completely unstiffened, he went with John and Bob Ashley on his first alligator hunt. Although cracker by blood, he'd been raised fatherless and brotherless, without masculine mentor of any sort, and thus had not been taught the usual wildland skills most crackers early acquired. He owned all the natural inclinations, however, and took to poling an Everglades skiff as one long practiced at it. At supper that night the Ashleys listened in high amusement to him tell all about how well he'd learned from John Ashley to bark like a dog to call alligators into open water for easier killing. He could not stop talking of the three gators he'd killed and the two he had skinned mostly by himself after the brothers taught him how to take the hide off the first one. None of the Ashleys minded listening to Kid Lowe's story three times over as they sipped at cups of old Joe's best. They knew the little cracker from the city was but happy to be among his own kind.

The next time they saw Gordon Blue he told them there had been but one recent mention in the Miami newspapers of a dead man found in an alley but the alley in question was not the one where they had fought the three men. "If that fella in the alley didnt, ah, make it," Gordon Blue said, "his friends must've taken him away from there."

John Ashley still slipped into West Palm Beach every now and then to visit Miss Lillian's and be with blind Loretta May. They were easy with each other now as they were with no one else, and had for a while even played a game whereby they would make bets as to what part of her he was looking at while they caressed each other's nakedness. At first they bet a dollar each time but after she lost the first five times she suggested they raise the bet to five dollars, saying maybe she could do better if there was more at stake. He said all right, but he hated taking advantage. She said he shouldn't feel guilty about it because after all it was her who wanted to raise the ante. She won the next five times in a row before he realized she'd conned him thoroughly, that she knew exactly where his eyes were on her at all times, and how she knew this did not trouble him as much as the fact that she used the knowledge to hornswoggle him. One more time, he said. On the next bet she said that he was looking at her left breast, which he was, but he told her she was wrong, he was looking at her belly, and she laughed with such delight that he knew she knew he was lying and he had to laugh too. He tried to summon a proper degree of indignation. "I dont know how you know what I'm lookin at, but knowin it and pretendin you dont know just cause you're blind, thats the same as cheatin." At which she could only laugh. "And it aint cheatin to make bets with a *blind* person about what you lookin at?"

After their lovemaking one night she asked if he had many dreams. Did she mean dreams like things he wanted to do real bad before he died, he asked, or dreams like the things you see in your sleep at night. "Night dreams," she said. He said it was funny she should ask that because, truth be told, he knew he'd been dreaming a lot lately but he could never remember the dreams when he woke up.

"Funny thing is," he said, "while I'm havin the dreams it's like I know they're showin me things that're real, or . . . *true* somehow. I mean, when I wake up thats the *feelin* I have, that I just dreamt about somethin true, only I cant remember what it was."

"You will," she said. "The time'll come you will."

He looked at her for a long moment, unsure whether to ask her what she meant. And now, as he stared at her smiling face, she said, "You're looking at my mouth—thats another five dollars you owe me."

He gave a mock roar and fell on her, saying, "You bat-blind little witch!"

And laughing, wrestling happily, they made love once again.

Gordon Blue's estimation of how long it would take to resolve Kid Lowe's Chicago troubles proved overly optimistic and two months later the Kid was still residing with the Ashleys, though he didn't at all mind and neither did the family. He was proud that the largest of the three turkeys Ma and the girls roasted for Christmas dinner was one he'd shot. In addition to taking him hunting and trapping with his brothers, John Ashley now allowed him to come with him on whiskey drops to the Indians and Kid Lowe marveled at the alien wonders of these primitive villages in the heart of the Devil's Garden.

The Kid liked Twin Oaks but he loved the whiskey camps. He loved their wildness. He loved the stygian nights when the orange pinefires under the great copper kettles were the only light save that of the moon and stars to hold at bay an encompassing darkness greater than imagination could conjure. The fires raised trembling shadows against the closely standing hardwoods hung with moss and twisted vines that held to the earth like umbilicals. The blackness beyond the fireglow stirred and rustled and splashed and sometimes sounded of fluttering wing. From the greater darkness came deep quivering grunts of alligators whose forebears had themselves looked upon dinosaurs. Came skin-tightening shrieks of panthers at mate, sporadic outcries of prey falling to predator. The night swamp was ever clamorous with blood. The air pungent with the redolence of muck and water seasoned richly with matter living and dead.

On nights as these they sat about the kettle fire into the late hours and smoked pipe and cigarette and sipped whiskey and told stories both real and invented to entertain each other. They never tired of hearing of the night John Ashley took a drive to Twin Oaks after several weeks of hiding out at whiskey camp and Ma Ashley stepped out on the porch and fired a doubleblast of her shotgun in the air to warn him of the policemen lurking in the surrounding brush.

"Old Johnny just hustled on up to the turnaround and stomped on the brake and kicked her into reverse and turned that Lizzie around on a damn silver dollar and right back out we went," Ed Ashley said, who had been in the car with John that night. "Cut off the headlamps so they couldnt see us but then naturally we couldnt see a damn thing neither. Lord knows how many times we run into the palmettos on either side of that little-bitty trail getting back to the main road in the dark. We was bouncing *all* over hell and I about got throwed right out the damn car more'n once, I mean to tell you."

It was early in the new year and their breath showed vaguely gray on the dark chill air. They were at the whiskey camp in the Hungryland Slough and about fifteen miles west of Juno Beach—John and Ed Ashley, Kid Lowe and Claude Calder, a rough and rangy bucktoothed youth, a longtime friend of the Ashleys and Old Joe Ashley's main deliveryman to most clients north of Fort Pierce. On this night Bob and Frank Ashley were helping their father out at the Sand Cut camp on Lake Okeechobee.

John Ashley spat into the fire and laughed with the others at the memory of that wild night ride. "Bet when Ma let go with that shotgun," he said, "them police in the bushes pissed their pants."

"They say Sheriff George about had a fit when he heard about it," Claude Calder said.

"He surely did," Ed Ashley said. "Came out to the house next day and told Ma she could get in trouble for aidin and abettin a fugitive from the law. Ma just looked at him like he was simple and said she didnt know nothin about no abettin nor any such gamblin talk, she'd just been shooting at some old hooty owl been tryin to get at a new litter of pups under the front porch."

"Them damn Bakers," Claude said. "You all heard Sheriff George done made Bobby his chief deputy?"

"I know it," Ed Ashley said. "That sumbuck Bobby's gonna be the sheriff before you know it, just watch and see." Even in the vague and shifting light of the fire, the cordlike scar across his mouth was visible and made him look about to laugh or about to cry, you couldnt be sure which. An Okeechobee catfisher had cut him with a filleting knife in a fight over a Hardieville whore named Della. Ed Ashley had then beaten the man senseless with a spitoon and had just snatched up the man's dropped knife and was set to shove it into his heart when he was pried away by the bouncer and a sheriff's deputy. He spent the night in jail and his father bailed him out the next day. He waited a couple of weeks until his wound was partially healed before he went back to Miami to see Della again but by then she had departed for places unknown. Another of the girls tried to console him by pointing out that he likely wouldnt have won her over anyway, not now, not with that awful scar, since Della always had been one to prize handsomeness. Ed Ashley had not spoken of her since, not even to Frank, but not a day passed that he did not think of her.

"Maybe Bobby'll become sheriff before *Sheriff George* knows it," Claude Calder said, and everybody laughed.

"I seen him up to Stuart just the other day," Ed Ashley said as he worked open a fresh jar of whiskey. He took a tentative taste and worked his tongue around it and considered and then nodded his approval. "You know, I do believe daddy's *still* gettin some better at his business, I truly do."

"You seen who? Bobby?" John Ashley said. "What was he up to? Still running his mouth about what a sumbitch I am to of run off and what a good man he is for not shooting me?"

"Like usual, yeah," Ed said. "Told me to tell you again, when you ready to meet him face-to-face just the two of you, you let him know."

"Face-to-face, my ass," John Ashley said. He spat. "You know as well as I do, he'll say he's gonna meet me just us two and then have a dozen damn deputies hid all around to jump me soon's I show up. Man's a born liar. If he said the ocean's made of salt water I'd expect it to taste like sugar. I tell you, I'm of a mind to slip up to his house one a these nights and call him out, just us two, and see what happens."

"I told him I'd take him on anytime," Ed said, "but he gimme a shit-eatin grin and said it's been between him and you. Before I could say another word he went on in the bank to add to his pile of money."

"I bet it *is* a pile, too," Claude Calder said. "Only I hear it's Sheriff George raking in the money, not Bobby. They say Bobby just runs it to the bank for him. But I bet anything he gets a cut."

"It's always been talk Sheriff George takes money, but I never heard anybody but a known liar say Bobby does," John Ashley said. "But he'll for damn sure do whatever his daddy tells him, and if Daddy says pick up money from someplace or take money to the bank, thats what he's gonna do."

"I heard from Miss Lillian that Sheriff George takes a cut from every gambling joint and whorehouse in the county—nigger and white both," Ed Ashley said. "She said he'd jacked up his cut to twenty percent and she cant hardly make a profit anymore unless she raises her own prices. Said she called him a thief and he laughed at her and said it aint thievin to steal from criminals."

"He got some interestin notions of justice, Sheriff George," John Ashley said. Nobody spoke for a moment and then he said, "They really keep their money in the Stuart bank? Maybe Bobby was just seeing to some kind of police business."

"Hell, John," Ed said, "he had a damn bag right there in his hand and if it wasn't fulla money I'll kiss your ass."

"How you know it was money in it?"

"Cause I seen him take it to the teller and hand it over to him and stand there while the fella went off with it to someplace in back and in a minute the fella comes back and hands him a piece of paper and Bobby sticks it in his shirt, thats how come I know it. I was waitin for him to come out. I said, 'Let's you and me step around back in alley and you take off that badge and we'll see whose ass is the blackest.' He just give that smile some more and said to tell you he's waitin on you, and off he went, the chickenshit son of a bitch."

For a minute none of them said anything, each man drifting on his own thoughts. Then Kid Lowe said: "You know, somebody ought rob that bank and all them Bakers' money in it."

Ed Ashley grinned his wretched grin and glanced at John, who smiled and cut his gaze to the fire. Bob had told the other Ashley brothers about John's Galveston bank job and John had then sworn them all to keep it secret from their father. Still, all of the brothers had a feeling their father somehow knew about it. "Hell, boy," Ed said, turning back to the Kid, "what-all *you* know about robbin a damn bank?"

Kid Lowe turned to him with a glower, then looked around at the others, then behind him, then spat into the fire. "I guess it's all right to tell you boys something." He looked around again as if checking the surrounding shadows for signs of spies. "The thing is," he said in lowered voice, "I'm a bank robber is what I am." He smiled with shy pride. "Dont guess any you all's gonna turn me in, are you?"

The others exchanged looks. Claude Calder chuckled. Ed Ashley snorted and said, "*Shiiit!* You never."

"Hell I aint," the Kid said. "It's how come I'm here. I robbed four banks all told in Chicago and was doing all right, if I say so myself, till I robbed this one bank on State Street. There was a dumbshit guard just couldnt do like I told him to put his hands behind his head and so he got himself shot." He paused to spit and take a sip of whiskey.

"You shot a bank guard?" Ed Ashley said. "You *kill* him?"

"Oh *hell* no," the Kid said. "Wasnt aimin to. All I did was wound him in the gut a little bit. He didnt die till long after, about two weeks later. Caught the pneumonia in the hospital and died."

"Well hell," John Ashley said, "he caught the pneumonia because he was bad wounded, thats what happened."

Kid Lowe flung his arms wide in exasperation. "That's just *exactly* what the damn cops in Chicago told everybody including the newspapers." The bitter memory gave his voice an edge. "Sorry sonofabitches. How do *they* know the fella didnt catch pneumonia for some other reason? How do *you* know he didnt? Maybe somebody with pneumonia sneezed on him. Maybe he wasnt warm enough in that damn hospital and he caught a cold and it got worser till it became pneumonia. That *could of* happened. They dont *know* thats not what happened. But *noooo*, they right away say he got pneumonia because he was wounded. And because *I'm* the one wounded him *I'm* the one to blame he's dead. Makes me so goddamn mad I wish the sumbitch was alive so I could shoot him again."

"So you down here hiding from the Chicago police?" Ed Ashley said.

Kid Lowe shrugged, spat, took another sip of whiskey, looked around at nothing in particular.

"How much did you get from these here bank robberies?" Claude Calder said. "You must got yourself a rich stash someplace, eh?"

"Dont I wish," Kid Lowe said. "Most the jobs didnt get me even two thousand dollars. And the way I was living—you know, girls, the racehorses, nice clothes—well, the money went pretty damn quick, you bet."

He took a drink of whiskey and looked sharply at Ed Ashley. "So dont be asking me what *I* know about robbing banks. I'm the only damn one here knows *anything* about it because I'm the only damn one here ever *done* it."

Ed Ashley met his stare for a moment, then turned to John and raised his eyebrows. John was grinning at the Kid and the Kid looked at him sharply and John Ashley said, "Well boy, that aint exactly right."

They hadn't been at all sure what Old Joe would think of the idea. While John Ashley explained it to him a few evenings later, all of them sitting around the firepit back of the Twin Oaks house, Old Joe gave no sign of his inclination as he listened without expression, puffing his pipe and sipping his whiskey and occasionally spitting into the fire. And when John had explained everything in detail and sat back to hear what his father thought of it, he who might dismiss the whole thing with a shake of his head, Old Joe did not answer right away but refired his pipe and refilled his cup and sat smoking and drinking and staring into the fire.

Nobody spoke for five minutes. And then, his eyes still on the flames, Joe Ashley said: "I don't understand it. All this trouble because of some worthless Injun. That goddamn George Baker's been a real mullethead recent and thats a fact. I hear tell he's drinkin moren usual. He looks it. Startin to get that yellow look around the eyes. But whatever's botherin him aint no good excuse for takin hisself so damn serious as he's been. I heard tell he said if he ran you down he'd take you in any way he had to. Heard tell those were his exact words: any way he had to. When I saw him up to Blue's store last month I went over and asked was it true he said that. He said it was. I said the day he did serious harm to any of you boys was the day I'd lay him in his grave. He knew I meant it. Bobby was there and started to run his mouth at me but George told him shut up." He looked skyward and regarded the stars. "You know Freddie Baker, Bobby's cousin? He's a deputy too."

John Ashley nodded. "More like brothers than cousins, some say. Spose to be a good old boy and a rough one, but he aint never looked all that rough to me."

"I heard tell," Old Joe said, "Freddie was in the Doghouse Bar the other night saying his Uncle George is gonna run the Ashleys out of Palm Beach County or know the reason why. Saying it like it's somethin good as done."

"I heard that talk," John Ashley said. "We all have. We waitin to see them try."

"Them damn Bakers are kindly startin to irritate me," Old Joe said. He spat hard into the fire.

They all sat silent and the minutes passed. Then Old Joe said: "You sure they keep they money in that bank?"

"Yessir."

Joe Ashley sighed and stared into the fire. "Cant imagine why *any*body'd trust his money to a damn bank."

John Ashley laughed. "Me either. Somebody's like to steal it."

Old Joe nodded in the manner of one being told something he already knew. "Bill says the fedral govment's sooner or later gonna pass the law against alcohol," he said. "Probly not for a coupla three four years yet, he dont think, but he says a smart man would start getting ready right now. Says the demand's gonna be way more than we can ever fill with just our own operation. Says if we get us a good fast boat and rig it proper we can bring in ever kind of labeled hooch when the time comes. Bring it from the Bahamas. Course now, a good boat costs plenty, and riggin it up for our purpose gonna cost more." He paused and spat. Then said: "I guess what I wanna know is, is it a *lot* of money in that bank?"

John Ashley shrugged. "Dont know, Daddy." He smiled. "But if it aint, there's plenty more banks."

Old Joe returned his smile for a moment, then his aspect went serious. "They already got so many warrants on you I guess it dont matter much if they add any more, even for a damn bank. But I dont want you takin no chances you aint got to. You see any police around before you go in, you forget the job. Wait and do it another time. You hear?"

"I hear you, Daddy." His heart jumped with excitement.

Old Joe turned to Frank and Ed and Bob. "But *you* boys, you aint none of you under warrant for a damn thing and I dont want you to be."

Bob Ashley cut his eyes to John whose look told him to keep quiet. Frank and Ed dug at the dirt with sticks, ready as always to do without objection whatever their daddy said.

"Damn Bakers," Old Joe said and spat hard into the fire. "They kindly irritatin hell outa me."

NINE

February 23, 1915

THEY GOT OUT OF THE CAR AT THE BEND IN THE HIGHWAY AND then Frank and Ed Ashley drove off to wait for them at the junction of the Lake Okeechobee Road. The four then walked the last quarter-mile into town on this midmorning of a brightly blue-skyed and cloudless Tuesday. The pinewoods fell away at the edge of town and they walked down the main street and nodded to storekeepers at their doors and tipped their hats to women on the sidewalk and paused to scratch the ears of friendly dogs. They waved casually to acquaintances driving past. All the while looking about for police cars or cops afoot and seeing neither.

There were three customers in the bank lobby and two tellers at work behind the cage and the manager sat at his desk behind a waist-high partition at the far end of the room. A pair of overhead fans hung motionless in the near-cool of this winter's day. None looked up nor noticed the four men until Bob Ashley shut the door hard enough to rattle the glass. Kid Lowe went to the windows and drew the curtains. Bob turned the little cardboard sign hanging on the glass front door so that the "Closed" side faced outward and then he pulled down the rollered shade and stood with his back to it. His grin was titanic.

John Ashley withdrew a .44 caliber revolver from under his loose shirt and grinned at the uncomprehending faces turned his way and announced, "Gentlemen, this is a robbery. Do like we say and nobody gets hurt. Why hell, you all gonna have an adventure to tell all your friends." His heart was at a gallop and he felt like laughing and thought maybe he was going crazy but so what. Claude Calder went to stand by the far wall with a pistol in his hand and his grin mirrored John Ashley's.

"All right now, folk," John Ashley said, gesturing at the customers, "sit on the floor. Sit on your hands."

There was no guard. The Stuart bank had been in business for years and never before been robbed. In this region, all notion of bank holdups was yet the stuff of Wild West stories, of Jesse James and his ilk, not any part of real life.

Kid Lowe moved to the other end of the room and vaulted the low partition and put his pistol to the bank manager's ear and told him to put his hands under his ass. The manager's name was Ellers. He appeared mildly dazed and his mouth moved as though speech were but an untried concept. Kid Lowe smiled and said, "Just stay hushed, mister. We'll tell you when to talk." He picked up the telephone on the desk. "This the only one?" The manager nodded. Kid Lowe yanked the line out of its connection and lobbed the instrument clattering into the corner.

The two tellers were Wallace and Taylor and both of them knew the Ashley boys and Claude Calder. Wallace said, "John . . . you boys . . . why are you all doing this?"

John Ashley laughed. "Well, shit, A.R., why you *think*? Open up the gate."

Wallace hastened to unlock the wire gate to the teller cage and John Ashley entered and handed him a croker sack and said, "Hold this open wide for Mister Taylor. Mister Taylor sir, you just empty all them little money drawers in the bag, hear? Do it now, sir, and do it quickly."

"Sorry, mam," Bob Ashley said loudly through the glass of the closed front door, holding aside slightly the roller shade and speaking to a woman insistently rapping on the doorglass with the handle of her parasol. "We're closed up a few minutes. Doin a inventory. Be open again shortly." The woman scowled and again rapped on the glass. Bob Ashley smoothed the roller shade back in place and turned his back on the door and shrugged at Claude Calder.

As Wallace and Taylor emptied the cash drawers John Ashley went into the bank's small vault and searched it and discovered but a half-dozen packets of twenty-dollars bills. He came out and dropped the packets in the croker sack. Taylor was redfaced and whitehaired, big-bellied, breathing like a man at hard labor. John Ashley patted him on the shoulder and told him to take it easy, everything was going to be fine.

"Tell me somethin, A.R.," John Ashley said, "is it true George and Bobby Baker keep their money in this bank?"

A. R. Wallace looked at him for a moment as though he didnt understand the question. Then said: "Well, they do keep an account here, but I believe their main bank is in West Palm Beach."

John Ashley smiled and said, "Just so they got some here."

The woman at the door was rapping harder now, her angry voice carrying through the doorglass: ". . . *open this door*, you . . ." The silhouette of a man in a suit and hat appeared beside her, the man trying to peek in through the slight gap between the roller shade and the frame of the door. Bob Ashley sidestepped over so as to block the man's view with his back.

Now Wallace handed the sack to John Ashley who hefted it as though trying to determine the sum of its contents by its weight. "How much you figure?" he asked.

"It's about seven thousand dollars you all got there," Wallace said.

"*Seven thousand!*" Kid Lowe said. "I know it's a lot more money than that in this place."

"There isn't any more," Ellers the manager was able to say. "This is a small bank. We never have much cash on hand." Kid Lowe put the muzzle of his .38 just under Ellers' right eye and the man's voice went high: "I swear to you it's all there is!"

Kid Lowe said, "You banker sonofabitches dont do nothing *but* lie about money."

"I *swear* . . ." Ellers said, his eyes shut tight but his head full of the terrible visions Kid Lowe's pistol pressed into it.

"Leave him be," John Ashley said. "He's too scared to be lyin. I checked the vault myself. It's no more money in there."

"You lucky *I* aint in charge of this operation," Kid Lowe said to Ellers and jabbed him hard in the forehead with the gun muzzle and raised a red spot there. "You be a dead man already for bein such a damn liar."

John Ashley ordered all the people on the floor to lie down on their bellies with their faces in their hands. "You too, Mister Ellers, get on down there. Mister Taylor, sir. You, A.R., I know you got a motorcar. Where's it at?"

"Around back."

John Ashley nodded at Claude Calder who went out the rear door of the bank. Two minutes later Bob Ashley peering out the front window said, "Here's Claude with the car."

Another man had now arrived at the door and both men and the woman were trying to peek past Bob and into the bank lobby and the woman all the while tapping on the glass with the whalebone grip of her parasol.

"God *damn* that racket," John Ashley said. "Get them sumbitches in here, Bob."

Bob Ashley unlocked the door and swung it open and said, "All right, then, come on in." But the three now saw the others on the floor and their faces went slack and they stood fast. One of the men started to turn away and nearly walked into Claude Calder who had come out of the Ford touring car idling in the street and stood before him, grinning wide and with a hand on the pistol butt jutting above his waistband. A pair of boys went running past, dodging the two men as unerringly as bats. Their mother came stalking behind, calling, "Albert! Samuel! You two are just *askin* for it!"

Claude Calder nodded toward the door and the two men and the woman went into the bank. The woman was middle-aged but not unattractive and Bob puckered his lips at her. She blushed and jerked her gaze away from him and he laughed. John Ashley told them to lie down in the same manner as the others. He asked Bob how things looked outside.

"Aint nobody noticin nothin," Bob Ashley said, looking out to the street. "I dont believe most people would take notice of a flyin elephant lessen it shit on their heads."

"All right, then, let's go," John Ashley said. He tucked the sack of money under his arm like a tote of groceries. "Listen, you folk—there's a fella with a rifle watching this door from the roof across the street. Anybody goes out that door before fifteen minutes gone by, you gone get a bullet in the brainpan and thats a promise. So you all wait, you hear? Fifteen minutes. And listen A.R., we'll leave your car out by the Okeechobee Road, you hear?"

Wallace said he much appreciated it, his voice muffled for his face being in his hands.

They went out all together and Claude Calder got behind the wheel of the Ford and the Kid got in the front passenger seat with him. Bob and John Ashley got in the back and pulled the cartop up and Claude and the Kid fastened it in place on the windshield frame. Then Claude released the brake and pulled on the throttle lever as he stepped on the low-speed pedal and the car lunged into motion. They were all of them but the Kid grinning and Bob Ashley's grin was the widest of them. "*This* how it felt in Texas, Johnny?" he wanted to know. "Good as *this?*"

John Ashley laughed. "About like this, yeah."

Claude Calder eased up on the throttle and worked the clutch pedal and the planetary transmission shifted with a lurch and the car rattled down the street. Kid Lowe turned around in his seat and said, "I dont know what-all you think's so damn funny. We didnt get but seven thousand dollars and I *know* there was more money in that bank—I *know* there was."

"I'll be go to hell," Bob Ashley said, suffused with good cheer. "Aint this the same little fella told us he never made more'n two thousand dollars from any of his big-time Chicago bank holdups—and here we get *seven* thousand and he's complaining it aint enough."

"Two thousand I get by myself is two thousand all for me," Kid Lowe said. "Seven thousand I get with six other fellas aint but . . . I dont know what it is, but it aint no two thousand."

They were almost to the end of town now and Claude Calder said, "Oh hell." All eyes in the car followed his gaze ahead to the left side of the street and saw parked there in front of Wilson's Cafe a county sheriff's car and a Stuart Police Dept. car and standing in the doorway of the cafe was Bob Baker. He was not in uniform and was saying something to someone inside and laughing and turning now and stepping out on the sidewalk and putting a toothpick to his mouth. As their car came abreast of him two uniformed sheriff's deputies and two Stuart policemen came out behind him. Bob Baker looked at their passing car and then at its occupants and his smile held for a moment longer and his eyes followed after them. They all looked back at him and Bob Baker's smile vanished.

"Kick this thing in the ass, Claude," John Ashley said.

And here came one of the bank customers on the run and behind him came Ellers as Claude's fingers busied themselves with the spark and gas levers and his foot worked the control pedal to drop the car into low gear and wind the engine higher and then he worked the pedal again and the motor issued a deep fluffing note and the car lunged forward and accelerated steadily. Even over the increased clatter of the Model T they could faintly hear the bankers shouting holdup, holdup, holdup. Women pulled small children to their skirts and hurried indoors as men came hustling out of the cafe and the barbershop and the hardware store.

Bobby Baker ran out to the middle of the street and raised his revolver and the other cops were pulling their weapons and now came the popping of pistols and bullets thonked into the back of the car and two rounds whooked through the car top and made starholes as they smashed through the windshield. Bob Ashley leaned out the right side of the car and fired back at the cops and they scattered in search of cover—all but Bobby Baker who stood his ground and aimed and fired as if he were taking target practice. Kid Lowe leaned over the front seat and fired at Bobby Baker in the receding distance through the cartop's open rear window and John Ashley was firing as well but the car was jouncing so much he could not have said where his bullets homed. Kid Lowe's pistol was inches from his ear and its reports deafened him to all else in the world.

Claude Calder hunkered over the steering wheel as if peering into bad fog, one hand on the wheel and the other still at the spark and gas levers. The Model T was now moving at thirty-five miles per hour and still gaining speed even as it shuddered so hard John Ashley was certain it was about to shake itself to pieces. A bullet ripped through the back of the cartop and flicked away a portion of Claude Calder's right ear lobe and fashioned another starburst in the glass before him.

The pinewoods again loomed high on both sides of the road as the Model T sped into the curve and out of sight of the shooting policemen. The car leaned hard to the left and raised a tall roostertail of lime dust as it swung out wide to the edge of the highway at the top of a grassy incline and its right wheels almost left the ground as Claude Calder fought to keep it on the road. Just as the curve began to straighten out and the car leaned back toward a level pitch its left front wheel dipped into a hole in the shoulder and the car bounced high and yawed sidewise with the wheel fluttering wildly and everyone rose and fell and Kid Lowe's head bounced against the cartop and his pistol discharged and the bullet angled into John Ashley's head at the juncture of his left eye socket and the nosebone and passed through the hard palate and struck his lower right jaw and instantly filled his mouth with blood and bits of teeth and bone.

The car plunged down the roadside slope into the brush and went snapping through a half-dozen saplings before crashing into a thick pine—and all in the same moment Claude Calder's forehead shattered the windscreen and the right front door slung open and Kid Lowe catapulted from it and just did miss hitting a tree and lit in a clump of palmettos and Bob Ashley lofted over the front seat and struck against the dashboard and felt one of his ribs stave and John Ashley slammed against the back of the front seat and crumpled to the floorboard.

He was yet conscious but his head felt strangely stuffed, his skull somehow askew. Blood overran his mouth and rained to the floorboard. He felt the vaguest pain. There was a loud hissing from the front of the car and now he remembered where he was and why. Claude Calder groaned. Bob Ashley grunting and cursing now and getting out of the car. Kid Lowe's voice at the car door, saying, "You hit?" Bob Ashley saying, "I'm all right. Claude? Claude, you?" Claude saying he didnt think he was hit. Bob Ashley saying for Claude to get up on the road and see was anybody coming after them. Now the rightside rear door sprang open and Bob said, "Oh *shit*. Help me with him."

Hands at his armpits. Lifting him, pulling him out of the car, turning him over and easing him to the ground on his back and he choked on the blood of his wound and turned his head to let the blood gush onto the grass. Then Bob was dragging him by the armpits to a pine tree a few yards away, helping him to sit up with his back against the trunk. Blood running off his chin and sopping the front of his shirt. His left eye throbbing now, its vision redly hazed but functioning. Bob looking close at it—then touching his jaw and pain bursting incandescent in his skull and he flinched from Bob's hand.

Bob asked if he was hit anywhere else and he was able to say quite clearly, "No."

"Just missed that eye," Bob said. "Dont know if you been hit twice or one bullet went through your whole entire head to end up in your mouth like that." He smiled weakly. "Lucky for you it was in the head, hey? Not much to hit in there." And then: "That *goddamn* Bobby Baker!"

"Wasnt Bobby's doin," Kid Lowe said. He stood over them and told what happened.

"Well, God *damn* it," Bob Ashley said, glaring up at him. Kid Lowe looked off to the woods.

"Aint his fault," John Ashley said. His voice deeply nasal, his tongue clumsy and feeling like an alien appendage. He marveled that he could talk at all, never mind with clarity.

And now here came Claude Calder on the run and shouting, "They're coming! Both damn cars!"

"Let's get our ass in the swamp the other side of this pineywood," Bob Ashley said. He tried to help his brother to his feet but John Ashley felt the ground undulate and he almost passed out from the effort of trying to stand. He slumped back against the pine trunk and waved his brother away. "Go! Go on!" he said, his voice gargled with blood. "I be arright, *Go!*"

"I aint leavin you!" Bob Ashley said. They could hear the police cars closing in.

"*GO!*" John Ashley said. "Won't help nothin they catch you too. *GO!*"

"Come *on,* Bob," Kid Lowe called from the edge of the pines. He held the croker sack of money. "Cant help him if you aint free. Come *on!*" And now Claude Calder was beside the Kid and the two of them turned and vanished into the trees.

"Go on, bubba—Goddamn it, *GO!*" John Ashley said, pushing at his brother. The police cars came shrilling around the curve into view and Bob Ashley said, "Shit!" and bolted for the trees.

The cop cars braked hard to a halt, raising a cloud of limerock dust. The driver's door of the sheriff's car swung open and the driver came out with a pistol in hand and from around the other side of the car came the other deputy and Bob Baker and both of them with shotguns. Now the Stuart policemen got out of their car too and stood beside the county officers and all of them looked down the grassy incline at the figure of John Ashley watching them from where he sat under the pine. John Ashley raised his hands slightly to show them he was not armed. He was sure they were going to shoot him anyway. He was conscious of the feel of the ground under him, the swell and fall of his chest with each breath, his heartbeat pulsing steadily against his ribs. He brushed the blood from his eye.

Bob Baker said something to the others and they started down the grade, spreading out and moving slowly. All of them keeping their weapons trained on the wrecked Model T but for Bob Baker who held his twelve-gauge pointed at John Ashley's chest.

"Anybody in that car?" Bob Baker said as he drew near. John Ashley shook his head and pain streaked through his skull like a cat afire.

Bob Baker gave a hand signal and the others began shooting the Model T. They stormed it with buckshot and .38- and .45-caliber rounds and they emptied their weapons into it and reloaded and continued shooting and shooting and the car seemed to flinch and sag under the fusillade and its glass flung in shards and John Ashley who sat but a few feet from the vehicle covered his head with his arms and reflected that A.R. was going to be mighty dismayed when next he saw his car. The cops fired on the Model T for a full minute before they finally stopped. John Ashley lowered his arms and saw that he'd been cut on a elbow and felt now a stinging on his neck and put his hand to it and his palm came away bloodstained.

The car listed like a ship afounder. Its tires were shot to ruin, its bodyshell pocked like something diseased, its glasswork reduced to sparse jagged remnant, its top in tatters. The two Stuart cops advanced cautiously through a thin haze of gunsmoke with their revolvers raised. They carefully peered into the car and now one of them jerked open each door in turn and then the cops lowered their pistols and one called to Bob Baker that the car was empty.

Bob Baker went to John Ashley and squatted down beside him and leaned on his shotgun like a staff. He pushed back his straw hat and mopped the sweat from his face with a bandanna and smiled at John Ashley. John Ashley smiled back and his whole face felt numbly weighted and overwide. One of the county deputies started to come their way but Bob Baker waved him off and the deputy shrugged and looked about and then headed into the woods.

Bob Baker smiled. "Guess you right there's nobody in the car," he said. His gaze moved over John Ashley's bloody and distorted face. "How you been keepin?"

"Doin all right, Bobby," John Ashley said. "How bout youself?"

"Lot bettern you, by the look of things." He leaned forward for a close examination of the wounds and John Ashley felt his breath warm on his face. "Pretty good shootin, hey?"

"Wasnt your bullet done it."

"Hell it wasnt," Bob Baker said. "Your face in the back window like that, I couldnt hardly miss. Had you square in my sights. But it wasnt really good shootin. I was tryin to blow your brains out." The yellow teeth of his closeup grin were huge. "I seen that Calder boy doin the drivin. And your brother Bob, seen him too. Who's the other one? The little fella?"

John Ashley shrugged.

"Whoo! Would you just look at this eye! How you seein out that eye, Johnny?"

"Still seein all right with it, Bobby, thank you."

"Well, I seen some bloodshot peepers before but nothin like this. Dont believe I ever seen a eye lookin so bad and still workin." He put his fingers to the shattered and swollen jaw and John Ashley winced and sucked air through his teeth and Bob Baker said, "I bet that does smart." He looked around and John Ashley followed his eyes and saw that none of the other policemen were about.

Now Bob Baker leaned closer still and gently laid a hand on the left side of John Ashley's face. *"Who'd* you say that other fella was?"

"Billy the Kid."

"Oh yeah," Bob Baker said. "I heard of him." He slid his thumb up to the corner of the bloody eye and John Ashley locked his jaws against the pain and the surge of bile in his throat. Bob Baker's teeth loomed large.

Came a whisper: "You ever even wondered what it's like not being whole?"

"Like somebody we know, you mean?" His head now felt to be swelling with pain, the very skullbone itself.

"I reckon I owe you, Johnny."

John Ashley tried to smile. "Ah hell, Bobby, forget it. I aint never been one to call a man's marker if he's down on his luck."

Bob Baker's thumb went into the socket and John Ashley screamed and saw behind the eye a radiant skyrocket burst of red light and then darkness.

TEN

February—October 1915

THE DOCTOR WAS A HEAVYSET BEARDED MAN NAMED BOYER. WITH the assistance of a horse-faced nurse called Rachel he worked on John Ashley's jaw in the narrow confines of an isolation cell of the Palm Beach County Jail. He was able to remove all bullet fragments and was obliged to scrape much less of the shattered jaw than he had thought would be necessary on his initial examination. He set the jawbone, then clamped it with a wire brace, and he put John Ashley on a liquid diet for the next few weeks. He assured him that there would be only a slight perceivable disfigurement to his face once the scars healed. The overall tissue damage had also proved much less severe than it had seemed to Boyer at first sight, though John Ashley's voice now registered lower than before and his sinuses would evermore trouble him at night and the wound in his hard palate would never heal completely and would occasionally become slightly infected. He had lost but two teeth—a bicuspid and adjoining molar.

He awakened with an eyepatch and a burning sensation under it. The doctor was at a loss to explain how the bullet could have done so much damage to the eye, which was outside the trajectory that took the round through the nosebone and palate to lodge in the jaw. He spoke of major trauma to the sclera and cornea and ciliary processes, of the loss of vitreous humor and of massive damage to the retina. John Ashley stared at him with his bloodshot right eye and saw him in a world gone skewed and narrow and he quite suddenly knew that the darkness under the eyepatch was greater than human vision could perceive and realized the socket was empty and thats what the doctor was trying to tell him. He had a instant's vision of Bob Baker's huge yellow teeth in the moment before his thumb set off the red explosion in his skull.

Bob Baker stopped by twice. The first time in the company of Sheriff George, who'd come to notify John Ashley officially that in addition to the charges of murdering Jimmy Gopher and escaping from custody, he now also stood charged for bank robbery and the attempted murder of five police officers. Sheriff George was all business and looked at John Ashley as if he were a stranger. Bob Baker said nothing but stood behind his father and smiled all the while. He looked well-rested. When Sheriff George turned to leave, Bob Baker put a thumb up to his own eye and turned his hand in a sharp corkscrew motion and shut the eye under the thumb and made a face of mock pain. Then he opened both eyes and grinned hard at John Ashley and left. Doctor Boyer watched the whole thing, and when Bob Baker had gone he sighed and shook his head.

A week later John Ashley lay on his bunk with his hands behind his head and thought of blind Loretta May and felt closer to her by virtue of his own half-blindness. He recalled the peach smell of her and the freshness of her yellow hair, the pale smoothness of her skin. He was enjoying the feel of the partial erection pressing snug in his pants when he sensed someone at the cell door. He looked over there and saw a pair of shadowed eyes at the small slotted window and even in the dim light he recognized them. "Hey, Bobby," he said. "How you keepin?" Come on, he thought—step in here for just a minute. The eyes pinched up in deliberation or amusement and a moment later they were gone.

He had begun to have dreams now such as he'd never had before. He saw things in his sleep and felt that what he saw was somehow real, though at times he knew too—without knowing how he knew—that what he saw had not yet happened. In one such dream he saw a woman he did not recognize, saw her vaguely. She smelled of the swamp, and under that redolence he caught the scents of her skin and hair and sex as keenly as if she were standing beside him. She seemed to loom over him as a wavering pale figure and he felt the heat of her skin and then her face was right in front of his and still he could not see her clearly but for her green eyes and a tiny gold quarter-moon in the iris of one of them.

In another dream he saw Kid Lowe in prison stripes and on a crutch and with a bandaged head, saw him redfaced and shouting and though for some reason he could not hear him he knew somehow that the Kid was cursing because he'd been proved right about the bank holding out on them. And so, when Gordon Blue came to visit and told him that the Stuart bankers were crowing to the newspapers about how they'd managed to withhold some ten thousand dollars from the bandits by simply not emptying all the cash drawers into the money bag, John Ashley was both irritated and a little embarrassed but not really surprised.

He was permitted no visitors but his lawyer, and Gordon Blue apprised him that the state's attorney had revived his motion to move his trial for the murder of DeSoto Tiger to Dade County. "I'm playing every ace I've got to keep it from happening, Johnny, but I have to tell you the odds aren't good. They mean to have the trial in Miami come hell or high water."

Gordon Blue told him of Old Joe's fury on learning that Bob Ashley had been in on the job after he had expressly forbidden any of his sons but John from acting on it. "I was going over some accounts with your daddy at Twin Oaks when Bob and Kid Lowe showed up and told him what happened. Your daddy was so mad at Bob for being in the holdup he took a strop to him like he was some disobedient *child.* I couldnt believe Bob would stand for it, but he took off his shirt and leaned against the side of the house like Joe told him to, and Joe let him have it with that strop a good dozen times. I mean, he gave him a hell of a hiding. Some of those welts were thick as your finger. Marked up his whole back all red and purple. Big as he is, Bob might've taken that strop away from Joe and beat *him* with it. It just *amazes* me that he stood for it."

John Ashley gave Gordon Blue a puzzled look. "Hell, Gordy, what else he gonna do *but* stand for it? It's our *daddy,* man. You dont hit your daddy, he hits you. It's who a daddy is—the one to hit you when you done wrong. Bob done wrong and he knew it."

Two weeks later the judge granted the state's motion to have the trial moved to Dade County. Within an hour of the judge's ruling a rock with a note wrapped around it came crashing through the window of the jail office and so tense were the police in the room that pistols cleared holsters before everyone realized what happened. The note said that if John Ashley wasnt released from jail immediately Sheriff George's house would be burned to the ground and no matter who might be inside it at the time. It was signed "the Ashley Gang." Sheriff George sent two armed deputies to keep watch on his house and family and deputized several friends to add to the jail guard force.

Barely an hour later a county deputy found a note on the seat of his motorcar. It read: "Tell Sheriff George to let johnnie go or perpare to pay the consequenses. We mean bisness. The Ashley gang."

Sheriff George affected to shrug it off, but his men could see the anger working in his jaw, the sudden distance in his eyes. He made secret plans with his son Bob and two evenings later and without advance notice to anyone he showed up at the jail a little past midnight and ordered John Ashley brought out of his cell. They manacled his hands behind him and put leg irons on him. They flanked him with guards carrying shotguns and hustled him out into a touring car with tarp covers tied over both sides of the rear of the car and put him in the backseat with two guards. Another guard got in the front with the driver and held a shotgun over the seat with the muzzle within inches of John Ashley's chest. John Ashley laughed and said, "Goddamn if you boys aint makin me feel like Jesse James."

Sheriff George appeared at the car window and put a finger in John Ashley's face. "One more word out of you, just one more—and Deputy Bradford's gonna blow a hole in you big enough to throw a dog through. Go ahead, say something. See if I dont mean it. I had all the trouble from you I aim to stand." John Ashley could see that Sheriff George was scared and absolutely serious.

"He opens his mouth again, Bradford," Sheriff George said, "it's the same as trying to escape and I want you to blast him, you understand?" The deputy holding the shotgun on John Ashley said, "Yessir." John Ashley heard Bob Baker laugh somewhere out in the darkness.

Sheriff George withdrew from the car and called, "Bobby, you and Freddie lead off. Let's go."

Bob Baker and Freddie Baker got into a roadster and led the prisoner vehicle out of the jailyard. Sheriff George and another deputy followed in a chattering coupé. They drove to the railroad station and the train was there and waiting. They put John Ashley aboard the baggage car and left the chains on him and put a double lock on the inside of the doors and kept two shotguns trained on him for the entire trip.

When the following sunrise broke like bright fire out of the distant rim of the Atlantic Ocean, John Ashley was watching it with his single eye from a barred window of the Dade County Jail.

"No," Old Joe said. "No. There aint gone be no tryin to break him out. It's just no need for anything risky as that. And hear me good, boy—you write even one more a them notes to George Baker and I'm gonna take a grub hoe to your head. You understand? You aint helpin a damn thing with them fucken notes."

"We got to do *something*, Daddy," Bob Ashley said. "They beatin on him ever day. They whippin him like a damn dog, whippin him all the time. They spittin in his food, pissin in his coffee. They wont empty his slop pail. You heard about it same as us."

"I heard it from people who dont know the facts of it anymore'n you do," Old Joe said. "Gordy saw him just yesterday again for about the tenth damn time and you heard him say it aint any of it true. They're feedin him all right and they aint pissin in his coffe or none of that bullshit. Gordy says he aint got a mark on him but from being shot in the face—and we know it wasnt *them* who did that, dont we?" He gave Kid Lowe a look and the Kid fixed his gaze on a sparrowhawk in the upper branches of a slash pine.

They were seated at a puncheon table alongside the Twin Oaks house—Old Joe and his four unjailed sons and Kid Lowe and Gordon Blue. The women were at washing clothes in big steaming tin tubs behind the house. The cicadas were loud in the oaks and a great flock of white herons was wingbeating across the purpling sky and past a low orange sun. Mosquitoes keened at the men's ears. The ripe smells of encroaching summer were on the air: hot wet earth and spawning bluegills and fresh nests of cottonmouths along the waterway banks.

"They hittin him where it dont show is why Gordy dont see no marks on him," Bob said. "They dont clean his cell nor give him nothing fit to eat but when Gordy goes to visit."

"How is it you know so much more than everybody else?" Bill Ashley asked. Though he was Old Joe's chief advisor, it was a rare thing for him to appear at a family council and even rarer for him to speak up at one. When he was in attendance he usually passed the time doodling in a notebook while everyone else did the talking. His brothers sometimes did not see him for weeks at a time. Unlike their own hands and necks, which were burned red-brown by the sun, his had the pallor of indoor life. He wore suspenders and sleeve garters and bow ties and wire-rim spectacles. He never asked any of them to visit his home and none of them had seen his wife but once or twice since the day of his marriage. In some ways he was less familiar to them than Kid Lowe or Gordon Blue.

That distance between him and his youngest brothers had widened even more after John and Bob robbed the Stuart bank. Bill thought they were fools to hold up a bank, which he saw as excessively risky. "There's too many other ways to make as much money," he'd said to Old Joe, "without near as much chance of something going wrong like it did in Stuart. As soon's whiskey's illegal all over the country you'll see what I mean."

Old Joe had shrugged and let the matter drop. A part of him knew Bill was right. He felt like a fool for having given John permission to rob the bank. He felt at fault that John was now one-eyed and in jail. But another part of him could not deny the pleasure of having more than $7,000 of the bank's money, having it because his boys had been bold enough to take it. He already had in mind a boat he could buy with that money—a sleek fast craft that with a few modifications would be perfect for carrying whiskey. But the news that the bank had cheated them of some ten thousand dollars was enraging. And it infuriated him further to think that Sheriff George might have convinced the bank that all the Baker money was with the cash the bank had saved and none of it gone off in Johnny's croker sack.

Now Bob Ashley gaped at Bill, at once surprised at hearing him speak up and angry at what he'd said. "Hey bubba," Bob Ashley said, "when I want shit out of you I'll squeeze your head."

"Ah hell, Bob," Frank Ashley said.

"Real bright," Bill Ashley said, looking at Bob with disdain. "You're a natural-born fool, you know that?"

"Go to hell, Billy," Bob Ashley said. "This aint never gonna be none your business—not while you sittin on your ass all day and markin in books while some of us are out there *doin* things."

"That's enough, the both you," Old Joe said. "Now I *told* you all how it's gonna be. We're gonna wait and see can Gordy get the murder charge dropped. If he can do that, then the bank robbery trial'll come back to Palm Beach and like as not we'll get us a good jury for it."

"He been in there more'n three months already," Bob said. "He's gonna serve life in prison before he ever gets to trial."

"Have a little patience, Bob—these things take time," Gordon Blue said. "You know how slow the law works."

"Dont *you* be tellin me too what I got to do!" Bob Ashley said.

Gordon Blue sighed and looked away.

"Daddy, look, we just got to—" Bob Ashley began, but Old Joe held up a hand to cut him short.

"*No,* I said. That's the end of it."

A week later Bob Ashley, Kid Lowe and Claude Calder sat at a corner table in the dim recesses of The Flamingo Restaurant across the road from the Fort Lauderdale depot and just two blocks removed from one of their favorite brothels, at which establishment they had passed the earlier part of the evening. They surreptitiously poured whiskey into their cups long since emptied of coffee and once more went over the details of the operation. They had been three days in Miami, ensconced in a rundown hotel a block from the Dade County Jail. They had watched carefully, made notes, followed people to and from the jail, established routines, set up an escape route to the Dixie Highway and an alternate route westward from Miami and into the Everglades. They had also been drinking steadily the while, a factor none among them considered important.

"Your daddy'd skin you alive he knew what you're up to," Claude Calder said. He fingered his mutilated right ear, a nervous habit he'd developed of late.

"Hell, bubba," Bob Ashley said, "tomorrow night Johnny'll be a free man and Daddy wont be doin nothing but pattin me on the back for it, you'll see."

"He damn sure will," Kid Lowe said. "Old Joe's a smart fella and smart fellas dont care about nothin but results. I'm proud to be in on this with you, Bob."

"Well I'm proud to have you in on it, Kid."

They raised their cups in a toast to their success. A whistle shrilled and a locomotive heaved a huge gasp and a train began its huffing, clanking departure and the smells of smoke and hot cinders carried into the restaurant.

They left for Miami before sunup, clattering along in a Model T touring car with the top down, the headlamps casting weak yellow light over the sandy road ahead. They'd stayed up late the night before, repeatedly toasting themselves for the boldness of their plan, and every man of them had walked at a list when they at last headed for the hotel and to bed. They'd directed the night manager to awaken them at five o'clock sharp and so had the man tried to do, but his pounding on the doors had failed to rouse them and he'd had to go in the rooms and shake each of them in turn to grumbling consciousness. Now they were all of them red-eyed and surly and their spirits did not lift until Bob Ashley reached under the front seat and withdrew a sealed bottle of true Kentucky bourbon.

"Was savin this for after we got Johnny in the car," he said, "but bedamn if I aint in bad need of a little bite of it right now." He unsealed the bottle and turned it up and bubbled it with a huge swallow. He blew a hard breath and said in a strictured voice, "Whoo! That oughta chase some of them snakes out of my head."

They passed the bottle around and they all quickly came to feel much better. By the time they went through the hamlet of Lemon City just a couple of miles north of Miami the bottle was empty. Kid Lowe threw it arcing from the car and it shattered against the trunk of an oak where several small Negro children were playing and the kids scattered like spooked grackles. The men's hard laughter trailed out of the car.

They stopped at a Little River gasoline station and alighted and removed the front seat to expose the fuel tank. Bob unscrewed the cap and poked the sounding stick into the tank and determined that it was more than half-full but went ahead and filled it anyway.

A pair of greasy dogs suddenly came together in a snarling snapping tangle alongside the garage and as quickly broke apart and one of them slunk away as the other stood growling after it. The day was brightly blue but uncommonly cool and dry for June in South Florida: a thermometer on the front wall registered but seventy-seven degrees. A sweetly briny breeze came off the ocean and rustled the palms. Despite the fair weather the three were avidly thirsty from the previous night's drinking and the morning's bourbon and they bought two bottles of cold beer each from the station proprietor's secret cache in the rear room and the beer did appease their dry tongues. Then they drove on into Miami.

They passed the Florida East Coast Railroad depot and all of them glanced down the adjoining road that led west to a fish camp at the edge of the Everglades and was their alternate escape route. They drove slowly down the boulevard and admired the beautiful schooners anchored offshore and the yachts moored in the bay and tied up at the docks. They pointed out to each other every pretty woman they saw strolling on the sidewalks and even some who were not so pretty.

They marveled aloud at the rate the town was growing and only Bob lamented this steady rise in population, predicting that the day would come when there'd be so damn many people in Miami they'd probably have to drain the Everglades all the way up to the river rapids. The more people came the more they'd have to drain just to make room for them—and then what would happen to all the good hunting, he wanted to know. Kid Lowe and Claude Calder snorted at this.

Kid Lowe said he sounded like some old fart who wanted everything to stay exactly the same forever. "This is progress, brother," Kid Lowe said. "It's what makes the world go round. Get in its way and it'll run right over your young ass."

"If this is progress, you all can have it," Bob Ashley said.

A couple of blocks above Flagler Street Claude turned off the bay boulevard and navigated the inner streets and they came now to the hotel where they'd stayed and went past it and then slowly past the Dade County Jail. Since John Ashley's incarceration within, the jail's outer doors were secured at sundown with double lengths of heavy-link chain and heavy padlocks, but during the day the chains were let off. A pair of policemen stood guard at the front door.

They went another block and parked at the curb on the other side of the street and from there had a clear view of the jail. A garage stood directly opposite the jailhouse and cars came and went through its wide front doors. To this side of the jail building and adjoining it was the small residence of the chief jailer Wilber Hendrickson. Bob Ashley checked his pocket watch. "Plenty of time," he said. "It aint but twenty after twelve." They had studied Hendrickson's routine and knew he came home for dinner every day at one o'clock.

The time passed slowly. No one talked. They checked their weapons and then checked them again. They affected to read the newspapers and magazines they'd brought along. None would have admitted it to the others but all were now feeling the pain of the morning's alcohol and every man of them was dry of mouth from hangover and apprehension. Few people passed by on this street and those who did paid them no mind. At five minutes to one the jail's front door swung inward and out stepped Wilbur Hendrickson, a tall sandyhaired policeman with a heavy paunch. Hendrickson chatted with the cops at the door a moment before coming down the steps and turning toward the house next door.

"Let's do it," Bob Ashley said. He and Kid Lowe got out of the car.

"Be ready, Claude," Bob Ashley said. He started across the street toward the jailer's house and Kid Lowe followed directly behind. They carried their pistols in their waistbands under their untucked shirts. Hendrickson was going through the fence gate and a smiling matronly woman waited for him at the top of the porch steps.

Bob Ashley believed that the more complex a plan, the more that could go wrong with it, and thus the best plan was the simplest. His plan was to get the cell keys from Hendrickson, get the drop on the jail guards and get into the building, get John out of his cell, and get away quick to the safety of the Everglades. Clean and simple. Should complexities arise he would deal with them when they did.

Claude Calder's job was to get the car in position and wait with the motor running, ready to pull up fast in front of the jail when he saw them bring Johnny out. He now went around to the front of the Ford to crank up the engine. The motor was a good one and usually started on the first good spin of the crank. Not this time. Nor did it fire up on the second spin, nor on the third. Claude Calder's face was suddenly dripping sweat, his shirt sopped. Kid Lowe and Bob Ashley were almost to the house and seemed not to hear the trouble he was having with the car. He dared not shout after them and draw attention from the cops at the jailhouse door. He hurried to the driver's side and reset the spark lever and then tried the crank again. No luck. Once more he adjusted the spark and this time reset the throttle too and then again spun the crank. Nothing. He felt like shooting the car for a traitor.

Bob and the Kid passed through the fence gate in front of the little house and went up the walk and up onto the porch which was shaded by a lush umbrella tree and Claude Calder could no longer see them. A car came out of the garage across the street from the jail and drove off in the other direction and it occurred to him that the place was full of cars for the taking. He restrained himself from running as he headed for the garage, affecting an air of casual passerby, lips pursed as if whistling, thumbs hooked in his belt loops. As he drew even with the jailer's house he looked across the street and saw Bob at the screen door and holding his .38 behind him. The Kid stood off to the side and held his own revolver low against his leg. Just then the Kid looked over and spied Claude Calder and he stepped into the sunlight at the edge of the porch and his aspect was perplexed. Claude was now at the garage entry and wanted to somehow let the Kid know what he was up to but the cops at the jail door were idly looking his way and there was nothing to do but go into the garage.

Kid Lowe said, "Hey Bob, you better—" but then a raspy voice said, "Who's there? Can I help you?" He turned and saw the large figure of the jailer filling the space behind the door, a bib napkin tucked into his collar.

"I'm Bob Ashley, you son of a bitch," Bob said, and brought the .38 around to brandish it in Hendrickson's face. "I'll have those jail keys and I mean right now. Your pistol too. Hand it over easy."

Hendrickson looked down at the ring of keys attached to his belt as if he was surprised to find them there. His gun was holstered on his other hip. Bob Ashley cocked the revolver and said, "*Now*, Goddamn you. Keys and gun."

Hendrickson'e eyes widened as if he'd only just now realized what was happening. "All right, son—you bet—all right," he said, and fumbled at the key ring.

A woman's voice called from the shadows within: "Will? *Will*, who is it?"

"Tell her get out here," Bob Ashley said. He leaned to the side to peer past the jailer into the dim living room.

"No!" Hendrickson said. "You leave her be!" And went for the gun on his hip.

Bob Ashley cursed and fired through the screen and the pistolblast was huge and all in an instant the round passed through Hendrickson's heart and broke through his shoulderblade and burst out his back and struck the wall behind him in a dark spray of blood. Hendrickson fell as if his legs had gone to water. The woman screamed. Bob Ashley yanked the door off its latch and was squatting to remove the keys from the dead man's belt when she came rushing from the hallway with a double-barreled shotgun. He dove out to the porch and went tumbling down the steps as she discharged both loads like a thunderclap and the screen door came apart and portions of the door-jamb sprayed over him into the yard.

Then he was up and running out the fence gate with his pistol still in hand and he caught a glimpse of policemen coming quick from the jail. He ran down the sidewalk ahead of the woman's screams and the shouting of the cops and saw the Model T still at the curb and Claude Calder nowhere in sight—only a spotted dog trotting away and glancing back at him fearfully. Came a gunshot and the dog bolted and Bob Ashley felt his innards constrict and his pounding heart surged higher into his throat. He ran past the car and around the corner and wondered whatever became of Kid Lowe.

He was on a glaring white street of boarding houses and small stores. People stood outside their doors and pointed him out to each other as he ran past and some of them up ahead ducked back indoors on seeing the gun in his hand and some simply crouched as though they might dodge any bullet he sent their way. Some behind him now yelling "Over there! Yonder he goes!" and he knew they were advising pursuers. His chest felt stretched to bursting and every breath seared and he saw at the corner ahead an idling bread truck parked before a grocery store and the driver just then getting into the cab.

He ran to the truck and opened the passenger-side door and clambered onto the seat and thrust the pistol into the driver's open-mouthed face and yelled, "Go! *GO! GO!*" The driver was young and freckled and his eyes were big as eggs and for a moment it seemed he would remain immobilized with fright—and then he worked the shift lever with a grinding of gears and the truck lurched into motion.

Behind them came policemen on the run and the lead cop stopped and aimed and fired twice, one round thunking into a bread case, the other ricocheting off the rear fender. Bob Ashley hunkered down on the seat and was glad of the protection of the bread cases back of him. He hollered, "Head for the train station! *Go!*" His thought was to get to the county road branching off the Dixie Highway at the FEC depot and take that short road to the edge of the Everglades and go it on foot from there. If he could make it to the Devil's Garden he'd be safe.

He looked back around the bread cases and saw a cop halting an oncoming Dodge and hustling into the car on the passenger side and now the car began to give chase. There sounded another gunshot and he heard the bullet hum past and he jerked back into the truck. The driver was bent low and peering at the road ahead from under the top of the steering wheel, eyes wild and knuckles white. "Oh sweet baby Jesus," he breathed.

A woman started to run across the street in front of them and then froze like a jacklit doe directly ahead of the truck. The driver stepped hard on the brake and the truck slewed to the right and bounced up over the curb and sideswiped the front of a hardware store in an explosive burst of window glass and veered left again and cases of bread tumbled off the truckbed and broke apart in the street and sent loaves scattering and the truck crashed into the rear of a parked Buick and both the driver and Bob Ashley hit the windshield with their heads and reduced it to shards.

For a moment he was addled and thought he'd been blinded and then realized his vision was but hampered by blood streaming from his forehead. Beside him the driver was slumped unconscious with his head on the door sill and blood running from his pulped nose. He heard an excited babbling and became aware of a crowd gathering at the truck, saw people gaping and pointing—men mostly, some women, some children, some of the faces awed, some horrified, some clenched in outrage. And then a portion of the crowd jumped back as a car braked squealing to a stop beside the steam-hissing truck and the passenger door flew open and a policeman spilled out and loomed over the unconscious driver and pointed a gun at Bob Ashley and said, "Deliver, you son of a bitch! Deliver or—"

Bob Ashley shot him in the face and the cop spun sideways and dropped from view. People screamed and fled in every direction and the other car sped away. He struggled with the door and it sprang open and he fell out onto the sidewalk. He got to his feet and the ground pitched slightly but he recovered his balance and looked about and saw here and there faces peering at him from around doors and from behind ashcans. He swept the pistol over them and they vanished as if he'd done a magic trick.

He thought to drive off in the Buick and went around the front of it to get to the driver's side. As he stepped into the street he saw the cop sitting alongside the truck. A small dark hole showed under one eye and he held his revolver raised and pointed. The gun cracked and Bob Ashley felt himself roughly shoved backward.

"You son of a bitch," he said—and shot the cop in the chest and the cop grunted and shot him in the belly and then they fired simultaneously and the cop's hair jumped and he fell over and lay still and his blood darkly stained the pale limerock paving.

Bob Ashley regarded the unmoving cop for a moment and then his legs quit him and he sat down hard. He looked down at his own bloody stomach and tried to curse but choked on something and he put his hand to his throat and his fingers came away bloodstained. He groaned wetly and looked at the cop and shot him again. Then felt in his stomach a pain beyond any he'd ever known and he could not help but holler with it. He tried to get to his feet but the ground tilted and he fell on his back and saw a pair of gulls winging overhead.

"Bob! You hear me, Bob?"

He opened his eyes to find himself on his side on a bunk. Sheriff Dan Hardie stood before him with his thumbs hooked in his gunbelt. Bob touched a thick bandage at his throat and then regarded his bloody fingertips. "Hey, Dan," he said in a voice gargly and foreign to him. "You still puttin it to that high-yella girl over in Little River?" The effort of speech felt such in his chest that he knew he was bad off. His feet were cold. Though the light was dim he could see he was in a jail cell. "Johnny in here?" he asked. *"Johnny?"* His intended shout came out a croak.

"He cant hear you, he aint in this block," Sheriff Hardie said. "Listen, Bob, I got to tell you straight. It dont look like you're goin to make it."

"Dont feel like it a whole lot, neither," Bob said, his face clenched against the pain in his belly. He saw now that there were two other men in the room and both of them in black suits and with serious faces pale as frog bellies and he knew at once who they were. "I'll wager you boys done got me measured for the coffin already," he said and coughed a gush of bright blood onto the bunksheet.

"Come on, boy—come clean of it," Hardie said. "Tell us who the others were. We know it was at least two more. Was it your brothers?"

"No," Bob Ashley managed to say through his teeth. "They never. Wasnt nobody but me in this."

"Bullshit!" the sheriff said. "Look, Bob, I been a friend to you and yours and you know it. I aint never braced any you. I always let you boys do your business and have your fun. But now—well hell, you're going over the river, son. Make a clean break of it and tell me: who was in it with you?"

Bob Ashley looked up at him and sighed wetly. With effort, he raised his hand and beckoned Sheriff Hardie closer. The sheriff squatted beside the bunk and leaned forward with his ear close to Bob Ashley's mouth.

Bob Ashley whispered, "Fuck you, Danny." And then a long exhalation issued from his throat and was gone into the world's vast mingle of last breaths.

Even before Sheriff Hardie had begun his interrogation of Bob Ashley, word had come to him that a mob was forming in front of the jail and demanding that John and Bob Ashley be delivered to it.

"It's a hundred of em if it's one, Sheriff," a deputy had told him. "They got guns, hatchets, clubs, ropes, ever-damn-thing. It's lots of Wilbur's friends out there and lots of old boys who knew J.R. too."

J. R. Riblett was the patrolman Bob Ashley had killed in the street. The deputy reporting to Hardie was barely nineteen years old and not yet four months on the force. He tried mightily not to let the sheriff see that he was afraid but Hardie heard the fear in his voice and smelled it on him. He put a hand on the deputy's shoulder and the gesture seemed to calm the boy. The sheriff then ordered that every man on the county force be called in to defend against an assault on the jailhouse—and now a force of some twenty deputies was standing between the jail doors and a mob of hundreds.

The mob's chanting cries for Ashley blood carried into the jail and down the corridors and into the cell where Bob Ashley lay dying—and carried deeper still to the corridor where two sweating deputies with shotguns stood outside John Ashley's cell. "Give us Ashley! Give us ASHLEY! Give us *ASHLEY!*"

The guards had told John about Bob's attempt to free him and of his failed try at a getaway. Since then they'd been receiving secondhand reports of Bob Ashley's condition and passing it on to John. The latest word was that Bob had choked to death on his own blood. John Ashley showed no expression when they told him. He lay on his bunk and listened to the mob's call for vengeance and it seemed to him but an echo of his own heart's cry.

When the sheriff appeared at the jail doors and the undertaker and his assistant behind him, the mob became frenzied as a zoo at feeding time. The officers on guard looked terrified to a man. Sheriff Hardie knew that if the mob should rush them, his men would start shooting or start running, one or the other, and of his untried officers it was hard to say which of them would do which.

The sheriff raised his hands to try to quiet the mob so he might address it but their cries for Ashley only grew louder. He turned and beckoned into the jail and two deputies came out bearing a sheet-draped body on a stretcher. The mob's chanting slowly gave way to a snaking murmur. And then one of the men at the front of the crowd cried, "It's a trick! They sneaking one out under the sheet like he's dead but he aint!"

"Let's see!" hollered another. In an instant the chant went up: "Let's see! *Let's see! LET'S SEE!*"

Hardie went to the stretcher and yanked the sheet away to expose the bloody corpse of Bob Ashley and the mob abruptly fell mute.

"Take a good look!" the sheriff shouted. "This here's Bob Ashley and he's as dead as he's ever gonna get! Now what you hardcases wanna do? String him up anyway? Wanna beat on him a while? Set him afire maybe? Wanna shoot him some? You all wanna bring your womenfolk up here to see him? Want your *kids* to have a good look?"

There were mutterings in the crowd but nobody spoke up. Dan Hardie pointed at the jail doors and shouted, "John Ashley's *still* in there, but he didnt have a thing to do with any the killing today. That man will stand trial for murdering a damn Indian and if he's convicted he'll be hanged. But he aint gonna be hanged today, not by you all or anybody else. Anybody goes in that jail without my say-so is gonna be one sorry son of a bitch and thats a goddamned promise."

He stood with his hands on hips and swept his gaze over them and every man's eyes jumped away from his.

And now in softer tone he said, "You all move aside now and let Doctor Combs get this body out of here. I dont want it stinking up my jail."

And move aside they did.

*   *   *

An hour later Bob Ashley's body lay alongside those of Wilber Hendrickson and J. R. Riblett in W. H. Combs' funeral parlor. By then more than a thousand people had gathered outside the parlor and were insisting on seeing the desperado's remains. Combs became fearful and telephoned the sheriff who advised him to let them look.

So the undertaker placed Bob Ashley's body in a room by itself and then permitted the public to come in and view it—men and women both, but no children under twelve. He posted a man next to the body to keep people beyond reach of it and prevent them from taking locks of hair or other mementos. The line of gawkers snaked through the front door and into the viewing room and out the side door to the alley through the rest of the afternoon. At nightfall Undertaker Combs pled exhaustion and promised he would show the body again in the morning.

At sunrise, the line of people waiting to go inside was already a block long. Word had spread that Bob Ashley's corpse was on display to any who cared to see him, and thrillseekers had come from as far off as Palm Beach. Combs was coming up the street toward the parlor when he was approached by two strangers in suits, one of them carrying a camera and rolling a toothpick in his mouth. The other, who looked too big for his clothes, said, "Mister Combs, sir, I'd like a word with you."

He guided Combs into the alley out of sight and earshot of the waiting line—and though his touch was gentle on Combs' arm the undertaker could feel the ready strength in his hand. The man said his name was Hal Croves and he would pay Combs thirty dollars for ten minutes in the room with Bob Ashley's body and no one else in attendance but the photographer.

"Oh, I'm afraid not, Mister Croves," the undertaker said. "We have a strict policy, you see—to protect the deceased from souvenir takers and such."

The big man laughed but his eyes roused in Combs a sudden unease. *"We,"* the big man said. "There aint no *we*. It's just you. It's *your* policy." The man's teeth showed large and yellow and Combs felt the grip on his elbow tighten slightly. "Fifty dollars," the man said.

"Fif—!" Combs said. He glanced about for eavesdroppers, "Well . . . I suppose if you were to promise not to actually *touch* the deceased, and if . . ."—he took another quick look about—"if you could make it, say, *sixty?*"

The man laughed again. "Sixty it is," he said.

Combs let them in by the alley door and showed them to the room where Bob Ashley lay. "I'll just wait out here," he said. He consulted a pocketwatch. "Ten minutes."

"Be just fine," the big man said. Combs went out in the hall and the big man closed the door and Combs heard the latch slide home. He went to the front door and opened it and announced to the crowd that he was running a little late but they would be permitted inside in just another five minutes. He turned up his palms at the chorus of complaints as if the entire matter were one of those things that couldnt be helped.

When the two men came out again, Combs was waiting in the hall with his hands clasped before him like a penitent. He raised his brow at them. The man named Croves paid him thirty dollars and showed his big yellow teeth and Combs stood there gaping, looking from the money in his hand to the retreating backs of the two men. The big man's laughter echoed in the high-ceilinged hall as he headed for the alley door.

At eleven o'clock that morning Edward Rogers, Bill Ashley's father-in-law, arrived haggard and disheveled on the train from Hobe Sound and went directly to the Combs Funeral Parlor and made arrangements to ship Bob Ashley's body the following day. He said no more than necessary and refused all reporters' requests for interviews.

There were rumors in the street all day that Old Joe Ashley and his other sons had been in town in disguise, though nobody had any proof of it and nobody could offer a reasonable explanation for their presence other than the possibility that they intended to try to break John Ashley out of jail themselves.

The moment Bob Ashley shot the jailer, Kid Lowe knew the plan was gone to hell. And because he knew Claude Calder had abandoned the car, he figured his best chance for escape was by the alleyway in back of the house. He vaulted the railing at the end of the porch and jogged around to the backyard, holding his pistol low and close against his leg. He nearly jumped at the sound of the shotgun blast from the front of the house and he knew Bob had been at the wrong end of it and was certain he'd been killed.

In the backyard a pair of Negro yardmen stood like statues with their tools in their hands and stared at him in stark fear. He pointed the pistol at them and said, "You aint seen nobody, you hear me?" The two men nodded jerkily and dropped their gaze and Kid Lowe hurried away down the alley.

He walked fast, restraining himself from running even when he heard a gunshot from somewhere near the jail. He reckoned Bob might yet be alive and was making a fight of it—or Claude Calder was. At the end of the alley he paused and heard now more gunshots but from greater distance. He slipped the pistol into his belt under his shirt and walked out onto the sidewalk and saw people hurrying toward the intersecting street that led back to the jail. He went in the other direction.

Two blocks away he stole a new Dodge sedan and made his way to the Dixie Highway and there turned north. At dusk he was just south of Stuart but did not even slow down at the branching oystershell road that led into the dark pinewoods and beyond to the Ashley Twin Oaks house at the edge of the swamps. The last man he wanted to meet with anytime soon was Old Joe Ashley.

He drove and drove and stopped only to take on fuel and buy sandwiches and soda pop and beer where he could find it. Just before sunrise he parked within the sound of breakers and slept in the car for a couple of hours and then drove on. He had decided on returning to Chicago to see if he might make his peace with Silver Jack O'Keefe's former competitors. If they should prove unforgiving he would push on to Detroit and try his luck there.

A few days later and just south of Macon, Georgia, the Dodge began to sputter and ten minutes later it quit altogether and coasted to a halt on the red clay road. In the absence of the motor's clatter the countryside silence seemed huge. The Kid sat on the front fender and smoked cigarettes and drank his last warm bottle of beer and regarded a pair of redtails wheeling on the hunt over a distant pasture.

Some time later a farmer happened along in his two-mule wagon and they hitched the Dodge to the wagon's rear axle with rope and the farmer towed it to a smitty shop at the edge of town. He absolutely would not accept the Kid's offer of a dollar for his help. The smith said the trouble was likely in the fuel line and he could fix it in about a half-hour but wouldnt be able to get to it for an hour yet. He directed the Kid to a barbershop down the block where a man might get a haircut in the chair by the front window or a shot of spirits in the backroom.

It was a dim place but cool and comfortable and the Kid sat on a stool at the makeshift plank bar and threw down two quick shooters before taking a third more slowly with a beer back. His very bones seemed to sigh with pleasure. An hour later he was glass-eyed drunk and ruminating bitterly about the way things had gone in Miami. A beefy fellow came in and straddled the adjacent stool and looked over at him and wrinkled his nose and said, "Whoo! Been a while since you was last near a tub of water, aint it, shorty?"

Kid Lowe squinted blearily at him and wondered if he'd been insulted and seeing no smile on the man's face decided that he had. In a single smooth motion remarkable in one so drunk he slid off his stool and punched the man squarely in the mouth and man and stool went over onto the floor and the half-dozen other patrons cheered and applauded with delight at this entertaining turn.

The man sat on the floor and gaped up at the Kid less in pain than in astonishment. He put his hand to his bleeding mouth and one of his front teeth came away in his fingers. Someone among the spectators said loudly, "Hey, Turner, you forgot to duck!" and there was a chorus of laughter.

"You half-pint son of a *bitch!*" The man scrambled to his feet and started for the Kid who in a sudden drunken panic perceived his antagonist as fearsomely and unstoppably huge and in an unthinking defensive reflex drew his pistol from under his shirt and from a distance of less than three feet shot the man through the throat. The man staggered backward with his hands patting at the blood jetting from his neck and spattering those nearest him. He reeled and crumpled to the floor and made rude guttering sounds and the blood was fast pooling round his head.

Now the bartender had the Kid in a headlock and was gripping his gun hand and several others fell to him in the midst of much angry shouting. The gun was wrested from him and the Kid went down flailing. They were cursing him and kicking him and it seemed to him a long time before they stopped. He was hauled to his feet and held by a man on either side of him and he could barely focus on the man before him who told him he was under arrest.

His arm was broken, his nose and ribs and one of his feet. Because he did not know his standing with the organization in Chicago he did not contact anyone there for legal help. He was sure that if he called on Joe Ashley the old man would come to Macon solely to kill him. And so when he went to trial still relying on a crutch and with his arm yet in a cast, he was represented by a court-appointed lawyer named Soames who smelled always of peppermint and had trouble remembering his client's name. The trial began at nine o'clock in the morning and an hour later he stood convicted of murder in the first degree and that afternoon was sentenced to life imprisonment in the state penitentiary.

Within the year he would escape from the Okeefenokee penal camp where he'd been confined. But he would get lost as he made his breathless way through the sunless depths of the swamp and unwittingly bore ever deeper into that wilderness where even the dogs could not follow. No one in the world would ever know that he plunged into a quicksand bog and drowned and his bones would remain in that muck to the end of time.

There had been no one in the garage but a mechanic at the far end of the room who was busy replacing a tire on a wheel and when he saw Claude Calder enter he called out that he would be with him in a minute. Claude said for him to take his time, he was in no hurry, and headed straight for a Ford touring car exactly like their own. He had just cranked up the motor when he heard the gunshot from somewhere out in front of the building and he was confused, thinking that Bob and the Kid and John Ashley were already making their break from the jail and he wondered how they'd managed to move so fast.

He got behind the wheel and saw the mechanic hurrying toward him saying, "Say there, mister, what you think—" when the shotgun blasted across the street. Both of them glanced in that direction and then Claude kicked the car into gear and worked the throttle and the car clattered forward. The mechanic came running as if he would jump into the car with him and Claude brought his gun into view and the mechanic veered and took cover behind a car.

He heard more pistolshots as he braked at the garage door and he expected to see Kid Lowe and the Ashleys shooting it out with police in front of the jail, but the jailhouse door stood deserted. Gunfire sounded to his right and he hunkered in the car seat as he looked down the street and saw policemen running around the corner. He drove after them as more gunfire sounded.

He made the turn and slowed the car almost to a stop at the sight of a dozen armed cops on the next block where a truck was crumpled and steaming against the smashed back end of a car. Shattered bread boxes littered the limerock pavement. A policeman and another man lay in the street and even at this distance Claude Calder could see that the street under them was stained with blood and that likely both of them were dead. And now he recognized Bob Ashley as one of the two bodies and he pondered the situation for one long moment and then wheeled the car around and headed for home.

He was slow about making his way back. He made frequent stops to take a glass of beer in the backrooms of filling stations and cafes, to shoot a game of pool in one roadhouse or another. When he was in sight of the beach he sometimes parked the car and stripped to his underwear and dove into the breakers to cool off. He knew he would have to go to the Ashleys and tell them what happened but he did not like the idea of having to face Old Joe. Two days after the break attempt he arrived at the oystershell road leading to Twin Oaks. He was hoping John Ashley would not be home, that the old man might be out at one of his whiskey camps.

The trail wound for several miles through palmetto thickets and heavy pine stands and he knew the Ashley lookouts had seen him from the moment he'd turned off the Dixie Highway and had already sent word to the house of who was coming. Now the Ford reverberated over a hundred-yard stretch of jarring corduroy road that carried him through a wide muddy slough flanked by shadowy stands of oak and gumbo limbo hung with vines as thickly as a jungle. The car's clangor raised a horde of storks from the shallows and up into the trees. And then he was off the logs and on a narrow sandy trail and the bushes scraped along both sides of the car. He negotiated a final sharp turn and the trees suddenly fell away and he came into a wide sunlit clearing and the house stood just ahead. The air was full of dragonflies hovering on blurred wings.

He saw Frank and Ed Ashley sitting on the front porch smoking and drinking and watching him come. He parked directly in front of the house and cut off the engine and got out of the car.

"Hey, boys," he said, and was just starting up the steps when the front door flew open and Old Joe burst out like an unleashed hunting hawk and swooped down the steps and onto him and struck him on the head with a grub hoe handle and Claude Calder never had a chance to say a word before Old Joe hit him again and again, grunting hard with every blow he delivered. Claude fell and got up and fell again and was trying to fend with his hands and he felt bones break under the slashing hoe handle and now there was blood in his eyes and Old Joe kicked him in the face and he felt his front teeth stave. And now he could not get up and the blows continued to fall but he felt little pain and only later would he find out that Frank and Ed had at last came down the steps and pulled Old Joe off before he killed him.

He was put up in a backroom of the Twin Oaks house while he healed. But he was permanently purblind in his left eye and would never again have full use of his left hand nor replace the two front teeth he'd lost. His bullet-maimed ear now seemed insignificant to him. Nor would his spirit ever fully recover. Evermore he would jump at sudden sounds and sometimes be the object of ridicule for it. He would for the rest of his brief life have bad dreams that woke him in the night in a soaking sweat.

Even after Claude was up and about, Frank and Ed had insisted that he stay on the place and they gave him simple tasks to let him feel he was earning his keep. Old Joe did not speak to him directly until nearly two months after the beating. One afternoon he came out to the Yellow Creek dock west of the house where Claude was cleaning a string of catfish. He expressed admiration for Claude's catch and sat on the edge of the dock and offered him a drink from his personal jug. He told Claude that he would always have a place to live, that even if he married and started a family he could live on the Twin Oaks property. Claude knew Old Joe was apologizing the only way he knew how, knew the old man might even actually be sorry for what he'd done to him. When Joe got up to go, he handed Claude the jug and said, "Here, son, you keep this." He accepted the jug with a smile and said thanks and watched Joe Ashley head off. And the thought of someday getting even with the old bastard was so sweet he could almost taste it. And then the thought of what would happen if Old Joe ever thought him faithless turned the taste to brass.

Scratchley ventured out of the Devil's Garden but once every three or four months, poling his dugout through the sawgrass channels and along the creeks leading in serpentine fashion to the canal connecting to Jupiter, there to get a new supply of matches and lamp oil and other such luxuries as he could not wrest from the Everglades itself like he did all the essentials of life. The money for these items he regularly received from Joe Ashley. To earn it he was required only to keep close watch in the swamp for any signs of encroaching strangers or known lawmen and, if he ever saw any—which he rarely did—to report the sighting at once to Joe's whiskey camp in the Hungryland Slough. The camp lay a few miles west of his weathered pinewood cabin in the Loxahatchee and he would go there once a month in any case to receive his stipend from Joe and take a cup of whiskey with him before poling back home. He was one of dozens—white, black and Indian—who served Joe Ashley in this employ all over South Florida.

On this late sun-bright Friday afternoon he had poled back up the canal from Jupiter with a fresh cargo of wheat flour and sugar, matches and lamp oil, a case of soda pop and sacks of rock candy, which was his weakness, and had just turned off into the creek leading to the Loxahatchee sawgrass channels when he saw another dugout laying to in the shadows of a live oak overhanging the creek ahead. Its three occupants were watching him and he knew there was no reason at all they would be there except they were waiting for him. To try to back up and outdistance them on the canal was out of the question. Two of the men had poles and they would overtake him easily. And so he slowly pushed ahead and closed the distance to them.

He saw now that the man in the middle—the one without a pole—was deputy sheriff Bob Baker. The forward man was one he'd sometimes seen roaming deep in the sawgrass country to the southwest, a halfbreed who seemed to know his way in the Devil's Garden. The fellow sitting behind Deputy Bob he'd seen before too, but could not recall exactly where nor if he knew his name.

He knew what they wanted and was already resolved to go to jail rather than give them the information. As his dugout drew near theirs he said, "Might's well just go on and take me in, Bobby, because I dont know a thing."

Bob Baker smiled. "Another fella was tellin me just yesterday he didnt know a thing neither and he didnt sound truthful to me anymoren you do. So I figured I'd test him. And do you know that not ten minutes later he was just jabberin like a parrot? I reckon I could make you do the same, Scratch, but truth is, I dont really need your information anymoren I needed his."

Scratchley hove up within ten feet of the deputies' boat. "Well then, what-all you want?"

"I want you to know you been makin a big mistake workin for the Ashleys," Bob Baker said. "You and all them others. And now you know it."

The breed stood up and it was as if the twin-barreled shotgun had materialized from the very air, so suddenly was it in his hands. He took aim and one of the muzzles flashed bright yellow and the buckshot load blasted through the forward hull of Scratchley's dugout and the great blue herons feeding along the banks broke for the sky in a terrified frenzy of wingflaps.

The impact jarred the boat under Scratchley's feet and he almost lost his balance and the dugout prow was already sunk as the breed raised the barrels and Scratchley saw the man's blue eyes behind the dark muzzles settling on him and the last thing he ever saw was the grin or grimace of the man behind Bob Baker who lacked both front teeth. Then the shotgun boomed again and he felt himself moving blackly through the air and then there was nothing.

Just after sundown they dumped his bloodymeat remains in a gator hole some five miles deeper in the Devil's Garden.

ELEVEN

The Liars Club

THERE WASNT ANYBODY TO GET EVEN WITH, THAT WAS OLD JOE'S problem. The man who killed Bob Ashley was killed by Bob himself in return and thats all she wrote. There wasnt nobody else at fault. Nobody ordered the cop who shot Bob to do it. Old Joe didnt have nobody to blame for Bob's killing, not even Dade Sheriff Dan Hardie. Truth be told, he was in Dan Hardie's debt for saving John from a lynch mob. Some said the old man snuck a whole carload of his best stuff out to Hardie for a present and the sheriff was appreciative. Anyhow, they say Old Joe went around for months looking like a man searching for something he couldnt even put a name on.

It didnt help Old Joe's spirits any that John Ashley was in jail down in Miami all this while. He was allowed one visitor at a time but they had to sit on the other side of a wide table from him and there was no touching allowed and there was always two guards standing right there and listening to everything was said. But Sheriff Hardie did allow Old Joe to bring John in some special dishes and treats Ma Ashley baked for him.

They dropped the attempted murder charges since there was no way they could prove he fired any of the shots at the cops who'd chased the Stuart bank robbers. But he stayed in the Dade County Jail under heavy guard for another year and a half before they finally let him out from under the murder of DeSoto Tiger. He mostly passed the time playing cards and exercising to keep from going soft. They say he got so he could do all kinds of card tricks and wouldnt none of the other jailbirds play him for money because he could deal himself any card he wanted and nobody could catch him at it. When he wasnt playing cards he was doing pushups and situps and such. He'd put his back to the cell door and take hold of the bars over his shoulders and then lift his legs straight out in front of him. He could do that a hundred times in a row. They say after a few months his belly looked like it was wrapped with rope and there wasnt a white man in that jailhouse could beat him at arm rassling.

The state said finally it was dropping the Indian murder case against him. *Nolle Prosqui* they called it—a high-sounding way of saying, "We cant prove it so we quit." Some said it was because they never could find their chief witness Jimmy Gopher anywhere—but they hadnt found him the summer before either and that didnt stop them from going ahead with the trial. Truth is, there was talk that Old Joe had passed a hefty sum of money to the judge and prosecutor by way of Gordon Blue and that the reason it took so long to bring the case to trial was all the negotiating over the deal. Supposedly the state's attorney and the judge each wanted ten thousand dollars. Back then that wasnt nothing less than a small fortune and Old Joe thought they were out of their mind to ask so much. He figured five grand each ought be way more than enough. But the prosecutor and the judge said they wouldnt even think about it for less than eight and they finally told Joe take it or leave it and he couldnt do a thing but take it. *Then* they argued about exactly what that sixteen thousand dollars would buy. Old Joe didnt see what there was to argue about. He naturally thought *all* the charges ought be dropped. Supposedly the prosecutor was willing but the judge wouldnt hear of it. The way the story goes, the judge was willing to see the murder charge dropped but Johnny would have to stand trial for the bank job—and plead guilty. If John pled not guilty and made the prosecution work for his conviction, the judge swore he'd give him thirty years, but if he pled guilty he'd only give him ten. Joe didnt like that deal for shit. Him and the prosecutor argued about it for a time before they finally agreed to a five-year sentence.

So John Ashley went to trial for the bank robbery and pled guilty— and the judge gave him seventeen years. Old Joe sat there like he'd been pole-axed. He musta felt like the fella who paid for a pearl and got him a pebble. The prosecutor looked at him and shrugged like he didnt know what was going on either and then quick skeedaddled. They say the judge was smiling as he left the bench, that the seventeen years was his way of letting Joe know he shoulda paid the ten thousand. The courtroom was about empty when Joe finally got up and walked out with Frank and Ed. The story goes that when he got outside he looked up at the sky and hollered, "The law aint nothing but a untrustworthy double-crossing son of a bitch!" Like it might of just come as news to him.

They transported John Ashley to the state penitentiary at Raiford in November of nineteen and sixteen. He was still there when the country went to war against the Hun. None of the Ashley boys went off to the army—Old Joe's view was that the family had enough enemies right here in Florida without having to go fight a new bunch a them on the other side of the Atlantic Ocean. Besides, he needed his boys to help him run his business. In 1917 the feds passed a wartime prohibition law that made it illegal to use grain for making whiskey, and a short time later they extended the law to include beer and wine. Naturally, the moonshine business just boomed.

They say Joe was paying protection money by the wheelbarrowful to the high sheriffs of three or four counties and to deputies and police chiefs and cops all up and down the East Coast and all around Lake Okeechobee. Supposedly he even had him a judge or two on the payroll. The more successful he got the more it was costing him to stay in business. Probably the only ones not on the Ashley payroll were the Bakers, but it wasnt no secret Joe Ashley had some of Sheriff George's deputies in his pocket and for sure Sheriff George knew it. By now George Baker's health was staring to go bad and he was giving Bob more and more authority to run the department in his place. Bobby knew a lot of the deputies were friends to the Ashleys or on Joe's payroll and he didn't trust many of the cops on the force except for about seven or eight he knew real well—the main ones being the Padgett brothers and Henry Stubbs and Grover Pass and Slim Jackson, a coupla others. His cousin Freddie was his closest bubba and sort of his personal lieutenant. He was a good old boy and easily the most popular policeman in Palm Beach County.

The rest of the department got to calling Bobby and his bunch the Baker Gang, and some say the most valuable man in the bunch was Heck Runyon. Even after Sheriff George was forced to fire him for killing a prisoner, he kept using him as what he called a special public agent. He said he needed him because there wasnt anybody on the county force as good at tracking a man in the Devil's Garden, and there wasnt. But there were rumors he used him to fight crime in other ways too, ways maybe not all that legal but ways Heck Runyon was awful good at. Hardly anybody was too bothered by these rumors because Heck wasnt really a policeman anymore and because when you got right down to it nobody really cared how Sheriff George and Bob Baker got rid of criminals, just so they did.

John Ashley hadnt been in Raiford but about six months when Bob Baker and his gang raided one of Old Joe's whiskey camps set in a clearing in the Hungryland Slough about twelve miles into the Devil's Garden west of Juno Beach. Old Joe himself was there and got caught redhanded along with two nigger helpers and a big old cracker boy named Albert Miller. They later on admitted they got took by such surprise they didnt even try to fight nor make a run for it. Bobby and his boys used axes to ruin the boiling kettles and bust up all the other whiskey equipment at the camp. They confiscated two of Joe's trucks and every weapon they found and all the cash money Joe had with him at the time which was said to be several thousand dollars. Bob Baker had wanted the judge to give them jail time but the judge—who some said was a friend of Joe's—made Bobby give back Joe's money and his trucks and then made Joe pay a fifty-dollar fine for himself and the same for Albert Miller and let them go.

Bob Baker was hopping mad but Old Joe was plenty put out himself. He even went to George Baker's office to complain about Bobby busting up his camp but Sheriff George told him he'd authorized Bobby to deal with moonshiners any way he saw fit and Joe would have to settle the problem with him. Old Joe told Sheriff George he could unauthorize Bobby just as easy as he'd authorized him and the sheriff said he didnt need anybody telling him how to do his job. They say you could hear the two of them a half a block away, they was hollering at each other so loud. When Joe Ashley came out of the office he looked ready to spit bullets and people just jumped out of his way.

That raid was the talk of the county for a month after. It was hard to believe anybody could find any of Joe's whiskey camps in the first place, never mind be able to sneak up on them if they even knew where they were at. Old Joe had about eight or nine camps by then—four or five round about Palm Beach County, the others strung out from south of Lake Okeechobee to just west of Miami—and it was common knowledge he had eyes working for him everywhere in the Devil's Garden, a whole grapevine of lookouts to send warning if the law ever started closing in on any the camps. The lookouts were said to be posted a good ways from the camps so that even if you caught one you still might never find the camp he was watching out for.

Bob Baker said he'd been able to find the Hungryland Slough camp because Heck Runyon knew his way in Devil's Garden as well as anybody. Maybe so—but not real likely. There was hardly a fullblood Indian who could find John Ashley's whiskey camps, never mind some halfbreed who'd lived way off in DeSoto County for seven years of his young life. More likely, at least one of the lookouts ratted. The talk was that Bobby had somehow found out who Joe's lookouts were for the Hungryland still and he'd run them down and made them tell where the camp was. Then ruther than put them in jail, he let Heck Runyon deal with them.

Mind you now, there aint never been a bit of proof put out in public that Bobby Baker was responsible for the death or disappearance of any of Joe Ashley's lookouts—but there *was* talk about it. Friends of the Ashleys said the talk was true and Bobby Baker was using Heck Runyon as his private executioner. Friends of the Bakers said it was a wicked lie of the sort nobody but the Ashleys was low enough to tell. Most of us didnt know what to believe—and still dont. It aint no denying that in them days bodies were always being found along the edge of the Devil's Garden and ever time one was found with its skull stove-in or showing a bullet hole, there were some who said it was one of Old Joe's lookouts. It was hard to say for sure because after just a coupla weeks in the swamp a body's nothing but rot on the bone and cant hardly be recognized by its own mother.

Most of the lookouts who vanished never turned up anywhere at all. But it's a true fact that a week or so after the Hungryland raid a nekkid dead man come floating up to the Jupiter docks with his throat cut. The men who first spotted him thought it was a fat nigger but it turned out to be a white man all swole up and rotted black. His name was Seth Thomason and he owned a house in Jupiter and he had a wife and baby girl. Nobody ever found out who done him in but the word quick got around that he'd been one of Joe's lookouts for the camp Bobby Baker had busted up. There'd been another lookout for that camp too—a swamp rat named Dog Scratchley who lived in a shack somewhere in the Loxahatchee Slough—and he just flat vanished is what he did. His shack was found burnt to the ground but there wasnt a sign of him nowhere and never has been. Most of us couldnt but wonder what-all was going on. Joe Ashley was said to be wondering too—wondering how Bobby Baker had found out that Scratchley and Seth Thomason were his Hungryland lookouts.

That Hungryland raid was just the first of more to come. Sometimes Bob Baker hit a couple of camps within just a few weeks of each other but more often months would go by between raids. Every time there was a raid, though, it turned out that the lookouts for the camp to get raided had disappeared a day or two before Bobby came popping out of the sawgrass or the pine trees to tear up the still.

Bob Baker never did catch anybody except now and then a few more of Joe's niggers. But he ever time busted up or burned all the equipment and stuff Joe and his boys were forced to leave behind in camp—boilers and kettles and barrels and tubing and jugs and sugar and mash and whatnot. He even burned up the vehicles the Ashleys had to abandon. He was tearing down Joe's whiskey camps faster than Joe could afford to rebuild them. We heard Old Joe was going crazy trying to figure out how Bobby was finding out who his lookouts were. It was a war going on is what it was, and Bobby was starting to win because he was making it so damn expensive for Old Joe to keep at it.

While all this was going on, John Ashley was doing his time at Raiford. He was kept in the main prison for a little over a year and while he was in there he worked in the laundry and got himself fitted with a glass eye. His natural eye color was brown, but for some reason the only color glass eye they could get for him in prison was blue. Some say they could of got him the right color but they just wanted to devil him some more by giving him different color eyes. The joke was on them though because John Ashley liked having one eye blue and one brown. He always did say the state had done him a favor and made him even more interesting to women.

Then he got transferred to a road camp not too far from Palatka there on the St. Johns River. And not three months later he escaped. The story has it that he was out with his road gang fixing up the ferry road north of Palatka one afternoon and two men wearing flour-sack masks stepped out of the bushes with shotguns and got the drop on the guards and manacled them to a magnolia tree. There's always been stories about somebody at Raiford being paid off to assign John Ashley to a road gang but it's just one more thing you hear that there aint never been no proof of one way or the other. Most stories say it was Frank and Ed who broke him out but there's never been no proof of that neither. For certain sure the Ashleys was behind the break—had to be. And they had to of planned the break real careful for it to work so smooth as it did. They freed all twelve cons on the chain but took only one with them, a fella named Tom Maddox who was a bank

robber out of North Florida and had got to be good friends with John
Ashley in the road camp but who nobody never heard nothing about
ever again.

Right after word of John Ashley's escape reached Palm Beach
County, Bobby and Freddie Baker were seen sitting at a corner table
in the Oleander Grocery in West Palm Beach drinking out of paper
bags and talking low and glaring like they'd like to shoot the whole
damn world.

TWELVE

July 1918–December 1919

THEY RAN THROUGH THE PINE SCRUBS TO WHERE ED AND FRANK had left the Dodge and they all four scrambled into the car and sped away jouncing and swaying on an old logging trail. They threw the flour sack masks out into the palmetto scrub a few miles farther on and just before the trail merged into a wider backroad. They drove north from Palatka and made their way to the ferry and were rope-pullied across the coppery St. Johns. They excitedly pointed out to each other a bald eagle wheeling from the sky with a fullgrown cat in its talons to alight at its nest atop a tall live oak overlooking the river. They pitched pennies at turtles sunning themselves on floating driftwood. They told the ferryman their name was Horton and they were headed for their uncle's funeral in Daytona. But when they reached the crossroad at Molasses Junction they turned the car north for Jacksonville.

His brothers admired his blue glass eye and asked him what it was like being half-blind and made jokes about how he truly could sleep with one eye open now. John Ashley asked about Kid Lowe and they told him the Kid had flat vanished and nobody had heard a word about where he might be. They talked then about their brother Bob and told Tom Maddox about some of the funny things Bob had done when they were boys and when they ran out of stories about him they fell silent for a time. Then Ed asked what it had been like in there. John Ashley shrugged and said it hadn't been all that intolerable. His voice was distant. His brothers raised their brows at Tom Maddox who shrugged and turned to look out at the passing pines.

The primitive roads of sand and limerock sometimes narrowed to hardly more than wagon trails winding through dense brushland and pine forest and they three times had to stop to repair flat tires and spell each other on the air pump before they made the Duval County line. Frank and Ed had brought several jugs of their daddy's product which helped to ease everyone's irritation with the delays.

As they puttered through the streets of Jacksonville in search of their sister's address they passed a police car and raised a hand in greeting and the two cops did likewise and all the while the Ashleys and Tom Maddox too had their other hand on a pistol. They found the house and got out of the car and their sister Daisy came shrilling out the door to greet them, her husband trailing her with a smile and leading their three-year-old boy by the hand. She hugged and kissed her brothers and let them swing her around in their arms and pat her fondly on the rump and she made a special fuss over Johnny, mussing his hair and kissing him all over his face and crying in her happiness to see him. As they trooped into the house Frank told her that Daddy sent his love. She looked at him and laughed and said she knew that wasn't one bit true. Frank flushed and shrugged and said, "Well, he ought of."

Her husband Butch had served a short sentence in Raiford for armed robbery back before Daisy knew him but he had since forsworn the criminal life. They'd met at a dance in Stuart four years ago shortly after his release from prison and while he was working with a crew building a cargo dock at Salerno on the Indian River. A few weeks later he asked her to marry him and move to Jacksonville where he had a good job waiting. Old Joe had no objections to the marriage but he was set against his daughter moving away from home. He offered to take Butch into his whiskey operation and told him he'd make more money in a month than he'd make in six months in a shipyard. When Butch politely turned him down Old Joe took umbrage and said he couldnt have Daisy's hand, not if he was going to take her away. "Ashleys dont desert they home," he said. To which Daisy said she'd damn well be the one to say who could or couldnt have her hand and whether she would or wouldnt move away. She had always known her own mind and this was not the first time she and her father had been at odds but this was their most serious set-to yet. "Then to hell with ye," Old Joe Ashley said, and left the room. By that night she and Butch were married and on their way to Jacksonville. That had been four years ago and she had not seen nor heard from her father since. She corresponded regularly with her mother, however, and Ma Ashley had been at her bedside to assist in the delivery when she'd borne Jeb. Ma later told her in a letter that Old Joe couldnt hear enough about his new grandson. She said she was sure he wanted to find a way to tell Daisy he was sorry. Daisy wrote back that all he had to do was say it. So far he had not.

For supper they barbecued huge smoking slabs of pork ribs on the backyard firepit grill and drank cold bottles of beer. Butch enjoyed hearing about the Ashley boys' exploits and telling them a few from his own outlaw past. Frank asked Tom Maddox which was the toughest jail he'd ever been in and Tom said his own house when he was married and they all had a good laugh over that. On first meeting his Uncle Johnny, the boy Jeb had stared in fascination at his eyes and said, "You got a blue eye and a brown eye—thats funny!" And John Ashley had said, "You think *thats* funny? Lookee here!" He removed his glass eye and held it out to the boy. The child's face went to horror and John Ashley hastily explained that it was made of glass and rolled it across the floor so the boy could see it was not real and nothing to be afraid of. He let the boy handle it and told him to wash it off and then showed him how to put it back in the socket. The boy was so taken with the glass eye he said he too was going to get one when he grew up.

Later that evening they went dancing at a riverside pavilion where a band was playing and there were lots of pretty girls and they had a swell time. Tom Maddox took a fancy to a bold red-lipsticked brunette from St. Augustine who was visiting her widowed cousin. She invited him to visit with them in St. Augustine for a few days. He told the Ashleys he was going to do that and would later make his way down to their Twin Oaks house.

The next day they motored to the beach after making a brief stop at the home of a fellow Butch knew who brewed the best beer in town and they had bought a dozen quart bottles and put them in two cartons of ice. At the beach they body-surfed in the big breakers and the Ashley boys helped their young nephew to build a sand castle. They all got sandy and sunburned and ate the sandwiches and boiled eggs and potato salad Daisy had packed. The men got half-drunk on beer in the sun and ogled and pointed at all the passing girls whose black wet washing suits clung so closely they could see the jut of their nipples. Daisy said all men were disgusting sex fiends. "I believe you absolutely right," Butch said, and grabbed her breast. She yelped and pummeled him with both fists and he pulled her down on the blanket and they ended up kissing deeply as Butch fondled her bottom and the brothers whistled and applauded. She broke off the kiss and stuck her tongue out at them and young Jeb laughed with delight. On the drive home into the setting sun they sang in horrid but vastly enjoyable harmony: "By the Sea, By the Sea" and "Abba-Dabba Honeymoon" and "When the Midnight Choo-Choo Leaves for Alabama" and "For Me and My Gal."

Over cigarettes and late-evening cups of coffee after Jeb had been put to bed the brothers all remarked how wonderful Daisy looked. Frank said life in Jacksonville had sure enough agreed with her. She told them how well Butch was doing at his job at the shipworks and Butch nodded and smiled shyly. She said they all ought to stay in Jacksonville too. "You can get jobs at the works with Butch," she told them. "You can rent a place until you get enough money together to buy you a house. It's no need for you all to ever go back to that trouble down there." Ma Ashley had kept her informed of circumstances.

The brothers shifted uncomfortably and exchanged sidelong looks. "Well," John Ashley said, "the thing is, Daddy needs help with the business."

"How is that any problem of yours?" she wanted to know.

"Hey, Daze, it's *Daddy*," Ed said, looking about to laugh, about to cry.

She looked about to spit. "You mulletheads, all you. You dont owe that man a solitary thing. He's used you all your lifes for his work. All you are to him is nigger labor."

"Quit that talk now," Butch said. "It's your brothers you talkin to."

"It's all right," Frank said. "She aint never been one to hide what's on her mind. We used to it."

"Why?" she asked. "*Why* you all got to go back there? You go back you cant even live in the house no more—not with police watching it all the damn time. You'll be livin out in the Everglades the rest of your lifes. What kinda life is that, livin out in the damn Devil's Garden?" She slumped deeper into the couch, her arms crossed tightly, her foot tapping in agitation.

John Ashley was sitting on the couch with her and reached out and put his hand under her hair and stroked the back of her neck. She closed her eyes and sighed and rolled her head under his caress.

"We just goin home, baby," he said. "That's all."

"Oh, Johnny," she sighed. "It aint no kinda home, not no more.
It's just a trouble place is all it is."

"It's our home, Daze," John Ashley said, kneading her neck.
"Trouble or not."

The next morning when they were all three in the car and ready
to go, Daisy told them once again that they always had a place to
come to, no matter why. Butch said that was for damn sure and shook
hands with all of them one more time.

The old man's smile on greeting John Ashley at the front steps of
the Twin Oaks house was the first anyone had seen on him since Bob's
death. He gave John a light punch on the arm and asked how he was
keeping. John stood before him with his hands in his pockets and
ducked his head at him and said he was doing all right, how about
himself, and Old Joe said he was just fine as a froghair split four ways.
He asked if they'd seen his grandson. Ma had told him the brothers
were going to see their sister and he wanted to know if Jeb looked
healthy and if he had a proper portion of wit. They told him all about
young Jeb—but when they started talking about Daisy and Butch the
old man dismissed the subject with an irritated wave of his hand.

John Ashley then went unaccompanied on the sandy path to Bob's
grave a quarter-mile into the pinewoods behind the house. The trees
were thick with squalling crows. In the high-ground clearing that was
the family burial ground were two gravemounds—Bob's, and a smaller
one where lay the remains of the youngest Ashley brother who'd
twelve years ago died within hours of birth and was never named. Joe
Ashley had buried him behind the house in Pompano but when the
family moved north to the Twin Oaks property the old man had dug
up the tiny coffin and brought the child's remains with them to be
reburied here. Both graves bore simple oak markers at their head. The
smaller darkly weathered one stated, "At Peace." The larger one read:
"Bob Ashley. A good son and true brother." A light breeze soughed
in the pine branches and the clearing was spattered with yellow sunlight. He stood gazing on Bob's grave for a time. And then said, "I'da
done the same for you but I guess you know that." He looked up at
the patches of sky showing through the pines and he felt a hot tightness
in his throat. After a while he went back down the narrow trail to
the house.

They sat to dinner at a long table set up on the front porch—cooter
stew, rice, greens, fried tomatoes, hot-peppered swamp cabbage, hush
puppies, cornbread and gravy and sweet potato pie. Ma and the girls

laid out the table and served the food and went back inside the house. At the table with the Ashleys were Albert Miller and a blond and ropily muscled young man named John Clarence Middleton. Ed and Frank Ashley had met him one day a couple of months before when they were driving through Stuart and spied him fighting three men in an alley. They stopped the car to watch the fight and were much impressed by the smooth cool way Clarence was holding his own against the three. He punched one of them down and fended even better against the others until the first one got up again and this time had a knife in his hand. Ed called "Hey!" and they all looked over at the idling Model T and he brought up his revolver and everybody stood fast. He beckoned the blond fellow and said, "Well come on, bubba, if you coming." The fellow came on the jog and hopped into the backseat and Ed waved goodbye to the other three as Frank got the car underway.

On the drive out to Twin Oaks John Clarence Middleton introduced himself and thanked them for saving him the trouble of breaking the knifer's arm and maybe having to cut him with his own blade. He said he did not need any more legal problems. "What you mean *more*?" Frank asked, grinning at him. Clarence said he'd had to leave Miami in a hurry after a misunderstanding about a stolen motorcar. He was easy-natured and quick to laugh and had a tattoo of the U. S. Marines' globe-and-anchor insignia on his right forearm. He didnt mind at all when Ed and Frank said they'd call him Clarence because their brother was named John and one John in the bunch was enough. The rest of the family took an immediate liking to him. He volunteered little about his past, yet none of the Ashleys was either so rude or so curious as to inquire into it. But they all admired his variety of skills. He'd learned to box in the marines and he displayed his fistic talent to them at a carnival in Fort Lauderdale where a challenger could pay a dollar to get in the ring with a carnie fighter and win five dollars if he could stay upright for three minutes. In the first two minutes Clarence broke the carnie's nose and closed one of his eyes and the carnie said fuck it he'd had enough.

He was an able woodsman, Clarence, and a good skinner, and impressively familiar with a variety of firearms. Through a military connection in Miami he had recently acquired four cases of Springfield rifles for about one-third their value and had let Joe have a case in gratitude for taking him in and had sold the rest to some Cuban insurrectionists who'd come across the strait to buy weapons. Clarence himself carried a new army .45 automatic. He'd let the Ashleys fire it one day and they were all taken with the piece's smooth action and striking power and Clarence promised to get one for everybody in the gang.

Having dinner with them too was Hanford Mobley, now fifteen and apprenticing at the whiskey trade with Old Joe and beaming proudly in the company of the uncles he revered. "That boy aint feared of a damn thing," Joe had told his sons before they sat to eat. "Got balls like coconuts. And a good head. Learns quick. Aint got to be told somethin but once. I always did say he was gonna be a good one and he is."

As they ate he told John Ashley all about Bob Baker's continuing war against their whiskey camps. His most recent raid had been two months ago when he and his boys swooped in on Joe's camp in the palm hammocks a few miles north of the railroad tracks running from Lake Okeechobee to Fort Pierce. They'd reduced it to crushed metal and busted glass and charred wood and made off with more than twenty cases of bush lightning. Joe now had but four camps in operation, fewer than half the number of stills he'd been running two years earlier. So deeply had the raids cut into his profits he could no longer pay off all the lawmen on his bribery list and so had lost much of the protection he'd enjoyed for a time.

"That damn Bobby's cost me a ton of money and trouble," Old Joe said. "I strained my brain a hundred times tryin to figure how in the hell he was findin out who my lookouts were. I knowed the lookouts was how he'd been doin it. He'd been catchin them some kinda way and gettin them to tell where the camps are at. I'll wager he got some interestin ways to get a fella to speak up. Anyhow, he wont be—"

"I'm meanin to pay Bobby a visit real soon," John Ashley interrupted. "It's a few matters we got to settle between us."

"*No!*" Joe Ashley said. "Now you listen good, Johnny: you aint payin Bobby Baker no kinda visit. If we do harm to Bobby Baker right now it wouldnt do nothin but bring police from everywhere down on us like a bad rain. It's too much at stake to fuck er up by putting away Bobby Baker over somethin personal."

"Hell, Daddy, it aint just personal—he's tearin up our camps!"

Joe Ashley paused to light his pipe and pour himself a cup of his own whiskey. He eyed John Ashley closely as he sipped, then he said: "Dont bullshit me, boy. It aint the camps got you bothered about Bobby Baker. You two aint never unlocked horns since the business with that little Morrell girl. I dont know what else it is between you, but seems to me you done got the better of him a lot more than he

ever did of you. I dont see what-all *you* got to settle with *him*. Maybe
you wanna tell me."

"It's between him and me," John Ashley said, and shifted his eyes
from Old Joe's intent stare. The others at the table were looking on
with interest.

Joe Ashley sighed. "Well, whatever it is, you cant be doin nothin
about it right now. I mean it, you hear? We cant have every cop on
the coast coming down on us and thats exactly what'll happen you do
any harm to either George or Bobby Baker right now. Bobby's time'll
come, boy, dont think it wont. Could be you'll be the one to see to
it. But the time aint now. You listenin to me, boy?"

John Ashley stared at the bowl of cooter stew congealing before
him for a long moment before he nodded.

Old Joe banged his palm on the table and grinned through a cloud
of violet smoke and said, "Old Bobby's anyhow gonna play hell findin
any more my camps to tear up from now on, because this fella here"—
he nodded at Hanford Mobley, who grinned proudly—"just this mornin told me somethin thats gonna put an end to it. I tell ye, boys, it's
a damn fine day when you get a son back from prison *and* you find out
who's been playing the rat on you, all in the same twenty-four hours."

What Hanford Mobley told Joe Ashley was how Bob Baker had
been learning who the lookouts were. The night before, Hanford had
been out netting mullet in the Indian River till around midnight. After
getting back to the Stuart docks he sold some of his catch to the night
dockmaster and left the rest in a tin tub of saltwater outside the door
of the dock baitshop and wrote in chalk on the slateboard fixed on the
wall, "U owe me—Mobley." He then headed for the train station
where he'd parked the car in the shade of a huge live oak that afternoon. As he turned the corner two blocks from the depot he saw Bob
Baker entering Molly's Cafe, an all-night eatery, on the opposite corner
of the street. Curious, Hanford Mobley crossed the street and walked
up to the cafe's front window and peeked inside. And saw Bob Baker
taking a seat at a table in the corner. And sitting at the table with him
was Claude Calder.

"I never figured Claude for the balls to do it," Old Joe said, "but
when Hannie told me what he'd seen, well, it all fell in place. Claude
knowed where the Hungryland camp was and he told Bobby—and he
told him Seth and Scratchley were the lookouts for it. Bobby had to
get them out the way before he could sneak up on the camp. I figure
Claude's heard us mention a bunch of the lookouts by name sometime
or other and he's told those names to Bobby Baker is what he's done.

All Bobby's had to do is track down the lookouts or lay for them somewhere or wait for them to come home sometime and then make em tell where the camps was at."

"Claude ratted our lookouts for no reason but Daddy give him a whuppin for runnin out on Bob in Miami," Frank said to John Ashley. "A whuppin he damn well had comin."

"I shoulda kilt the sonofabitch the minute he come back here," Old Joe said. "I meant to."

"We shouldnt of pulled you off his sorry ass, Daddy," Ed said.

"Well hell," Hanford Mobley said. "Let's set the business straight right now. I know for a fact he's over to the Yella Creek dock right this minute sandin a skiff bottom."

Old Joe looked at Hanford Mobley and grinned. "I want you all to just listen to this one here. Fifteen year old. Aint he a bull gator though!"

"Let me set it right, Gramps," Hanford Mobley said. Old Joe looked around the table at the other grinning men, then smiled and nodded at his grandson.

Hanford Mobley beamed. "Yall excuse me," he said and stood up and pushed his chair in under the table and adjusted the pistol under his shirt. Then skipped down the porch steps and jogged out to the sidetrail leading through the pinewoods and down to Yellow Creek, about a quarter-mile away.

The men passed the bowls and platters around the table for third helpings and they poured more ice water and Old Joe served himself another drink and told John about a boat he had his eye on, a forty-foot trawler for sale in the Stuart boatyard.

"She'll make a fine rummer we fix er up right," he said. "But she'll cost a pretty penny and the work she needs wont come cheap neither." He took a slow sip of whiskey and eyed John Ashley intently. "Frank and Ed, they always was the best of us with boats, so they gonna be my main whiskey runners," he said. "I dont want them goin in no banks, you hear? I dont want no warrants on them."

"Banks?" John Ashley said as though he'd never heard the word before. "What-all banks you talkin about, Daddy?" But he could not keep the smile off his face.

"Whatever ones you and Clarence and young Hannie was whisperin about when you all was over there fishin in the creek. Hell, boy, I aint gonna object. We need money to get the boat and fix er up right if we ever gonna start running booze from the islands. All I'm sayin is Frank and Ed wont be havin nothin to do with it. I want them able to come and go and take care of business without havin to look over their shoulder for the law all the time."

"How could you tell what we was talkin about from way over here?"

"Boy," Joe Ashley said with mock tiredness, "I known the lot of you since you was whelped. I can look at any a you from a quarter-mile off and know exactly what the hell you got on your mind, so dont play the innocent with me." His grin was as wide as his son's.

A pistolshot sounded from the area of Yellow Creek and the crows fell mute in the pines. All heads at the table turned in that direction as a second sharp report carried to them. And then only silence.

And then Joe Ashley said, "Damn pretty day, aint she?"

A month later deputy sheriff Bob Baker drove out to the Ashley homestead. He let the motor idle as he got out of the car and was met at the porch steps by Ed and Frank Ashley and Hanford Mobley, each of them with a .45 automatic snugged out of sight at the small of his back, the pistols only recently presented to them all by Clarence Middleton.

A lookout had come running to tell them Bob Baker was coming and that he was alone. John Ashley had gone upstairs to his father's bedroom where Old Joe lay abed with one of his chronic attacks of ague. John positioned himself with his automatic in hand to peek out from behind a curtain and Old Joe, brighteyed with his fever, had slipped his pistol out from under his pillow and sat up so he could peek out too.

In the three years since John Ashley had last seen him, Bob Baker seemed to have grown even larger, wider of shoulder, deeper of chest. Even his hands looked bigger, of a size unreal. He put his booted wooden foot up on the bottom step and hooked a thumb in his gunbelt and rested the heel of his other hand on the butt of his pistol. He told Ed and Frank Ashley that lawmen all up and down the Florida east coast were on the alert for sightings or reports of John Ashley as an escaped convict who was armed and dangerous and they had orders to shoot to kill if he attempted to resist arrest. He advised them to tell John to keep to the Devil's Garden if he knew what was good for him.

"My boys'll throw down on him the minute they see his face in public," Bob Baker said. "He even looks like he'll make a fight of it, they got orders to shoot him where he stands. And those're Daddy's orders, not just mine."

"Well now, Bobby," Ed said, rolling a toothpick in his twisted mouth, "we'll be sure and tell what you said if ever we see him, though we aint seen hair of him since he got sent to Raiford, no thanks to you and your daddy."

Bob Baker glanced up at the second-floor windows and then spat off to the side. A horsefly bigger than a bumblebee lit on his arm—purpleheaded ugly and amber-winged, with a bite like a cigarette burn that could raise a welt the size of a clamshell. Bob Baker smacked it hard with the flat of his hand and the horsefly dropped to the ground and lay still for a moment and then fluttered its wings tentatively and then flew off so fast none of them saw the direction it went.

"Them sumbitches are some hard to kill, aint they?" Ed said. "Damn near everything out here is."

Bob Baker spat and looked at him.

"If we ever *do* see Johnny sometime," Frank said, "you bet we'll tell him what you said."

Bob Baker now inquired after Claude Calder. No one had seen him in well nigh a month or so, he said, and some people couldnt help wondering what might've become of him. "Everbody knows he been living out here with you all."

Hanford Mobley chuckled and Bob Baker fixed his gaze on him. "Is it somethin funny, boy?"

Hanford Mobley smiled and said, "I just remembered me a joke I heard is all."

"That a fact? I like a good joke my ownself. Tell me it."

"Damn if I aint just this second forgot it," Hanford Mobley said.

Frank and Ed snorted and smiled. At the window upstairs Old Joe grinned and nudged John Ashley and whispered, "Aint he a damn pistol!"

Bob Baker's eyes narrowed. "You way too runty and wet behind the ears to think you so tough, sweetpea. You sass me again I'll come up on that porch and slap you sillier than you already look."

Hanford Mobley lost his smile and pushed off the porch post he'd been leaning on and stood with legs apart and a hand behind his back.

"Whatever you got there, boy," Bob Baker said, "dont show it to me unless you want it way up your ass."

"Oh hell now, Bobby, he's just funnin," Frank said as he gave Hanford Mobley a sharp look and came halfway down the porch steps to stand between them. "Truth is, Claude went off to Atlanta nearbouts a month ago. Said his sister was real poorly and he wanted to see her one more time fore she passed on. Hell, we didnt even know old

Claude had him a sister. We anyhow aint heard a word from him since—have we Ed?"

Ed allowed they surely had not.

"Wish we could be more help to you, Bobby," Frank said, "but thats all we know about ole Claude."

"Could be ole Claude was lyin about havin a sister," Ed said. "Hell, he mighta been lyin about goin to Atlanta. That Claude, he was bad to tell lies. Aint that right, Frank?"

Frank Ashley allowed he surely was.

Bob Baker spat again and worked the spit into the dirt with the toe of his boot. Then scowled and said, "You tell John we aint foolin. Your daddy too. Tell em I'm gonna find ever one of his stills sooner or later and tear em all down and I dont need Claude Calder to do it."

He looked up at the curtained window and then at Frank and Ed Ashley and Hanford Mobley. "You tell em I said so. Tell em both."

As Bob Baker got back in the car and wheeled it around and headed back for the narrow pineywoods trail to the Dixie Highway, Old Joe turned to John Ashley and said, "It'll be ass-deep snow in hell before he finds another one of my stills. But goddamn I hate that son of a bitch standin on *my* property and talkin about tearin em up."

He looked out the window again as Bob Baker's car vanished into the trees. "I surely hope I dont never regret not putting a bullet in that fucker's brainpan just now." He held up his thumb and forefinger a quarter-inch apart. "I mean, I was *this* close."

John Ashley was still staring at the trailhead where Bob Baker had driven out of sight. "Tell me about it," he said. And let a long breath. And reset the .45's safety with his thumb.

As he'd walked back to his car he'd felt the sweat rolling coldly down his sides. He'd half expected to get a blast of buckshot in the back from the upstairs window. He knew John Ashley was up there, he could feel he was. The old man too most likely.

And after those pictures . . .

The eye was fair desserts for Johnny backjumping him and smacking his head on a wall and near busting out his brains, damn if it wasnt. For breaking his worthless Ashley word and escaping and making him look so bad. For stealing his gun. For . . . lots of things. A damn eye was letting him off *light*.

But those pictures . . .

He figured John wouldnt have shown them to his daddy or anybody else. He'd want to keep them secret. Who wouldnt? Jesus. He could not have said then or now what had possessed him to do such a thing. The mean shame of it had been welling under his ribs like a poison gas ever since he awoke one night with the thought that John Ashley wouldnt have done anything like that and probably saw it as cowardly. The notion that John Ashley saw him as a coward was enraging and added weight to his shame.

His car jounced over the uneven trail and out of sight of the house. He blew a long breath.

All right then, he thought, you gave him a chance to do something about it and not a one of them can say you didnt. And if he did show the pictures to any of the rest of them, well, they'd just had their chance to do something about it too, didnt they? He figured that counted for plenty, going there and giving them the chance to do something about it. Took some balls—damn if it didnt. His shirt sopped now with sweat.

He wouldnt go back there again, nor go hunting after him. He'd given warning and that was enough. As for the Calder boy, hell, he'd been found out sure and done for. They'd somehow come to know he was fingering the lookouts and they'd done him in and fed him to the gars in one of the hundred creeks back in the pine swamps. No surprise to it. It's what every snitch had coming to him sooner or later and one way or another.

He figured he'd been clear enough: keep out of the county towns, keep to the Glades from here on, keep to your whiskey camps you got left. Keep to your ground and we're quits. It was a damn fair deal and just show him somebody who could say it wasnt.

His hands tremored on the steering wheel and he cursed the rugged car trail that shook the car so.

After they'd made love Loretta May brought him up to date on the happenings around the place in the nearly four years he'd been gone. She told him Miss Lillian had steadily gotten bitchier as she got older but had been nice enough to give Jenny the Horse a big wedding and reception right there in the house when Jenny married a hardware dealer who had been visiting her every Tuesday night for almost a year. Jenny and her husband had gone to live in Delray and she every now and then wrote a letter addressed to all the girls to let them know how married life was going and to break the news when she was pregnant the first time and to announce when her first kid was born. Quentin the redhead had run off one night with some trick and never even said goodbye to any of them but nobody really cared since nobody had ever liked the bitch anyway. Sheryl Ann had gotten married too but it only lasted about five months before she'd come right back to Miss Lillian's.

She said she'd cried when she first heard about his eye. She asked if he'd really got a glass one and when he said yes she sat up in bed and asked if she could touch it. He took the eye out and placed it in her hand and watched as she felt of its slight heft and rolled it between her fingers. She dropped it from one palm to the other and back again and giggled. What shade of blue was it, she wanted to know. "Real light," he told her. "Like the sky was today when it's sunny and cool and there's no clouds at all."

"Pretty," she said. She placed it between her breasts and rolled it from one to the other and her caramel nipples puckered enticingly and he gently plucked at one and she smiled. She reached out and found his face and the empty socket and gently fingered its ridge. "Oh baby," she breathed, her face soft with pity. He leaned forward and lightly kissed each of her cheeks and then held her face between his hands and kissed her mouth.

He put his eye back in the socket and she put her fingers to it again and smiled. "I bet you seen some real interestin things with that one."

He said he didnt know what she meant.

"Yes, you do," she said. She lay back and pulled him down beside her and held him close and hid her face against his throat. "You said before you couldnt hardly ever remember what you dreamed but it was like you was seein true things while you were dreamin them. Now you rememberin a lot of what you dream, aint you?"

He tried to pull back to look at her but she held him fast and burrowed her face under his chin.

"It's some eyes cant see any of the awake world but can see a whole lot in the sleepin world," she said barely above a whisper.

"I think you turned crazier'n a coot while I was gone," he said. But he suddenly felt uneasy and couldnt have said why.

"I saw you sometimes while you were away," she said, her voice so low now he had to strain to make out her words. "Not every night and most times not real clear and sometimes I'd wake up before I could see exactly what you were doin. But I saw you."

They lay in silence for a time and then he said, "What'd you see?"

She told him. Told of seeing him standing at a steaming tub and stirring clothes in it with a wooden pole and that she could smell the strong lye soap he was smelling. Told of seeing his bare shoulder real close up and a sharp instrument dipped in dark ink and its nib pecking into his shoulder and the image of a skull taking shape there. As she spoke she slid her hand up his arm to his shoulder and her fingers found the black skull with the paleskin eyes and nosehole and teeth.

"How'd you . . . *see* that," he asked in a hoarse whisper. "The laundry at Raiford . . . the tattoo?"

She murmured into his neck but he could not make out the words. And then she told of seeing him in a cramped dark place. And though it was dark she knew he was naked and knew too that it was so cold and damp in that place it made his bones ache. "I saw you and could feel how much it hurt to be so cramped like that. I could feel how thirsty you were and how . . . lonely. I swear I could smell how awful bad it stunk in there. Tell me, Johnny . . . where were you at?"

In the hole, he told her. He'd been put in there for three days and nights the first time for backsassing a guard. That had been in winter and he'd been colder than he'd ever been in his life. The next time was in late summer and he was put in there after a fight with a convict who'd tried to get ahead of him in the chow line. He'd stabbed the con in the face with a fork and the guards had both of them headlocked and manacled before the fight really got started and they'd each been given a week in the hole. In this season the hole had been an oven and it baked the human waste sliming the floor and walls, the foetor nearly palpable and the steamed air a labor to breathe. The cockroaches so many they felt like a crawling blanket. Rats squirmed into the cell as he slept and bit him awake into a panicked hollering and always escaped his wild blind grabs for them in his rage to kill them with his hands. He'd been too weak to stand when his time was up and they'd had to drag him out by the heels, rife with festering sores and sightless against the sudden light of day and nearly rank as a dead man.

She'd seen him too in bright sunshine once when he was dancing back and back and flinging his arms out to the side each time he leaped rearward and another man in striped pants like his own was lunging at him and both of them barechested and then there were bright red stripes across John Ashley's chest and stomach. As she spoke her hand went to his chest and belly and her fingers trailed softly along the scars there. She'd seen then that the other man had a knife and they were fighting near piles of brush. John Ashley tripped the man down and ran to a stack of tools and grabbed a shovel and she saw other convicts gathered around and watching. She could see them cheering though she could not hear them and she saw too a man in a uniform and holding a shotgun and he too was watching and grinning

as the man with the knife came running after John Ashley. She saw
John strike him in the head with the shovel and the man fell and John
straddled him and with both hands gripping the shovel handle he drove
its blade into the man's throat as if he were plunging into the earth
with a postdigger. She saw the man's head come loose of its moorings
and his face of a sudden looked sleepy and the gaping neck heaved a
bright gout of blood four feet in the air and it splattered back on the
face of the killed and on the shoes of his killer like a quick fall of
red rain.

"Burchard," John Ashley said lowly. "I didnt have no idea why
he come at me. Somebody said later he'd thought I was the fella his
wife run away with in Tallahassee. He was always looking hard at me
but he never said word one to me, not even when he just all of a
sudden was standin in front of me and started cuttin at me, the son
of a bitch."

He stroked her hair and put his face to it and breathed deeply of
its sweetness. "I didnt get in no trouble over it. The walking boss,
Sobel, he was a old boy from Alva where my family used to live, and
me and him got along pretty good and he didnt care for Burchard at
all and was glad to see him get it. He told the warden the truth—that
Burchard had went crazy and attacked me with a knife he wasnt supposed to have and I didnt do nothin but defend myself. The warden
never questioned it, neither, even though all the cons on brush detail
that day saw what happened and some were sayin I didnt have to kill
him. Hell, sometimes I wish I hadnt. Took me a while to quit thinkin
about . . . about what he looked like after. A time like that, you just
wanna stop the other fella, just make sure he cant cut you no more.
I admit I was blackassed about gettin cut. Anyway, the bosses dont
like a fella they dont care much what happens to him or who does it."

They lay quietly for a while. Then she said: "This other time, I
seen you sitting on your bed in a little-bitty room and you, well, you
were cryin. You had some papers in your hand and you were cryin.
I couldnt see but the back of them. Whatever they were, they made
you so awful sad I couldnt stand it. I didnt have that dream but two
minutes before I woke up and I was cryin too. I cried all that day and
didnt even know why. What was it, Johnny, made you feel so bad?"

He shrugged. "I dont recall nothin about it."

He could feel that she knew he was lying. The papers had been
photographs. Four of them. They had come for him in an envelope
with no return address and bearing a Tampa postmark. In the first
picture Bob was sitting up and naked and his open eyes were dead as

glass and his mouth shaped into a grotesque smile and he held his own shriveled dick in his hand. In the next he was still showing the horrid smile but this time holding a pistol to his head, his hand supported by the large hand of someone standing beside him but out of the picture. In the next, his head was turned sideways toward the same large man standing very close to him and holding Bob by the hair with one hand and a penis to his mouth with the other so that the skinned-back glans was between his lips. In the last photograph Bob was lying on his back and someone visible only from the waist down was standing beside him on the table with one booted foot on his chest in the manner of a hunter posing with his trophy. On the front ankle of the boot was embossed a white star.

He had looked and looked at the pictures and sobbed in his fury and his helplessness. He did not want to risk that anyone else might ever see them and so had studied them very hard for a while longer and then burned them to ash.

How could he have told his father? Told anyone? The day Bob Baker had stood at the foot of the porch steps while he watched from the window above with a .45 cocked in his hand and his daddy sitting in bed beside him, it had been all he could do not to shoot the bastard then and there. He dreamed of those pictures more often than he did not and would waken enraged in the dark of night, his jaws clenched and aching.

"What're you thinkin?" Loretta May said. "You're wantin to hurt somethin. Not me, is it, baby? I didnt say nothin wrong, did I?"

He heard uncertainty in her voice and blew a deep breath and kissed her shoulder and stroked her hip and said, "How'd you *see* all that?" His breath was tight in his chest. "You some kinda geechie woman?" He hoped she wouldnt say she was a witch because he did not believe in witches but had no trouble believing in her.

"I dont reckon," she said, still nuzzling his neck. "I just see things in my sleep sometimes." She pulled back and held her face toward him. "You had any more of them dreams you told me about? Them that seem like they're trying to tell you somethin but you wake up and cant remember?"

"Yeah," he said, "sometimes. I can recollect some of them fairly clear ever once in a while." The dreams always disquieted him, and even now, simply thinking about them, he felt his pulse quicken.

"I *told* you the time would come when you'd start to remember them." She said, smiling. "I dont reckon you'll ever see as much as I do because you only blind in *one* eye. Tell me one you remember."

He thought for a moment and then said, "I recent had one about a funeral. It was in St. Augustine. I could see the old fort out yonder of the graveyard and see the ocean behind it. But it was strange because it was like the graveyard was on top of a high hill. There wasnt anybody there but me and a woman with real red lipstick and it was like she didnt even know I was there. I could see the casket down in the grave but it didnt have no top to it and you could see the man lying in there. I knew him. A fella name of Tom Maddox. He'd been with me in prison and he come with us when Frank and Ed busted me free of the road gang. He went to Daisy's with us and met a girl in Jacksonville with red lipstick and said he was gonna stay with her a few days and catch up with us at Twin Oaks but he never did show up. I looked down at him in that grave and I knew it was real, even though it aint real that people get buried in coffins with no tops and there aint no big hill like that in St. Augustine. But I knew it was true he musta gone to Augustine with that girl and died there for some reason and was buried and thats why we never saw him no more."

"You could go and find out if he's really buried there."

"Dont have to. I know he is."

"What do you reckon happened to him?"

"I dont know. Somethin."

"Do you care to find out?"

"No. It was his own business."

They lay in silence for few minutes and then she said, "Tell me another one. A nicer one."

"Well, it's one I had it a few times now," he said. "It's a woman in it but not one I ever knowed. I dont see her, not really. More like I . . . *sense* her, like she's *right* there but I cant really see her too clear. I swear I can almost smell her. She got this thing in her eye . . . like a little gold piece of the moon, it looks like." He glanced at Loretta May and saw her smiling and he flushed and looked away. "Ah hell," he said.

Loretta May laughed. "It's always a woman in what men dream. Either that or somebody dead or somebody chasin after them. Men's dreams either give em a hard cock or a cold sweat."

He leaned over and kissed her breast and tongued the nipple and felt it go rigid, then did the same with the other, then looked up and saw that she was smiling happily. Her hand sought him out and closed around his hardness and she made a face of mock astonishment and said, "Oooh. Sometimes they aint even got to be dreamin, do they?"

He laughed with her and mounted her in a smooth practiced motion and began rocking and rocking into her as she grinned up at him clutching tight to his shoulders.

They entered the Avon bank with .45's in hand just before closing on a Friday afternoon and relieved the guard of his revolver before he fully comprehended what was happening. They did not wear masks. The customers' mouths hung open but the gang assured them nobody would be hurt if they all just stayed put and did as they were told. John Ashley went to the head teller's window and asked his name.

"George Doster, sir," the teller said.

"I'm John Ashley, George. Open the cage."

The teller did so, and while Clarence Middleton and Hanford Mobley kept the patrons under watch, John Ashley went around behind the tellers' windows and himself emptied all the cash drawers into a gunnysack. He then went into the vault and filled another sack with all the paper cash he found in there. The bags now held about eight thousand dollars. Then he came out and asked the manager, a balding man named Weatherington, if there was any more money in the bank and the manager said there wasn't.

John Ashley grinned at him. "I heard that song before, bubba. Cost me ten thousand dollars to believe it." He turned to the head teller and said, "George, is he tellin me true? Is it any more money in this bank?"

"I . . . I dont know, sir."

"Listen, George," John Ashley said. "If I read in the newspapers that you boys cheated me, I'm gone be mad, you hear? I'm gone be *real* mad. I'm gone come back and see all of you one by one and aint none of you gone be happy to see me. So now—one last time—any more money in this bank?"

George Doster licked his lips and glanced sidelong at the bank manager who kept his eyes on the floor. "Mister Ashley, sir," he said, "I *think* there might be some money in Mister Weatherington's top desk drawer."

John Ashley went to the manager's desk and in the top drawer found an envelope from the Tarpon Construction Company containing nearly twenty-five hundred dollars. He stepped up to the bank manager and hit him across the bridge of the nose with the pistol barrel and his nosebone cracked like a nutshell. The manager let a yelp and sagged to his knees with blood spurting bright from his nose onto his white shirtfront and spattering the floor.

"Damn, but I hate a liar," John Ashley said. He gestured for Middleton and Hanford Mobley to go out ahead of him and then he paused at the door and said, "Listen, Weatherington, I dont want to hear that George lost his job for tellin me the truth. You understand?"

The bank manager had both hands to his nose and blood ran through his fingers and into his shirtsleeves and his eyes were red and flooded with tears. He nodded vigorously and blood shook from his hands in thick drops.

Three months later they ranged back to the central highlands once again and this time hit the bank in Sebring, announcing themselves loudly as the Ashley Gang. They were in and out in less than ten minutes and took seven thousand dollars. Four months after that they drove down the coast and robbed the Boynton Beach bank of sixty-five hundred. People came out on the sidewalks to watch them make their getaway and some of them waved to the bandits as they went by. Hanford Mobley tooted the horn and waved back.

They let pass another three months and then again picked a job west of Lake Okeechobee and well away from their own territory, this time robbing a bank in Fort Meade of a little more than five thousand. Their reputation had spread and some of the patrons seemed thrilled to be part of an Ashley Gang holdup. "I do believe that teller was about to ask you for your autograph," Clarence Middleton said to John Ashley as Hanford Mobley steered with one hand and worked the levers with the other and his foot danced on the Model T's left pedal. They made away into the pinelands on the Frostproof Road. "You all see that pretty thing was standin near the door?" Hanford Mobley said happily. He was sixteen years old this day and feeling very much a man. "I thought she was gonna kiss me on my way out. I shoulda slowed down for a minute and give her the chance, what I shoulda done."

Newspaper accounts of the robberies used such phrases as "bad actors" and "desperadoes" in describing the Ashley Gang. They referred to the "menacing Wild West deportment of these fearless outlaws."

When they walked into the Avon bank for the second time they did not even take out their guns. The customers nudged each other and whispered, "It's them! It's them!" as Hanford Mobley and Clarence Middleton stood by the door with their hands in their pockets and smiled pleasantly at everyone. John Ashley walked past Weatherington at his desk and nodded at him and the manager nodded jerkily in response and dropped his eyes back to the open ledger in front of him.

George Doster had seen them come in and had already put all the paper money into two bags by the time John Ashley arrived at his window.

"Hey George," John Ashley said.

"Good afternoon, Mister Ashley, sir." The other teller had seen what was happening and now hastily filled a bag with the contents of his cash drawer and handed it to George Doster. Doster pushed the three bags of money across the counter to John Ashley.

"How much, George?"

"About four thousand five hundred, Mister Ashley. We dont keep as much on hand as we used to before your visit last time."

"You aint lying now are you, George?"

"Nossir, I wouldnt lie to you, Mister Ashley."

"How about the vault, George?"

"There's only about fifteen hundred back there, sir, and, well, I was hoping you might let us keep that so we could at least stay open for business through the rest of the day. If we have to close up for lack of money I dont get paid for the lost time, sir, and, well . . . I've got a family, Mister Ashley. Surely you understand."

"Got kids, George?"

"A boy and a girl, sir. And one on the way."

"Oh hell, George, keep the damn fifteen hundred." John Ashley picked up the bags of money and headed for the door. As he passed Weatherington's desk he said to the manager, "You ought give that Doster fella a promotion, saving you money like he just did. Got a good head on his shoulders."

Shortly before Christmas John Ashley walked by himself into the bank at Delray with no intention but to exchange a sack of one hundred silver dollars for a hundred in paper money. The silver had come to him in payment for a load of Old Joe's bush whiskey from a long-time customer who owned a grocery store at the edge of town. The bank manager glanced out the front window and recognized John Ashley coming across the street and he ordered the head teller to empty the cash drawers into a sack and do it quick.

Now John Ashley came inside but before he could say a word the manager handed him the bag and said, "That's most of the paper money, Mister Ashley, a little more than four thousand dollars. I swear I'm not lying. There's about five hundred left in the vault and I wish you'll leave us with that, Mister Ashley—like you let that other bank keep some. To stay open for business."

The man was near breathless and his face shone with sweat despite the cool dryness of the winter morning. John Ashley stroked his chin and peeked into the bag and saw the money in there and he smiled at the manager whose left eye was twitching.

"Well now, sir," John Ashley said, "thank you kindly." He walked out with the bag of silver dollars in one hand and the sack of paper currency in the other and went across the street to his car. Albert Miller cranked up the engine while a Delray policeman stood on the corner not twenty feet away with his hands behind him and stared up at the sky as though utterly entranced by the blueness of it. Now Albert got behind the wheel and they chugged on out of town. As the car passed by, people heard them guffawing.

THIRTEEN

January 1920

On New Year's Day Bill Ashley and his pretty but reticent wife Bertha took supper with the rest of the family at Twin Oaks.

The Volstead Act, by which the Eighteenth Amendment would be enforced, was within three weeks of passage. During the meal the talk was of family matters, of Butch and Daisy's new baby—about whom Ma had lots of news by way of a recent letter from Daisy—and of which neighbors had married and which had died. When everyone had done eating, the women cleared the table and left the room and the men rolled cigarettes and fired up pipes.

Bill beamed at Old Joe and said, "I told you a long time back this Prohibition business was coming, didnt I? Well, pretty soon now we're gonna be makin so much money we're gonna need us a whole *bunch* of wheelbarrows to carry it all in."

Old Joe puffed his pipe and nodded without expression.

"We're still doin good with the shine," Bill said, addressing the table in the manner of a finance manager at a stockholders' meeting. "We're selling more to the Indians than we ever did and we put up two new camps since Bobby Baker last busted one up. That gives us six in operation. We're makin enough of the stuff to supply our regular customers all up and down the coast." He paused to sip at his cup of shine, the only one he would drink all night. "The thing is, we ought to be sellin more to the townfolk, specially to them down in Miami, and it's two reasons we aint. One is, they been stockpilin the factory stuff since before the Eighteenth got passed, and the other reason is they know can *still* get the factory liquor they used to drinkin and they dont care they got to pay way more for it than they did before. It's a lot of money to be made off an attitude like that."

"By smuggling, you mean," Frank said, his smiling face brightly eager.

"That's what I mean," Bill said. He took off his rimless spectacles and cleaned the lenses with a bandanna and put the glasses back on and adjusted them carefully and then looked at them all and said, "Soon as we start bringin factory stuff over from the islands we'll be makin some real money."

"Damn right," Ed said. The scarred grin pale against his brown face.

"I believe it's *real* money we been gettin from the banks, aint it?" John Ashley said, irritated that Bill should neglect to mention the family's most lucrative source of income these past sixteen months. "Aint you the fella who once upon a time didnt think bankrobbin was such good business? Guess maybe you weren't real right about that, huh?"

"It's been a payin proposition, I'll admit," Bill said, his tone patient. "But you been luckier'n any bankrobber I ever heard of. I always said the returns on bankrobbin werent worth the risks and I still dont think so. The longer you keep at it, the less money you're like to get from any one bank and the more chance there is you'll get caught or shot, one. On account of you robbin them, none of the banks are carryin as much money as they used to and so the take's been gettin smaller. And now every town between Fort Pierce and Miami and all the way over to Fort Myers has got an armed guard in it. The local police everwhere are keepin a closer eye. They're all just hopin you'll try robbin them next so they can shoot you dead and get a reward. Truth be told, Johnny, bankrobbin's about the worst business there is right now in terms of risk against likely reward. Smugglin aint near as much risk, not yet anyway, and it pays as good as banks and it's gonna way pay better still when all that booze they're stockpiling in Miami starts running out."

Old Joe looked at John Ashley. "Man's got a argument," he said.

John Ashley drummed his fingers on the table. Something there was about his elder brother that irritated him every bit as much as it had his brother Bob. He couldnt say what it was exactly but it was always there. Just the same—and as much as he hated to admit it— he could not deny that Bill was making sense.

"Yeah," he said, "he's got a argument."

*   *   *

Some of the bank loot had gone to the cops on Old Joe's payroll, some to the women of the family to cache in the house and use as they saw fit for coal oil, housewares, for clothes and pretties for themselves. But the bulk of the take from the robberies had gone to Frank and Ed that they might buy the forty-foot trawler Joe had long had his eye on. The money had also gone toward the best materials and for the hire of the best boatworkers and mechanics in the Indian River region to help them refit the vessel and make of it a proper rumboat.

Frank and Ed had narrowed the trawler's prow slightly to cut down on water resistance and add speed. They sanded and planed and caulked and painted, replaced every cleat and fitting. They removed some of the bulkheads belowdecks for greater cargo capacity and to allow for easier loading. They installed additional fuel tanks and beefed up the lower decking from bow to stern. They reworked a brace of new engines, refitting them with stronger main bearings and higher-lift cams and more powerful magnetos, then mounted and turned the powerplants as precisely as bank clocks. They installed heavy-duty drives and screws. When Ed said the boat's name was *Della*, Frank and John smiled at each other and raised no objections.

On a warm January morning they took the boat on her maiden run. They put her in the river behind the boatyard and chugged down to the Stuart harbor and into the blaze of a mountainous orange sunrise. They ran through the trickily narrow St. Lucie inlet and then bore east-southeast for Grand Bahama Island some seventy-five miles distant as the crow flies. They would in fact have to cover about one hundred miles because of the Gulf Stream, the great river of northbound current flanking the length of Florida's east coast. As the land fell from view behind them the turquoise water gradually darkened to a blue the same shade as the sky's and when they were about seven miles offshore the seabottom abruptly plunged and the water went to dark royal blue and they knew they'd arrived at the fast depths of the Stream. It was usually running strong by this time of year but it flowed gently on this windless day as unseasonably warm as early summer. To maintain his true course against the Stream's northward push Ed had to hold the wheel only slightly more to southward than his desired heading of east-southeast.

They were all three shirtless and bareheaded and wore rolled bandana headbands to keep hair and sweat out of their eyes. John stood at the stern and trolled with rod and reel and mullet chunks for bait and brought up three flashing blue-yellow bull dolphin in quick succession. He filleted them and roasted the meat on a makeshift charcoal grill set on the deck and fashioned of a wire screen over the shallow sawn-off end of a metal barrel and they ate the fish with their fingers. A pod of dozens of porpoises appeared off both sides of the boat and like sailors everywhere the brothers were glad to be accompanied by these creatures of good luck. The porpoises leaped and ran with them for miles before suddenly veering away and out of sight as though to some urgent summoning in some other region of the sea.

The Gulf Stream's breadth varied from one locale to another and sometimes from day to day within the same latitude. At some points it might be fifty miles wide one day and constrict to thirty the next. By the increasing pressure against the wheel under his hands a seasoned skipper could sense when he'd reached the strongest vein of current and thereby know when he was halfway across the stream. When Ed reckoned they were at the current's midpoint he opened up the throttles and the engines roared and the bow rose smoothly as the boat surged forward and the wake behind them fanned white and thick.

"Whooooo!" Frank hollered, all of them with their faces windward and their hair slicked back by their swift passage.

"She'll do!" Ed yelled, "She'll do!" He stroked the wheel as he might the bare arm of a favored woman.

They held their course and speed for the next hour and a half before they cleared the eastern edge of the stream and found themselves less than four miles from their destination of West End at the tip of the island. Ed cut back on the engines and his brothers clapped him on the shoulders for his expert navigation and piloting and he showed his about-to-laugh-or-cry smile.

"Daddy'll be proud to know she's a worthy boat," John Ashley said. "And even he dont say it, he'll be just as proud to hear how good you can cross the Blue River."

The sun was hot and bright and the eastern horizon now marked by distant cumulus clouds rising like dense white smoke off great distant fires. The waters about the island were glasstop smooth and shimmered brightly green. As the *Della* closed on the mouth of the harbor Ed cut the engines down to just above idling speed and they eased into port. Dozens of boats were tied up at the docks and dozens more lay at anchor in the bay and all of them taking on liquor for the mainland. The imminence of the Volstead Act had every drinking business in South Florida dealing frantically for factory stock to hoard against the coming dearth. Every day the West End harbor saw more rumboats than the day before. Within weeks and for years to come the harbor would be jammed around the clock.

They had intended to tie up just long enough to go into the bait-house and drink a cold beer before heading back home to report to their father on the boat's performance. But even as Ed carefully steered his way through the busy harbor and made for the dock, there came a small launch toward them and a corpulent whitebearded man in shirtsleeves and white skimmer stood at the bow and hallooed them. "Say, you boys!" he called out. "Are ye negotiable for carrying a load across?"

The brothers looked at each other, all of them grinning. "Load of what?" John Ashley called to the man. "And to where?"

The man scowled and spat and said, "Of what'd ye think, bucko—sassafras tea? It's a hundred and fifty cases of prime Irish whiskey and another hundred of the queen's best gin I need to have carried across to West Palm Beach—and I'm needing it carried today. I had a deal with a fella but the bloody fool got drunk last night and opened his hull on a reef this morning. I'll pay ye seven dollars a case. Are you my men or not?"

John Ashley looked from Ed to Frank. "What you boys say?"

"Gordy said ten's the usual rate," Ed said softly.

"Wouldnt Daddy be tickled if we run a load our very first time?" Frank Ashley said.

"Be tickled by the money we hand over for it is what he'd be tickled by," Ed said.

John Ashley called to the man: "Ten dollars and it's a deal!"

"Ten?" The man looked stricken. "Ten's what I pay experienced hands. You boys and yer craft there look like ye might be equal to the job, but ye aint never carried booze, have ye? I've an eye for it and I can tell. Prove yourselves to me this time and next time we'll talk ten."

"We done carried plenty a loads," John Ashley said. "But even if we hadn't—*if* we hadnt, mind you—we'd still be takin the same chance as anybody who has and we ought be paid the same."

The man spat and looked glumly all about at the other boats taking on their cargo. "Nine dollars," he said. "That's more than fair now, you got to admit."

"*Ten,*" John Ashley said. His brothers chuckled.

"Goddamn it," the man muttered. He checked his pocketwatch and swore again. "All right, ye cockers, ten it is—but it's got to go out *right* now, do you hear me? There's people'll be waiting for this shipment on the West Palm bar and they want it before dark."

"You got a deal, mister," John Ashley said.

An hour later the last of the 250 cases was taken aboard at the docks and lashed down in the hold and the *Della*'s gunwales still rode well above the waterline. The boat could have taken 400 cases if the man but had them. His name was Leonard Richardson and he said he'd have at least 350 cases for them next time and would try for more. He gave them $1,250 and said they would get the rest from the people waiting for the shipment.

"They aint gonna try and crawfish on us, are they, Leonard?" John Ashley said. "World's just fulla dishonesty, now aint it?"

Richardson snorted. "If anybody's got cause to be leery it's me. I dont know you boys from Adam's wild-oat sons and can only hope ye aint such fools as to try to make off with me booze. Whatever ye sold it for would be the last money ye made in the trade out of West End, thats certain sure." His arm swept the harbor and he said, "These fellas'll steal from anybody but each other, and you know why? Because it's bad business to cheat them ye want to *keep* doin business with. You'd be killing your own goose, you see? Better we stay straight with each other and we can make plenty for years to come."

"We're good for our word, Leonard," John Ashley said.

"That's fine, lad," Richardson said. "So are the boys who'll be meeting you. Good to know we can all trust each other now, aint it?"

The sun was past its zenith as they made ready to slip their mooring and head out of port. The clouds in the east had now grown to massive black thunderheads and were coming in a rush.

"Looks a mean storm building," Richardson said. "I was told it never rained here this time of year."

"Nothin to fret," John Ashley said. "West Palm's but a hundred miles and just about dead-west across the stream, so we aint got to buck much and she's runnin real soft today anyhow. I figure us to easy outrun them clouds. Hell, Leonard, like as not we'll be unloaded at the West Palm bar before the first drops hit the deck."

But as they quickly found out when they reached the deeper blue, the Gulf Stream was running stronger now, as though energized by the force of the encroaching storm. Ed had to hold the wheel hard to port to keep from drifting off course. And though he held her throttles open wide and the bow was reared high they were but a few miles past the stream's midpoint when the storm overtook them.

All in the same abrupt moment the wind struck like a thing becrazed and the sky went black and the sea began to heave and plunge. The rain slung sidewise in dense flailing sheets. Waves burst over the deck in stinging drenching spray.

Now lightning flared in white jagged branches and thunder cracked and blasted as though the sky were breaking apart. The ocean seemed bent on detaching itself from the earth.

Again and again the waves carried the boat up and up as though to crush it against the sky—and then fell away beneath it to bring it skidding down the steep black walls of water to such depths as made the dark surrounding ocean seem to John Ashley the very maw of the world.

He clung with both arms to the port gunwale and swallowed seawater with every gasping breath and the boat pitched and swayed as though drunk on its own cargo. Each smash of water over the port side pulled his legs out from under him and had stripped him of his shoes—and then the vessel would abruptly reverse its yaw and slam him against the bulwark as the water rushed out the scuppers and he several times almost rolled over the side.

Through the wind's howling he faintly heard laughter and wondered if he'd gone insane. He looked to his brothers in the blurring rain and saw Ed clutching to the wheel as though to a hard-dancing woman and Frank gripping the starboard gunwale and trying vainly to gain his footing and both of them laughing wildly into the teeth of the storm. Thunder persisted in its roll and boom across the darkness, lightning in its flickering blue casts which made his brothers' movements awkward and unreal and made deathly hollows of their eyes and mouths.

Ed turned to him, his mutilated mouth moving as though in shouts, but John Ashley could not make out what he was saying and he shook his head. And now his belly spasmed and the swallowed seawater roiled by the boat's undulant antics and in mixture with the lunchtime dolphin came surging up and out his gaped jaws and the wind smacked a good portion of the vomitus back in his face and some of it streaked over his cheekbone to fill his ear. Ed and Frank showed all their teeth in laughter. He was enraged that they thought this was fun—and terrified he would any moment be swept into the rioting black sea.

The storm seemed to him to rage for hours but not twenty minutes passed before the wind fell to fitful gusts and the driving rain reduced to drizzle. The cloudmass broke and the sky lightened to gray and the sea slowly settled to a high gentle roll. Frank and Ed were exhilarated in their sodden dripping state. John Ashley worked his grip free of the gunwale and washed his face with the rainwater running from his hair.

And reflected that his daddy was right—these two were the sailors in the family. He stood up carefully, unsteady on his feet.

"Goddamn man—this smugglin business is *fun*, aint it?" Ed said, standing easy at the wheel now and grinning his wide maimed grin. Frank sat on the cabin roof with his legs dangling and smiled at John.

John Ashley glared at them and they both started laughing hard and then he was laughing too.

"*Whoooo-eee!*" Ed said. "Aint no storm can get the best of *us!* Not the fucken Ashleys!"

Coughing for all his laughter, his hair yet shedding water in his face, Frank said, "Tell you true, it was a minute or two there when I thought we might were goin down certain sure."

"*You* thought?" Ed said. He cackled. "You see *Johnny?* He looked like a decked snapper the way his mouth was goin gulp-gulp-gulp. You *see* him?"

"I'll tell you all what," John Ashley said. "I was wishing I *was* a fucken fish. I was wishin for goddamn *gills* what I was wishin!"

Their laughter was hard and lasting and they all three clutched their stomachs against the aching cramping pleasure of it.

The storm had carried them several miles north of their intended latitude and the Gulf Stream was running even stronger now and they had to buck the brunt of it as they mended their course to southwestward. They made the bar off West Palm barely an hour before sundown. The sky was clear and the easterly breeze at their backs soft and cool. And now they saw that they were being watched by four men standing beside a pair of large motor launches beached in the shadow of a long ridge of dunes showing patches of sea oats and backed by the reddening western sky. John Ashley passed his binoculars over the rest of the long strip of beach. To the horizons north and south it stood deserted.

"Can see anything coming at us by water from north or south for a long way before they get to us," Ed said. "No wonder these boys wanted us here before nightfall. I'd say they knew what they doin when they picked this spot for the transfer."

They hove to and dropped anchor a hundred yards offshore to avoid the tumult of the breakers and make easier work of the unloading. The men on shore shoved off in the long launches and the rapping of their engines came to the Ashley brothers as they checked their .45's to ensure full magazines and chambered rounds. John and Ed stood their .44 Marlin rifles close to hand against the cabin bulkhead. Frank set his brother Bob's old Winchester atop the cabin with the stock jutting out for easy grasp.

The men in the launches had taken precautions of their own—each carried a revolver in his waistband. The launches made fast against the *Della*'s port side and a husky blond man came aboard and introduced himself as Morris. His quick eyes inventoried each Ashley in turn and he saw their .45's and the rifles at the ready and he stared for a moment at John Ashley's bare feet. No one made to shake hands. Morris said he wanted to have a look at the cargo and John Ashley took him belowdecks. When Morris was satisfied, he handed John Ashley a small cloth bag containing the rest of their money and called for two of the other launchmen to come aboard and they set to relaying the cases from the hold to topside to the gangway and then down to the man in the forward launch. When the Ashleys made to lend a hand, Morris did not object.

The launches had been smartly adapted for their present purpose. Each could carry forty cases and its gunwales yet stand a half-foot above the waterline, and even with a full load they could skim the water as smoothly as an eel. As soon as the first one was loaded it headed for shore and the other launch moved up in its stead under the gangway and began taking on cases from the relay man. In the gathering twilight, the Ashleys now saw other men hastening from behind the dunes and splashing into the surf to meet the first launch. They pulled it up on the beach and began relieving it of its cargo, working like a team of ants to bear the whiskey into the shadows.

Though the work went swiftly, nightfall was almost on them when the last launchload was ready for shore. "Luck to you," John Ashley called out as the Morris fellow dropped down into the launch and nodded at the helmsman and the launch swung about to port as its prop churned up a froth and the bow rose slightly as the boat made away. If Morris heard John Ashley's last remark he gave no notice of it.

And now Ed had the *Della* underway too and heading for the St. Lucie Inlet and home to a father they knew would be pleased to learn they had made $2,500 on a trip they had all supposed to be nothing more than a shakedown run.

"You know," Frank Ashley said to his brothers above the rumble of the *Della*'s engines, "I believe Bill's right and this smugglin business gonna work out just fine."

"I kindly agree," Ed said. He showed his twisted smile. "But I aint too sure about Johnny here. You reckon that little breeze and drizzle we went through back there mighta sopped some a his enthusiasm for bein out on the salt?" He winked at Frank and both brothers grinned at John Ashley.

"I reckon it mighta," Frank said. "I mean, a fella pukes in his own face, he cant be havin a *real* good time."

"You damn mulletheads," John Ashley said, and spat over the side. "All you can do better'n me is swallow down your own puke, and hell, a goddamn *dog* can do that. And you maybe can handle a damn boat better'n me. But *on land* where all normal people belong anyway I'm twice the man of either of you any damn day of the week."

And then they were all three laughing hard once again and showing their teeth white in their sun-darkened faces, punching playfully at each other, their jaws aching with their laughter, their eyes burning with the joy of being alive and in their own company, these brothers Ashley.

FOURTEEN

April 1920

ONE WARM FORENOON IN LATE APRIL JOHN ASHLEY AND HAN-
ford Mobley sold three skiffloads of gator hides to a dealer named
Phil Dolan on the Salerno docks and then repaired to the backroom of Toomey's Store down the street to drink a few mugs of cold
beer before heading for home. Frank and Ed Ashley and Clarence
Middleton were away on another liquor run to Grand Bahama. They'd
made more than a dozen such trips now, no longer transporting for
Richardson or anyone else but buying loads on behalf of Old Joe to
resell to backroom buyers for hotels and restaurants and groceries all
along the southeast coast but chiefly in Miami. Old Joe also continued
in the moonshine trade, selling most of his product to Indians, though
business had grown too large to assign deliveries to the various villages
directly anymore and he now dealt with middlemen in Pahokee and
at a central waycamp in the Big Sawgrass Slough. The profits were
streaming in. Frank and Ed were buying cases of island rum for as
little as six dollars each and selling them for sixty in Pahokee, for
eighty-five in Miami. They'd fast become old hands at the business.
And Clarence Middleton had proved to be as capable at handling a
boat and running whiskey as he was at so many things else. The only
thing he could not do well was the only thing he would not do at
all—take charge of men. Whenever Joe Ashley needed someone to
supervise an immediate enterprise and his sons were all occupied with
other duties, he gave the charge to young Hanford Mobley who rel-

ished the authority and exercised it well. And though Mobley was barely seventeen, Clarence Middleton liked him and admired his grit and willingly accepted his leadership in the absence of the Ashleys.

As always before he went into a town in Palm Beach County John Ashley first checked with his local informants on the whereabouts of the Bakers. Old Joe had made John swear not to show himself any-place where Sheriff George or Bob or Freddie Baker might be. "Why-ever it is you champin to get at him, you keep a tight leash on it," Old Joe had told him. "I want you to stay wide of the Bakers till I say different and I dont want to hear you didnt." For months now John Ashley had not laid eye on Bob Baker nor Bob Baker on him. On this day all the Bakers were about their business in West Palm Beach, where they usually were.

Toomey's backroom was cool and pleasant and smelled of fresh sawdust and seafood and beer. A single paddle fan revolved slowly from the ceiling. They took a foamy pitcher and two mugs and a big iced tray of unshucked oysters to a table against the wall opposite the bar and sat there shucking with their knives and slurping oysters and sipping their beer. A friend known to them as Shadowman Dave sat on a bench next to the pool table at the far end of the room and softly plunked his five-string. Toomey's trade was strictly crackers—fishermen and trappers, mostly—who were friendly to the Ashleys and took pride in one of their own being such a notorious public figure. Whenever John Ashley stopped in for a quick one, those in attendance would greet him in raucous fellowship and Toomey would nod at his young son and the boy would happily leave off sweeping up shells and go sit in front of the store and whittle and keep an eye for any show of county lawmen not known to be Ashley friends.

The place was nearly empty at this morning hour and Toomey came to the table to sit with them and gossip over a mug of beer. John Ashley had just poured a second mug for himself and young Hanford when the door swung open and someone entered carrying a twin-barreled shotgun and wearing baggy overalls and brogans and a faded black slouch hat. It took a moment for John Ashley to realize he was looking at a darkhaired woman of hard sunbrowned face. As she went to the bar she glanced at them without expression. Her eyes were moistly red and the underside of the left one was slightly swollen and discolored. She was not truly pretty and he would not have argued that she was, yet something in her aspect deepened his breath. She leaned the gun against the front of the bar and slid up onto a stool and the seat of the overalls abruptly snugged into a configuration to engage John Ashley's full attention. He thought that an ass that looked so fine in overalls must be a marvel in the flesh.

Toomey got up and went behind the bar and said, "Yes mam?" She murmured and Toomey nodded and set to drawing a mug of beer. He cut the head with a spatula and flicked the foam on the floor and finished filling the mug and set it before her. He poured a doubleshot of Joe Ashley's shine in a glass and placed it beside the beer and scooped up the money she'd put down. He nodded to her and put the money in a box on the backbar and then came back to join John and Hanford.

"They lord Jesus," John Ashley whispered. "Who's *that*?" Hanford Mobley grinned at his uncle.

"Name's Upthegrove," Toomey said softly. "Dont sound real, do it? Dont know her first name—nobody does. They say she lives with her daddy way to hell and gone south of Okeechobee in what they call the Thousand Hammocks."

"I know the place," John Ashley said. "Naught out there but sawgrass and so many hammocks look alike even a Indian can get lost in em."

"I heard nobody *but* Indians ever seen their house," Toomey said. "She got a brother used to bring Phil Dolan a load of hides ever month or so, but the word is he got sent to Raiford last year for killing a fella in a fight. About five-six months ago she started bringing in skins. Dolan says she brings in ever kinda hide—gator, otter, deer, bobcat. Brung in four goodsize painter skins one time and one of em black as ink and of a size to cover the most of a pool table, Dolan says. He asked her did she kill them big cats her ownself and she give him this *look*. Said to him, 'Well, mister, they didnt none of them say goodbye cruel world and shoot *theirselfs*.' Got a mouth on her. Just as well she dont talk much."

"I aint never known a woman to come in here before," John Ashley said.

"Aint her first time," Toomey said, "About a month ago she brung Dolan a load of hides and then instead of gettin in her boat and heading right back downriver like she always done before, she comes in here and sits herself right there where she is now and says to me to give her a pitcher and a shot. Place was about half full and you shoulda seen the jaws hangin open. Hellfire, I been runnin this place for five-six years and never had no woman come in here. Shadowman back there was grinnin and pickin and that banjo was the only sound in the place. I musta stood there gawpin at her for a full minute before she says, 'Well?' I finally think to tell her this aint no place for ladies, and she says thats just fine because she *aint* no lady and to hurry up about that pitcher. Well, I'll admit to you boys I didnt know whether to shit, spit or go blind. Understand now, she's settin there with that shotgun acrost her lap and lookin like the last thing she's gonna do is anything she dont want to. So I think it over for about two seconds and figure the hell with it, man or woman makes no difference to me as long as they puttin up cash money. So I pull a pitcher for her and put a mug next to it but she just goes ahead and drinks from the pitcher like a lot of old boys do. I bet she didnt take two breaths before she finished off the half of it. She sits there a minute and then lets go with a burp to rattle the windows. It aint that many *men* I ever heard burp like that, never mind no woman. Everbody was lookin at her like she was some kinda show but she wasnt payin nobody the least notice. Just drinkin her beer like she's the only one in the place. Well sir, she's startin in on the rest of the pitcher when Harvey Roget leaves off his pool game and comes up behind her with a shit-eatin grin. He says loud enough for everbody to hear how her ass looks ripe enough to take a bit out of and he grabs a handful of it. If he'd been figurin to charm her some more he never had the chance to do it because she come around on that stool and laid that half-full pitcher upside his head like she was thowin somethin sidearm. Pitcher didnt bust—just *WHONK!*—and beer goes everwhere and old Harvey goes quicksteppin off to the side like a man doin a jig and he didnt hardly get his balance before she was off that stool and had the shotgun by the barrels in both hands and smacked him over the head with the flat of the stock like she was drivin home a railroad spike. I tell ye, ole Harv went down like a killed man. Turned out he was only coldcocked but it's another dent in his headbone he'll carry to the grave for sure. The one half of his face was swole up all red and ugly and he lost him a eyetooth. By the time he come around she was long gone. The boys naturally give him a pretty good ribbin about getting the shit beat out of him by a woman. Harv got all blackassed about it and cussed a blue streak and stomped on out. Aint seed him since. Dont know where-all he's been doin his drinkin lately."

They had all three been furtively eyeing the woman at the bar as Toomey told his story. Now she shifted her weight on the stool and John Ashley felt his cock stir and he sucked a breath between his teeth.

"Just last week she brung Dolan another boatful of hides and then come in here again," Toomey whispered. "She'd just recent got that shiner under her eye and it was lots worse-lookin than now, I'll tell ye. That eye was swole near shut. Some of the boys thought maybe Harvey give it to her but I misdoubt it. Harvey aint *so* dumb he dont know he'd only make hisself look worse if he was to beat up on her. All he can do is hope that after a time nobody'll remember much about what she done to him. But like they say, hope in one hand and shit in the other and see which fills up first. Wont nobody who saw it ever forget the way she laid him out nor ever quit tellin about it. Anyhow, this last time, she had herself a pitcher and a coupla shots of your daddy's good stuff and then left. Never said a word except to order the spirits. And didnt nobody get bold with her neither. Hell, nobody come within four feet of her, not after how she done poor Harvey."

Toomey gave her a sidelong look and he leaned farther over the table as he said, "I tell you, boys, that aint no woman to get gay with. It's things about her just aint natural."

"It's somethin about her," John Ashley said.

"You right about that," Toomey said. "And it sets on that stool real nice."

Hanford Mobley chuckled and John Ashley said, "That aint what I mean."

Toomey and Mobley grinned at him. He said, "Well, it *is*—but it aint *all* I mean." He could not have said what he meant.

Now the woman drained the last of her beer and slid off the stool and took up the shotgun and headed for the door.

"She gonna make her getaway, uncle," Hanford Mobley said, nudging John Ashley with an elbow.

John Ashley got up and went to the door and watched the woman cross the street to a battered Model T he guessed to be ten years old. It angled awkwardly on a bent frame and its top was in tatters. She laid the shotgun on the seat and adjusted the levers under the steering wheel and took the crank around to the front of the car and fitted it and gave it a hard turn as forcefully as most men might and the motor coughed several times but didnt ignite. She glared at the car and tried again and this time the engine did not even cough. She reset the spark lever and tried again. After she'd cranked the motor a half-dozen futile times John Ashley went across the street and gave her his best smile and asked if he might be of assistance.

She studied him narrowly. She was breathing hard and her shirt was darkly damp and sweat beaded under her chin and nose. Her mouth was set hard and her eyes were shadowed by her hatbrim though he could see they were brightly wet. She looked like she might be resisting an urge to cry. Standing this near to her he was surprised to see she was almost as tall as he was. Now she held the crank out to him.

He used the marking stick to make sure there was gasoline in the tank and then checked to see that gas was getting to the carburetor. Whistling the while to convey an air of casually assured proficiency he made certain all ignition wiring was properly affixed and then went to the steering wheel and adjusted the spark lever and throttle and then set himself in front of the car and readied the crank and gave it a turn.

The engine emitted a hollow rasp on each of the first four tries. Passersby averted their eyes when he turned his glare on them. He reset the spark advance. The woman looked on without expression, her arms crossed over her breasts. The motor hacked on the fifth and sixth and seventh attempts but still would not start. When it coughed not at all on the eighth try, he blew a hard breath and muttered "Son of a *bitch!*"

He was huffing hard and dripping sweat. The woman sat down on the edge of the sidewalk with her elbows braced on her knees and her chin in her hands. He rolled up his sleeves and gripped the crank as though he meant to strangle it. He turned to the woman and smiled and winked and she reacted not at all. He gave the crank a mighty turn but his sweaty grip slipped and he fell to his knees as the crank recoiled and clipped him on the chin and snapped his teeth together with a clack. He saw an instant's darkness lit with sparks and swayed and nearly fell over but managed to keep his balance. He heard laughter from Toomey's across the way and turned to glare over there but the door stood empty. He got to his feet and tasted blood and felt of his mouth and found that he'd bitten his lower lip.

The woman was laughing into her hands and he felt a rush of anger—and then pictured what he must have looked like when the crank hit him and he chuckled and shrugged and sat down beside her on the plank walkway. He mopped at his lip with his shirttail and said, "Bedamn if that car aint got it in for me."

She laughed harder and covered her face with her hands and rocked to and fro and stomped a foot on the ground and people passing on the sidewalk glanced at them and gave them wider berth. He felt himself grinning. He looked across to Toomey's and saw a pair of heads at the door pull back from sight.

And then she was crying. He gaped and wondered what he'd done to upset her so suddenly. He stammered, "What's—what're you—"

He put a hand to her shoulder and said, "Hey now, darlin, what's all *this*? What's the matter?"

She dropped her hands and turned to him, her face bright with tears, her eyes bloodshot. "All I want is to get em back," she said. "It's all I want to do. But nothin ever works out right, not a goddamn thing! Now the goddamn car's no good and I cant get out there to get em back."

"Get *what* back?" he asked. "What all you talkin about?"

"My kids, goddamn it—my *kids*. They all I got and I want them back and I dont know how I'm gonna get out there to get them without no goddamn *car*!"

"Kids?" he said, as though he'd never heard the word.

"It's all I want from him," she said. "But *noooo*, he cant let me have em. Says they ruther be with him, the liar."

"*Who* wont let you have em?"

"My son of a bitch *husband*, who you think? Lord Jesus, I wish he'd drop dead this minute. I wish he'd dropped dead a long time ago. I wish his momma'd sat on him when he was just a baby. Goddamn it, I wish I had a *car*!"

"Hey, darlin," he said, "*I* got a car. And thats the same as you got one."

She wiped at her nose with her sleeve and looked at him.

"I'd be proud to take you to get them children."

Once again her eyes went thin. "Oh yeah? And just why you want to do that? You dont even know me."

"Well I know you're a nice person. And I know you need a car to go get your kids. And I know I can help you with that. What else I got to know? Let's just say I got a hankerin to help. Course now, if you don't *want* my help. . . ."

His hankering went well beyond wanting to help out, of course, but he knew that the best way to approach these nervous half-crazy ones was slowly and roundabout.

Her name was Laura Upthegrove. Her husband was E. A. Tillman but she had never taken his last name for her own. She called him Eat.

She sat leaning against the passenger door as John Ashley drove his Model T roadster over the narrow and dusty rockfill road flanking the St. Lucie canal that ran through scrub pine and palmetto prairie in a long easy curve of about twenty miles southwestward from the lower fork of the St. Lucie River to Indiantown and then went on another dozen miles or so to Lake Okeechobee. The sky was palely

blue and fathomless, the sun as light yellow as a baby chick. The wind
was from the south, soft and redolent of ripe sawgrass and spawning
bream. Osprey nests showed in the high pines and the parent raptors
wheeled in hunt far out over the savannah.

She'd wanted to bring her shotgun but John Ashley wanted no part
of spousal murder and had told her there'd be no need of it. He'd given
it to a passing boy to take across the street to Toomey for safekeeping.

"Eat's not only his initials, it's what he likes to do best," she said.
"And it's about what he's done to ever old boy who ever messed with
him—just eat him up."

She looked at him carefully when she said this last, and he grinned
and said, "Well I aint fixin to mess with him. I'm just takin a friend
to get her children is all."

Snakebirds stood on the canalbanks with their pointed beaks up-
thrust and their wet black wings spread to the sun. White herons—
which some called johnny cranes—winged gracefully over the prairie
and bore south to roosting destinations in the sawgrass country.

He asked if Eat Tillman had been the one to black her eye and
she nodded. "I guess I give him reason," she said, biting her thumbnail
and looking out at the passing pine stands and the vast stretch of
savannah grass behind them. He tried not to gawk at her shirted breast
where it swelled out from under the overall bib or at the snug cling of
the denim to her crossed thighs. "I just did miss takin his head off
with a frying pan," she said. "Caught him a little on the ear is all.
Shoulda seen, though—it was swole it up like a damn plum. I was
just fixin to swipe at him again when he laid one on me to make me
see stars for the next night and day." The fight had been ten days ago
when she tried to take the kids from him. She said she wished she'd
thought to shoot the bastard while she had the chance but she was so
addled from the punch she didnt think of it until she was miles away
from Indiantown and by then the sun was set and she was feeling too
low to turn around and go back and kill him.

"Just as well you didnt," John Ashley said. "If you'd killed him
and the police run you down for it, you'd gone to prison and been
separated from your kids anyhow. Most like for a long time."

She looked at him. "I aint afraid of the damn police." She said
this as though it were something he ought well have known. "I didnt
think you were neither."

"Me?" He smiled. "What you know about me?" He had told her
only that his name was John.

"I know who you are," she said. "The law's been after you forever.

I heard about them different color eyes, how you got one shot right out of your head. I reckon you must be tough to kill as a gator gar."

He looked at her and then back at the road ahead. "I guess so far," he said.

"They say you killed a half-dozen Indians. Killed a coupla white men too, they say—some gambler in Miami, and a guard when you made your getaway from prison. They say there aint a bank in South Florida you aint robbed."

"*They* say a hell of a lot, dont they?" he said, irritated by such reckless general surmise about his crimes but a little proud of his notoriety as well. "Too bad *they* dont know what in the hell they're talkin about."

"You mean you aint done all them things?" she said in a tone of disappointment. Because she wasnt smiling he couldn't be sure if she was teasing. He couldn't see her eyes in the shadow of her hat brim.

"I expect there's probably a bank or two I aint robbed."

"Not yet, anyway. Desperado like you, you'll get around to them, I'm sure." And now she smiled out at the road and he felt himself grinning.

"If I'm such a dangerous fella and all, how come you ridin with me way out here in the big empty where any ole thing might happen?"

"Oh I'm scared to death," she said in a voice of mock fright. "I'm just hidin it real good. And I'm ridin with you cause you takin me to get my kids." She looked out at the road ahead for a moment and then back at him. "I never woulda figured such a bad man like you bein scared of the police."

"Oh yes, mam, all the damn time."

"You are not, neither."

They rode in silence for a time and then she said: "And I wouldnt of thought a man like yourself would hold with a man beating up on a woman."

"I didnt say I hold with it," he said. "I said you'da made things worse for youself if you'da killed him. My daddy raised us to know there aint never a right excuse to hit a woman." He mulled for a moment before adding, "Unless she be fooling with some other fella. But thats the *only* reason." He paused again, and then: "*Or* if she tries to steal your money. But thats it, them's the *only* two reasons. No, wait—there's one more: if she kicks your dog. For damn sure if she kicks your dog." He twisted his face in mock hard thought. "*Or* if she's late with supper on the table, almost forgot that one. *Or* if she wont leave you be." He looked sidelong at her and saw that she was trying to look put out but her smile would not be restrained.

"Yeah, I know," she said. "It aint no excuse but whatever one you got to hand." They both laughed.

She told him Eat Tillman was a dredge operator her daddy had brought home to supper one evening after Eat had stopped to help him get his car out of the mud. It was raining hard and the shoulder of the South Shore road had given way and her daddy's car had sunk on its right side to midway up the wheels. Eat chained the cars together and after several tries in which he'd almost got his own car stuck, he managed to tug her daddy's car free. They put up the cars at Bobby Raines' shop in South Bay and got in her daddy's skiff and went down the canal a few miles and then portaged the skiff over the canalbank and into the sawgrass channel and poled a few hours more out to the Thousand Hammocks. She said Eat started making eyes at her from the minute they were introduced. Two months later they were married and living in Indiantown where Eat had inherited a small house from his daddy who managed a trading post. That was seven years ago.

"I didnt do it cause I loved him," she said. "I liked him well enough I guess, but what I really wanted was to get away from home and, I dont know, do somethin *else*. Somethin . . . *excitin*."

They were clear of the pines now and she looked off to the savannah horizon and blew a long breath. "He's the quiet sort, old Eat. Dont never get drunk and hardly ever raises his voice and never hit me but a few times and never once used his fist. Not till this last time, and I guess any man would at least use his fist if you took a frying pan to his head. The thing is, what he most likes to do when he aint out workin on the dredge is sit home and play his harmonica. Lord." She rolled her eyes.

About seven months ago she'd finally got to where she couldn't stand the boredom of Eat Tillman another day. She packed a bindle and took her shotgun and a few tools and headed off in a skiff to live in her family's house in the Thousand Hammocks. Her parents had left it to her when her daddy got his foot bit by a gator and was left too crippled to make his living by taking hides anymore. They had moved back up to Georgia to live with kin on a farm. She'd long ago learned to hunt and trap from her daddy and she got along just fine on her own, getting whatever money she needed by selling hides every now and then to Milt Jessup's store in Jupiter or, lately, to Dolan's in Salerno, which was worth the longer trip because she could usually get a better price. She didnt say anything about her brother in the penitentiary and John Ashley didnt ask.

Eat didnt come looking for her. "I guess he was as glad I was gone as I was," she said. The kids were five and four by then and she figured he could take care of them well enough. "I anyway didnt think I'd miss em all that much, truth to tell. And I didnt, not for the longest time, not till about last month. I asked Eat for em but he said no and so I stewed about it for a time and then last week I went and tried to take them anyway and thats when we had the fight."

She stared out at the vista of scrub and grass. "I guess I miss em," she said. "I mean, all of a sudden I come to have this feelin of somethin missin real bad and must be it's them because it sure's hell not him." She paused and took out a pipe and tin of tobacco and packed the bowl and got it burning with the fourth match and puffed on it a few times and then looked over at John Ashley and said, "You know, I dont usually talk this much."

"Glad to hear it," he said—and they both grinned.

The sun was huge and pale and only slightly past its meridian when they hove into Indiantown, a hamlet sprung up around a longtime trading post. It was composed of a combination store, a grocery, a small tannery hung with drying hides of every description, a smokehouse, several boathouses, a small cafe, a few houses scattered near and about in the meager shade of scrawny oaks. A trio of men in widebrimmed fisherman's hats stood smoking and drinking beer in front of the cafe and turned away from their conversation to watch them go by.

The air was cast in a thin haze of smoke. On the far side of the canal stood a cluster of Indian chickees—raised platform huts with open sides and roofs of palmetto fronds—and a row of dugouts along the bank where an Indian in white shirtdress and a black bowler was gutting a deer hung on a gumbo limbo branch. She directed John Ashley to drive on for another quarter-mile until he came to an abutting road and then turn onto it. The road was of raised rock and sand and ran through a stretch of marshland flanked by high pines. Then they were out of the trees again and a half-mile farther on arrived at a small shadeless house with a railed porch.

He turned into the sandy yard and shut off the motor. One of the porch posts bore the skin and rattles of a diamondback more than six feet long. A rusting old landaulet of uncertain make without canopy or windscreen stood just off the porch. Behind the house the pale green savannah extended flat as a carpet to the horizons west and south.

The children were playing in a dirt patch alongside the landaulet, the boy and his younger sister both wearing only short pants and digging with spoons and tin bowls and their faces and limbs smeared with mud. For a moment they sat gaping at the woman who stepped out of the car and smiled broadly and opened her arms wide to them. John Ashley slouched behind the wheel and rolled a cigarette. As the woman stepped toward them the children scrambled to their feet and ran around the side of the house, the boy yelling "Pa! Pa!" and the girl at his heels glancing back fearfully over her shoulder.

"No!" the woman called. "You get back here, Billy! I'm your *mother*, dammit!"

John Ashley lit his cigarette and reflected that unrequited affection was for certain sure one of life's most melancholy circumstances. As the woman started after the kids, a man appeared from around the other corner of the house and she looked over and saw him and stopped as short as if she'd hit the end of a leash. The man was very large and his sleeves were rolled and his arms were blood to the elbow. He held a skinning knife in one hand and a raw length of indigo snakeskin in the other.

John Ashley came upright in the car seat. The man looked unhappy to see this woman who was yet his wife. He tossed the snakeskin onto the porch and wiped the knife on his pant leg and slipped it into a belt sheath. He glanced at John Ashley in the roadster and then shambled over to the woman and stood before her with his hands on his hips and said something to her that John Ashley couldn't make out.

He reached under the seat and withdrew the .44 Colt and checked the loads and slipped the pistol into his waistband at the small of his back. He got out of the car and closed the door and stood leaning against it with his thumbs hooked in his belt loops. The man looked at him again and then said to the woman, "I done tole you and tole you—they stayin with me. Hell, girl, you dont really want them except I do."

"They're *my* children too, Eat," she said, her voice strained.

The man turned to the front door and called, "Billy! Rayette! Come on out here."

The two kids came in view behind the screen door and hesitated, and then the boy pushed it open and he and his sister stepped out on the porch. "You kids," the man said, "your momma's still wanting you to go with her. Either of you changed you mind and wanna go, you can. Do you? Either you?"

Both kids shook their heads and the man said, "You gotta say yes you do or no you dont. Say it so she can hear."

"No," the boy said, glowering at his mother. He looked at his sister and nudged her and she said, "I dont *wanna* go with her."

"All right," the man said. "Get back inside." The kids disappeared into the interior darkness. The man looked at the woman and turned up his palms. "I guess it aint nothin else to say, is there? Why dont you just quit all this anymore and go on and leave us be?"

"I *want* them kids, Eat." Her voice was drawn to an edge. She smacked her fists on her thighs. She turned now to John Ashley who thought she looked becrazed. He was suddenly sorry he'd come out here, but there was nothing to do now but see the thing through. He stepped forward and said, "Look here Mister Tillman, everybody knows kids ought be with their momma. It's the most natural—"

"Who the hell are *you*?" Eat Tillman asked, his voice utterly absent the placatory tone he'd used with his wife.

"I'm a friend of Laura's come to help her take her children home."

"They *are* home, hoss, not that it's any your business."

"I aint leavin without them kids, Eat," Laura said. "Not this time."

"You sure's hell not leavin with em," Tillman said, looking from John Ashley to her and back to Ashley.

"You talk like some kinda hardcase," John Ashley said. "You a hardcase, mister?" He noted now how very large Eat Tillman's hands were, noted their scars and sizable knuckles.

"I'm all I need to be to deal with you."

"You fixin to deal with me with that skinner?" John Ashley said, gesturing at the knife Tillman wore on his belt.

They were slowly sidestepping further out into the yard where they would have more room. Tillman withdrew the knife and half-turned and threw it end over end to impale quivering into the porch pole opposite the one with the rattlerskin.

"I don't need no weapon," Tillman said. "Not for you."

John Ashley reached around behind him and brought out the Colt. Tillman's eyes narrowed and his mouth went tight and he nodded as though confirming his own suspicions that this stranger was not a man to be trusted. For an instant John Ashley considered holding him at gunpoint while the woman snatched up the kids. How much easier it would be that way. Then he turned and held the pistol out to Laura and said, "Hold this. That's *all* you do with it, hear? Just hold it." Then he took the glass eye out of its socket and handed it to her too. "And this while you at it." For a moment she stared at the eye in her palm like it was some object of rare imagination, and then smiled at him and put it in her overalls pocket.

He turned to Eat Tillman and said, "Winner says who gets the kids."

Tillman was gaping at the empty eyesocket in John Ashley's head. "I dont know I can fight a man got but one eye," he said. "Dont seem fittin."

"How fittin's it gonna seem to you when that one-eyed man stomps your sorry ass whether you fight back or not?" John Ashley said.

Tillman shook his head resignedly. "All right, mister, suit yourself," he said. He started to take off his shirt and John Ashley hooked him hard to the belly and crossed him to the jaw. The man staggered back a few steps but his eyes held their focus. His thick belly was firm as a shipping-sack of sugar and his jaw stung John Ashley's hand. Well hell, John Ashley thought. And knew he was in for some pain.

Fifteen minutes later his face felt overlarge and numb and his vision was blurred and every huffing breath ached in his ribs. He had thrown up his breakfast and had to spit blood constantly to keep from choking on it. Now Eat Tillman hit him in the face again and again he fell down. He saw the blue sky whirl and he rolled over and pushed up on hands and knees and rested a moment. He tasted mud and blood. The first time Tillman put him down, the man had kicked him even as he tried to get up and Laura had cursed her husband and shrieked for him to fight fair goddammit. John Ashley had told her to shut up. But Tillman had not kicked him again.

John Ashley stood up and swayed and wiped blood from his good eye. Tillman waited with fists ready, showing one swollen eye and bloated lips and an ear outsized and purple. But he could still see clearly and looked hale in contrast to John Ashley. He moved with the quickness of a truly dangerous big man.

John Ashley charged with his head down and grabbed him about the waist and tried to pull him off his feet, hoping to straddle him, pin his arms with his knees and then punch him until he couldnt punch anymore. But Tillman stood fast and hooked him hard with lefts and rights to the ribs and kidneys and then braced himself and brought his knee up hard and John Ashley went sprawling.

He got to hands and knees and then set one foot on the ground and rested with an arm on the raised knee. And now heard Laura crying and wanted to tell her to stop it but the effort of speech was too great to muster. He tried to stand and his head spun and he fell over on his side. And then hacking and gasping began the struggle to rise again.

A gunshot shook the air and John Ashley flinched on all fours and looked up to see Laura with her arms stretched in front of her and holding the revolver in both hands and pointed at Eat Tillman. She was crying and Eat Tillman's hands hung at his sides and he was staring at her and looking very tired. "I'll put the next one in your teeth," she told him. She snuffled hard.

"You gone have to shoot me you want them kids," Eat Tillman said in a voice now deeply nasal.

"Just dont you hit him anymore," she said. She looked at John Ashley and said, "Get on up and kick him in the balls if you want."

John Ashley spat blood and sat back on his heels with his hands on his thighs. He slowly shook his head. He could not stand by himself, never mind kick anyone. She sidled over to him and held a hand to him. "Come on, baby," she said.

John Ashley took her hand and she helped him to his feet. With an arm about each other they shuffled to the car and she helped him get in on the passenger side. Then she went around and got in behind the wheel and kept the pistol on Eat as she held out the crank to him and told him to turn the motor. He did it and the engine fired up and he handed the crank back to her and stepped away from the car.

John Ashley said, "I dont think it's anymore need of that gun, do you?" but so battered was his mouth that she did not understand what he said and he had to repeat it before she nodded and laid the pistol on the seat.

As she backed the car around in the yard John Ashley saw the children come out of the house and go to their daddy and each one hug tightly to one of his legs while he stroked their heads and told them it was all right, there was nothing to cry about, not anymore.

Then they were rattling down the road and past the pines and then came to the crossroads and turned toward Indiantown and sent up a flutter of chickens that had wandered out from a nearby yard. As they went through the hamlet they once again drew stares. And then they were down the road and around the bend and Indiantown fell away behind them.

"Eye," he said, and held out his hand. She gave him the glass eye and he fitted it in place and then put his head back on the seat and closed his eyes and thought of nothing at all.

After they'd driven in silence for a time she pulled over onto the shoulder and stopped the car. He sat up and saw but the road ahead and behind and boundless blue sky and nothing else to see in the world but open prairie and distant hammocks and the bluegreen horizon shimmering hazily in the rising heat like a world badly imagined.

She slid across the seat and up against him and hugged his neck and kissed his battered face. He flinched and her face drew with concern and she kissed him more softly. He said he was sorry he didnt get her children back. She said she wasnt. She said that while he was fighting for her she'd come to understand that what she'd been missing wasnt the children at all but something she hadnt even known existed. What it was she'd been missing in her life was him.

She straddled him on the seat and kissed him again and then stroked his hair and looked down into his one-eyed face. Her eyes bespoke a tenderness beyond any he'd ever known. He saw then for the first time that her eyes were green. And that one of them held a tiny gold quarter-moon.

FIFTEEN

The Liars Club

LORDY, THE STORIES WE HEARD ABOUT JOHN AND LAURA! THE kinda stories no one could know were true or not except for the two of them their ownselfs. Stories about the sort of things they'd do in the house Laura was give by her daddy. They say it was way down in the Devil's Garden, that house, down in the Thousand Hammocks where there's nothin for miles around but sawgrass and snakes and gators, hooty owls and skeeters and frogs ranging on your ears all the night long. Nights out there just black as blindness. It wasnt any way at all to get within a mile of that house but by the twisty sawgrass channels out there where the grass was just shy of sufficient height to hide you. By the time you'd get close enough to see just a tiny bit of the house through the highground pines, a lookout up in the trees would of had you in his gunsight for a half-an-hour. They say there was getaway sawgrass channels all around that hammock that nobody but Laura knew about and the only one she ever told about them was John Ashley. It was probly the best hideout house John Ashley ever had. Them wild-ass lovebirds didnt live out there all the time, only when they wanted to be alone for a few days and nights way off where there wasnt no law of man nor God to keep em from doin whatever they felt like as loud as they felt like. Ever now and then some hunter or frogger would claim to've been out in that part of the glades of an early evening and from a mile away heard em howling like a couple of painters. We heard that when they first moved into the sidehouse on the Twin Oaks property Old Joe couldnt stand the ruckus they made when they went at it late at night. He said if they were going to carry on so awful loud they could damn well do it someplace where they wouldn't keep everbody awake by it. The Ashleys liked Laura real well and everbody in the family was glad John had found him a true love and all, but we heard the whole family was bad to joke about the caterwauling John and Laura'd make out in the sidehouse.

And so the lovebirds started going out to her house every now and again. Out there they could make all the noise they wanted and nobody around to make fun of them for it nor tell them to quit.

In the spring of nineteen and twenty Sheriff George Baker whose health hadnt been gettin nothin but worse woke up sicker than usual one morning and stayed home in bed and only got worse and by that night he was dead. Bob Baker was appointed to finish out his daddy's term and then in November he ran for election to the job. He had a photographer take his picture throwin his hat in a ring like he was Teddy Roosevelt. Dont none of us recall who it was ran against him that November. It didnt matter. Bobby was about popular as religion by then and there wasnt a chance in hell he wouldnt be elected—and he was. In his victory speech he said his number one aim was to rid Palm Beach County of what he called the criminal element. Actually he'd been claiming credit all during the campaign for having cut crime a goodly bit already. There hadnt been a bank robbery in the county in nearly a year and he promised the voters there'd not be another one, not while he was sheriff. He didnt mention the Ashley Gang by name but everybody knew that was who pulled the last bank job. It pretty soon became clear, though, that as long as the Ashleys didnt show their face to Bob Baker or any of his officers nor harm any of the good citizens of the county, Sheriff Bob wasnt gonna go out hunting for them. In a way it was like he was letting bygones be bygones as long as the Ashleys didnt do any new crimes, not in Palm Beach County—not in public anyway. Oh he knew they were runnin booze, everybody knew it, but hardly anybody around here saw moonshiners and rumrunners as criminals anyhow, except for some of the good Christian people who'd favored the damn Prohibition laws in the first place.

If the Ashleys had done their booze business out in the open like some bootleggers were doin in some places, Sheriff Bob wouldnt of had no choice but to come down hard on them. But they was careful and quiet about the way they made deliveries to their Palm Beach

County customers and Bobby knew better than to work too hard at stopping them. Just about all the hotels and restaurants had speakeasies and they couldnt have done much business without em. And the fish camps liked to keep spirits on hand for their customers who liked a cold beer or a drop of something stronger after a day of fishing. If Bob Baker had put a stop to the Ashley bootlegging in Palm Beach County he'd of hurt a lot more businesses than just Old Joe's. And if you do something that harms a man's business, he aint about to vote for you come next election—not him nor his family nor his friends.

John Ashley was another matter. There was a warrant on him and arresting him wouldnt of put Joe Ashley out of business. But John Ashley was mostly keeping to the Devil's Garden or down to Miami, where Bob Baker couldnt touch him. As far as anyone knows, the only times he showed hisself publicly in Palm Beach County anymore were now and then when he'd bring a load of hides to a buyer. He never caused trouble on those visits and never stayed long, and he seemed to know exactly when neither Bob Baker nor any of his main deputies would be around. Sheriff Bob have to of known about those appearances but he didnt seem to care all that much. All in all, over the next few years it was like there was an unspoken truce between Bobby and John.

Which aint to say the Ashleys didn't have their troubles in that time—especially once national Prohibition came along. Supposedly a gang of Yankee bootleggers tried to run hooch through Palm Beach County and the Ashleys took exception to the intrusion on their territory. None of us knew—then or now—what the real truth of all those stories was, but we heard a lot of things. We heard the Ashleys was hijacking ever booze shipment the Yankee rumboats were landing on the local beaches. There were rumors of gunfights out on boondock stretches of the Dixie Highway where they was stopping every Yankee rum truck to come down the road. There was stories of men gettin shot dead. Mind you, we only *heard* most of this—the local newspapers hardly ever mentioned any of it. There was talk that Sheriff Bob had told them not to print any stories to worry the public with secondhand reports of things that were no threat to the civic order, of things going on in the dead of night way out in the lonesome reaches of the Dixie Highway or on stretches of beach where not a soul lived for miles around. More than one person made bold to whisper that Bob Baker didnt want anything to put an end to that whiskey war because he was hoping every one of the Ashleys would get killed in it.

*   *   *

Miami really started booming during the Great War and just kept at it after the Armistice. When Deering finished building his Vizcaya estate in 1915 the town lost a lot of jobs—then the war come along and everthing got all better in a hurry. Thousands of servicemen got stationed in Miami and at the end of the war some of them stayed. All the military branches—army and navy and marine corps—set up flying centers of one kind or another in Miami and us kids loved to watch them military planes making their practice flights ever day. We were all just crazy for aeroplanes. Some of us are old enough to remember the first aeroplane flight in Miami back in nineteen and eleven. The mayor wanted to do something special to celebrate the town's fifteenth birthday so he passed the hat and scraped up a whopping $7,500 to pay the Wright brothers and they sent down an aeroplane on the train and a pilot named Gill to fly it.

It was one of them old bi-wing jobs that looked like a giant dragon-fly. They hauled it out to the country club golf course and when Gill took off you didnt hear nothing but his motor and a coupla thousand people going *"Ooooh!"* and it was one or two ladies fainted from the excitement. The plane went up over the pines and a bunch of the girls from the Hardieville houses had come out to watch and they waved their white hankies at the pilot as he flew over them and he wagged his wings from side to side and you could see his big white grin under his goggles. But the plane scared the daylights out of a herd of cattle in a neighboring pasture and them cows went right through the fence and come stampeding across the golf course just as the plane circled around low and started coming back our way. All the horses and mules started rearing and bucking in the traces and the drivers were yelling "Ho! Ho now!" and trying to rein them in as hard as they could, but here come the cattle stampeding at us and here come the plane not more'n fifty feet overhead with its motor loud as bejesus and them horses and mules were flat terrified and there was no holding em back. They lit out with their teeth showing and their eyes big as baseballs and the drivers and passengers went ass over teakettle off the wagons and out of the buggies. People were shrieking and scattering out of the way of the cattle and the runaway vehicles and some folk went tumbling into the sand traps and some fell in the ponds. All you heard was the rapping of that aeroplane motor and the cattle bawling and horses and mules galloping and whinnying and women screaming and men cussing and kids laughing and . . . well Lord, aint none of us who was old enough to be there have yet forgot that fifteenth birthday celebration and the first aeroplane to fly over Miami. We found out later that one fella drowned in the water trap in front of the sixteenth green and wasnt found till the next day when a golfer's fairway shot bounced in front of the hazard and ended up between the dead man's shoulder blades, which was about all of that was showing above the water. Some say the golfer waded on in and played the lie off the fella's back before reporting the body, but likely as not thats just a mean story. Anyway, not six years later we were watching the navy's flying boats—flying *boats,* mind you—takin off and landing from the bay at Dinner Key and asking each other what they'd think of next. But by the end of the war we'd seen so many planes we didnt even look up anymore when one flew over. A body can get used to anything, no matter how mysterious or strange, and it pretty soon becomes a commonplace, even if its mystery aint any better understood than it ever was.

Lots of mysterious things happened around that time. There was a story in the newspapers about a baby born in Fort Lauderdale that no sooner came out of his momma's womb than he said just clear as a bell, "It will rain for forty days and forty nights." And bedamn if it didnt start coming down that very evening and rain from Lauderdale to the keys all through the next day and all the day after that. Newspaper reporters went to the baby's home and asked his momma and daddy to ask the infant what was going on but apparently the child had spoke his piece and wasnt about to say another word about rain or anything else. You can imagine how people carried on when the rain kept falling and falling day after day. Some good Christian folk sold everything they owned and got ready for the second coming of Noah's Flood. Most the houses in town put a boat ready in the yard and loaded it with provisions. In the worst flooded neighborhoods alligators swam across the yards and ate ever dog around. Ever day there was news of somebody got bit by a water moccasin. The churches did steady business in sinners stopping in to make theirselfs right with the Lord. Others went the other way and took to the bottle. They say half the men in Miami didnt see a sober hour during that steady fall of rain. There were drunken public fistfights ever day and the cops mostly didnt do anything about them except make bets on who'd win. We heard that some men drowned in the streets when they fell down and were too drunk to even lift their heads up out the water. It rained ever single day for three entire weeks before it finally quit and the sun come out again and started to dry out all the craziness. Some said the rain was God's way of punishing Miami for its wicked ways but others said that was just superstitious nonsense and that the real reason for

the rain was them enormous Krupp guns the Germans was using to
shell Paris from seventy-five miles away. They said the blasts of them
huge guns was upsetting the atmosphere and causing all kinds of
strangeness in the weather all over the world.

Then there was the Spanish Lady. That's what everbody called the
influenza that went around so bad during the war. For a time it seemed
all South Florida was sick, the whole damn world. People pretty much
stopped visiting with their neighbors for fear of sickness in their house.
Some of the grownups called catching the flu being kissed by the Spanish Lady. It was a kiss to make you out-of-your-head sick is what it
was. For some it was the kiss of death. Everbody knew somebody who
was took by the influenza. It was lots of people in mourning dress at
that time. For reasons nobody ever figured out, the only ones in Miami
who seemed immune to it was the Hardieville girls. Some said it was
because God had meaner ends in mind for them sinful women and
wasnt about to let them die of anything so easy as the flu.

Anyhow, the war brought more servicemen to Miami than you
could shake a picture postcard at and the doughboys brought money
and things were mostly good most of the time during the war and got
even better afterward. Business was fine all over town—it was money
money everwhere. Some restaurants were open for business round the
clock. Clothing stores couldnt resupply their stock fast enough, there
was so much demand for the latest fashions. Every man wanted a silk
shirt and a white boater. Pink and yellow were the favorite colors for
shirts during the war but after the Armistice candy-striped became most
popular. Wages went way up—but so did prices. A carpenter who
used to make two dollars a day now got paid a dollar an hour but his
twelve dollars for a day's work was about what one of those new silk
shirts cost.

Of course what them doughboys wanted more'n anything else during the war was whores and booze and gambling games—and of course
the town was quick to provide all they wanted and no matter it was
all illegal. The Hardieville houses never closed. Some of the houses
had gambling and some didnt but damn near ever hotel in town had
at least one room reserved for dicing and cards at any hour. The
politicians and cops were gettin rich on the payoffs. With all them
cathouses and gambling rooms doin round-the-clock business the call
for booze was constant and the Ashleys had all they could do to satisfy
it. When Prohibition came in after the war the market for hooch in
Miami was so great it's no wonder the gangsters from up north wanted
in on the action.

* * *

After the war the Ashley boys started going to Miami more often than ever. The town was building up a boom that wouldnt do nothing but get bigger and bigger till it'd finally get blowed away by the hurricane of nineteen and twenty-six—but by then the Ashley boys were history, all but one. Once Prohibition become the law there wasnt any kind of fun a man couldnt find in Miami. The Ashleys still went there to gamble sometimes and to sport with the fancy ladies like they always had, but by now they all of them had a steady girl and they liked to go down to Miami in a bunch and have a big time together.

Frank had took up with a gal from Stuart named Jenny, a real pretty thing with black hair to her waist. Ever chance he got he'd take her for drives in his roadster. Now and then people saw them having a picnic in the harbor park. Ed's girl was named Rita somebody. She was a reclusive thing and nobody'd ever seen much of her till she became Ed Ashley's girl. She was half-Indian and a few years older than Ed and lived somewhere midway of the St. Lucie canal near an Indian camp. They say she had tits like grapefruits and an ass like a perfect turned-over heart—a body to make a man just howl with want. But her face was another story. They say one side of it was real pretty but the other side of it was a scary thing to behold. The story is, she got that face when she was about fourteen from a bad Indian named Tommy Fox Shadow who later got killed in a fight with a game warden who caught him taking egret plumes. One night in a drunken argument the Indian hit her across the face with a flaming chunk of pinewood off the campfire and knocked out a coupla upper teeth on that side and embers got stuck in her cheek and just burned her to the bone. After that nobody ever saw her to smile nor heard her to say a word. But if her face wasnt much to look at, well hell, neither was Ed's, what with that scarred mouth and all. It was lots of jokes on the quiet about how the two of them must of had to put a bag over each other's head just to do the deed.

Hanford Mobley was said to of fallen for some redhead in Miami, and Clarence Middleton had a girl in St. Lucie he was sweet on. Clarence would go off by himself to see her and hardly ever went to Miami with the others. Roy Matthews now, he never did have a steady girl as far as anybody knows. From the time he joined the gang he pretty much took his pleasure where he found it and they say he found it everwhere. For reasons no man's ever understood, women just cant seem to resist a naturalborn sonofabitch and they say Roy Matthews could have his pick of them like oranges off a tree.

The way we heard it, the boys were taking their girls to Miami nearly ever weekend. They say Old Joe had foaming fits about them spending so much time in the city. He believed all cities were naught but sin pits and he was fearful his boys might get too fond of Miami's ways. The fact is, the Ashley boys liked Miami plenty well. They liked wearing snazzy city suits and going dancing in the Elser Pier hall. They liked eating in fancy restaurants and going to the moviehouses and singing along to the music at the park bandstand. They for damn sure must of liked them big hotel beds for fooling on. As for their women, well, they loved the city. They didnt have to work while they were there. Didnt have to cook nor wash laundry nor chop wood nor nothing. They could take bubblebaths, they could wear perfume and pretty theirselfs up. Those visits to Miami were the only times Laura Upthegrove was ever known to put on lipstick and a dress.

SIXTEEN

October 1920–January 1921

THE ELSER PIER WAS AN ORNATE THREE-STORY BUILDING THAT stood at the foot of Flagler Street and extended on pilings into Biscayne Bay. It was as big as a warehouse and from its blazing confines every evening came a rich medley of smells to waft through the streets on the inshore breeze—a redolency of popcorn and roasted peanuts, hot dogs, cotton candy, pastries. This was the place to go in Miami for almost any sort of fun that wasnt illegal. The Pier contained a dancehall and an arcade comprising food stands, a shooting gallery, a tattoo parlor, game booths where fast-talking pitchmen challenged every passing fellow to win for his sweetie a teddybear or gewgaw of colored glass by throwing a baseball at a pyramid of wooden blocks or pitching a penny into a cup or tossing a plastic doughnut at a peg, by shooting an arrow at a fistsized balloon or lobbing a horseshoe at an iron stake in a box of sawdust. There were viewing machines in which one could see short loops of moving pictures by depositing a penny in a slot and turning the crank on the side of the machine—slapstick scenes, quickdraw Western gunfights, exhibitions of horseback highdiving. One viewer showed Hawaiian hula dancers in grass skirts and every night this machine did a brisk trade. Here and there along the arcade aisles were benches and small tables where one might sit with an ice cream cone or a bottle of pop and observe the passing parade. Each time the Ashley gang visited Miami with their women, the Elser Pier was where they took their fun.

The man who ran the shooting gallery would groan at the sight of them headed for his concession. The first time they'd come to Elser Pier each of the men had taken several turns shooting with the pellet rifle and they cleared the pitchman's shelf of every prize it held. They would have required a sizable sack to bear away their booty except the man looked so dejected they took pity on him and gave back most of it. He'd suggested that thereafter they just give him their fifteen cents and point out the prize they wanted and he'd hand it over and they'd all save some time. The brothers laughed and said that wouldnt be sporting. But on every visit since, they'd made only a single trial apiece with the little rifle, each in turn always shooting a perfect score and laying claim to whatever trophy his ladylove desired off the shelf. Later the girls would give away their prizes to children in the arcade or to women in the dancehall who looked to need cheering up.

The lot of them loved to dance and would still be taking a turn on the floor when the bandleader announced the night's final number. The dancehall was on the second floor and had tables along the walls and several tall windows to either side overlooking the bay and admitting the seabreeze to swirl the haze of cigarette smoke in the dim yellow light. From these windows the music carried out to the shadowed sidewalks to draw in happy couples and hopeful stags and the always and ever lonely. When the band was between sets you could hear the bayswells slapping at the pilings under the building. Laura loved the Elser Pier dancehall. She told John Ashley it made her feel like she was dancing on a ship at sea.

One warm October night when John and Laura came off the dancefloor to sit at a table and cool off with a glass of lemonade they were approached by a lean man wearing a seersucker suit and a white skimmer. "Pardon me," the man said. His angular face seemed carved of stained oak. He leaned on the table and said in lower voice, "Might you be John Ashley?"

He spoke with a soft drawl that was neither of Florida nor Georgia. John Ashley wondered if he might be a cop even though his manner bespoke the city and he did not look the type common to the local police department. The Miami chief was partial to hiring beefy young crackers for his force, most of them plowboys whom he enlisted off farms all over Florida and even up in Georgia by way of itinerant agents he'd send out on recruiting missions a few times a year. The plowboys were all tough and afraid of nothing and deeply beholden to the chief for a livelihood other than the backbreaking dullness of life on a farm. They were loyal to him as dogs. And as cultural kin to South Florida crackers they spoke a common language. This lean fellow of quick dark eyes was of another tribe.

John Ashley casually leaned on the table and surreptitiously put his hand to the pistol under his jacket. The day before, he had delivered his father's monthly contribution to the Miami Police Chief's "civic fund," and he did not really think this was a plainclothesman sent to serve warrant. The chief held no quarrel with the Ashleys—nor with any other association of entrepreneurs, however outside the law their enterprise might be—so long as they did not commit robberies or public violence within the city limits and so long as they made regular donation to his fund. The chief would not in any case have sent a lone man to arrest an Ashley and never mind three of the brothers at once. This one could be a detective thinking to solicit for some civic fund of his own. The world was full of fools who knew no better and John Ashley thought this might be one of them.

"Who's askin?" John Ashley said.

"Somebody who might put you onto somethin I think you'd like to know about. Somethin that might make us some money."

"Us?" John Ashley said. He exchanged a look with Laura who seemed somewhat amused by the stranger.

On the dancefloor with redhaired Glenda—more than a year older than he and two inches taller, even in flats—Hanford Mobley whispered in her ear that he couldnt wait to give Mister Cooter a kiss when they got back to their room at the hotel. Mister Cooter was their pet name for the small green turtle he'd a week ago persuaded her to have tattooed just below her navel. The tattoo artist had done the job behind a drawn curtain and had smiled the whole time he worked on her smooth belly under the skirt bunched at her waist. Now Hanford Mobley caught sight of the skimmered man talking to John Ashley and he danced Glenda over toward the bandstand in front of which Ed Ashley was whirling with Rita the Breed to the strains of "A Pretty Girl Is Like a Melody." Some of the couples nearest Ed and Rita would gape on catching sight of her face and she'd whisper to Ed and he'd turn to the gawkers and they'd gawk no more.

Hanford Mobley tapped Ed's shoulder and gestured toward the table. Ed looked over there and nodded and then deftly maneuvered Rita through the other dancers until they were near enough to Frank and Jenny for him to catch Frank's eye and direct it to the stranger with John. Then all three couples danced their way toward the table.

The man made bold to sit without invitation. He removed his hat to expose freshly barbered brown hair neatly combed straight back and brightly oiled. He smelled of bay rum. His upper lip was lighter than the rest of his face and John Ashley suspected he had recently shaved a mustache. A short broad scratch was crusted darkly on his left cheekbone. "*Us* is me and you all," he said. He put his hand out to John Ashley across the table. "Name's Matthews. Roy Matthews."

John Ashley regarded the hand for a moment. The fellow might be city mannered but the calluses and knucklescars on his hands informed that he had known both hard work and skirmish. Any Miami policeman was likely to have such hands but something of this Matthews' aspect and in the cast of his eyes now decided John Ashley that the man was no cop. He shook the proffered hand and leaned back and said, "If you tryin to interest me in the real estate around here, bubba, save it for the suckers."

"What if I was tryin to innerest you in somebody who's runnin whiskey through Palm Beach County?"

John looked at Laura who raised her brow. And now Frank spun Jenny so close to their table her skirt brushed John Ashley's arm. Then Hanford Mobley whirled Glenda past the table and John Ashley grinned at his narrow-eyed nephew.

Roy Matthews glanced up at them too. Then said to John Ashley: "*Besides* you all I mean."

John Ashley's smile eased off his face. "What you mean?"

"There's somethin I want first."

The number ended and Frank and Ed Ashley came to the table with their arms around their girls to listen in and look more closely on the stranger. Hanford Mobley moved up behind John and Laura, Glenda beside him and holding to his arm with both hands. When Roy Matthews' gaze fixed on her for a moment, she flushed and averted her eyes.

"I asked you what you mean," John Ashley said.

"I want in," Roy Matthews said. "Whatever you do with this, I want in on it."

"On *what*, dammit?"

The band surged into "Second-Hand Rose" and the floor once again began to spin with dancing couples.

"Tell me I'm in."

"You might could be in your grave you dont tell me what I'm askin."

Roy Matthews sighed deeply and regarded John Ashley with a bored look. "I aint been scared in so long I dont even remember what it feels like. I'm gettin up and leavin if you dont say I'm in."

Hanford Mobley said, "You aint doin a damn thing but what we—"

John Ashley cut him short with an impatient wave of his hand. Hanford reddened but held silent. John stared at Roy Matthews as if trying to hear the man's thoughts. Then smiled. "Bedamn if you dont believe you some kinda hardcase, dont you? What'd you say you name was—Ray?"

"Roy."

"All right, *Roy,* you're in. There. *Now* tell me what I just let you in on."

Roy Matthews smiled tightly and leaned over the table and said in low voice, "This bunch from Chicago, they're bossing a big clan of moonshiners in Georgia and they're runnin the stuff from those camps down to Miami."

John Ashley stared at him. "That's right," Roy Matthews said. "Right down the Dixie Highway. Right through Palm Beach. And I dont mean a few cases at a time. I mean they're runnin truckloads. Sometimes one truck and sometimes two or more at a time. Might be only a coupla hundred cases come down one time and then five or six hundred the next. Depends on how many trucks and how big they are."

"God *damn,*" Frank said. John Ashley glared at him and Frank said, "Well I dont like it, Johnny, and I dont give a shit who knows it."

"I didnt quess you would care for it," Roy Matthews said. "Nary you."

"Daddy aint gonna be real happy about it for damn sure," Ed said.

"It aint all," Roy Matthews said. "They bringin in stuff from the islands too. But there's so much Coast Guard off Miami and Lauderdale it's too big a risk anymore to beach the booze there. A coupla weeks ago they started puttin some of it off in Palm Beach and drivin it down the rest of the way."

The Ashley Gang men exchanged narrow looks.

"Might innerest you to know," Roy Matthews said, "some New York fellas tried gettin in on the Miami trade too but the Chicago boys pretty quick discouraged them. Chicago wants Miami for theirself, I mean to tell you."

"Discouraged them New York fellas how?" Ed Ashley asked.

"How?" Roy Matthews said. "Told them they wanted to talk about bein partners. Took a couple of them for a boat ride on the Gulf Stream. About a mile out they got the jump on them and tied them hand and foot and hung a concrete block around their neck and gave them a little push over the side. All but their ears. Sent their ears back to their bosses in New York by way of the U.S. mail." He took his time about lighting a cigarette. "They know all about you fellas. Know all about your daddy bein the big-dog moonshiner round here. They probly gonna want to see him pretty soon, talk some business. They probly wanna talk to him about bein partners."

John Ashley's eyes were gone thin. "Tell me somethin, Roy. How you know so much about it?"

Matthews blew a blue plume of smoke at the overhead lights. "I was workin for them Chicago boys until recent. A friend of mine in Memphis knew a fella who knew a fella who got us hired on as load runners to Miami. Job like that, you hear things now and then, here and there. You know how it is."

"How come you tellin *us*?" John Ashley said.

Roy Matthews took a deep drag and exhaled a series of small perfect smoke rings to sail slowly between John and Laura and bear directly for Glenda's nipples jutting against the clinging bodice of her satin dress. Hanford Mobley abruptly batted the rings to haze before they lit on her. Glenda had started to smile and then blushed brightly and seemed not to know where to direct her eyes. Hanford Mobley glared furiously at Roy Matthews who affected not to notice.

"The fella who runs things for Chicago in this town," Roy Matthews said, "is a sumbitch named Bellamy—excuse my language, ladies." He smiled with boyish rue at the women, who all showed smiles in return. Frank looked at Ed and rolled his eyes.

"Anyhow," Roy Matthews said, "him and my friend Cormac never did like each other for spit. He shorted us on our cut the last two deliveries we made and we knew it. So last week we went over to the Taft Hotel to see him about it. Now it so happens I dont like this Bellamy even more than Cormac dont like him, so Cormac figured it'd be better if just him went up to see him and I wait downstairs. That was all right by me. So I'm waiting around in the lobby and old Cormac hadnt been up there five minutes before there's gunshots. I look over and the desk clerk's gone, the bellboy, everdamnbody's gone. It's just me in that lobby. Then I hear them comin down the stairs and I can tell it's more than one and I'm already headed for the back door when they come off the landing and I see they got guns in their hands and brother I hit that door on the fly. I hear *bam* and a chunk of wood tears off the doorjamb yay close to my head and thats how I got this scratch here. I run down so many alleys and crawled under so many cars and clumb over so many fences that by the time I was sure I'd lost them I was damn well lost myself. I looked like somethin the cat drug in, I mean to tell you."

"They were shootin in a goddamn *hotel*?" Frank Ashley said. "Didnt it bring a bunch of cops down on them?"

"Well now I wasnt around to find out. But the Taft's been their headquarters since before I started runnin hooch for Bellamy and ever cop I ever saw in there was gettin his palm greened or was havin hisself a drink or was there for a free one with one of the third-floor girls. I'd say if the shootin brung any cops it was only from upstairs to tell them hold the noise down."

Ed Ashley said, "Hell, you could fire a machinegun in this town and nobody's hear it a block away or pay it any mind if they did, it's always so damn much noise in the street."

"Why they wanna shoot you and your partner anyway?" Frank Ashley said.

"*Why?*" Roy Matthews said. "Well I'd guess old Cormac probly irritated the man some, dont you reckon? Irritated or scared him, one. Maybe he told him pay up what he owed us or else, and Bellamy figured or else meant he best shoot Cormac while he had the chance— then me too for bein the partner. Hell man, I dont know why and I dont give a damn. Coupla sumbitches—scuse me ladies—coupla fellas come at you with guns in they hand you dont stand there and ask how come they upset. *Why* dont matter a damn. *What's* all that counts—and they tried to shoot me is the what of it."

John Ashley smiled. "So you're gonna get even by tellin us where they're landin the stuff and we take it from them."

"And I get a cut," Roy Matthews said.

"Hell, boy, what makes you think we need your help to find where they landin their booze?" Ed Ashley said.

"I guess you dont," Roy Matthews said. "I'm just hopin you'll do the sportin thing and let me in on it since I'm the one who told you."

Hanford Mobley snorted and said sardonically, "The *sportin* thing."

"We'd of heard about it soon enough," Frank Ashley said. "Dont nothin happen in Palm Beach County we dont hear about it soon enough."

Roy Matthews nodded. "I reckon. Still, I'm the one brung it to you first."

Hanford Mobley said maybe they ought to go over to the Taft Hotel and see this Bellamy fellow and ask him if Matthews was telling the truth. "If this one's tellin us true." Hanford said, gesturing at Roy

Matthews, "we can take care of Bellamy right then and there. And if this one's lyin, well, we can take care of that too."

John Ashley chuckled. "Hey now, Hannie, we dont want to go startin no war." He looked at Roy Matthews. "He's sore-assed about them smoke rings is what it is. Tell him you didnt mean nothing by it."

Roy Matthews glanced at Hanford Mobley and then turned back at John Ashley with a look that wondered if he was kidding.

"Be best if you tell him," John Ashley said. "He dont fool that way with other people and dont care to have them fool that way with him."

Roy Matthews shrugged and turned to Hanford Mobley and said, "Sorry boy. I didnt mean ary thing." He put his hand out to him.

Hanford Mobley stared at him. Glenda nudged him and stage-whispered, "*Han*-nie! Dont be mean. Do it." Hanford exhaled loudly and took Roy Matthews' hand.

"All right then," John Ashley, "let's get on over to the hotel where we can talk some more about this over a jug."

As they all headed out of the dancehall and toward the stairway the band was playing "I'm Always Chasing Rainbows." Frank and Ed Ashley were groping at their girls who squealed and pulled away in feigned protest at their liberties. John Ashley was pointing out to Laura a particularly graceful pair of dancers and Hanford Mobley was admiring them too. None among them saw Glenda glance back at Roy Matthews over her shoulder nor see the wink he gave her nor the quick wide smile she showed him in return.

They took Roy Matthews out to Twin Oaks and introduced him to Old Joe and let him tell their father what he'd told them. Lambent sunlight filtered through the tall oaks flanking the house and made pale yellow mottles on the pine-needled ground. A family of scrub jays clamored in the high branches. Old Joe listened to Roy Matthews and then spat off the porch and went through the ritual of loading and lighting his pipe before saying he wasnt surprised the Yankee gangsters were bringing their booze through Palm Beach. "Hell, they bound to been doin it for a while and we just now findin out about it because we aint been payin no kinda attention worth a damn."

Bill Ashley sat beside his father on the porch. He took off his spectacles and held them up against the light to check for cleanliness. "I told you this problem was like to come up," he said.

Old Joe turned a thin look on him. There were times when Bill's know-it-all manner could wear on him as much as it did on his brothers. "Yes, you did tell me that, boy. And I told you we'd do somethin about it when it happened."

Bill fit the glasses back on his face and looked at his father for a moment without expression and then stared off at the swamp pines.

"It aint right, Gramps," Hanford Mobley said. "Them bringin they whiskey right smack through our territory without so much as a by-your-leave."

Old Joe grinned wide at Hanford Mobley and turned to his sons and said, "Listen at him. Damn pit bull, ready to tear ass."

Now he fixed his attention on Clarence Middleton who was sitting on the ground beside the porch steps with his back against the lattice-work fronting the crawlspace, legs crossed at the ankles, hands folded on his stomach, eyes closed. He'd just returned from another night with his girlfriend Terrianne in St. Lucie and his face was sagged with fatigue and lack of sleep. Every few minutes he'd wince and hustle his balls to ease the ache of their strained condition. Over the past two months he seen the girl every night that he wasnt out on a rum run, and his exhaustion was beginning to tell.

"You, Clarence," Old Joe said, and Clarence Middleton opened one watery red eye to look up at him. "You best ease up on all that hunchin or we gone have to wrung you out that girl's bedsheets one these mornings. You listening to me, boy?"

Clarence sighed heavily and shut his eyes.

Old Joe smiled at him and then turned to Roy Matthews. "Tell me, young fella, you know boats?"

"Grew up in Myrtle Beach and learned to sail when I was but ten year old," Roy Matthews said. "Know motors too. Aint ary kinda boat I cant handle nor motor vehicle I cant drive."

"Real high-powered package, aint he?" Hanford Mobley said with heavy sarcasm. Old Joe gave him a smiling glance. Roy Matthews ignored him.

"Myrtle Beach, hey?" Old Joe said to Roy Matthews. "That aint where you spent your first years though was it? You didnt learn to talk in no part of South Caroline. Say you was borned in Tennessee?"

"I didnt say," Roy Matthews said.

"You surely did, boy," Old Joe said. "Said so with the first word come out your mouth. East part I say."

Roy Matthews grinned. "You say about right. Borned and spent my first years just outside Rogersville."

"Reckoned it was thereabouts," Old Joe said. He leaned back and scratched his chin, then swept his hard gaze over them all and said:

"Anybody bringing whiskey through our territory has got to pay us a tax."

The others looked at each other. Then Frank Ashley whooped. "A *tax*! Damn, daddy! Who you think we are, the *government*?"

"Well boy, if we aint the government of ourselfs, who is?" Old Joe said.

Ed Ashley laughed. "Bobby Baker'd have an answer to that."

"Piss on Bobby Baker," John Ashley said. "Him and the mangy-ass dog he rode in on."

The Ashley boys and Hanford Mobley all laughed and grinned at each other. Clarence Middleton chuckled with his eyes closed. And even Bill Ashley's eyes were bright with excitement behind his spectacles.

They posted lookouts along the Dixie Highway about ten miles apart and ranging from Fort Pierce in St. Lucie County all the way down to just above Palm Beach County's southern line. Each lookout was kin or a trustworthy hired man of Joe Ashley's and each was positioned near a telephone. Some were set up on secondary roads that connected with the main highway at points between Stuart and Delray. Three or four of the gang at a time were now living in a pinelands camp just outside of Boynton Beach near the south county line and a scant quarter mile from the highway. Their Boynton lookout could get word to the camp in twenty minutes of any suspected whis-key carrier reported by telephone to be coming their way, and in min-utes the gang could be on its way to intercept the load.

Their first stop was a truck just south of Jupiter. They got report of the truck and its description from their Fort Pierce lookout and then drove north to a desolate spot flanking Hobe Sound and parked the car on the highway's narrow shoulder alongside the palmetto thickets. John Ashley and Hanford Mobley and Roy Matthews got out and hid in the bush. Clarence Middleton raised one of the Ford's hood flaps and stood smoking a cigarette and leaning on a fender. The midmorn-ing was bright and clear and passing traffic was sparse. One motorist stopped and asked if he needed help and Clarence thanked him and said help was on the way and the motorist waved and went on.

When the truck came into view Clarence stepped out on the road and raised his hand. The truck slowed and started to go around him but he sidestepped in front of it again and the driver braked hard and the truck halted on the wrong side of the road. The man sitting on the passenger side was wearing a Chicago White Sox baseball cap and he stuck his head out and began to curse Clarence for a fool. Then John Ashley and Hanford Mobley and Roy Matthews came out of the trees with shotguns ready and the man shut up.

John Ashley directed the driver to park the truck on the shoulder and turn off the motor. The two men then got out of the truck as ordered and John Ashley told them to keep their hands down at their sides while Hanford Mobley quickly searched them and found a revolver on each one. On the floor of the truck cab he found a shotgun and he took it and the pistols to the Ford and laid the weapons on the rear seat. He put up their own shotguns too and they went to their .45's.

"Car comin!" Clarence Middleton called. John Ashley and Hanford Mobley hid their Colts against their legs and John walked up to the driver and put an arm over his shoulder in the manner of an old friend. A roadster made its way toward them. Hanford Mobley affected to engage the baseball-capped man in conversation as Clarence leaned over the sedan's exposed motor like a man at repairs and Roy Matthews knelt in the grass and slowly retied his shoes. Now the roadster came abreast and at the wheel was a young man wearing a duster and goggles and a car cap and beside him a pretty girl in a summer dress who brushed her wild blonde hair from her face and smiled at them one and all as the car sped past in a pale cloud of dust. They all looked after the roadster a for a moment, and then Clarence Middleton said, "Kiss my ass if that aint one lucky sumbitch!"

The highway again lay deserted in both directions but for the turkey buzzards that lit from the pines to the shoulder some fifty yards up the road to feed on the crushed and moldering carcass of a possum whose stench came faintly to the men where they stood,.

John Ashley and Hanford Mobley again brandished their guns and the man in the Sox cap said, "What is this, a robbery? You want our money?" He was a tall lean man with prematurely gray hair cropped close as a convict's. A short but vivid purple scar curved from the corner of his mouth to just under his chin.

John Ashley laughed at him. He went to the truck and loosened the rope holding a tarp cover across the back of the enclosed bed and he lifted a corner of the tarp and looked in and gave a low chuckle. He asked the driver how many cases it was. The driver glanced at the man in the Sox cap and John Ashley looked at him too and the man hesitated and then said fifty. Hanford Mobley and Clarence Middleton grinned.

Now the man in the Sox cap spotted Roy Matthews and looked

at him hard and said, "Well hell now, look who's here. I heard you and your Scotchman buddy had a fatal accident down in Miami."

"I'd say you heard half-wrong, White," Roy Matthews said. He was smiling broadly.

"So now you're in with these jackers? Bellamy'll have your ass for breakfast."

"Bellamy best pray he dont never see me again."

The man called White gave a derisive snort. "Bold talk." He looked around at the others. "Must be all these hillbilly guns makes you so bold."

"Who you callin hillbilly, you son of a bitch?" Hanford Mobley said.

"Hell, it aint hardly a hill *in* Florida," Clarence Middleton said. "Everbody knows that except dumbass Yankees."

White smiled and said, "Sorry, friend. I guess Roy's just feeling brave because he's in your company. I think I know who you gents are, but I'd rather not guess." When he smiled the scar on his chin went thinner and lightened almost to blue.

"Name's Ashley," John told him. "Palm Beach is our grounds. You ask anybody. Any whiskey you bring through this county anymore is gonna cost you a tax of ten dollars a case. It'll cost you five hundred dollars to take these here fifty cases on through."

"A *tax*?" White said. He looked around as if suddenly unsure of where he was or if he ought to laugh. "Listen," he said, "if I *had* the fucken money on me I wouldnt pay it, not to you guys. This here's a public road, brother. We got as much right to use it as anybody." He smiled at the folly of his own argument.

"I aint your brother," John Ashley said. "And considerin how much you stand to make on this load in Miami, I'd say five hundred is a fair cut to us for lettin you take it by. It's anyway cheaper than losin your whole entire load like you gonna do."

White heaved an exaggerated sigh. "Do you know whose booze you're stealing?"

"Sure do," John Ashley said. "A fella's who wouldnt pay us the tax on it."

White showed a wry smile. "Say your name's Ashley?"

"That's right."

"Which one are you?" White said.

"John. You heard of us, huh? What's your name?"

"James White," the man said. "Some people as soon as you're introduced to them as James think it's all right to call you Jim, but I let them know pretty quick I dont care much for that name. Care even less for Jimmy."

"Where you from, Jimmy?"

James White laughed. "Chicago."

John Ashley said, "Ah."

"You heard of it, huh?" James White said. "Listen, you gonna take the truck too?"

John Ashley spat to the side and grinned. "Well you dont reckon I'm gonna bust a sweat hauling all that booze out of your truck just to heave it up on mine?" He gestured at Hanford Mobley and the boy hastened to the truck cab and set the levers and got out the crank and went around to the front of the vehicle and cranked the motor and it fired up on the first try. He got in the driver's seat and tooted the Klaxon in sheer exuberance, then put the truck in gear and it lurched into motion and he wheeled out onto the road. They all watched it move away down the highway until it clattered around a bend and was gone.

James White let another long sigh. "How far to the nearest depot?"

"Olympia station, back the way you came," John Ashley said. "Aint but a few miles."

White tugged his White Sox cap low on his eyes and put his hands in his pockets. "You know, John: there's people in Miami gonna be real unhappy about this. I'm responsible for the transfer of our Georgia stuff. I've got other drivers working for me. I got a half-dozen trucks to keep track of. You're making me look bad at my work is what you're doing."

"Damn if that aint a sad story, Jimmy," John Ashley said. "But the plain and simple of it is, we cant have somebody else making money by runnin whiskey through our territory without us gettin a share of it. I know you can understand that."

"Oh hell yeah, John, I understand it just fine. But I dont think my bosses are gonna be near so understanding."

"You explain it to them real good and maybe they will be," John Ashley said. "They're businessmen. They know taxes is part of doin business. They dont wanna pay the tax they can either take their hooch around Palm Beach County or they can lose it to us." He headed for the Ford. Clarence Middleton was already behind the wheel and Roy Matthews in the backseat.

James White morosely shook his head. "You're fucking with the wrong people, John."

"Tell Bellamy I said his momma sucks nigger dicks," Roy Matthews called back to him.

"You always been a silvertongue, Roy," James White said.

Then Clarence Middleton was accelerating the Ford down the road and all three of them were laughing and James White and his driver stood in the raised dust and watched them go.

The next one came through at night and didnt even slow down nor try to go swerve around Clarence Middleton who stood stark in its headlights and was obliged to dive off the road and into the palmettos to avoid being run over. As the truck roared past them John Ashley and Hanford Mobley and Roy Matthews opened fire on its wheels and the flaming rifleshots blew out three of its tires. The truck veered and then straightened out and tried to go on with its useless tires flapping and its rims cutting rasping grooves in the whiterock road but the engine was laboring hard and now it began stuttering under the heavy drag and the truck slowed steadily and finally stalled. And here came John Ashley and Hanford Mobley and Roy Matthews on the run through the dust with Clarence Middleton behind them and cursing the bastards who'd tried to run him down but by the time they got to the vehicle the driver and shotgun rider had fled into the woods.

They repaired the flattened tires and took turns on the air pump and when all the tires were inflated Clarence got in the truck and drove the load of booze to Twin Oaks with John Ashley and Hanford Mobley following close in the Ford touring car.

Some weeks later, on a cool January evening, John Ashley and Hanford Mobley lay hidden among the sea oats on the crest of a Jupiter Island sand dune and watched a whiskey sloop bobbing easily on the swells fifty yards offshore as it unloaded its cargo. Although the bigger rumships that could carry several thousand cases were now careful to conduct their load transfers outside the three mile limit of the Coast Guard's legal authority, the captain of this sloop obviously had no fear of doing business so close to shore. A trio of large motorboats operating without running lights was nestled against the sloop's hull and taking on the booze. The Ashley gang had pulled a half-dozen road hijackings by now but this was their first beach job.

They could see that the booze was in sacks instead of wooden crates. The smugglers were always learning new tricks for their trade and this was a recent one in the way they packed whiskey for transport. The bottles were now commonly packed in burlap sacks jacketed with straw—three to six bottles to the sack—and the sack tied tightly to hold the bottles snugly together. Because of the resemblance, these booze sacks were called hams. They made for easier handling and more compact loading. Twice as much liquor could be put in a cargo hold when it was packed in hams rather than crates, and pairs of hams tied together with lengths of cord could be hung around a man's neck for portage from beach to trucks. Frank and Ed Ashley themselves now insisted that the whiskeyloads they took aboard the *Della* in the Bahamas be packed as hams.

The Ashleys had also adopted another common rummer's trick, one intended to avoid capture with a load of booze. They securely glued a light ball of cork about as big as a baseball to a fist-sized bag of salt, then tied one end of a six-fathom length of fishing line to the cork and the other end to a ham, then hung the coiled line over the neck of the ham. They did this with about dozen hams in every load. If it should ever look to them like they were going to be intercepted by the Coast Guard, they would jettison the load before they hove to— and then later, after the salt dissolved and released the cork markers to bob to the surface, they could come back and use divers to retrieve the cargo.

They knew the tactic was not assured of success. They had heard stories of rummers who dumped their loads in water too deep for the markers to reach the surface. And of instances when somebody else came along and spied the markers and stole the whiskey before the rummers could come back for it. Smuggling was a lucrative enterprise precisely because it was fraught with risk. To the outsiders now landing their booze in Palm Beach County, the Ashley Gang was about to present itself as one of the more severe risks in the business.

A dozen yards fore of the sloop a school of silvery fish broke the water in a sparkling phosphorescent rush ahead of a pursuing pack of dark dorsal fins. A half-moon pale as a skull hung high in the east. The sky was cloudless and swarming with stars. A cool saltwind came softly off the ocean. John Ashley felt the beauty of this world as a tight clutching in his chest. A comet cut across the night in a fine bright-yellow streak and vanished in the measureless void and he wondered if it now existed anywhere at all.

Between the island and the mainland was the Jupiter Narrows, a labyrinthine tangle of mangrove channels pungent with marine decay. At this location the channels were shallow enough to ford and on the mainland side of the Narrows an oystershell trail had been hacked through the mangroves and laid to a clearing in the hardwoods and pines farther inland. The clearing stood within a hundred yards of the Dixie Highway but was fully hidden from its view. A pair of trucks was waiting there to receive the whiskey. In each of the cabs sat a driver and a guard, smoking and quietly talking, unaware of being watched from the trees by Roy Matthews and Clarence Middleton, both of whom held shotguns charged with buckshot.

Now the transfer was complete and the motorboats swung away from the sloop and came churning for the beach, their motors rapping on the night air. Behind them the sloop weighed anchor and hoisted sail and made away on the wind like a pale phantom. The motorboats rose and dipped over the swells and came through the cut in the bar where the waves broke. The pilots throttled back their engines and the boats glided up onto the beach in front of a line of dunes some thirty yards from where John Ashley and Hanford Mobley lay watching.

A shore party of ten men scrambled from the shadows and began unloading the booze. Soon all the hams were on the beach and the motorboats were heading for open water again and bursting through the combers in sprays of spume and then one after another veering to the south and a minute later not even their foamy wakes were in evidence.

The men of the shore party now hung hams around their necks and began trudging over the dunes and through the sea oats and down to the meager mangrove path leading to the Narrows. One man was left on the beach to watch over the rest of the whiskey. The shore party filed into the shallow lagoon and made their way across under the blazing moon.

The Ashley Gang waited and watched—John Ashley and Hanford Mobley from the dunes, Clarence Middleton and Roy Matthews from the trees at the edge of the clearing—watched as the shore party went back and forth over the Narrows, carrying whiskey to the trucks. When the last of the hams was retrieved from the beach, John Ashley and Hanford Mobley followed the shore party at a distance through the mangroves and across the Narrows and into the trees. They hung back in the shadows while the last sacks of whiskey were put aboard the trucks under the supervision of one of the drivers, a man wearing a longbilled fishing cap. Illuminated by a pair of kerosene lanterns hung on a pine branch, the clearing was cast in a ghostly yellow light. The shore party spoke little as it went about its work. Then the fishing-capped man pulled down in turn the rear tarpaulin flap on each truck and tied it snugly in place and the trucks were ready to go.

John Ashley and Hanford Mobley stepped out of the shadows and

took positions a dozen feet apart and aimed their cocked shotguns at
the guards and drivers. John Ashley said, "You even think about them
pistols on your hips, boys, and your brains'll be all over the bushes."
The drivers and guards put their hands up and stood still but for
breathing.

Some in the shore party glanced around as if thinking to bolt. But
now Clarence Middleton and Roy Matthews appeared from the darkness of the trees with their shotguns ready and Clarence Middleton
said, "Stand fast, cousins."

John Ashley ordered them all to clasp their hands on top of their
heads and then told everybody in the shore party except the drivers
and guards to bunch up in the middle of the clearing. Hanford Mobley
hastened for the pump shotguns the truck guards had left propped
against a pine tree. He pitched one to Clarence Middleton and one to
Roy Matthews and now they both brandished a shotgun in each hand
like a pair of huge pistols. Mobley then went to the drivers and relieved
them of the revolvers in their hip holsters—a .38 and a .44 caliber. He
tucked the .38 in his waistband and lobbed the bigger piece to John
Ashley, who kept it in hand.

"Hey, Johnny," Hanford Mobley said, "lookit here who's ridin
with these boys."

One of the truck guards had been trying to keep his face averted
from the light and shielded by his upraised arms. He was short and
thickshouldered and when he looked directly at Mobley and grinned
his mouth looked almost toothless for the blackness of his teeth. It was
Phil Dolan who operated the trading post on the Salerno docks. "How
do, Hannie," he said. "How you keepin?"

"Well damn, Phil," John Ashley said, coming up to him, "what
you doin ridin shotgun for this bunch?"

Dolan showed an abashed smile. "Aw hell, it's just for the money
is all. I aint been doing a lot of business lately. The trappers're havin
to go way out farther in the Glades than they used to get a full load
of hides. You know thats true, John. Nowadays by the time they get
theirselfs a load they usually closer to the Okeechobee or the Indiantown trade posts. They aint about to tow them hides all the way
back to me if they can sell them just as good over there. I mean, my
business gone all to hell recent, I aint lyin."

He'd been talkin rapidly and now paused to lick his lips. The look
he gave John Ashley beseeched understanding. "A while back these
fellers come to my place and said they was from Miami and they'd
pay me two hundred dollars for ever back road I could show them

through Palm Beach County and another hundred for just ridin with the trucks when they come through. Said they'd pay me another two hundred for ever good spot I could show them for unloading stuff on the beach. Well hell, John, I couldnt rightly turn down no offer like that, now could I?"

"Dont look like you could, Phil," John Ashley said. He was surprised to be bothered as much as he was by the fact of a local cracker in the employ of the Yankee bootleggers. He nodded at the man with the fishing cap and said, "This the party chief?"

Phil Dolan glanced at the fishing-capped man and nodded.

"I can talk for myself," the party chief said.

John Ashley told him to shut up. Then asked Dolan: "Who were these fellas sweet-talked you so easy, Phil?"

"They had Yankee accents, the both them. Wore suits. They never said their names and I never asked. I heard one say they worked for a fella called Ben Mead, I think he said. But—"

"Bellamy," Roy Matthews said.

Phil Dolan glanced at him and shrugged. "Could be, I guess. Anyway, it wasnt sweet-talk like you say, Johnny. It was just the money, is all. You should see the money they had. Big roll of hundred-dollar bills like you wouldnt believe. Said they'd pay me in advance and then did it. Hell Johnny, how was I gonna turn down somethin like that? Would you have, you was me?"

"I aint you, Phil," John Ashley said. His impassive air unnerved Phil Dolan the more.

"Oh hell, John," he said, "it's just the money, man. It dont mean nothin."

The party chief hawked and spat. He was stocky and wore several days' growth of whiskers. The look he held on Phil Dolan was hard with disdain. The other driver and guard looked as fearful as Dolan.

"How about that shotgun you was carryin, Phil," Hanford Mobley said. He'd perceived John Ashley's intention to make Phil Dolan sweat a little for going on the Bellamy payroll and he thought to get in on the fun. "Aint that for shootin anybody tries to hijack this load?" He was smiling at Dolan's fear. The men of the shore party stood still as a painting.

"Jesus, I wouldnt shoot none of *you,* Hannie," Phil Dolan said, his face gone even paler now. He knew John Ashley for a reasonable man but Hanford Mobley was of a more volatile nature. He turned back to John Ashley and said, "It's just for show, that shotgun, it's just . . . ah hell. Johnny, you wouldnt shoot *me?*" His attempt at a smile was pitiful. "We *know* each other, man. We done business for years, you and me."

"Quit your whining, you pussy son of a bitch," the party chief said.

John Ashley turned to tell him that if he said another word without permission he'd break his jaw—and in that instant Phil Dolan broke for the trees and Roy Matthews shouted, "Watch it, Johnny!"

All in one motion John Ashley whirled and raised the revolver and fired. The pistol blasted an orange streak and bucked hard in his hand and a chunk of Phil Dolan's skull jumped off his head and Dolan lunged forward with his arms out to his sides like he was flinging himself into the surf. He lit on his face and lay still.

A pair of shotguns boomed almost simultaneously and John Ashley spun in a crouch with the revolver ready and saw Hanford Mobley and Roy Matthews jacking fresh shells and both of them looking to the edge of the woods where the party chief lay in an awkward tangle a few feet shy of the trees which was as far as he'd gotten before the buckshot took him down. In the hazy lantern light his left forearm was ripped open to the bones and his back looked scooped of a spadeful of flesh and rib to expose to the indifferent stars his mutilated organs. The air smelled of gunsmoke.

Everyone held mute. John Ashley slowly lowered his gun and turned and walked over to Phil Dolan and stared down at the lanternlit spill of blood and brainmatter around his broken skull. You dumb cracker, he thought—it wasnt no need. He wasnt sure if his thoughts were directed at Phil Dolan or himself or both. He stood perplexed by his own angry sorrow.

He saw Clarence Middleton looking serious and Hanford Mobley grinning widely at nobody in particular. Roy Matthews was squatting beside the shotgunned man and now looked over at John Ashley and shook his head. The men of the shore party had all put their hands up high. They looked terrified. "Put your hands down," John Ashley said to the shore party, and some did, and some put them back on top of their heads, and some seemed reluctant to bring them down at all.

"I said put them *down,* goddammit!" John Ashley shouted. "Not on your head, just *down!*" He looked ready to shoot them all. Some of them were petty criminals but most were simply unemployed laborers who'd thought themselves lucky to be recruited for the shore party. Excepting two veterans of the Great War and a man who'd seen one bum stab another to death in a St. Louis alleyfight, none among them had ever before witnessed a killing.

John Ashley sighed heavily and put the revolver in his waistband and rested the shotgun barrel against his shoulder and rubbed his face hard. He regarded the frightened men before him, then walked up and looked closely into every man's face in turn. Then he directed Clarence Middleton to give each man five dollars. As Clarence dispensed the money, John Ashley told them they had until sunup to get out of Palm Beach County. They could not go back to Dade. They could not go south at all. They could go only north to at least Jacksonville or north-westward to at least Pensacola. "Be best if you get all the way out the state," John Ashley said. "Now I know what all you look like and I never forget a face. I ever see any of you anywhere in Florida outside of Jacksonville or Pensacola, I wont even ask you what you're doin. I'll just shoot you where you stand. Do you all believe me?"

They nodded, all of them quickeyed and tightfaced. John Ashley told them to get on the trucks, he was taking them to the train station. The men loosened the tarp covers and clambered aboard and positioned themselves carefully so as not to upset the hams. When every man of them was on the trucks, John Ashley and Hanford Mobley drew down the tarps and tied them tightly in place. Then John took Roy Matthews and Clarence Middleton aside and told them to dispose of the bodies where they wouldn't be found.

An hour later John Ashley and Hanford Mobley were watching the Midnight Flyer pulling out of the West Palm Beach station with its whistle shrieking and its smokestack huffing high black plumes and tossing sparks as the train headed for Jacksonville and points north with all ten men of the shore party aboard. At the same moment, Clarence Middleton and Roy Matthews, with a pair of dead men stretched at their feet, were on an eighteen-foot launch cutting through the ocean and heading for the Gulf Stream under the high half-moon. When they reached the Stream they would cut back the motor and the boat would rise and fall on the silvery swells as they tied concrete blocks to the dead men's feet and cut their bellies open with a buck knife and felt the boat bottom go slick under their shoes. They would roll the bodies over the side to plunge into the dark fastrunning depths with blood billowing and intestines uncoiling and sharks closing fast to rid the world of all mortal evidence that these men did ever exist.

SEVENTEEN

February–June 1921

OVER THE NEXT FOUR MONTHS THEY HIJACKED NEARLY A DOZEN
truckloads of booze coming through on Palm Beach County roads
and another half-dozen shipments that landed at various beaches
along the county shoreline. The word was out among rumrunners in
Florida: you paid the tribute the Ashleys demanded or you risked
having them hijack your load—or you found some roundabout route
to bypass their territory and get your stuff to Miami. Some of the
runners coming through Palm Beach were smalltimers trying to build
up their portion of Miami trade and most of them grudgingly paid off
the Ashleys rather than lose their cargoes. But Nelson Bellamy stead-
fastly refused to pay for the right to move his product through Palm
Beach County. Now and then one of his crews managed to sneak a
load through Palm Beach without being spotted, but the Ashley Gang
continued to intercept most of his truck imports and beach drops and
cut deeply into his profits.

From the time of their first hijackings Gordon Blue had pleaded with
them to desist from stealing Nelson Bellamy's booze. "Take anybody else's
stuff but not his," Blue told them one afternoon at Twin Oaks. "He works
for the Chicago organization, for God's sake. I represent his legal interests
down here. He knows I represent you too, but he says he doesnt hold me
responsible for your actions. That's what he *says*. But every time you jack
one of his shipments, he gives *me* a hard look. You're putting me in a
tight spot with the Miami people, boys, is what I'm saying."

"If he's so mad at us, why aint he done nothin about it when we're in Miami?" Frank Ashley said. "We're down there all the time—dancin at the Elser, eatin in restaurants. We do a little gamblin in Hardieville, we stay in hotels. It aint hard to find us. If he's so mad why aint he tried to shoot our ass off like he tried that one time with old Roy here?"

"Believe me, Frank, he would if he thought he could get away with it," Gordon Blue said. "But the chief of police told him if there's anymore public violence he'll come down on him and his organization with both feet, no matter how much they juice him. Too many citizens have complained to him about the rough stuff in the streets. No, you boys are all right in Miami as long as you stay together so he cant take you down one at a time. But *me*, I'm the one getting heat from the son of a bitch."

Joe Ashley said he didnt see what Gordon was so worried about if Bellamy wasnt holding him to account for the Ashleys. "It's between him and us," Old Joe said. "Got nothin to do with you, so you got nothin to fret about." He dismissed with a handwave any rebuttal Gordon Blue might have thought to make.

Bill Ashley had sat in on the meeting but said nothing, knowing well when his father's position was adamant. But he had earlier argued in private with Old Joe that the hijackings were bad business and could only lead to greater troubles, that the wiser course would be to seek some sort of accommodation with Bellamy. The look Old Joe gave him was rawly scornful. "You dont go askin for *accommodation* with some sumbitch dont show you the proper respect, boy," he said. "Aint you learned that by now?"

Most of the hijackings during those four months went fast and smoothly—but on three occasions Bellamy's truck crews made a fight of it. In both of the first two scraps, a truck guard got wounded but neither was killed. The sole Ashley Gang casualty came in the second fight, during a hijacking in March and less than a mile south of Boynton Beach. Albert Miller had been pleading with John Ashley for weeks to take him along on a job, and in this, his first one, he got his ring finger shot off. "To hell with this Jesse James stuff," he said on the drive back to Twin Oaks, holding tight to the bloody bandanna wrapped around the finger stub that Ma Ashley would cauterize and bind properly. "You boys can have it."

The most recent skirmish came on a moonlit night in April. They'd stopped a truck loaded with Jamaican rum on a desolate stretch of the

Dixie Highway south of Hobe Sound and were walking up to the vehicle with their guns in hand when suddenly one of the tarpaulin sideflaps flew up and two men inside began firing wildly into the shadows with steadily flaring automatic rifles. Bullets ricocheted off the road and hummed through the air and chunked into the pines as the Ashley Gang dove for cover every which way and then counterattacked with a blazing fusillade of riflefire and buckshot into the rear of the truck. A third guard was shooting from the cab with a Winchester carbine. Hanford Mobley snaked his way on his belly through the palmettos and across the road and then stood up in the driver's side window and said, "Hey!" The guard turned from the other window and his last vision in this world was of the bright blast of Hanford Mobley's .45 two feet from his face—in that instant the back of his head burst open and portions of his brain sprayed over the roadside brush.

When the shooting was done, both of the guards in the rear of the truck were sprawled on the floor, their mortal remains pickling in the wash of sprits from the shattered bottles, their blood mingling with it. John Ashley looked in at them and sighed and said, "Well hell."

Hanford Mobley said they werent worth feeling sorry for. "Them boys could be standing there breathin and thinkin how good they next piece a ass was gonna feel, but no, they had to make a fight of it. Fuck em."

John Ashley shook his head but couldnt help smiling. "You're a hard man, Hannie." To which a grinning Mobley responded goddamned right he was.

The vapor of rum stung their eyes. Clarence joked that he was getting drunk just breathing the air. Half the load was yet intact and the gang transferred these hams to their own truck. Some of the sack bottoms were soaked with bloody rum. They took up the rummers' weapons and were delighted with the pair of .30–06 Browning Automatic Rifles. They found also a pouch of extra 20-round magazines and Hanford Mobley released the empty magazine in one of the rifles and snapped in a full one. "I just got to try this thing," he said. He stepped out into the road and aimed from the hip at the trunk of a tall pine silhouetted against the moon. He squeezed off a long deep-popping burst, the muzzle flaming and momentarily pulling to the right with the recoil before Mobley swung it back on target without easing off the trigger and the rounds kept pouring forth and began ripping chunks off the pine trunk and then the magazine was empty. Mobley lowered the BAR and gaped at grinning John Ashley and said, *"Damn!"*

Clarence Middleton had the other BAR and now he opened fire on the tall pine also, shooting in short bursts as he had been taught in the marines, and bark flew off the pine to either side and then his weapons too was empty. He smiled broadly and said, "I believe we gained us a tad more firepower, what I believe."

They aligned the three dead men side by side on the truck bed and John Ashley ordered the driver—who'd survived the fight by diving under the truck—to deliver the bodies to his bosses in Miami. As the truck clattered away to the south, the Ashley Gang made bets among themselves as to how far it would get before the cops flagged it down to investigate the effluence of rum and inquire after the bullet holes.

A few days after that skirmish Gordon Blue came to see them at Twin Oaks. He was nervous and looked paler even than his usual milkiness.

"This war has *got* to stop, Joe," he said at the supper table. "How about if I tell Bellamy you'd like to sit down with him, tell him you'd like to see if something can be worked out?"

"How about he asks *us* to sit down with him because *he* wants to see can something be worked out?" John Ashley said. Old Joe smiled around his pipe and nodded.

His eyes bloodshot and baggy, Gordon Blue obviously had not been sleeping well. His goatee was in need of a trim, his suit was rumpled, his tie hung loose at his collar. He rubbed his haggard face and sighed deeply. "Joe, please—let me arrange a meeting. Hell, they dont like losing loads to you, but they dont like bad publicity either. Did you know the Lauderdale cops stopped that truck with the dead guys in it? They said it smelled like an open rum barrel rolling down the street. Said it looked like something from the war. Naturally they pulled it over. Then they open the back and see the dead guys. 'What the hell's this?' they ask the driver. 'Who're these dead men?' The driver says, 'There are *dead men* in there? Oh sweet Jesus!' The cops said the guy was so good he nearly made himself faint."

Everybody laughed except Gordon Blue who but smiled weakly and shook his head. Frank Ashley winked at his brothers. He had won the wager about how far the truck would get.

"Could use more fellers like that driver," Old Joe said, still chortling. "Shoulda hired him, Johnny, while ye had the chance." John Ashley smiled and nodded.

"It's not really funny," Gordon Blue said. "The papers in Lauderdale and Miami both ran a story about it. Bellamy was as hot about the bad publicity as he was about getting jacked again. I'm serious, Joe, he's ready to work something out and we ought to take him up on it. If we dont, there's no telling what'll happen but it wont be any good for anybody, thats for sure."

"I'll tell you what can be worked out," Joe Ashley said. "He can agree to give us a cut of everything he brings through Palm Beach. He agrees to that and he can run all the hooch he wants through here. You reckon he'll go for *that*?"

"Well yes, sure—sure he will," Gordon Blue said, surprised by Old Joe's sudden amenability. "Bellamy's a reasonable man, Joe. It's cheaper for him to give you a cut than keep losing loads to you and he knows it. Hell, giving you a cut is the only compromise that makes sense. Let me arrange a meeting and the two of you can talk about it."

Old Joe looked at Bill Ashley sitting beside him. "I reckon I know where you stand on this."

"It's time we made some kind of deal so we can do business without more shootin," Bill said. "I've said that from the start. We can quit jackin him and start concentrating on bringin more booze in from the islands."

"Bill's absolutely right," Gordon Blue said to Old Joe. "You'll make more money if you strike a deal with Bellamy. Everybody makes more money all around. The main thing is, the shooting's *got* to stop. Sheriff Baker's let us operate in whiskey without interference, Joe, but if this war with Bellamy starts scaring the citizens he'll have to do something about it. That Boynton Beach fight a few weeks ago was way too close to town. People heard it, Joe, they got woke up by it. A stray bullet broke the window out of some fellow's car a half-mile away. They were a dozen complaints to Bob Baker. He told the newspapers he was thinking of organizing a special force to do nothing but track down whiskey camps and catch bootleggers on the roads and the beaches. Nobody needs *that*—not you, not Bellamy."

"Shit," Ed Ashley said. "Bobby Baker's too busy anymore gettin his picture took by the newspapers at the openin of ever new bank and restaurant and hotel in the county. He anyhow dont give a shit what rummers do to each other, everbody knows that."

Old Joe turned to John Ashley. "Boy?"

"I guess it's worth it to try and make a deal."

"You caint trust that sonofabitch!" Roy Matthews blurted. All heads at the table turned his way. "I know what I'm talkin about. I done business with Bellamy before. He'll cross us sure."

"I know he kilt you friend, Roy," Old Joe said softly. "But thats somethin between you and him and got nothin to do with business. This is business we're talkin. Now, if the man *does* cross us, well, we'll deal with that if the time ever comes."

"It aint because of his friend," Hanford Mobley said. "He just dont wanna run into his old bossman again." He tucked his hands up under his armpits and flapped his arms like chicken wings. "Bawk-bawk-bawk." He had never forgiven Roy Matthews for the business with the smoke rings and everybody knew it.

"You keep runnin you mouth, boy," Roy Matthews said. "You just about to the edge with me."

Hanford Mobley affected a look of fright—and then laughed and looked around at the others that they might join in.

"It's enough of that, Hannie," Old Joe said.

"You best listen to me on this," Roy Matthews said, pointing a finger at Old Joe. "Bellamy'll mean trouble to you some kinda way, you mark me."

"You made your point, boy," Old Joe said, staring hard at him. He was not one to have a finger pointed at him or be told what he'd best do. Roy Matthews threw up his hands and looked away and said nothing more.

"All right, Gordy," Old Joe said. "See to it."

They met in a West Palm restaurant called The Clambake on a warm humid forenoon in latter May. Gordon Blue made the arrangements. They had a private backroom to themselves and sat at a long table bearing pots of coffee and baskets of biscuits and doughnuts. Nelson Bellamy and three of his men sat on one side of the table, and on the other, Old Joe Ashley and his boys Bill and John. As mediator, Gordon Blue sat at the head of the table. He was the only unarmed man in the room. Clarence Middleton had stayed outside with the car to act as lookout. He passed the time chatting with Bellamy's driver about the best way to fish for snook.

Nelson Bellamy was tall and broadchested and hairy, and his suit coat was tight across his shoulders. Gold winked from his cufflinks, from his tie clasp, from a chain bracelet on his wrist, from a front tooth. He smoked cigarettes from a slim gold case he kept in his coat pocket. His right thumb was absent its forehalf. His eyes were dark and deep-set and moved constantly from one to another of the men across the table. One of the men with him was James White. On entering the room and seeing him at the table John Ashley had grinned and said, "Hey Jimmy, how you keepin?" White had smiled slightly and nodded but said nothing. The other two men with Bellamy were introduced as Bo Stokes and Alton Davis. Davis—tall, ropy, acne-scarred—was Bellamy's "chief of import operations." Stokes was larger even than Bellamy, thicknecked and heavyshouldered, his blond hair cropped almost to the scalp, the bridge of his nose off-center. His duties were not explained, but Gordon Blue now told the Ashleys that Bo Stokes had two-and-a-half years ago fought Jack Dempsey in the ring. John Ashley grinned at this information and said to Stokes, "That so? Did you win?" and Old Joe laughed but not Bill. Stokes turned to gaze out the window like a man profoundly bored. In the manner of their employer all three of Bellamy's men wore well-tailored suits, but all three were sunbrowned and scarred of hands and were clearly not indoor types.

Bellamy's voice was without accent and strained for sincerity. He said he wanted an end to their differences. It was costing him too much in lost product, he said, in lost trucks and reduced manpower. "You've run off a lot of my workers," he said to Joe Ashley with a small smile void of all cheer. "A bunch more got scared just hearing the stories about your people and took off too. It's all James here can do to put a truck crew together anymore." He looked at John Ashley. "And you got a couple of my Brownings. I paid top dollar for those guns. They shoulda been enough to keep anybody off those trucks."

"A gun's only as good as the man to use it," John Ashley said with a smile. Old Joe nodded like an approving professor.

"Looks that way," Bellamy said. "Anyhow, they're my guns and I'd be grateful if you gave them back."

John Ashley laughed. "And I guess people in hell would be grateful for icewater. The thing is, I reckon we earned them guns."

Bellamy's smile thinned. White and Stokes and Davis wore no expression whatever. Bellamy turned to Gordon Blue and asked, "What do you think, Gordy? You're an attorney-at-law. These boys got right to those Brownings?"

Blue seemed taken aback. "Well ah, I dont know, Nelson," he said. "I guess so. I mean, your boys *did* start shooting first, so I guess—"

"Who says they shot first?" Bellamy said, voice and eyes going tight.

"Well, actually," Gordon Blue said—looking nervous now, adjusting his tie—"he did." He gestured at John Ashley, who smiled and nodded at Ballamy.

"Oh, I see," Bellamy said. He nodded at John Ashley. "If *he* said so, then it *has* to be true, is that it? *That's* the way the law works."

Joe Ashley chuckled and grinned at John and Bill, but Gordon Blue saw no humor in his situation. He gestured awkwardly and said, "No, Nelson, thats not what—I dont—what I mean is it seems like—"

Joe Ashley cut Blue off with a handwave. "Look here, Mister Bellamy," he said, "I aint the least innersted in settin here watchin you scare ole Gordy who aint all that hard to scare anyways. All I wanna know is are you and me gone do business or aint we?"

Nelson Bellamy's hard gaze cut to Joe Ashley and then back to Gordon Blue for a moment longer—and then his face abruptly softened and he leaned back in his chair and lit another cigarette. "By all means, Mister Ashley," he said, "let's do business."

"Good. I guess Gordy told you what we want?"

"He did," Bellamy said. "And I've given the matter some thought. The only question is, how much? What's the percent?"

"Twenty," Old Joe said without hesitation.

"That's pretty damn steep," Bellamy said. "I was thinking ten would be more like it."

"I guess you *would* think so."

"I cant see twenty."

"I guess we could set here the rest of the day and argue about it," Old Joe said.

"What say we split the difference and put it to rest?" Bellamy said.

Joe Ashley affected to ponder this suggestion. "Fifteen percent?"

"It's still damn steep but I'll shake on it if it'll put an end to the trouble between us."

"It might could if we're talkin fifteen percent of *every* load that comes through Palm Beach, land or sea."

"We are."

"We got people who'll be keepin count. Cant a load go through we wont know about it."

"I'm sure thats true, Mister Ashley. I've heard about the grapevine you got up there. They say even the local cops cant get near you."

"They say correct."

"Well, we'll be square with you on the count—trust me. What say to payment on the fifteen of every month, starting next month?"

Old Joe looked at Bill, who put the last bite of a doughnut in his mouth and licked the cinnamon sugar off his fingers and nodded.

"Good enough," Old Joe said to Bellamy and they shook hands on it over the table.

"See there?" Bellamy said. "It's not hard for reasonable men to come to agreement. Most people have no idea."

In truth he was seething about Gordon Blue's siding with the Ashleys in the matter of the automatic rifles. And it had occurred to him that fifteen percent was probably the cut this redneck old goat Ashley'd had in mind from the start. Now the sonofabitch would go around telling everybody he'd got the best of Nelson Bellamy. He smiled and smiled at Joe Ashley across the table and hated him and all his trash kind.

He asked if they'd care for a drink but Joe Ashley politely declined for them all and the Ashley party took its leave. Gordon Blue went with them.

A few minutes later they were all in the Ford touring car and Clarence Middleton drove them out onto the Dixie Highway and headed for home.

"What you think, Daddy?" John Ashley said. "We trust Bellamy to pay us every month like he said?"

"I wouldnt trust him if he had one hand on a stack of bibles eight feet high and the other one glued to his dick," Old Joe said. "We'll just see. A deal's a deal and we'll hold to our end of it. But the first time he dont pay our cut we'll be right back to jacking his damn trucks and every fucken boatload he puts down on our beaches is what we'll do."

That night John Ashley had a dream in which he saw Gordon Blue sitting crosslegged in some hazy setting. His suit was sopping wet and he was staring at him with unmistakable sorrow and then opened his mouth as if he would tell him something and his tongue became a fish and swam away on the air. The dream was still nettling him the next morning, but at breakfast Gordon Blue was in high spirits and joking with Ma Ashley and feeling very optimistic about the deal they'd made with Bellamy, and so John Ashley shrugged off his lingering unease. That afternoon Blue took his leave and Albert Miller drove him back to Miami.

Three days later as Gordon Blue came out of his office building at the end of the day, the man Stokes appeared at his side and took him by the arm and said, "We got business to discuss, Counselor." A car was idling at the curb with Alton Davis at the wheel and its back door open wide. James White was seated in the back and beckoned Blue into the car. Gordon knew that to resist would be folly. Stokes could snap his arm like a broomstick if he took the notion—and he looked to have it in mind.

They drove west through the heavily trafficked streets and then the town buildings were behind them and the road turned to packed shell. They went through a few small but well-kept neighborhoods and then the road went to rutted dirt and now there were no more residences but for occasional shacks. Nobody made conversation. Now the road was flanked by dense palmetto scrub and slash pines and Davis turned south onto a rough narrow road hardly wide enough for one car. A few minutes later they came to a clearing on the north bank of the Miami River at a point about two miles from town. They parked in back of an empty fishhouse that looked out on a pair of rotted piers where Indians had until recently come to trade. The sun had lowered behind the redbark gumbo trees and the western sky was the color of raw meat. As he got out of the car Gordon Blue looked hard at the trees and at the long shadows they cast on the river surface. A flock of white herons was winging toward the fiery sunset and the deeper reaches of the Devil's Garden. It had showered earlier and the grass was still wet and frogs rang in the high reeds. Blue breathed deeply the ripe redolence of vegetation and pungent muck and he rued that he'd never spent much time outdoors. Then he was steered inside the dark fishhouse whose windows were covered with burlap and he was made to sit at a small table that was the only furnishing in the room. The table held an oil lamp and James White lit it.

White did the talking. He reminded Blue that not long ago he had mentioned in passing to Mister Bellamy that the Ashleys were about to expand their whiskey distribution to places where they didnt have the legal protection they enjoyed along the southeast coast. Mister Bellamy, White said, was very interested in knowing where these new distribution points would be.

Gordon Blue said he didnt know. He'd now and then overheard the Ashleys discussing the possible expansion of their business, but he had no idea which places they had in mind as new drops. They did not share such information with him.

Bo Stokes let a heavy sigh and took off his jacket and hung it carefully over the back of a straight chair. James White told Blue that Mister Bellamy had been disappointed by his having sided with the Ashleys in their claim to the automatic rifles. White suggested this would be a good opportunity for Blue to prove to Mister Bellamy that he was truly on *his* side. Mister Bellamy didnt expect Blue to know all the new places where the Ashleys would be delivering whiskey, but he would be grateful if he would pass on the name of at least one or two of those locations.

Stokes lit a cigarette and expelled a stream of smoke at the oil lamp. Alton David stood leaning against the wall, idly picking at his crooked brown teeth with a matchstick and looking on without expression.

Gordon Blue's throat was tight, his mouth spitless. He'd never even pretended to be physically brave. His bladder was in distress.

Mustering all the sincerity possible to him he said he'd like to help Mister Bellamy, he truly would, but he really did not know much about the particulars of the Ashleys' business. If he knew where the Ashleys intended to sell their whiskey he'd say so. And why not? He didnt owe them anything except his legal counsel. It wasnt like they'd ever done anything personal for him.

James White studied Blue's eyes closely as if he would read the truth there. Then moved away from the table and gestured to Davis. Davis came to Gordon Blue and locked an arm under his chin and pulled his head back and held it fast. Blue could hardly draw breath. His attempt to plead with them emerged as a strangled groan.

Stokes took a deep drag off the cigarette and then blew on its tip to produce a red glow. "You let me know, now," he said as he loomed over Gordon Blue's terrified upturned face, "just as soon as you start remembering."

She never knew when he'd show up. She might come home from her typist job at the Seward Land Title Company and find him waiting on her stoop, smoking a cigarette and reading the sports items in the newspaper in the light of the late afternoon, his skimmer tilted back on his head. He'd look up with a smile full of devilment and she'd laugh and rush through the front gate of the apartment-house yard and into his arms and he'd fondle her bottom as they kissed and men driving past would toot their horns or whistle at them and grin. Five minutes later they'd be in her second-floor apartment, entwined naked on her bed. Or she might be reading a magazine after supper and listening to her phonograph when there would come a soft tapping at her door and she'd open it to find him leaning against the hall wall with his ankles crossed and his thumbs hooked over his belt buckle and a toothpick waggling between his grinning teeth. Sometimes, after not hearing from him for two or three weeks, she'd be startled awake in the middle of the night by his hand clamped on her mouth and his other hand stripping her of her pajama bottoms and she'd feel his hard cock against her and his warm breath at her ear whispering fiercely, "I'm Captain Dick the Pirate and I'm gone fuck you till you faint." Her heart would jump and her breath leave in a rush and she'd seize his erection and hasten him into her. Later she'd feign pique and slap at his chest and tell him he was awful for scaring her like that. She'd every time say she was going to change the lock on her door and he'd laugh and say the doorlock hadnt been invented he couldnt tease open.

Roy Matthews came to see her only when Old Joe sent Hanford Mobley off with a crew on some assignment that would keep him away for days—picking up beach unloadings or making deliveries to middlemen in the deeper Glades. Joe Ashley never put him on a crew under Hanford Mobley's charge. Old Joe wanted no confrontation between them that might jeopardize a delivery or a pickup, and so he had begun using Roy for most of his one-man jobs—collecting delinquent payments for deliveries, meeting secretly with law officers on the Ashley payroll to give them their monthly bribe, making drops of bush lightning to some of their smaller clients from Fort Pierce to Miami. Sometimes he would not see her for weeks, sometimes he'd be with her for two or three nights running.

Hanford Mobley was with her every Sunday, as well as whenever the Ashley gang came to Miami with their girls to make a high time of it. He had but recently declared his love for her and had begun to hint about marriage at some time in the nebulous future when he would be rich and carefree and could afford to give her the best of everything and take her everywhere. She liked Hannie, liked his devotion to her, his boyish enthusiasm for sex. Liked above all his outsized phallus, which, as she'd measured it from base to slit with a seamstress' tape, stood at very nearly nine inches in its enpurpled readiest state. It was her bad luck that the boy owned no discipline whatever. Within seconds of entering her he would be pumping wildly and ejaculating like a firehose. *He* had wonderful times. She—despite that supremely thrilling moment when he entered her with that elephantine thing—would be left in a tight tangle of frustration.

Roy Matthews was the dark side of the moon. He never spoke of love and she knew he never would. She had tried to make him jealous by speaking in awe of Hanford's huge member but he had affected to be unimpressed and came back at her with the ancient male bromide, "It aint the size of the tool, it's the knowin how to use it." And he did know how to use it, Roy did, she had to give him that. He knew how to use every tool God gave man for pleasing a woman—cock, fingers, mouth, words. For all his jokes about Dick the Pirate, he very nearly *would* make her swoon every time they did it. She'd once rather tentatively urged Hanford to kiss her farther down than Mister Cooter, her turtle tattoo, and he'd gaped at her and said, "You mean . . . down *there*?" as if he'd been asked to put his face in a chumbucket. She'd been glad for the darkness that hid her furious blush and she had not broached the matter with him again. But she couldnt help thinking sometimes how Hannie was *such* a boy.

Roy required no supplication. His mouth was a wicked thing and he loved to use it on her. He'd suck her breast tips to hard puckers. He'd roll the hood of her clitoris under his tongue. He'd lap expertly at the little pearl within until she'd shriek her pleasure. Her neighbor had more than once pounded on the wall and made threat to call the cops. Roy thought she should get another tattoo, a snake tail curling out of her public patch. "Could call it your snake in the grass," he said. Like somebody else I could name, she'd thought, but kept it to herself.

On those occasions when the Ashley bunch would come to Miami for a good time at the Elser Pier and at whichever hotel they were staying, she would of course be with Hanford. Roy came with a different girl every time, and every one of them a looker. She would tell herself that she wasnt jealous, she wasnt, yet she'd be all the more demonstrative in her public affections toward Hanford, all the more suggestive in the way she'd press against him as they danced. Hanford Mobley of course loved it when she was so ardent. He'd sometimes question her with a grin about what had gotten into her and she'd kiss him and then whisper, "That's for me to know and you to enjoy," which was good enough for Hanford. As she'd insinuate herself against him on the dancefloor or tickle his ear with her tongue or grope him under the table, she'd now and then glance Roy's way to see his reaction. Sometimes he would be smiling at her antics—but usually he was too absorbed in his girl of the moment to even take notice.

"We've been told John Ashley himself is the one going to make the drop," the pockmarked one said, the one calling himself Baxter. "It's a fishcamp, a one-man drop, but it's their first time there and they aint bought any police protection there, not yet anyway, and so maybe he'll have a backup. It's not likely there'll be more than two of them if there's that many." The man's smile was a brown ruin of skewed teeth.

The big blond called himself Williams. He rarely spoke but his eyes were quick and didnt seem to miss much.

The waitress came to the booth and asked if anybody cared for more coffee and they all shook their heads. They were in the Cove Cafe in West Palm Beach. Bob Baker had agreed to meet them here after one of them called him on the telephone and said they had information about John Ashley he might be interested to know.

Freddie Baker had come along with Sheriff Bob and had been observing Baxter and Williams carefully. Now he said, "Where you all get this information?"

"We have our sources," the pockmarked one said.

"Name one."

The pockmark showed his bad teeth.

"Dont matter the source," the blond one said. "I guarantee you he didnt lie."

"Listen," the pockmark said, "we thought you'd be interested, thats all. We heard you been wanting to catch this particular fella for a while and we thought the information might be of use to you, thats all. If you're not interested, well, all right. We'll be one our way."

Freddie Baker said: "Maybe we'll just lock up both your big-city asses for withholding information pertainin to a criminal investigation."

The pockmarked man and the blond one stared at him.

Bob Baker laughed lowly. "Hell, Freddie, these boys dont want to withhold nothin. They come to make a deal. So get to it, boys. What is it *you* want?"

The pockmark cleared his throat and looked about. Then said: "We heard you're putting together a special squad to stop runners through Palm Beach. That would cause problems for us. What we want is for you to let our whiskey trucks slide. Let our boats unload on the beaches."

Bob Baker regarded them for a moment. Then looked at Freddie Baker who pursed his lips in order to disguise his smile. Freddie knew Bobby had no intention of interfering with the booze supply coming through Palm Beach County. Certain interested parties in Broward County, which lay just south of the Palm Beach line, had recently advanced to him some sizable "campaign contributions" in exchange for his assurance that the Palm Beach portion of the booze pipeline would not be shut down.

"How much you givin the Ashleys?" Bob Baker said.

The pockmark regarded him intently for a moment before answering. "Who says we're giving the Ashleys anything?"

Bob Baker smiled thinly. "Hell, boys, I know that family bettern you know the feel of your own peckers. Only way you could be runnin booze through Palm Beach is they're lettin you—and if they're lettin you it's because you're payin them."

"If thats true—*if*—why aint you done something about it?" the pockmark said. "Sounds like they're shaking people down. That's against the law, aint it? Why aint you pinched the bunch of them?" He was smiling too, and as humorlessly.

"Because if they shakin anybody down it's only people like you," Bob Baker said. "I aint never felt it ought be illegal to steal from a thief." He grinned.

"And we never felt it should be illegal to make a buck selling the public what it wants," the pockmark said. "We aint crooks, we're businessmen. If you dont like booze, Sheriff, take it up with the folks who voted you into office. I'll give you two-to-one most of them like a drink now and then and are doing their part to keep us in business."

"I never said I didnt like booze," Bob Baker said. "I just dont much care for crooks. And what I said in the first place was, how much are you givin the Ashleys?"

The pockmark looked at the blond man as if he could read some meaning in his neutral aspect. Then turned to Bob Baker and said, "What the hell, we're payin em, yeah, so what? They get seven percent of every load that comes through. It's worth it to avoid the headaches they can give us."

"Bullshit," Bob Baker said. "You aint gettin by for no seven, not past them. They gettin ten if they gettin a dime. Come on, boy, tell the truth and shame the devil."

The pockmark looked away and heaved a huge sigh, then looked back at Bob Baker and shrugged, "It burns our ass that they get ten. They had us over a barrel."

"Eleven," Bob Baker said.

"Huh?" the pockmark said.

"They get ten percent, I want eleven."

The pockmark laughed and looked away again. Then nodded and said, "Well hell, I guess you got us over a barrel too."

Bob Baker went through the careful ritual of lighting a cigar. Why not, he thought. Grab him and put him away for good. He wouldnt be cutting off Ashley whiskey to the local businesses who needed it, not if he put the arm on John but let the old man's business be. And it would be good publicity for a crime-fighting sheriff sworn to keep the county safe. So do it. He could give himself a half-dozen reasons to do it. Practical reasons. Not that he didnt have plenty of personal reasons too. The humiliations. Julie. *Julie.* Hell yes, he had reasons to put the man away. Damn good reasons. And never mind anything else. Never mind he sometimes woke in the night from the vision of an eyeball under his thumb and the sound of screaming. Or from the dream of posing with a dead man in ways that now seemed more shameful than he could bear to think about. What happened happened and was done with. Never mind that sometimes, right in the middle of the day, he'd feel a sudden inexplicable surge in his heartbeat, an abrupt dryness of mouth and tightness of chest that had nothing to do with ill health. Never mind his suspicion that he had to put the man away soon because he was only biding his time before seeking his own retribution.

Now he had the cigar burning evenly and took a few puffs and then looked at the pockmarked man and said, "All right, Tell me."

Laura Upthegrove had a sense for things amiss. Raised from childhood in the Devil's Garden she possessed a wildland creature's acute sensitivity to the surrounding world and all things in it. She could intuit trouble in a subtle tightening of her skin, in the altered hum of her blood.

It was commonplace for John Ashley to take his leave of her every so often on an early evening with the explanation that he had to pick up a load or deliver one, and she'd never questioned his need to do it. Bootlegging was mainly a nighttime business, after all. One evening as they lay in a tangle of arms and legs and both of them still breathing hard from the thrash and tumble of their coupling, he told her he had to make a late delivery in Riviera, and he slid out of bed and began to get dressed. But as she watched him from the bed she quite suddenly knew he was lying. There was nothing in his manner to rouse her suspicions. There had been no abatement at all in his ardor for her when they made love (they'd learned to grip sticks between their teeth to mute their mating sounds when they coupled in the sidehouse at Twin Oaks). And yet she knew he was lying, knew it just as surely as she'd always known when a moccasin was nearby or a panther was watching from the shadows or Indians were in proximity of her house. She could *feel* it. And her feeling at this moment—her inexplicable but utterly certain feeling—was that he was off to see another woman.

He checked the magazine in his .45 and then snicked it back into the pistol butt and slipped the gun into his waistband at the small of his back and pulled his shirttail over it. He put on his hat and gave her a wink and went out the door. She listened to him crank the truck and heard the motor catch and then stutter until he was behind the wheel and adjusted the levers and the engine's idling became smoother. Then the gears chunked into action and the truck clattered away toward the pinewoods trail leading to the highway.

She flew into her overalls and pulled on her brogans without lacing them and went out hatless into the moonlight-dappled yard just as his headlamp beams disappeared into the trees. She jogged to the Ford roadster and cranked it up and got behind the wheel and set out after him without turning on her lights.

Sipping bush lightning and smoking in the recessed darkness of the front porch, Old Joe Ashley and his boys Frank and Ed watched the truck and then the roadster depart. Ed spat out into the moonlight and said, "Looks like ole Johnny might could be in for more excitement tonight than he bargained for," and they all laughed lowly. Ma Ashley came to the door and looked at them and then out to the woods where the Ford chugged away faintly in the dark. She sighed tiredly and said, "Kids," and shook her head and went back inside.

Laura kept a quarter-mile back from the single red taillight of his truck as they bore south under a white crescent moon and a sky so thick with stars she thought she might reach up and swirl them with her hand and they'd trail sparks of every color. They'd been driving for almost an hour when they reached Riviera and when he didnt stop there she knew her hunch had been right. She almost shouted her anger into the night. Goddamn him! Goddamn all men and their stupid hankering dicks!

At West Palm Beach he slowed and turned off on a side street. She followed at a distance. A few blocks farther on he turned onto a muddy street where the air assumed the smell of brackish water. He drove past a row of darkened boathouses and then pulled into a weedy half-full parking lot near a three-story building with a small front porch illuminated bright orange by a lamp over the door. The building stood at the edge of a towering pinewoods and was flanked on both sides by areca palms and clusters of bamboo standing in high black silhouette against tall openshuttered windows ablaze with yellow light. The truck's headlamps cut off and he got out and went past a pump shed at the edge of the lot and through the shadow of a large umbrella tree and up to a lighted screendoor that she guessed opened to a kitchen. She knew what the place was without knowing how she knew. Her fury swelled in her breast. Bad enough another woman—but a whore! God*damn* him!

She parked at the end of the street and reached under the seat and withdrew the .44 revolver he always kept under there. She checked the loads and then tucked the pistol in the deep sidepocket of her overalls and got out of the car and stood there for a moment with fireflies blinking greenly all about her. She wondered what she was going to do. The front door was out of the question. The idea of simply leaving and confronting him later made her want to curse out loud. Whatever she was going to do about this she was going to do it now.

She crossed the parking lot and headed for the screendoor. She went up the low wooden steps and stood in the shadow of the eaves' wide overhang and looked in through the screen. In a kitchen spacious and bright a young Negro girl was taking a cut-glass bowl out of a cupboard. There was a wide door at the far end of the room, a narrower one near the pantry. Muttering to herself the girl went out through the larger door.

Laura eased the door open against a softly creaking spring and stepped inside. The air held the mingled aromas of bread and perfume, pipe and cigar smoke, sex and whiskey. She paused and glanced nervously from one door to the other, expecting somebody to come in at any moment and demand to know what she was doing here. What could she say? She was suddenly quite conscious of her nakedness under the overalls.

Plinking piano music carried faintly through the wider door—"Frankie and Johnny"—and she felt like both laughing and crying at this tune so perfect to the circumstance. Now the muffled laughter of men and women came through the wider door and she guessed a parlor lay that way. She went to the narrower door and saw a shadowy hall with a stairway at the far end. Her mouth was dry and she felt her heartbeat throbbing in her throat. She touched the pistol for courage and then went down the hall and slowly ascended the stairs and came to a landing and yet another door, this one shut. She turned the knob and the door opened onto a red-carpeted hallway with a half-dozen doors to either side and another closed door at its far end and she knew this was there the whores would be.

Gripping the pistol in her pocket she stepped into the hall. She could think of nothing to do but put her ear to each door in turn. At the first one on her left she heard nothing. She opened it silently to reveal a man and woman lying naked and in spooned fashion, their eyes closed, the man idly fondling one of the woman's breasts. For a moment she stood and stared, and then eased the door shut. In the next room an unfamiliar male voice was talking about Australia. From the room on the other side of the hall came a low urgent chanting, "Yes-yes-yes," but she did not know this voice either. The next door to her left was open and she saw there was no one inside. The room after that was also deserted. The following door was closed and silent and she opened it and saw a thin naked brunette with pear-shaped breasts sitting astraddle a man so hairy he seemed of another species. They looked at her and the man grinned through his beard but the girl scowled and said, "The *hell* you want?" She quickly closed the door and stood there for a long moment with her heart hammering. The man was laughing, the girl cursing that you couldnt get any privacy in this business anymore, just anydamnbody could come walking in on you.

At the last door on the left she heard him. He was saying something about seeing Bobby in a dream. She didnt know if he was talking about his dead brother or the sheriff or somebody else. She didnt care. She took out the .44 and swiftly opened the door, stepped inside and closed it behind her.

The room was dimly illuminated by a small bedside oil lamp turned down low. They were lying naked on the bed, his back to the door, the bedsheets in a tangle at their feet. He looked over his shoulder and saw her and then saw the gun in her hand. His mouth opened but he made no sound.

"Who is it?" the woman said. She sat up with her face to the door and in a quick glance Laura saw that her hair was short and blonde and that she was pretty.

She strode quickly to the bed and put the pistol muzzle against John Ashley's forehead and forced his head back into the pillow and said, "Give me one good reason I ought not to shoot you here and now, you no-count whore-mongerin son of a bitch." She cocked the hammer.

His good eye fixed on her. He was trying to affect indifference but she knew him too well to be fooled. He was scared—she could see it in his eye, in the pale tightness of his mouth. She wanted to laugh, she suddenly felt so good, but she kept her aspect deadly serious the better to preserve the mood and her authority.

"I aint got no good reason," he said.

"I'll give you a reason," the blonde said quickly. "He loves you."

Laura looked at the woman whose stare was strange and unfocused. "Who the hell asked—"

John Ashley grabbed her wrist with one hand and clapped his other hand tightly over the cocked hammer so it could not fall as she squeezed the trigger. She tried to pull the pistol free but he locked both hands tight and yanked her off balance and onto the bed. She punched at him with her free hand and cursed him and he rolled over on top of her and straddled her stomach and she shouted, "Get offa me—*get off!*" and vainly bucked and writhed and tried to unseat him. He wrested the revolver from her and eased the hammer down and Loretta May's hands scrabbled over his shoulders and her arms locked around his neck and she said, "Get *offa* her before you squash her!" With a hard choking tug backward she pulled him off Laura and he went tumbling to the floor. He scrambled away from the bed on all fours and got to his feet and stood with his back against the wall and the gun in his hand as Laura sat up and rubbed her wrist and glared at him like she might come at him yet. Both of them were gasping for breath.

"You damn crazy woman," John Ashley said.

"You hush, John Ashley," Loretta May said sharply. "It's no way to talk to the woman you love."

"The woman I love was ready to blow my damn brains out, is what she was—"

"Goddamn right I was, you cheatin, lying son of—"

"*Hush* now, the both you!" Lorreta May said, reaching out and finding Laura's back and then scooting up beside her. She put her arms around Laura's shoulders and said, "It's all right now, honey, it's all right."

And then suddenly Laura was crying—crying hard with her face in her hands—and Loretta held her closer and rocked her gently and crooned, "There now, baby, there now, dont you cry. It's no need to cry, it's no need. Everthing's better than you know. It is, it is."

Laura's unlaced brogans had come off in the struggle, and one of the overall straps had slipped off her shoulder to expose a breast and even as she wept she became aware of the soft warmth of Loretta May's naked breasts against her arm. She snuffled and wiped at her tears with the back of her hand and turned to look at Loretta May and saw the strange lack of focus in her eyes. And even as the realization came to her she said, "What's the matter with you? Are you—? I mean—"

"She's blind, for chrissake," John Ashley said. "Cant you *see?*"

Laura stuck her tongue out at him and then said to Loretta, "Are you *really?*"

"As a damn bat, honey. Aint you never knowed anybody blind before?"

"Uh-uh. You been blind since always? Since you was borned?"

"No. Just since I was ten."

"You *used* to could see till you was *ten* year old?"

"Used to could."

"And now you cant see *nothin*? Nothin at *all*?"

"Well. Nothin you can put your hand to."

"But thats . . . it must be so awful *dark* all the . . . you poor . . . that's just *terrible*!" Laura said. And broke out crying again. She pulled Loretta May to her and kissed her on the forehead and hugged her around the shoulders.

Loretta May stroked Laura's hair and kissed her cheek and they hugged more closely still and Laura caressed Loretta May's bare back and kissed her perfumed shoulder and then each of her eyes in turn. She looked into her sightless eyes a moment and then kissed her quickly and lightly on the lips.

Loretta May smiled and brushed at Laura's tears with her fingers and put her fingers to Laura's mouth and whispered, "I always known why you love him. Now I see why he loves you."

Laura smiled against Loretta May's fingers and took a fingertip in her mouth and rolled her tongue on it and then blushed brightly and grinned and Loretta May grinned back at her and put a hand to Laura's face and kissed her full on the mouth. And Laura held the kiss. And then they were kissing deeply and with tongues and Loretta pushed down the other of Laura's overall straps and lightly touched her breasts. They kissed and tentatively put their hands to each other in shy exploration and they both made soft sounds of pleasure. Now Loretta May eased her hand down Laura's taut belly and playfully wriggled her fingers into her pubic bush and Laura's eyes came open wide and she pulled back slightly in Loretta's embrace and the two women faced each other and burst into giggles like mischievous schoolgirls.

"You know what?" Lorretta said. "We forgettin somethin." She put her hand over her eyes like a sun visor and turned her head in one direction and then the other, as if she were scanning the horizons. "Wherever he's at."

Laura looked at John Ashley still standing with his back to the wall. He'd put the pistol aside on a chair and was smiling. He bore an erection as sizable as any she'd ever seen on him. It was nodding in time with his heartbeat like an approving bystander. She laughed and shook her head and said, "He's over there with that ugly thing all swole up and pointin at us like it aint seen a nekkid woman in a year."

He looked down at himself and said, "I dont know it's so ugly."

"How you, ah, feel about this, Johnny?" Loretta May said, lightly touching Laura's breast. Laura put her hand over Loretta's and held it to her and grinned at John Ashley.

"I feel like everbody's gone to a hell of a good party," John Ashley said, "and I aint been invited."

The girls tittered. "Poor boy feels left out," Laura said.

"Well now, you one-eyed gator skinner," Loretta May said, "maybe you wouldnt be left out of nothin if you just quit bein way over *there* and got your outlaw ass on over *here*."

His grin widened the more and he bounded for the bed with his bobbing erection pointing the way like a compass right and true.

One of their informants brought the news to Twin Oaks. He'd heard it from a West Palm Beach cop who got it from some Miami cops just a couple of days before.

The corpse had been weighted by something heavy tied to its neck by quarter-inch cord. Whatever the weighting object had been—a concrete block, a section of scrap metal, a limerock boulder—it had to have been rough-edged because the action of the current's steady tugging on the body had eventually severed the cord where it rubbed against the anchor. The body had then carried downstream and floated up near the mouth of the river at Biscayne Bay and in front of the Royal Palm Hotel where it was spotted by a guest taking an early morning stroll. The police were summoned and they pulled it out of the water and even though the dead man was eyeless several of the cops recognized him as Gordon Blue.

Much of his face bore small dark pocks about the size of bulletholes, particularly around the empty sockets. The cops figured them for burns. The body was conveyed to the city physician who surmised that the victim had been dead at least a week. He found that several fingers on each hand were broken and that the victim's scrotum had suffered severe trauma. "The man went through some goodly pain before he went in the river," the informant told the Ashley Gang. "And he went in still alive. The doc said he died of drowning."

The Ashleys figured it was most likely Bellamy's doing. The question was why. If Bellamy didnt like the deal with them why take it out on Gordy? Hell, if Bellamy didnt like the deal why even bother to shake on it? If he'd intended to crawfish why make the first payoff as he already had?

"What we gone do about this, Daddy?" Ed said.

Old Joe knocked his pipe against a porch post to dislodge the dottle and then put the stem in his mouth and blew the remaining ashes from the bowl. "Nothin," he said. "We dont *know* it was Bellamy— not for a fact, we dont. And even if it was, it dont look to have nothin to do with us. Bellamy's holdin to his end of the deal, so we'll hold to ours. I dont know why he'd do Gordy such as he did but I figure it for somethin personal between them."

For a moment no one spoke. Then Frank Ashley said: "Gordy was our friend."

Bill Ashley snorted. "He was a lawyer. A lawyer aint nobody's friend." The late afternoon light played off his spectacles and made them look like circles of tin.

John Ashley glared at him. "You do best when you do like usual and keep you mouth shut."

Bill turned his glinting lenses toward him but said nothing.

"Quit now," Old Joe said. "You both right. He was our friend and he was a lawyer and sometimes I wasnt real sure when he was being the one and when the other. But it was his choice to do business with them Miami sumbitches. I always told him he oughten to truck with them—some you heard me tell him. But he always said he knew what he was doin. Well, he took his own chances is what he did and we had nothin to do with it then and we dont now. And thats the end of it."

Shortly thereafter John Ashley made a delivery of Old Joe's bush lightning to a new customer, a man named Goren, who operated a fish camp on the Peace River just east of Wauchula in brandnew Hardee County barely two months old. Goren had been informed he could get booze at a better price from the Ashleys than from the Arcadia moonshiners he'd been dealing with for the past year, and he sent word to Old Joe that he could use twenty cases a month if the Ashleys could see fit to get him off the hook with the Arcadia dealers. They were some pretty rough old boys and he didnt want them to get mad at him for quitting them. Old Joe told Goren he'd settle the matter with the Arcadians, but it would be a month before he'd have a suffi-cient store of hooch on hand to make the fish camp's first delivery. He promised that thereafter the hooch would come around as regular as the moon. He said his boy John would deliver the first load to

ensure that everything went all right and that Goren was satisfied with
the stuff. Goren said they had a deal. He was impressed that Joe
Ashley would take so much trouble for such a smalltime customer.
Old Joe said he treated all his customers the same whether they bought
a thousand cases or just one jug. He then sent Clarence Middleton to
apprise the Arcadians of Goren's switch in hooch suppliers. The Arcadians didnt like it but knew better than to make an issue of it. And
now John Ashley was delivering the Wauchula fish camp's first load
of Old Joe's hooch.

The camp stood on a stretch of riverbank in the deep shade of live
oaks hung thick with Spanish moss. A dozen small boats were tied up
at a trio of piers jutting into the river. Ten yards back from the river
was a bait and tackle shop set on six-foot pilings and engirt by a wide
planked deck with rough-hewn tables and benches. Goren's two Negro
workers were quick to unload the truck and store the cases in the bait
shop's backroom next to Goren's tiny living quarters. The fishing camp
fellas were good old boys and all of them were excited to have John
Ashley in their midst. John accepted their invitation to have a short
one with them before heading back and they sat themselves at one of
the long tables on the portion of deck overlooking the river. As the
fish camp owner poured a round of Old Joe's shine a school of mullet
broke the surface of the river like silver shards of a bursting mirror.
The men were just raising their glasses to one another's health when
police cars came roaring down the shell drive and cops with shotguns
came running out of the flanking trees yelling, "Hands up! Get your
fucken hands up, you sons of bitches!"

His first thought was to dive over the railing into the river. But he
knew the cops would open fire and there were too many of them to
miss and that would be all she wrote. Either that or they'd get in one
of the ready boats and go out and pluck him from the water before
he was halfway to the other bank. So he stood up with the others and
raised his hands high as the cops closed in and Goren whispered
fiercely, "We dont know no Ashley, none of us, got that, boys?" The
others nodded and grinned, their faces bright and unable to hide their
excitement at this adventure of a police raid and John Ashley in
their midst.

There were a dozen or so Hardee County deputies in the raiding
party and some of them shoved the fishcamp men up against the wall
face-first and frisked them while others went into the bait shop and
found the cases of hooch. The deputy who patted down Ashley relieved
him of the .45 in his waistband and called, "Sheriff Poucher, right

here!" The sheriff came over and examined the pistol and then looked at John Ashley as though he might smile at him. He said, "You the one brought the shine in?"

John Ashley said he sure as hell was not, he was just passing through and thought he'd stop and see if there was aught to drink at this camp and there was, and he was just having a short one with the fellas is all. The sheriff asked what he was doing with the .45. He said it was for protection, a present from his uncle who'd fought against the Hun to defend the American way of life and freedom for all. He told the sheriff he was a sewing machine salesman and he'd heard that south Florida roads were bad for bandits and he was afraid of being robbed on the road. He'd sold every machine in his truck between Fort Lauderdale and Avon Park was why the truck was empty and why he had a fat roll of money in his pocket. He said was on his way home to his wife and three little children in Tampa who he'd sorely missed these past few weeks on the road and couldnt wait to see again. The sheriff nodded as though seriously considering this explanation and then asked his name. "Murphy, sir," John Ashley said. "Art Murphy."

A man laughed loudly behind him and John Ashley abruptly felt a great sagging weight in his chest. He turned and saw him standing there, large and beaming, his thumbs in his gunbelt, his yellow grin showing teeth the size of thumbnails.

"Hey, Johnny," Bob Baker said. "How you keepin?"

Hardee County Sheriff John Poucher relinquished custody of the prisoner to Sheriff Robert Baker who'd brought him the tip about the hooch drop at Goren's fish camp and who had a handful of outstanding warrants to serve on the bootlegger. By the following sunrise John Ashley was once again in the Palm Beach County Jail.

The jail had just begun to undergo renovations and the clamor and dust of construction was daylong. He was manacled by both wrists to the solid-piece iron bunk in one of the windowless isolation cells along the back wall of the block, the chain just long enough to allow him to sit up but not stand fully. The single other furnishing was a half-gallon tin can for his waste. The only light was a black-crossed yellow shaft angling in through a small barred window in the door. Just outside the cell a pair of guards with shotguns were stationed round the clock. They were under Sheriff Baker's orders to shoot the prisoner dead if anybody tried to break him out. Two more guards were posted in the outer room and two more just outside the front door. The rein-

forced fence around the jail was patrolled by a dozen cops with carbines. For the whole time John Ashley was in the Palm Beach County
Jail Bob Baker put most of the sheriff's department on duty there. It
was a plum time for robbers and burglars and holdup men working in
other parts of the county.

He was permitted no visitor but his lawyer, one Ira Goldman,
who'd been recommended to Joe Ashley as the best criminal defense
attorney in Miami. Goldman was at his side at every court session
and filed a steady progression of motions and briefs all of which were
rejected just as quickly as the judge scanned them. Goldman forth-
rightly informed Joe Ashley that there was no chance of keeping John
from going back to prison to serve out the rest of his original sentence—plus time added for his escape. Old Joe refused to believe he
couldnt buy John out of jail one way or another. "Just find out who
we got to grease," he told Goldman. "The judge, the guards, whoever.
No matter how much they want, I'll get it."

Goldman told him to forget it. There wasnt a thing the judge could
do. As for the guards, their fear of what Bob Baker would do to them
if John Ashley should escape was even greater than their greed. No
payoff of any size, Goldman said, not to anybody, would suffice to
get John free. Not right now anyway. He'd heard they even planned
to shut him up in solitary confinement at first—and no, they couldnt
buy him out of that, either. There had been too many escapes off the
road gangs the last few years. Too much written in the papers about
corruption in the penal system. John Ashley was the perfect example
for them to show they meant business up in Raiford. In a couple of
years, Goldman said, they might be able to make some arrangement
with somebody up there. "When our chance comes," Goldman said,
"it'll cost us plenty. But first John's going to have to do some time."

Old Joe glared at Goldman and nearly quivered under the urge to
kick him until he hollered that yes, there was a way to get John Ashley
out of jail. But he held his fury in check. In his bones he knew Goldman was right. John Ashley wasnt just a captured fugitive from the
law—he was a political issue. The newspapers were crowing about the
arrest of Florida's most notorious desperado. Politicians from Fort
Pierce to Miami were blowing hard about this being the beginning of
a long-overdue effort to rid South Florida of its festering criminal element. Day after day Bob Baker smiled for the cameras and reminded
reporters that he'd sworn to bring John Ashley to justice and now he'd
done it. He wanted to thank the people of Palm Beach County for
putting their trust in him by electing him to office and he hoped they

would continue to support him in his fight against crime. Up at Raiford the warden awaited the desperado's transfer and told reporters it would snow peach ice cream in hell before John Ashley was assigned to a road gang again where it would be easier to try another escape. Mister Ashley, he said, was going to become very familiar with the penitentiary's walls.

To avoid crowds of gawkers and the possibility of confederates trying to free John Ashley in transit, Bob Baker made no announcement public or private of when he would move the prisoner to Raiford. One humid morning an hour before first light ten armed sheriff's deputies escorted him from his cell to the train depot. The only witnesses on hand besides cops were the station agent and the train crew. He was hustled aboard a prison car which on the outside looked no different from the other boxcars but whose interior contained a cell with bars as thick as baseball bats and a padlock the size of a bible. He looked around for Bob Baker as he boarded the car, curious to see his expression of the moment, but he did not spot him among the policemen milling in the station platform's weak lamplight. During the weeks he had been in county custody they had seen each other only at the court sessions and had not exchanged a word since his arrest. He'd expected Bobby to say something about the pictures of his brother in the morgue, to at least make some allusion, and he'd decided to try to strangle him with his manacle chain if he did. In court he'd a few times caught Bobby staring at him, his expression each time unfathomable in the instant before he realized John was staring back and his face broke into a yellow grin.

By sunrise he was miles to the north and bearing for the penitentiary. The transfer detail planned to arrive at Raiford at midmorning of the following day and the officer in charge so notified the warden by telegraph from the Titusville station. The warden and his assistant met them at the prison's front gate. They had tipped local reporters to the infamous desperado's arrival and now smilingly obliged the photographers by posing for a picture of themselves aflank the prisoner. In their black suits and smiling pallors they looked like celebrant undertakers. Dressed in white and his aspect rueful John Ashley looked bound for the grave.

EIGHTEEN

Liars Club

A FEW MONTHS AFTER JOHN WENT BACK TO PRISON ED AND FRANK
Ashley went on a whiskey run to Grand Bahama like they'd done
a hundred times before, only this time they didnt come back.
Nobody was sure where that story came from but at first nobody believed it. We all thought it was a phony rumor put out by the Ashleys
themselfs for some reason of their own. Ed and Frank were hiding out
from somebody and the Ashleys wanted everybody to think they were
dead—that was what we told each other.

But the story persisted and picked up a little more detail as it made
the rounds. After a time we had to believe it. We heard Old Joe sent
Clarence Middleton to West End to ask after Ed and Frank. Clarence
was told they'd been there and bought the biggest load they'd ever
taken on—more than seven hundred cases of Canadian whiskey done
up in burlocks. The Ashley boys packed the hams into every foot of
space in the *Della*'s hold. With that much whiskey on board, the *Della*'s
gunwales couldnt of showed hardly more than a foot of freeboard.
To make it worse a black storm was bearing in from the northwest.
The harbormaster advised the boys to wait it out. They just laughed
and said the *Della* was sealed tight as a cork and they were old
hands at crossing the Stream in ever kind of weather. They cast off
and set for home and that was the last anybody saw of them. The
storm was a rough one and tore through West End a half-hour after
the Ashley boys left. The harbormaster told Clarence it likely caught

up to them before they'd cleared the Gulf Stream and took them down.

They said Old Joe refused to believe the boys had drowned. He said they were too good a sailors, Ed and Frank, and the *Della* was too good a boat. What they'd done was, they'd taken the load someplace else for some reason and would show up any day and explain things. They say Joe Ashley held tight to that idea for more than a month. Then one night everybody at Twin Oaks was woke up in the dead of darkness by what sounded like a yowling panther got into the house. It wasnt but Old Joe, wailing with realization that his sons were dead at the bottom of the sea.

All that happened in the fall of nineteen and twenty-one.

Bobby Baker was reelected sheriff in 1922. He campaigned on his record for cutting crime in Palm Beach County and as the man who put John Ashley back behind bars. Even some of the folk who liked the Ashleys couldnt help liking Bobby Baker too. The man was becoming a real smooth politician. He gave talks to political organizations, to women's clubs, to classrooms full of schoolchildren. He showed up at ever damn civic function in the county, at ever holiday parade. He almost always wore a suit with vest and tie now, even in the summer heat. He passed out little American flag pins to everybody he met. He'd never been one to take his family out in public, but now you'd see him at the moviehouse with his wife and three little girls. You'd see the whole family of them at a restaurant or eating a lunch together on a blanket under a tree after he'd give a speech at some holiday picnic. She was a quiet but gracious woman, his wife Annie, and his little girls were always perfectly well behaved. More and more the pictures you saw of him in the newspapers had his family in them too.

We didnt hear anymore such stories, neither, as we used to about what Bobby Baker had done to the Ashley whiskey camp lookouts. Some who used to believe them stories now said they always knew they was bullshit. Bobby Baker wasnt the kind of man to do such a thing, they said, they could see that now. That's what a lot of folks said. But there was some of us always figured it took a special kind of man to handle himself with the Ashleys, and if Bobby Baker was that kind, well, then there *had* to be sides to him nobody wanted to believe or even think about.

NINETEEN

July 1921–August 1923

HE WAS LOCKED INTO A SEVEN-BY-NINE CELL IN A SPECIAL BLOCK
set apart from the rest of the prison and he did not come out
again for one year and eleven months and four days. The door
was of iron bars and faced a narrow dimly lighted corridor. If there
were any other cells close by he could not see them nor did he raise
response when he hallooed loudly from his door. The concrete floor
was slightly concave and in its center was a shithole three inches wide
and engirt with the umber wastestains of countless convicts over the
decades. Once a week a guard flung a pail of water through the door
to give the cell a rudimentary rinse. John Ashley quickly learned to
anticipate these occasions and would sit naked near the door to receive
the brunt of the water and thus wash himself somewhat.

In the rear wall was set a small barred window eight feet above
the floor. It was a foot square in dimension and its top was even with
the ceiling. It was brightest with daylight in the late afternoons.
Through it came birdsong, leaves off a looming water oak, the frost
of winter nights. During hard storms of westerly wind the rain spattered into the cell and he positioned himself to receive the drops on
his face. He loved the thunder and sporadic flaring of lightning at the
window. His narrow bunk was bolted too far from the window to
serve as a platform and there was nothing else on which he might
stand, and so the only way he could look out was to pull himself up
by the bars and hold there by arm strength and with his toes effecting

the barest purchase on the wall. In this way would he gaze out on the trunk and branches of the oak that stood almost near enough to touch, on a portion of a highwalled weedgrown yard littered with broken wagon wheels, torn harness, and rusted parts of automobiles and other machines. At various times of the day he would cling to the window until the burning in his biceps became unbearable and he'd drop back to the floor. To straighten his cramped arms was then so painful he'd nearly cry out.

He never saw nor heard anybody in the little yard but often saw birds—mostly jays and crows and mockingbirds—come to feed on insects in the grass. He sometimes spied cats hunting in the yard and once saw a scruffy tortoiseshell catch a mouse and devour it on the spot in less than a minute. One time a sparrow flew into the cell and couldnt make its way out again and it flew wildly until it hit the wall in exhaustion and lit on the floor. He picked it up and felt its tiny heart quivering against his palm and the light in its eyes dimmed as if some wick within were being turned down and it died in his hand. He pulled himself up to the window and dropped the bird outside and felt foolish in his notion that it was now freer than he was.

Since the day of his arrival at Raiford he'd not again seen the warden nor anybody else except the guards who twice a day brought his meals on a tin plate they slid through a narrow slot at the bottom of the door. In the beginning he'd tried to make small talk but neither of the hacks ever made reply nor even looked directly at him and so he quit trying. He was as hungry for conversation as he was for food but would be damned if he'd let them know it. Almost without variance he was fed on fatback, cornbread, molasses and coffee every morning, on blackeyed peas, greens, rice and water every night. Occasionally his plate held a thin watery stew of pork or rabbit. Besides the exercise of holding himself up to the window several times a day, he also did daily pushups and situps and stretching routines of every sort. He took to punching the wall every day, one hundred times with his right fist and then one hundred with his left. He punched the rough stone lightly at first but as the months went by and his knuckles enlarged and gained thicker callus he could hit harder and harder without breaking the skin. He stood on his head for a count of two hundred every morning and again every evening because he'd heard that the habit improved your upright balance and that such regular infusion of blood to the head would make you smarter.

He talked to himself to keep in the practice of speech and hear a human voice if only his own. He described the splendors of the Devil's

Garden, the vast sawgrass horizons and the skies without limit, the veils of heat that rose and shimmered in the heart of summer midday as if the air itself had been crazed by the sun. He held forth on thunderheads that swelled like encroaching mountains of coal until they overwhelmed the sky and sparked with lightning and detonated with thunderclaps and burst into storms as explosive and incandescent as heaven's own war. He remarked on the ripe smells of verdure and muck that followed hard rain. He talked of whitetailed deer bounding through the pinewoods in misty dawn silence, of redtail hawks wheeling in graceful hunt over wide savannahs, of the dogbark call of alligators and the ruby glint of their eyes just above the waterline where the lanternlight found them in the dark. He spoke of the cold blue colors and fast deep currents of the Gulf Stream, of the exhilarating sight of porpoises cavorting alongside a boat far out to sea, of the sound of ocean nightwinds and the strange faint melodies they sometimes carried which graybeard sailors said were ancient songs of drowned women whose undying love had transformed them to mermaids. To cockroaches skittering across the floor he confessed that the sea had always scared him.

He was determined not to break under the weight of his isolation nor to dwell on the length of his sentence. But he sometimes found himself thinking he'd missed forever his chance to even the score with Bob Baker and he cursed himself aloud for not havin settled things with him when he had the chance and to hell with his daddy's order to leave Bobby alone. Such ruminations made him want to howl like a dog forlorn. He'd punch the walls till his knuckles looked like purple grapes.

On clear nights he stood with his back against the door bars and gazed on the small patch of stars framed in the window and among the oak branches. In phases of the lunar cycle he'd see the moon for brief periods of the night and his chest would tighten with the beauty of it. He sometimes saw the moon showing after daybreak like a bruised pearl or a segment therefrom against a soft patch of blue sky.

Excepting the mermaids and their sea-songs he did not speak of women, not even to the cockroaches. He tried hard to keep women from his waking mind. But from the start of his isolation he dreamt almost nightly of Loretta May who was blind but could see across time and distance and into the heart of things, she whose nipples were sometimes the color of caramel and sometimes of brown sugar, depending on her state of excitement, whose skin smelled of peaches and her hair of daybreak dew. And he dreamt of course of Laura who smelled always of the swamp and whose joy in sex was as abandoned as a cat's. He dreamt of dancing with her at Elser Pier to plinking ragtime and blatant jazz bands. In his sleep he sometimes revisited the three occasions on which they had all frolicked together in Loretta's bed and he sometimes ejaculated as he dreamt and he sometimes woke with a throbbing erection that flexed like a snake in his hand as he came. He dreamt also of seeing them together without him, kissing and caressing each other's bare flesh, and he knew the dream was true but he did not mind that they took comfort from each other that way. He could not have explained how he knew they were doing it as much for love of him as for any other reason. But so rousing were these visions that by the end of his fourth month in isolation he was masturbating several times a day. He continued this excess for weeks. The deepest reach of his rectum developed a chronic ache. Not until his raw and discolored cock became infected and too painful to touch was he able to free himself of the mania. Once his penis was hale again he refrained from choking the chicken—as he and his brothers had called it since boyhood—but a few quick times a week. Over the next months the practice palled to the point that he abandoned it altogether. He thereafter spent himself only as he dreamed of Laura and Loretta May.

In his sleep one cool night of his first October in isolation he saw his brothers out at sea. It was like watching a moving picture show without the accompanying piano music—all action and no sound at all, not even the whirring of the projection machine. He knew somehow that his brothers were on the back leg of a whiskey run, knew they were in the Gulf Stream and bearing westnorthwest. The *Della* rode low on the gathering swells under an amber crescent moon running through ragged purple clouds. High black thunderheads were closing from the west, sporadically backlit by shimmers of sheet lightning. Ed was at the wheel, smiling and talking, and though he could not hear his words John Ashley knew he was relating some recent sexual adventure with Rita the Breed. Frank clung one-handed to the cabin railing and laughed.

But now the brothers both looked out into the night and John Ashley knew they were hearing the sound of powerful marine engines. The boats materialized from the cloud shadows into the brightness of the moon, two sleek craft and each perhaps thirty feet long and running without lights, one bearing on the *Della* from southwestward and the other coming at her from the north. Ed opened the throttles wide as Frank swooped belowdecks and came back up with a Browning Automatic Rifle. The *Della* cut smoothly through the water but even though the engines were churning at full speed the bow was hardly raised at all, so heavy was their cargo, and the speedboats were closing fast.

Now automatic fire sparked from both boats and John Ashley saw where the bullets spouted the water aft of the *Della*'s stern and then the shooters had the range and rounds were gouging into the hull and the after bulkhead and shattering the cabin ports. He saw Frank kneel at the transom and fire a long burst with the BAR—and then he jerked sideways and he fell down clutching at his forehead, his mouth wide and showing all its teeth. Ed looked back at him, yelling something, yanking at the throttle as though he might wrest greater speed from the engines through sheer will. And then he suddenly flung forward against the wheel and John Ashley saw the brilliant red blossoms on his back as Ed slumped to the deck with blood overrunning his scarred mouth.

The *Della*'s freed wheel spun wildly and the boat veered to starboard as bullets continued ripping into her and first one engine must have quit and then the other must have died too because the boat ceased its forward progress and rode the swells adrift. The shooting stopped and the speedboat pilots backed off their engines and the boats closed in slowly.

Now the moon was vanished into the roiling black clouds and enormous rays of lightning illuminated the night sea as bright as day and John Ashley in his tossing sleep felt the force of the thunderclaps he could not hear. He saw Frank rise to all fours in the gathered darkness and slashing rain and crawl to Ed. Saw the darkly gaping wound over Frank's eye running with blood and rainwater. Saw him shake Ed by the shoulder. Frank was yelling now and Ed's eyes opened. Grappling hooks lofted over the gunwales and caught hold and the hooklines went taut and Frank was searching the deck for the BAR and spied it several feet away and started for it but a booted foot planted on his hand. He looked up half-blinded for the blood in his eyes and John Ashley saw as Frank saw the grinning face of Bo Stokes above the cocked .45 almost touching Frank's face. Saw too a tall lean man standing unsteadily over Ed in the pitching boat with a pistol in his hand. In a spectral cast of lightning the pitted face of Alton Davis. Ed stirring weakly and Frank's mouth moving and John Ashley knew Frank was cursing them. Bo Stokes laughing. And then the pistols flashed and his brothers fell still.

They found the other Browning belowdecks and passed both rifles to one of the other boats. They made no effort to unload the whiskey, maybe because of the storm or maybe because they had no interest in it from the start. They emptied a gasoline can into the cabin and set a match to it and then hurried back onto their boats and made away just as the brunt of the storm rolled in.

The *Della* pitched and yawed to every direction and flames leaped from the cabin ports and hatch. The boat spun crazily and traced great sparking loops of fire above the bucking black sea and in the clarity of his dream he saw his brothers lying dead in the driving rain. Then the fire broke through the cabin deck and found the whiskey in the hold and the entire hull burst into flame. A huge wave hove the vessel high and turned it on an awkward axis and the boat was poised on its stern for a long shimmering moment before capsizing and tumbling down the wave's steep slope in scaling sheets of fire and the wave broke over the upturned keel in a great raise of smoke and the *Della* whirled under the sea and was gone.

He woke in a soaking sweat, gasping for air as though he'd been drowning. Woke to the sounds of rain and weeping. And found that it was in fact raining. And that the weeping was his own.

In the late spring of 1923 he was removed from isolation and taken to a shower room where his first full soapy wash in two years gradually unloosed from his hide scales of dirt and clogs of casefied bodily exudates that ran off him as a rank gray gruel. His flesh was rashed and splotched and scabbed, coated with sores both old and fresh. Then to the prison barber who grinned at the sight of his wild shag and beard and cheerfully set to work upon him. His hair was cropped to a buzz and lice burrowed in the thick locks tumbled to his sheeted lap. His beard was scissored and then shaved with such dexterity he showed but two bloodspots when the job was done. The barber finished up by rubbing kerosene into his scalp. He was then led to the supply room and issued a fresh set of convict stripes and told to put them on. Then to the warden's office where he learned he was being assigned to the Rockpile Gang.

"You wont be in general population," the warden said, "but it's better than that damned isolation cell, isnt it? Two years in isolation's enough to make some men loony but you look to be all right in the head. Of course now, we cant always judge by looks, can we?" The assistant warden stood against the wall with his arms folded and looked to John Ashley like he was trying not to yawn.

The warden chuckled and paused to light a cigarette. It was the first tobacco smoke John Ashley had smelled since arriving at Raiford and the aroma was so heady he felt mildly faint. Sweet Jesus, boy, he thought—the things you done without.

"There's no escaping from the Rockpile Gang, take my word," the warden said. "You'll see that for yourself. But if you're fool to try it anyway, you'll get shot dead, I promise. I surely hope you believe me, John."

John Ashley said he did.

And now the warden cleared his throat loudly and glanced out the window and then looked at the assistant warden and then at John Ashley and cleared his throat again. "There's somethin more," he said. He told John Ashley that his brothers had been reported drowned while fishing in the Atlantic Ocean. The accident had occurred in October of the previous year but prison policy prohibited giving information of any sort to inmates in isolation. He regretted that he had been denied this knowledge for so long but it simply couldnt be helped. John Ashley looked at him but said nothing. The warden studied his face for a moment and then nodded as though he'd been told something satisfactory.

The Rockpile Gang was quartered in a windowless cell block secured tight as a tomb. He shared a cell with a convict named Ray Lynn, a weathered sandy-haired Florida native from Crawfordville who was serving six years for armed robbery. The Rockpile Gang's membership, Ray Lynn informed him, varied from six or seven men to nearly two dozen, depending on the warden and the assistant warden's whims. "You never know what either a them fuckheads will do next. Puttin a fella in isolation right off, thats the warden's way of dealin with dangerous convicts. Likes to try to bust they spirit first thing. But I gotta say, you was in there a lot longer than anybody else I know of." The rockpile was for convicts the warden considered particularly high risk for escape, Ray Lynn said. "Or for fellas the underwarden just flat fuck dont like."

The rockpile stood in a remote sideyard—a huge sprawling heap of limerock boulders brought in on a half-dozen trucks once a week. The gang was shuffled out to it on a common legchain. Only at the rockpile itself and in their cells were they ever off that chain. They broke the boulders apart with sledgehammers until no piece remained bigger than a fist. Then shoveled the broken rock into trailers to be hauled away to various construction projects. They broke and shoveled stone from sunup to sundown six-and-half days a week and always under the eyes of wall guards armed with shotguns.

Ray Lynn had been on the Rockpile Gang for nine months—longer than anybody else except Ben Tracey who'd been on it for nearly eighteen months. On John Ashley's first day on the rockpile, Lynn introduced him to Tracey whose grin was absent a front tooth and whose aspect suggested that nothing this world might show him would be cause for surprise. He was doing five years for second degree murder and two for attempted murder, but he'd cut almost a third off his sentence for good behavior and was due for release in another two months. He'd killed a man he caught coupling with his sister in a barn back home in Tallahassee. "He might of got her to claim it was rape and he'd been free as a bird," Ray Lynn said in low voice later that evening in their cell. "Probly wouldnt of even gone to trial. But after beatin the sumbitch dead with a shovel, he started in on *her* too." He paused to glance at Tracey in his cell across the way. "All told, I'd say he got him a pretty light sentence." His voice was barely at a whisper. "Especially since the way some tell it, he'd been shagging little sister his ownself, you see, and he had just a awful shit fit when he seen her doing it with somebody else."

John Ashley looked over at Tracey. Ray Lynn read his aspect and said, "I dont know if it's true about the sister. It's some say he's a bug with all women. I dont know. I just know he's a damn good one to have on your side when things get hairy."

Ray Lynn was on the Rockpile Gang because he had tried to escape from a turpentine camp. "Hell, I didnt have no idea of tryin to light out when they sent me there," he told John Ashley. "I just wanted to do the two years I had left on my three-year sentence and get out. But goddamn, you ever *been* in a turpentine camp?" John Ashley said he had not, but that all he'd ever heard about them was bad. "Closest thing to living hell is all it is," Ray Lynn said. "I thought I was tough but I couldnt take that fucken place. It's only niggers can work turpentine and not die of it and even some a them dont fare too good. You dont even *want* to hear about them turpentine camps. After three months of it I didnt give a shit if they killed me tryin to escape. I figured being dead all at once would be better than stayin there and dyin little by little. So I made my break. I was two days and nights in the swamp before the dogs caught me and run me up a tree. When the posse showed up they were so mad at having to slog through the swamp after me the captain shot me in the leg as I was startin to climb down. I hit the ground so hard it knocked the breath out of me all the way to next week. When they realized they were gonna have to carry me back through the swamp on account of I couldnt walk on the leg they'd shot they kindly got hotter about the whole thing and sict the dogs on me for a while and then give me a good kickin besides. I mean to tell you I looked like hammered shit by the time they brung me back. They stuck me in solitary till my leg healed up some and then put me in the hole for fifteen days and then doubled my sentence and put me on the Rockpile Gang. And thats how come I still got moren four years to go instead of the three I had when I first got here."

John Ashley came to learn that at age sixteen Ray Lynn had impregnated his sweetheart, a girl a year his junior, and willingly married her. But their families had been feuding for generations—and both families cut all ties with them. Ray Lynn could not say what the feud was about and doubted that anyone in either family knew either, not anymore, and yet the feud persisted. He worked at a lot of menial jobs to try to support wife and child but it had been rough times. Their second winter together was particularly hard and the baby contracted pneumonia and died. His wife withdrew into her grief and he could not bring her out of it. He took to drinking and keeping bad company. One day he helped a couple of buds rob a lumberyard office in Tallahassee. His share of the take was fourteen dollars. He took it home and gave it to his wife. She suspected he had stolen it and wept. He was trying to placate her when the police arrived and arrested him. One of the others had been caught and ratted out the rest. He served six months in the Leon County jail and when he went home his wife had moved away and no one knew where and he had not seen her since.

At noon every day the captain on the wall would blow his whistle and the gang would lay down their hammers and shovels and line up to receive the common leg shackle before being taken to the mess hall for dinner. On his fifth day on the rockpile and just after the captain sounded his noon whistle, John Ashley was lined up in front of a gang member named Pankin who suddenly yelled, "You aint so fucken tough!" and stabbed him in the short ribs with a shank fashioned from a spoon. John Ashley seized Pankin in a headlock and pulled him down to his knees and began beating him on the head with a melon-sized chunk of limerock. Pankin's backup man was set to stab Ashley in the neck but Ben Tracey tripped him down and started kicking him and Ray Lynn ran up and joined in. The guards came running with their clubs to break up the fight. Pankin was unconscious for two days and woke up dimmer of wit than he'd already been. But the guards reported the incident truthfully, and the warden sent Pankin and his confederate to the hole for thirty days and then assigned them to a turpentine camp. Ben Tracey—who'd risked losing his accumulated good time when he jumped into the fray—stood exonerated, as did Ray Lynn. John Ashley was hospitalized for ten days and then returned to the rockpile. He told Ray Lynn and Ben Tracey they had a friend for life.

The last Sunday of July was a visiting day and that afternoon he was permitted his first visitor since arriving at Raiford. His father sat across from him at a table extending the width of the room and partitioned with chickenwire. Guards stood against the walls on either side of the partition. John Ashley smiled to see that the old man's movements were still quick and his eyes yet alert and full of fire.

"They aint overfed you, thats certain sure," Old Joe said, assessing the leanness of him, the edged planes of his face.

"Shoulda seen when I first come out that solitary," John Ashley said. "Looked about like a broomstick. Looked like I never in my life seen the sun. I'd get fattened up quick enough I reckon if I could get some of Ma's cookin in me."

"She sent a basket but they say you caint have it. She and your sisters wanted to come but I said no. I wont have them in such place as this."

Now Joe Ashley leaned close to the screen and told John it wouldnt be long before he got a chance to slip away. Ira Goldman had found out that if you wanted to make a deal with Raiford you didnt talk to the warden, you went to see his assistant, a man named Webb. Ira was close to working something out with him.

"This underwarden sumbitch wont guarantee nothin except the chance for you to slip out," Old Joe said. "Told Ira it'd be just him and one guard and one driver in on it." He looked around to be certain nobody had closed to earshot distance, then leaned to the screen again. "He's asking for the moon, this Webb. We aint settled on a sum but I do believe he's lookin for me to retire him for life. I guess I caint rightly blame him. He aint gone have a shadow of a job after you fly this coop, thats sure."

John Ashley said the plan would cost even more than Old Joe thought it would. "I want a fella here to get put on a road gang," he said. He told his father about Ben Tracey's and Ray Lynn's help in the rockpile fight. Ben was due for release soon but they'd have to deliver Ray Lynn. "Cant do that unless he's outside these walls," he said.

"He took your side in a fight, hell yes we'll deliver him," Old Joe said.

The problem was the money. Old Joe's profits had fallen off badly in the time John Ashley had been locked away. Bellamy had found some better beaches for landing his smuggled whiskey—down in the upper keys and in Florida Bay—and had cut down on the amount of stuff he brought through Palm Beach County by boat and truck both. "We aint been makin near as much as we used to on our deal with him," Old Joe said.

He was still operating the whiskey camps—five of them, all told, in the pinelands and the Devil's Garden both—and had more customers than ever. But the money from moonshine and Bellamy's payoffs was hardly sufficient anymore to cover much else beyond operating and living expenses. The cost of distillation equipment and ingredients had gone high as the sky since Prohibition and the cops on their payroll were greedier than ever—and there were always more and more of them to pay off.

To fatten their treasury, Joe told him in a whisper, the gang had hit a couple of banks. It had been Hanford Mobley's idea. Bill Ashley had argued against it for all the same old reasons but nobody wanted to hear it. Even Laura was in favor of the bank jobs, Old Joe said, keeping a sidewise watch on the guards. "Insisted she'd do the driving. The boys all know damn well she can outdrive any a them and shoot just as good too, so nobody argued the point. You got you a good one in her, boy. She got a right amount of sand, that girl."

John Ashley grinned and said, "Naturalborn outlaw aint she? Just like Ma." He did not mention that two months ago he had dreamt of seeing Laura with an army .45 on her hip and driving hatless down a sandy pinewoods road with her hair tossing in the wind. She was laughing along with the boys around her—Hanford and Clarence and Roy—and all of them with money in their fists. He'd awakened smiling.

The gang had robbed the bank in Arcadia of ten thousand dollars, Joe told him. Back in April. Hanford, Clarence and Roy did the job in under five minutes and Laura scooted the getaway car out of there like a scalded dog. And then three weeks ago they hit the bank in Wauchula. They'd heard that the money for a big cattle deal was on deposit there but it turned out they'd been misinformed—there was only seven grand in the vault. It was worth it anyway, Old Joe said, just to even the score a little with that dickhead Sheriff Poucher who'd put the arm on John at Goren's fishcamp. "Would of been better if we could of let him know we did it," Old Joe said, "but I didnt want to draw no more heat from the cops than we already got." They'd not only hit banks far from home, but on both jobs had worn bandannas over their faces as well, and none of them had been recognized.

"We figured not to do any robbing in Palm Beach," Joe said. "Bobby Baker's let us alone since you been gone and we didnt see no need to agitate him and get him troublin our whiskey business." He looked around and leaned so close to the wire his nose almost touched it. "The thing is, we just got word a big construction company's about to put more'n forty grand in the bank at Stuart. They got a contract to rebuild most of the city docks and the money's for payrolls and operatin capital and such. It's too fat to pass up. That job'll give us all we need to pay off this Webb. It's worth takin a chance with Bobby."

John Ashley asked how he knew the information about the Stuart bank was accurate.

"Your old bud told us. George Doster. Remember him from the bank in Avon? That good family man that talked you into leavin some of the money when you robbed him for the second time? He's the assistant manager at the Stuart Bank now. But he's a unhappy fella, George is. Thinks he aint gettin paid near enough for as hard as he works and all the responsibility he got. Been feelin real sorry for hisself. That's why he come to us with a deal. Said he'd tell us just exactly when a big bunch of money would be put in the bank. Said he'd tell us on one condition."

"You had to promise that good family man a cut," John Ashley said.

"Ten percent he wanted," Old Joe said. "I told him five and he better take it, and he did."

They grinned. And then as if they'd both had the same thought at the same time, their grins faded and they stared at each other without expression and Old Joe sat back. John felt his chest tighten as he said, "You aint had much to say about Frank and Ed."

Old Joe looked off for a moment. Then told him flatly his brothers had drowned nearly two years ago on a whiskey run when they got caught in a bad storm out on the Gulf Stream. "I'm sorry to tell you this way, boy, and I'm sorry to tell you so long after the fact of it. Your Ma was near distracted by it. Didnt hardly say a word for the better part of three months. Just sat out on the porch in her rocker and looked out at nothin. It were hard on her when Bob got killed, but that was somethin she'd pretty much been expectin from the time he was a boy and she saw how nobody could tell him nothin and how reckless he was. Boys like Bob dont never get to be old men and she knew it. But Frank and Ed, well, they was rough boys but they was good to mind me and her, they wasnt reckless. And it bein the both of them at once, well . . . it went hard on her."

He told John that just nine days before he died Frank had asked Jenny to marry him and she'd said yes. When she got the bad news she shut herself up in her parents' home for nearly two months in her grief and when she emerged she was wasted and pale and carried herself like an old woman. She had taken a train for Charleston where her family had kin and she had not returned nor was expected to. As for Rita the Breed, she'd simply vanished. One story held that she'd taken up with some mean Indian who lived on the far side of Okeechobee and they hadnt been together three weeks before they had a bad fight and he killed her. Another rumor said she'd gone to Apalachicola and was working in a whorehouse. Nobody knew.

Joe Ashley kept his eyes away from his son's as he said these things, and John knew it had been harder on the old man than on anyone else, even Ma. Now Old Joe swallowed hard and snorted and narrowed his eyes as he looked at John. "This warden here, he told Ira you couldnt be told about Frank and Ed cause you was in isolation. Prison policy, he said. Sorry bastard. I'd like to show him what I think of his fucken *policy*. Anyhow, I'm truly sorry, boy, that—"

"Listen, Daddy," John Ashley said, "it's somethin I got to say." He said it so softly that Old Joe knew what would follow was bad. He knew his boys, knew their tones. He put his ear close to the screen.

John Ashley recounted for his father his dream of Frank and Ed, a dream he'd had but once and yet recalled as vividly as if he'd awakened from it a minute ago. When he was done with the telling his chest was tight, his voice strained. Old Joe eased back from the screen and stared at him. His face looked carved of limerock.

"It wasnt but a dream," John Ashley said, "but—"

Old Joe shushed him with a raised hand. "Dont say nother word." He told him to keep out of trouble and stay ready. Then took his leave.

Ben Tracey had no visitor that day. The story around the yard was that the only visitor he'd ever had was his sister who came but once. During his fourth month at Raiford she showed up to let him see for himelf the ruin he'd made of her face with the shovel. Even the most hardened cons who'd looked on her were moved to pity. She made Ben Tracey look at her face and cursed him to hell and then broke into tears and fled the room. Back in the block Tracey joked that if he'd had to look at her a minute longer he would've horked his dinner. None of the cons who'd seen his sorrowed sister laughed. Most of them hated Ben Tracey. But they feared him even more and so held their opinion mute.

Ray Lynn received no visitor that day nor any other.

A hot August night in Miami. The air unmoving, congealed with humidity. A cat's-eye moon in a hazy sky holding but distant promise of rain and few stars to be seen. The Hardieville streets poorly lighted and sparsely trafficked this midweek eve.

Two men emerge from the front door of The High Tider—formerly The Purple Duck owned and operated by Miss Catherine Mays who'd departed for California shortly after her fiancé Gordon Blue had been found dead in the Miami River. The men stroll down the street and turn at the end of the block and approach a parked roadster. One chuckles at something the other says. As they pass under a streetlamp their faces are for the moment clearly exposed, the pockmarked aspect of Alton Davis and the chin-scarred visage of James White. Davis cranks the motor to life and settles himself behind the wheel. White lights a cigarette. Davis stares at a pair of young couples going down the street a block away with their arms about each other and one of the boys fondling his girl's ass. Now two men step from the shadows and into the hazy light of the streetlamp and stand directly before the car and each of them aims a pair of .45 automatics at the two men through the windshield. James White's mouth sags open and the cigarette drops burning from his lips as he looks on Hanford Mobley and Roy Matthews grinning behind the guns and he wonders what it feels like to be shot and he wants to turn to Davis but cannot and only manages to say, "Alton, shit . . ." and Davis turns to him and does an almost comic double-take back to the men holding guns on them and he makes a low grave sound as he grabs for his shoulder-holstered revolver knowing he will never touch it and he doesn't for in that instant Mobley and Matthews start squeezing off rounds as fast as they can work the triggers.

The windshield flies apart and Davis and White jerk and twitch and lurch like dire epileptics and blood jumps from their heads and faces and several bullets glance off the roadster and ricochet off the building across the street and one stray round makes a starburst hole in a shop window and almost as abruptly as it began the rapidfire gunblasting ceases, all thirty-two rounds of the four Colts spent. In the jaundiced haze of gunsmoke under the streetlamp Roy Matthews steps around to the passenger side and spits in James White's ruined face uptilted against the car door. Then the shooters are gone in the darkness.

Only now do heads cautiously appear at some of the doorways to peek out at the death car. Blood runs in a thin line from under the driver's door and pools darkly in the street as though the automobile itself has suffered mortal wound. Only now do the girls on the street who watched the whole thing in open-mouthed shock begin a hysterical wailing. And not until this moment does one of the young men with them realize he has pissed in his pants.

In a late hour of the same night . . .

Bo Stokes comes out of a restaurant at the north end of Biscayne Boulevard where he has dined on a superbly broiled red snapper and his thoughts now are of a particular woman he is to meet at the McAllister Hotel. She is lean and lovely with firm breasts and a pubic bush soft as a Persian kitten. He feels himself heavy in his loins as he walks along this northern portion of boulevard lit only by the narrow moon and the lights from the train depot across the street. He glances skyward to check for possibility of rain and sees none.

A car draws up to the curb alongside and a voice calls, "Hey, Bo, wait up! Look here who wants to meet you, man."

He stoops slightly to look into the coupé and sees a man behind the wheel and a woman sitting by the passenger window and both silhouetted against the light from the depot. "Who's that?" he says.

"It's me, man," the driver says. "Look here who wants to meet you." A bare female arm extends from the interior darkness and the fingers flutter in greeting and then quickly withdraw as the woman giggles.

Bo Stokes laughs and steps up to the car and leans one arm against the car roof and peers into the gloomy interior and still cannot make out the driver's face nor the woman's. "Who the hell is it?" he says.

"Me, man," the driver says. "This here's Wanda. She been wanting to meet you. She's seen you around, you know, at the Taft. She knows Nelson. Been telling him she wants to meet you."

"She has, huh?" Bo Stokes says. He grins at the woman's silhouette, "You told Nels you wanna meet me, huh?"

The woman nods and giggles. "Wanda, meet Bo," the driver says. "Bo, meet Wanda." She slides over closer to the driver and pats the seat beside her.

"Well now darlin," Bo Stokes says. He opens the car door and crowds his bulk onto the seat and slides an arm around the woman's shoulders and his hand closes on her thigh and the woman puts her hand to the back of his neck and he glances at the driver and even in the dim light sees now that he does not know him and he starts to draw back but the woman locks both arms hard around his neck and pulls him against her and the driver grabs him by the coat lapel and holds him fast and presses a pistol up under his chin and before Bo Stokes can gain the leverage to break free, before he can even believe this is happening to him—he who fought Jack Dempsey almost even for two rounds and scored several good shots before the Mauler caught him with a right hook that brought the stellar sky down on his head—he sees an explosion of stars to surpass all imagination and where the bullet goes through the car roof it leaves a dark viscid smear.

Laura Upthegrove pulls the door shut as Clarence Middleton wheels the car into the street and if anybody along the boulevard heard the pistol report there is no sign of it.

"This dress is just ruint," Laura says as Clarence makes a right turn at the corner and heads around the block. She holds the heavy press of the dead man to her like a lover so that any who sees them might take them for such. She feels the blood seeping warmly over her breasts and down her belly, smells it ripe through the scent of cordite. "Good thing I never did like it worth a damn."

Clarence drives back onto the boulevard and heads north. In another hour he will be dropping Bo Stokes' mortal remains in a canal miles off the main highway and fourteen feet deep and swarming with gators.

Near midnight of yet the same evening . . .

Nelson Bellamy is lying supine and fondling the heavy breasts of the naked woman mounted on him and rolling her hips with expert technique. The bedside lamp is lit but the woman has draped Bellamy's undershirt over it to effect a more subdued cast of light. So engrossed are the lovers in what they are doing—and so loud is the music booming through the open window from the dance pavilion next door—that neither hears the small clack of the doorlock Joe Ashley has opened with a ring of keys appropriated from a downstairs maid. He is masked with a bandanna and holds a shotgun with cut-down barrels and the stock reduced to a pistolgrip.

They had pulled up their masks and entered the Taft Hotel—he and Albert Miller—through the kitchen. Albert Miller put a pistol to a cook's head and asked which room was Nelson Bellamy's and the man said 302 without hesitation and they could see he was too frightened to be lying. Just then a maid came in from the adjoining linen room and at the sight of the key ring on her waist Old Joe smiled and said the Good Lord was making it all too easy. Albert Miller remained downstairs to hold the cooks in place as well as any other who might come to the kitchen in the interim. On the third floor landing Old Joe came on a pair of guards playing rummy, men so long without challenge they'd grown lax and dull and they sat with their cards in their hands and one asked in raised voice to be heard over the music who he was. Joe Ashley brought the cutoff up from behind his leg and cocked both hammers and the guards went still and mute. He disarmed each of them in his turn and ordered one to lie on the floor and the other to use cords off the *window curtains to bind his partner's hands tightly behind him and tie his feet together. Joe then clubbed the untied man in the back of the head with the muzzle of the sawed-off and the man fell to his knees and clutched his head and swore vehemently and said, "What the fuck you do that for?" He started to get up and turn around and Joe hit him again, harder, squarely atop his crown. The man fell on his side and gripped the top of his head with both hands and rocked on the floor and wept with the pain and swore heatedly. Old Joe gaped and said, "Son of a bitch." And once more hit the man in the head with the shotgun—this time behind the ear—and this time the man fell still. Blood ran in a thin rivulet from his hair and stained the carpet under his head. "Shit man, you killed him," the tied man said. Old Joe told him to shut up. He knelt beside the bleeding man and checked his pulse at his throat and felt that he was still alive. He took the cords off another window curtain and tied the unconscious man tightly hand and foot. Then checked the first man's bonds and found that they been left just loose enough that the men might with effort work himself free, and so he tightened them. He dragged the unconscious man around and using their belts tied the two men together back to back, each man's hands belted to the other's feet. He pulled off their shoes and socks and balled the socks and stuffed a pair into each man's mouth. He studied his handiwork and picked up his shotgun and saw the conscious one watching him:*

"You try callin out or you make a fuss any other way before I come back through, I promise you'll die."

Now he gently pushes the door open and the hallway light falls across the bed within. The girl ceases her pelvic gyration to look over her shoulder and she sees a masked man with a wild tangle of white hair coming toward her with darkcircled eyes glowing like coalfires in a nightwind. He motions her away and she scrabbles off the bed and against the wall where she huddles with her arms crossed over her breasts. Bellamy rises on his elbows, his cock yet upright and gleaming, and sees a shotgun muzzle two inches from his face and at the far end of the shortened barrel and the extended left arm holding it the maniacally grinning face of Joe Ashley, his bandanna mask pulled down around his neck so the man might see clearly the agent of his death. Bellamy's erection folds.

"I dont never care to come to this snakepit town," Old Joe says, "but this trip's damn well worth it."

"Hold on," Bellamy says in halting voice. "Let's talk this out."

Joe Ashley shoves the gun muzzle against Bellamy's cheek and forces his head back into the pillow. Bellamy shuts his eyes and says tightly, "Listen, listen to me, we can work this out. We're businessmen, you and me. We can work it out."

Holding the gun to Bellamy's underchin Joe Ashley withdraws an ice pick from his belt and all in one fast action shoves it to the hilt in Bellamy's heart and slips it out and steps back as Bellamy convulses but once and then lies still with eyes wide but done with seeing in this world. Joe Ashley pulls his mask up again and heads for the door. The girl whimpers into her fist at her mouth and her eyes are shut tight as if she would subvert the memory of this horror by not paying visual witness.

He exits the way he came—past the belt-bound and sock-gagged guards who have not made effort to free themselves and down to the kitchen where the cooks are seated now and drinking coffee and Albert Miller is flirting with the maid. Albert pulls his bandanna down just long enough to give her a quick kiss on the lips and then follows Old Joe into the night.

Every couple of weeks or so Laura presented herself at the kitchen door of Miss Lillian's to be admitted by Wisteria, the daytime head-maid who adored Miss Loretta and delighted in the special charge of conveying Miss Laura to and from her room. A few weeks earlier Wisteria had told Loretta May of seeing a scruffy one-eyed marmalade kitten wandering about in the alley behind the house and being re-minded of Mister John by it. Loretta had insisted that she go find the kitten and bring it to her and the maid had done so. Loretta named the cat Johnny and it had lived in her room ever since.

Laura always arrived shortly after sunrise, at which hour Miss Lil-lian and the girls were just retired until the midafternoon and no one was about in the house but the Negro help. If any of the domestics were curious about her visits they kept their curiosity to themselves. She would usually stay but an hour or two, sometimes longer. Some-times they fell asleep in each other's arms and in those instances the good Wisteria would do as Miss Loretta had instructed and tap on her door at one o'clock to rouse Laura so she could be on her way before the rest of the house came awake.

They never questioned their actions together, these two. They held each other close and kissed and caressed and their mutual affections now and then were of such intimacy to render them both breathless. Sometimes they spoke of John hardly at all but he was ever on their minds. As they held each other close Loretta May would tell Laura in low voice what she had seen of him in recent dreams, what she had heard him say. She told of his lonely isolation and the things he called to mind to keep a steadfast spirit. Laura smiled at her renditions of his visions of their swampland world and of the sea—though she was fearful of the ocean even more than he was and would not venture on

it. When Loretta spoke of the near-madness of his desire for them and
the physical torment it caused him they both wept and Laura said she
wished they could fuck him for real in his dreams and then cried the
harder because they could not. When Loretta May announced one
morning that John had been released from isolation, albeit he was now
swinging a sledgehammer all day, Laura pulled her from the bed and
danced her around the room as she sang, "Johnny's in the sun again,
Johnny's in the sun again." But another day when Loretta related the
dream of seeing him stabbed, Laura was beside herself and demanded
more details and grabbed the blind woman by the shoulders and shook
her hard before collapsing in tears on her lap.

"He'll be all right, honey," Loretta May had crooned to her, stroking her hair. "It's all I know for sure but it's enough. He'll be all right."

"I made up my mind," she said. "I'm moving to Jacksonville.
Going next week."

"That so?" Roy Matthews said. They lay naked under the bedsheet,
the glowing tips of their cigarettes alternately brightening and dimming,
a steady baybreeze belling the gauzy curtains of her bedroom window
against which was framed a bone-white gibbous moon.

"My best girlfriend Rose Sharon says I can easy get me a job at
the insurance company where she works because I know how to use
a typewriting machine so well."

"I thought you liked Miami. I thought you said it's lot more lively
than Jacksonville."

"Yeah, well, it's gettin a little *too* lively, you ask me. Hardly a
week goes by there's not a shooting or some other kind of murder
going on. There's no being safe here anymore, not for any respectable
girl, anyhow. You can't even walk down the street anymore without
total strangers giving you the wolf whistle or saying something so awful
nasty you just cant believe your ears."

"That's what I hear," Roy Matthews said, snuffing their cigarettes
in a bedside ashtray. "Damn town's just chock fulla criminals and bad
actors and no-counts of all kinds. It's no place for a right citizen like
me or you to live."

"Ho ho, look who's talkin," she said.

He kissed her shoulder and said, "You gonna give me a number
so I can call you I'm ever up there?"

"Oh you with all your girls. You wouldnt call me."

"Sure I would. I'm gonna miss you plenty, sweetheart."

"Oh, *you*."

They lay facing each other and he slid his hand under the sheet and held her breast. "Does he know you're goin?"

"Well of course he does. He's not real happy about it, naturally. I *told* you he wants to marry me."

Roy Matthews chuckled and lightly tweaked her nipple and she slapped at his hand through the sheet. "If he wants to marry you why you goin to Jacksonville?"

"Cause he says he doesnt wanna live nowhere except down here in South Florida is why. You know he built a house up there where the Ashleys live?"

"Sure. For his momma and daddy. Cleared and filled some ground a quarter-mile from Twin Oaks and built the place and laid down a trail and everthing. He lives there too. So what?" His feigned puzzlement was belied by his grin.

"Dont *you* shine me, mister," she said. "When I first met him all he talked about was how much he wanted to travel around and see the country. That's exactly what I always wanted to do—travel around, see things, *do* things, you know, while I'm still *young,* damn it. For more than two years he's told me it's what he wanted to do too. *Now* he tells me he wants to stay where his roots are. His *roots!*" She snorted with disgust. "I told him, 'You know what I want and you know where I'll be. You got Rose Sharon's address and I guess you know how to write. I guess you know how to get to Jacksonville from here if you want to come see me.' That's exactly how I told him."

Roy Matthews laughed and said, "Good for you, girl. Hell, you dont need that peckerwood no way. I'll go up and see you now and then and help you keep your mind offa him." He squeezed her breasts and nuzzled her neck.

"Oh you." She pushed his hands out from under the sheet and drew it around her breasts and made a face at him. "You're *such* a liar. You and all your girls."

He grinned and tried to insinuate his hand under the sheet again but she rolled onto her back with the sheet held to her chest under her crossed arms and affected to glare at the ceiling. "And I used to think you were a nice fella. Jeepers!"

"I *am* a nice fella," he said, kissing her bare shoulder. He pulled the sheet off her breasts and she said, "Oooo, *chilly,*" and put her hands over them. He pushed one hand aside and ran his tongue over the erect nipple and prickled aureole and she made a low purr and rolled into his embrace with a smile.

TWENTY

September 1923

THEY HIT THE STUART BANK FIVE MINUTES AFTER IT OPENED FOR business on a warm and humid morning. Although Hanford Mobley was disguised as a woman his voice and demeanor identified him to the two tellers on duty who had done business with him in the past. A bank patron who ran a haberdashery and had once sold Mobley a pair of trousers recognized him as well. The tellers were also certain that one of the other two robbers—both of whom wore bandanna masks—was Clarence Middleton. Neither the tellers nor the customer were so foolish as to let the bandits know they'd been recognized. The identities of the third robber and the getaway driver were yet mysteries.

They rushed from the bank with guns in hand and people fell away from their path. A rumbling green Dodge sedan waited at the curb, Laura at the wheel in overalls and large sunglasses and with her hair tucked up under a highcrowned hat of wide floppy brim. The holdup men tumbled into the car and she gunned it away northbound on the Dixie Highway.

Sheriff Bob Baker was attending an outdoor inauguration ceremony for a new circuit judge in West Palm Beach when Deputy Henry Stubbs sidled up to him and whispered that the Stuart bank had been robbed ten minutes ago. The sheriff made apologies to the judge's party and took his leave. As they hurried to Sheriff Bob's unmarked car Stubbs told him that Hanford Mobley and Clarence Middleton were among the robbers. "I knew that little son of a bitch would be trouble," Sheriff Bob said. "Knew it the first time I laid eyes on him."

He strove to affect a cool demeanor but his blood was in a fury. He had been fair with them, damn it. More than fair. After he'd put John away he'd let that peckerwood family be. He hadn't bothered their moonshine business since way before John went back to prison. Hellfire, he'd let them hijack *other* bootleggers at will. He was no friend of the Ashleys and never would be (never again, anyway) but what was past was done with, and his past troubles with John hadnt kept him from doing the smart thing, which was to let the Ashleys go about their whiskey business any way they wanted, so long as they didnt upset the good citizens of Palm Beach County. As long as the Ashleys didnt make him look bad as sheriff he'd cut them slack. They knew that. It was a condition unspoken but understood. And now look how they'd gone and broken their side of the bargain. And for what? For putting John back in the pen? For not bothering to keep his pleasure a secret when he heard two of the Ashley boys got drowned during a whiskey haul? Hell, those things happened a couple of years ago at least. Why would they wait so long to do something about it? But *if* thats why they'd done it—*if* they'd put personal feelings above good common sense, *if* they couldnt see that bygones were bygones and live and let live was the way to go—then they were just plain damn stupid, thats all, so damn stupid they were dangerous. Crazy goddamn swamp-prats. Hell, you didnt see *him* going around eating himself up with wanting to get even with John Ashley, and he sure enough had plenty of reason. Whoever lived in the past was dead to the present—he'd heard that somewhere and thought it was sure enough true. If *he* could let the past go, why in the purple hell couldnt they? (He had the briefest flash of a thumb gouging an eyeball, of a dick at a dead man's mouth—and instantly had to remind himself of being stripped of his leg and pistol. Of being coldcocked in the jailyard in the rain. Of Julie. Julie who he loved.) Anyway, it wasn't as though it was *his* doing Frank and Ed Ashley went down in the Stream. Old Joe had no reason to go and rob a bank in *his* county where a bank had not been robbed in years. He'd given that crazy old man no call to make him look bad in the public eye. But by God if this is how the bastard wanted it, well, they'd just see who got the last laugh. He'd put *all* their asses in jail or know the reason why. In jail or in the ground.

Made no damn difference. Not to him. Not anymore.

Stubbs told him the robbers had fled north. As he got in his car Bob Baker told him to send a bulletin to all police departments as far north as Jacksonville and as westward as Tallahassee. He asked where Heck Runyon was and Stubbs said he was still in the Everglades tracking an Indian wanted for murder—but Fred Baker was in Fort Pierce. Bob Baker told him to send word to Freddie to put up roadblocks at that town's exits. It'd likely be too late to catch them going into town but if the robbers lingered there for any reason it might not be too late to catch them trying to come out. He also wanted Freddie to have two fast unmarked cars ready to go—and six good men with arms and ammunition. Stubbs ran off to send the messages and Bob Baker headed off to Fort Pierce.

He paused in Stuart long enough to go in the bank and make quick interrogation of the robbery witnesses. The tellers said they had no doubt whatever that Mobley and Middleton were two of the bandits. George Doster who appeared to be ill said he wasn't so sure as all that. Sheriff Bob accepted the majority opinion. He dispatched four deputies to the Ashley place at Twin Oaks with explicit orders not to engage in a fight should they find Mobley or Middleton on the premises. "If they're there, you just let me know," Bob Baker instructed them. "Dont do anything but keep the sonsofbitches under watch till I get there."

Twenty-five minutes later he rolled up to the south town limits of Fort Pierce where Fred Baker stood waiting beside his own police car. They'd found the green Dodge getaway car in an alley at the west end of town. It had been stolen. A witness saw four men get out of the Dodge and into a Ford sedan and head out on the Yeehaw Road. Fred had two cars ready to go and in them sat the Padgett brothers, and four other Baker Gang deputies, all of them as heavily armed as soldiers.

Bob Baker bit off the end of a cigar and spat it out and tugged down his hat and looked off to the flat horizon in the west. "I figure they got less than a hour's headstart. Let's go!"

They were unaware they'd been identified in the bank. As he stripped off his female disguise Hanford Mobley yelled, "Anybody comin?" Roy Matthews was looking out the car's rear window and said, "Nary soul."

Clarence Middleton watched Mobley taking off his woman's clothing and now hollered as though at a cooch show, "Put it *on*, baby, put it *on!*" Roy Matthews laughed and said Mobley was sure enough about the skankiest woman he'd ever seen. Hanford Mobley told them to fuck themselves, the disguise had been a real smart idea.

"That's right, honey," Laura said, glancing at him sidewise and grinning as she sped them down the dusty road. "Pretty is as pretty does and dont you let these peckerwoods tell you different." But she couldnt help laughing along with Clarence and Roy. "And you watch your goddamn language, hear? There's a lady present in case you didnt know." Mobley glared at her but held his tongue.

He swiftly counted the take and said, "Forty thousand, my sorry ass. It aint but a little over twenty-three thousand here."

"I think Old Joe ought to figure Doster's five percent out of the difference," Roy Matthews said.

"I think he should pay Doster *with* the difference," Laura said. "He ought say, 'Hey bubba, you know that seventeen grand that wasnt there? Well it's all yours. And it's *all* thats yours.' "

Hanford Mobley put twenty thousand dollars in one satchel and the rest of the money in another. Laura slowed as they came in sight of Fort Pierce. They followed the highway through town and saw but one police car and it parked in front of a cafe. Near the north city limits and the Yeehaw Road she turned down a street and then into an alley behind a closed roadhouse where Clarence had parked a Ford sedan he'd stolen in Vero before sunrise that morning. They abandoned the Dodge and got into the Ford and did not see the bum watching them from his nest of crates and cardboard twenty yards away—he who would wait till they drove from sight on the Yeehaw Road and then be rummaging through the Dodge when a police car pulled up and a pair of cops pointed guns at him and told him to freeze or die. They had no inkling of the telephone call Fred Baker was receiving even as they swapped cars, no notion that ten minutes after their departure on the Yeehaw Road every exit from Fort Pierce would be posted with police.

Thirty miles west at the Okeechobee crossroad they were met by Albert Miller in a coupé. Laura took the twenty thousand dollars and got in the car with Albert and they headed back the way Albert had come—south to the town of Okeechobee and around the lake's east side to the Indiantown Road and then east through the swamp and pineywoods toward the road to Twin Oaks. Hanford Mobley took the wheel of the Ford and he and Matthews and Middleton pressed on to westward, bound for Lakeland. The plan was for them to take refuge with Mrs. Ella Fingers, a trusted woman friend of Joe Ashley's whose lucrative business was to shelter and feed men on the dodge, no questions asked. There the three would lie low for a week or so until Old Joe sent word whether they could return to Palm Beach County without fear of arrest or would have to slip back surreptitiously.

They did not think they were being followed but thought it the wiser course to proceed as though they were. Rather than take the

Sebring Road they drove on a narrow dirt road flanking the Seaboard rail line. The road was of sand and rock and even more rugged than most backcountry routes. The Model T jounced and pitched as it made its way through pinelands thick and dark that periodically gave way to marshy savannah rife with palmetto scrub. A covey of white herons took to wing like fluttering scraps of paper falling upward. A hawk swooped into the prairie grass near the edge of the road and arced back for the sky with a rabbit flailing in its talons.

Thunderheads purple and blue as fresh bruises were shaping in the western sky. At the Kissimmee River the railtracks crossed on a narrow trestle but the road veered north and followed the river to a bridge at Fort Basinger two miles away. Not wanting to be seen by anybody who might inform pursuers of their passing, they chose to cross over on the trestle rather than show themselves at the bridge. Hanford Mobley eased the car slowly onto the elevated tracks and the Model T lunged and yawed as it advanced from tie to tie in the manner of a cautious cockroach. Roy Matthews and Clarence Middleton gaped at the green river rippling below the tracks and arched their brows at each other and clutched tightly to the door posts against the car's erratic sway as it forged ahead. Hanford Mobley caught their stricken looks and laughed.

Once across the trestle they continued on the tracks for nearly another mile before the narrow backroad from Fort Basinger came curving out of the pinewoods and again ran alongside the track bed and Hanford steered the Ford down the embankment and onto it. Five miles farther on, the rail line met with the Sebring Road and ran parallel with it for almost ten miles to the north end of Lake Istokpoga before road and track once again diverged, the raised track bearing directly for Sebring through its bordering swampland and the highway curving around the swamp to come up into Sebring from the south. They had just gone around the bend of the lake when the radiator sprang a leak and began hissing loudly. A handpainted roadsign announced the Lorida Fishcamp just a mile ahead and down a narrow dirt lane to Lake Istokpoga. They drove on with steam keening before them and blowing back with a smell of hot metal and came to the camp under high wide oaks hung with Spanish moss. Here they bought cold bottles of bootleg beer and a raw egg. Clarence Middleton wrapped his hand with a bandanna and removed the radiator cap with a whoosh of steam. He cracked open the egg and dropped it into the radiator and while they drank their beer and chatted with a couple of locals about the best ways to rig a trotline the egg circulated in the steaming water and found its solidifying way to the leak and plugged it. Clarence then filled the radiator with water from a dispenser can and replaced the cap. They finished off the beer with huge sighs and ripping belches and got back in the car and pushed on.

They drove into Sebring under an early afternoon sky darkening with storm clouds. A wind had kicked up and was shaking the trees. They topped off the gas tank at a filling station and then went to a cafe and bought sandwiches and bottles of soda and asked for the food to be bagged so they could take it with them before the rain hit. While they waited for their order they flirted with the waitresses. Roy Matthews told the prettiest, a blonde named Marybelle, that he was going to be visiting an uncle in Lakeland for the next week or two and asked if she ever got up that way. She said it so happened her best girlfriend lived in Auburndale which was only a few miles from Lakeland and she would be going to visit her this coming weekend. She gave him her friend's telephone number and he winked at her and said he'd be sure to call on Friday night. Hanford Mobley had been first to speak and smile at Marybelle but after Roy Matthews caught her attention she had eyes for no one else. As they went back out to the car Mobley said it surely was pathetic to see a fella practically having to beg women for a date just because he couldnt get him a steady one. "I'm sure glad I got Glenda," Mobley said. "She makes both them girls back there look like skanks." Roy Matthews spat and laughed and let the remarks pass. Now they got on the paved main highway and bore north for Lakeland, still nearly sixty miles distant, but the roads from here on were all good and they would be there in two hours.

Barely fifteen minutes after the fugitives' departure from Sebring a three-car caravan of Palm Beach County police officers swept into town in a crashing rain. At the Fort Basinger bridge fishcamp they'd learned that two men who'd been fishing from a skiff just upriver from the railroad had seen a Ford sedan drive over the trestle earlier that afternoon and Sheriff Baker knew it was the robbers.

"They say it was only three men in the car," Fred Baker said as he drove off in the lead car with Bob Baker in the passenger seat beside him.

"Dont matter," Bob Baker said. "One might of been laying down. One might of gone off on his own for some reason. I know it's them, I *know* it. Let's move, Freddie, goose this thing."

Bob Baker had already considered that from Sebring the robbers could go north, south or west—and he planned to send a car in each direction in hopes that one of them would pick up the trail. But first all three cars pulled into a filling station for gasoline and the attendant there recognized Bob Baker's description of two of the robbers and pointed out the cafe where they'd gone after they'd fueled their car. Ten minutes later Marybelle had told him about Lakeland. Ten minutes after that he was in the Sebring police chief's office, forming a puddle of rainwater at his feet as he talked on the telephone to the Lakeland chief of police, shouting into the mouthpiece to make himself heard above the steady sequence of thunderclaps and the clatter of rain on the roof. The Lakeland chief said he'd post cars at every end of town and have any suspicious vehicles stopped for questioning. Bob Baker said he was on his way and rang off.

The police cars motored north through the swirling storm and flickering lightning, their speed hindered by poor visibility, the cars weaving sharply in the windgusts and raising little roostertails of water as they went. At Avon they turned west to Fort Meade and there cut north again and bore for Bartow and Lakeland some twenty miles beyond. Sheriff Bob Baker had been holding his own silent counsel and studying the regional map he'd been given by the Sebring chief.

"What would you do if you were them and you spotted a bunch of cops all over when you got to Lakeland?" Sheriff Baker shouted at Fred over the rain drumming on the car.

"Try to get away to someplace else, naturally," Fred yelled, staring hard into the slashing rain. "Find me another road out of there if I could."

"Wouldnt you figure the cops would probly be watchin *all* the roads around there?"

Fred Baker considered for a moment. "I reckon. Leastways the main ones."

"So wouldnt you maybe figure it'd be smarter to quit the car and travel some other way?"

"Like how?" He glanced at Bob Baker. "Like by train?"

"That's what I'm guessin."

"Not the Lakeland depot. Not with cops all over."

"No," Bob Baker said, "they wouldnt go there. Stop the car." Fred pulled off onto the shoulder and the other two cars fell in behind. The rain swept over them in torrents and the cars were jostled by the wind.

Bob Baker was staring at the map spread open in his lap. "Here's where." He put his finger to a spot and Freddie leaned over to look.

"How you know?" Fred Baker said.

"*I* dont know," Bob Baker said. "I just *know.*"

A moment later Freddie was out of the car and the rain knocked

down his hatbrim and pasted his clothes to his flesh as he went to the
car directly behind and told the Padgett brothers to bring the shotguns
and get up in the first car with him and Chief Baker. He put Henry
Stubbs in charge of the rest of the detail and told him to proceed with
both cars to Lakeland and take custody of the suspects if they'd been
apprehended or to render whatever assistance the Lakeland police
might ask for if the robbers were still at large. He told Henry that
Chief Baker would join them in Lakeland later that night.

They were almost to the Lakeland city limit when Roy Matthews
said "Cops!" and pointed to the two cars bearing police insignia on
their doors and looking ghostly in the whipping rain on the shoulder
just ahead. Mobley slowed the Ford and pulled off the road and into
a filling station as if that had been his intention all along. He wheeled
the car in a U-turn to park it next to the pumps on the side away from
the highway and further under the overhanging roof for better protection from the rain—or so, he hoped, it would seem to anybody watching them. The maneuver also put the pumps between them and the
cops and positioned the car so it pointed back the way they had come.
They all three stared back over their shoulders and through the rain
at the police cars which remained as before.

"What you boys think?" Clarence Middleton said.

"I aint sure they even seen us," Hanford Mobley said. "I aint sure
they even on the lookout for us. Could be they waitin on somebody
else. Could be they just waitin out this damn rain."

Roy Matthews grimaced. "Who the hell you kidding, boy? You
bet you ass they waitin on us. How many other people you know
robbed a bank today?"

Hanford Mobley glared. "Who knows? Maybe there was a goddamn dozen robberies today. How would we know?"

"It's *us* they're lookin for and you best know it," Roy Matthews
said. He alternately checked the loads in his shotgun and looked out
at the cop cars as he spoke. "I dont believe they seen us. Not yet. But
we can forget about goin to Miz Fingers'."

"We best get a move on before this rain lets up and they can see
some better," Clarence said.

"It's that fucken girl!" Hanford Mobley said. "You told her we
was comin to Lakeland and now here the cops are, just waitin for us.
You and your big mouth!"

"Why would she of called the cops on us?" Roy Matthews said.
"She didnt have the first damn reason to call the cops on us."

"What if the cops went callin on *her?*"

"Well why in the hell would they do *that?*"

"I dont know! But who the hell else knew we were comin here?"

"Goddammit thats enough," Clarence Middleton said. "This aint hardly the time. What we gone do here?"

An old man stepped out of the station and was struggling into a rain slicker as he started toward them. Clarence Middleton waved him away and yelled, "Never mind, bubba. We dont need no gas after all." The old man shrugged and went back inside.

"Shit!" Hanford Mobley hammered the steering wheel with the heel of his fist. "They're like to have cops set up on *all* the roads around here."

"Listen," Roy Matthews said, "Plant City's not but ten miles from here and there's a backroad to it—about half a mile yonderway. I know cause I took it once. No way in hell they'd think to watch that little bitty road. Dont nobody hardly ever use it."

"What the fuck's in Plant City?" Hanford Mobley said.

"A fucken train station," said Roy Matthews.

The rain did not slacken and they nearly got stuck in the mud several times but Hanford Mobley each time adroitly maneuvered the car free and they pressed on. It took them the better part of an hour to traverse the ten miles. As he drove, Mobley proposed they take the next train to Tampa, a big enough town so strangers didnt arouse suspicion. They would check into a hotel and call Old Joe to tell him of the change in plans and let him say what they should do next. Clarence said fine by him. Roy Matthews shrugged and nodded and said sure, why not.

They deserted the Ford two blocks from the depot. Each of them carried a .45 under his coat but they had no means for concealing the shotguns and the automatic rifle and so had to leave them with the car. Hanford Mobley took the little grip containing the three thousand dollars and tucked it under his arm and they set out down the street at a quick walk. The rain had abated but little and before they were halfway down the block they were sodden. At the corner was a small store with a Chesterfield ad in the window that reminded Roy Matthews he was nearly out of cigarettes. Clarence Middleton said to buy him a pack too. A train whistle squealed and Hanford Mobley said that might be the train for Tampa and called to Matthews to hurry and catch up and he and Clarence set off at a jog.

"Think it'll rain?" the clerk said as he handed over the two packs of smokes and laughed at his own lank humor. Roy Matthews grabbed up the cigarettes and threw a bill on the counter and hastened from the store just as the rain assumed a new intensity. At the next corner he had to wait for a few cars to go by and the train whistle blew again and he saw a locomotive huffing steam on one of the sidings in preparation to move out, but the train was a long freight carrier facing north, not the passenger transport to Tampa.

And then through the rainy gloom he saw Bob Baker. With him were three other men, none of whom he recognized except to know with absolute certainty that they were cops too. They were coming from the parking lot at the south end of the station and he figured they must have only just arrived. All four were without raincoats and all carrying shotguns and keeping the breeches dry under their arms. Roy Matthews backed away from the curb and stood under the awning fronting a real estate office at his back and slipped his hand under his coat to the Colt automatic and pushed the safety off with his thumb.

The cops paused at the far end of the depot and conferred and every man checked his pocketwatch. Now Bob Baker pointed and two of the cops went off around the corner of the building and Roy Matthews knew he had sent them to cover the depot's trackside doors. As Bob Baker and the other cop started for the front of the station a man approached them with his hands deep in his raincoat pockets and his head down against the rain and he didnt see them until he was almost on them and then he saw the guns and stopped short and backed against the depot wall. Bob Baker said something to him and gestured for him to go on and the man nodded jerkily and hurried away. Now Bob Baker and the other cop paused at a depot window and the other cop carefully peered inside and then turned to Bob Baker and nodded and they both checked their watches yet again.

And now here came the store clerk around the corner and clutching an umbrella and looking intent. His face brightened on seeing Roy Matthews under the awning. "Hey, mister!" the clerk said, and held up a sheaf of dog-eared dollar bills. "You give me a ten-dollar bill and probably thought it wasn't but a one. Here's you change." Roy Matthews barely glanced at him before turning his attention back to the other side of the street. The clerk stood there with the rain running off his umbrella and his handful of money extended toward Roy Matthews and nothing in his experience told him what to do now.

Bob Baker and the other cop stood waiting by the front door and Baker kept looking from the front door to the pocketwatch in his hand. The freight whistle keened again and let a great blast of steam and the locomotive lurched forward and the couplings of the cars behind sent up a great clash and clamoring of iron and the cars shuddered one after the other as the train began to move. Roy Matthews saw a pair of men scurry from the bushes fifty yards south of the depot and clamber up onto the side of an empty stockcar. The bigger of the men clung to a slat and struggled with the door and now pushed it partly open and both tramps slipped into the car. The door slid back again but remained open just a little.

Roy Matthews walked quickly down the street and when he was a block north of the depot he jogged across the road and scaled a low wooden fence as lithely as a cat and dropped into the railyard. He loped to the siding on which the freight was slowly rumbling past and ran alongside the cars and looked over his shoulder and saw the cattlecar with the partly open door coming up behind him. He half-expected to hear the warning shout of railroad bulls but this was no big city railyard plagued by tramps and hobos and no warning shout came nor did any bull appear. The train was picking up speed now and here came the car he wanted and as he ran alongside he grabbed a slat near the door and swung his feet up and planted them against the edge of the door and he pushed hard and the door slid open enough for him to wriggle himself into the car feet-first.

The two tramps were standing up and looking at him as he lay gasping on the floor. "Pretty neat trick, mister," the bigger one of them said. "But this here car's spoke for, so you can just roll your ass right back out again." The floor of the car was littered with dirty hay and smelled of cowshit.

Roy Matthews sat up, his breath slowing, and looked at him.

"Ah hell, Bosco," the other tramp said. "It aint no need to be like that. It's plenty room for him."

"Fuck him," Bosco said, and advanced on Roy Matthews. "Now you gone jump out or I gone throw you out?"

Roy Matthews stood up and stepped away from the open door and pulled out his .45 and cocked the hammer. He pointed the gun in Bosco's face and said, "Now you gone jump out or I gone kick your dead ass out?"

Bosco stood fast.

"I dont care either fucken way," Matthews said. "I'll count three."

"Hold on," Bosco said.

Roy Matthews said, "One . . ."

Bosco raised a hand as though he might deflect the bullet as he stepped back and snatched up his bindle. He went to the door and stared out at the passing world a moment and then glanced at Matthews and then tossed his bindle and leaped after it and was gone.

Roy Matthews put up his pistol and told the other tramp he was welcome to stay. The tramp said he'd as soon stick with his buddy if it was all the same to him. Matthews shrugged and said to suit himself. As the tramp took up his bindle and went to the door Matthews asked if he knew where this freight was headed. The tramp said Jacksonville.

Roy Matthews smiled. "No shit?"

"No shit," the tramp said. Then looked out of the car and picked his spot and jumped.

Hanford Mobley thought their luck was running just swell. According to the ticketseller the Tampa train would be arriving in eighteen minutes. The man punched out three tickets and passed them through the arched window to Mobley and then counted out his change.

As Mobley scooped up the money he heard Clarence say "Shit!" He turned and saw Clarence leap over a bench and bolt for the trackside door and he was looking back over his shoulder just as Freddie Baker came in through the doorway with a shotgun at port arms. Clarence turned face-front just in time for Freddie to hit him full in the face with the stock of the shotgun like a boxer throwing a right cross and the sound was like a shingle splitting. Clarence's feet ran out from under him and for an instant he was completely supine in the air before he crashed to the floor like a full sack of feed and with an explosion of breath.

Waiting passengers scattered shrilling from their benches like birds flushed from a roost.

"Duck down, mister!"

Mobley heard the words clearly through a woman's scream and caught a sidelong glance of the ticketseller dropping out of sight behind the counter and he knew the voice even before he turned and saw Bob Baker pointing a pump action .12 gauge at him from a distance of ten feet. And beside him Joel Padgett with a shotgun pointed at him too.

"You can live or you can die, sonny," Bob Baker said. "You dont put them hands way up right now, I know which it be."

Hanford Mobley gave an instant's thought to making a fight of it, to jumping aside as he drew his piece and they'd just see who lived and who died—and then remembered that the safety of his .45 was on and knew he'd never fire a shot before Bob Baker and Joe blew his head off.

He put his hands way up.

The store clerk came across the street to the depot to see what all the excitement was about and learned that the Palm Beach County high sheriff and his deputies had just captured two members of the notorious Ashley Gang. A porter told him that the sheriff had asked the little one over there getting the chains put on him hand and foot where the other two were and the bandit had said it'd be a cold day in hell before he ever ratted.

The clerk presented himself to the Palm Beach sheriff and said he'd seen something that probably didnt have anything to do with this but he thought he ought to know it anyway—and he told Sheriff Baker about the man he'd seen jump aboard the freight train.

Fifteen minutes later Sheriff Baker had contacted the Duval County Sheriff and given him a thorough description of Roy Matthews—who was yet but an unidentified suspect. The Duval sheriff said he'd post men at the freight yard to watch for the train's arrival and agreed not to arrest the suspect right away if they saw him. Rather, they would do as Sheriff Baker suggested and follow him to see if he might lead them to the fourth member of the holdup team. The Duval sheriff said he'd be in touch as soon as he had something to report.

Bob Baker now borrowed a car from the high sheriff of Hillsborough County so the Padgett brothers could transport Clarence Middleton to the hospital at West Palm Beach. One side of Clarence's faced was hugely and darkly swollen and his articulation was reduced to a guttural groan. He was manacled hand and foot and put in the front passenger seat of the car and Joel Padgett sat directly behind him with a shotgun muzzle pressed to the back of his head. Elmer Padgett got behind the wheel and looked at Clarence and said, "Hey, bubba, is it true what they say in the adventure books about the outlaw life bein so much fun?" Joel Padgett laughed and poked Clarence sharply in the back of the head with the shotgun muzzle. Clarence turned and glared at him with eyes so bloodshot they looked like cranberries. Joe jabbed the muzzle lightly against his broken jaw and Clarence jerked back shrilling through his teeth. "You just face front and stay that way, tough guy," Joe Padgett said.

Bob and Fred Baker took Mobley with them. Before heading back to the east coast Sheriff Bob contacted the sheriff of Broward County and asked if he might house a special prisoner in his jail for a time. The Palm Beach County lockup was undergoing renovations and its security would be frail until the construction work was finished. The Broward sheriff said to bring the rascal on down.

During the drive to Lauderdale Bob and Fred Baker chatted with each other about their families and about a fishing trip to Lake Okeechobee they were planning for upcoming weekend. They were in such high spirits they couldn't keep from laughing, whether anything was funny or not. Hanford Mobley sat in the backseat with his ankles cuffed against the frame of the front seat and his hands manacled behind him. So completely was he ignored by the lawmen he might not have been in the car with them. Only twice did they pay him heed, the first time was about midway through the trip when Bob Baker adjusted the mirror to look at him and laugh hard and then repositioned the mirror off him again. The other time was when Freddie Baker turned to look at him and grinned and then suddenly lunged and punched him just under the right eye.

Mobley saw stars and his eyes welled with tears and he cursed Freddie Baker for a son of a bitch.

"That's enough now," Bob Baker said, glancing casually at Fred Baker.

"Shit-eatin son of a nigger bitch," Hanford Mobley said.

"You *hear* this little boy's mouth?" Freddie said.

Without turning to look at him, Bob Baker told Hanford Mobley that if he didnt keep his trap shut for the rest of the drive he'd gag him with a piss-soaked oilrag balled in his mouth.

Hanford Mobley snorted but kept mute the rest of the trip.

The Ashley grapevine brought Old Joe the word about Hanford Mobley and Clarence Middleton even as Clarence was being manacled to a bed in the West Palm Beach hospital where he would have his broken jaw wired and be under round-the-clock guard by armed deputies. Old Joe told Bill Ashley to get Ira Goldman up to Twin Oaks immediately. That evening the three of them talked well into the night. On the following afternoon the assistant state's attorney announced that John Clarence Middleton had been charged with bank robbery and his arraignment was set for the day after tomorrow. The prisoner's legal counsel had insisted on exercising his client's right to a speedy trial and the state was happy to oblige. Trial was scheduled to begin in two weeks.

"Good," Old Joe said when Ira and Bill reported how things stood. "I wish they was tryin him tomorrow." They had recently come to secret agreement with Assistant Warden Webb at Raiford—at a price of twelve thousand dollars for John Ashley and five thousand for Ray Lynn. The underwarden had enlisted into the plan a trusted guard and one of the drivers of the trucks that delivered limestone to the rockpile twice a month. The confederates' cut would come out of Webb's seventeen thousand, which was part of the reason his price was so high. The rest of the reason was John Ashley's notoriety and the fact that his escape had to be from inside the walls. Assistant Warden Webb had the authority to assign Ray Lynn to a road gang—from which escape was easier—but could not reassign John Ashley, whom the warden was sworn to keep inside the penitentiary for the full length of his sentence. The underwarden told Ira Goldman that John Ashley's escape could be effected only on one of the two days each month that the limestone trucks delivered to the prison. The plan depended on the truck. That was fine with Old Joe, but he wanted Ray Lynn—and now Clarence, as well—to make their break from the road camp at the same time John was slipping out of the pen. If John got free too soon before Ray and Clarence, the warden might get the idea of locking them up in isolation to keep them from getting away too.

"I want Clarence up in Raiford just as quick as we can get him there," Old Joe said to Ira. "Go see that Webb fella again and tell him hold off on John till Clarence is up there too and can come out with the Lynn boy."

"It'll cost more to include Clarence," Ira Goldman said. "The bastard will probably want another five."

"I know it," Old Joe said. "Offer three and settle at five if you have to. Five's way more than enough and he knows it. But he's got to wait for Clarence. That's the condition."

Hanford Mobley he could help more directly and immediately. When he heard that Mobley was being put in the Broward County Jail Old Joe grinned like he'd been told a good joke and Ira Goldman asked him what was so funny.

"You know W. W. Hicks?" Joe said, looking from Ira Goldman to Bill Ashley. "Either you?"

They neither one did.

"Well, I do," Old Joe said. And he laughed again. "Knowed him from the time he was a pup and his daddy and me used to fire-hunt deer together in the Big Cypress."

"Who is W. W. Hicks, daddy?" Bill Ashley said.

"The night jailer at the Broward County lockup."

Hanford Mobley had been in the Broward lockup three days when W. W. Hicks sidled up to the bars of his cell late in the evening and introduced himself as a friend of his granddaddy's and said he'd spoken with Old Joe earlier that day. He informed Mobley that as the night jailer he was authorized to appoint two inmates every evening to the jail cleanup detail. "You know," Hicks whispered, "if a inmate on the cleanup detail was to somehow overpower the guard and tie him up, and if he was to get aholt of a small crowbar, and if he was to know that one of the skylights in the storeroom off the other hallway got a real old rusty lock on it, and if he was to boost hisself up to that lock some kinda way, why, he'd probably be able to bust it open with no trouble at all. Then he'd be up on the roof and would find out that in a back corner of it is a drainpipe he could skinny down. Then he'd likely do well to get his ass into the swampwoods back of the jail and make his way to Turtle Creek and follow it about two miles to the intracoastal. If he was real lucky he might could find him a skiff there. Then he'd like as not pole his way up through that mangrove channel where not even the dogs could follow in case the jailbreak had been found out and a posse was after him. Once he got past the mangroves he'd practically be to Pompano and if he was to put in at Skeet Massey's fish camp there, why, it might not be too much of a surprise to have somebody waitin there for him in a car."

Hanford Mobley was smiling. "You can put *me* on the cleanup detail?"

"Like as not your sheriff dont know thing one about how the sheriff runs things here," Hicks said. "And for a fact my sheriff aint give a whole lot of thought to you—you not bein one of his own prisoners and all. What I'm gettin at is, aint nobody said to me you *caint* be on the detail."

"Well now damn," Hanford Mobley said, his smile wider.

"You feel like maybe doin some cleanup work round here tomorrow night?" Hicks said, smiling back at him. "You know, make yourself useful?"

"I always was raised to believe that cleanliness is next to godliness," Hanford Mobley said.

The Duval County sheriff had posted men at the station to watch for anybody coming in on the freight from Tampa, especially somebody riding in a stockcar. The sheriff was proud of his law enforcement heritage—his daddy had been a respected sheriff of DeSoto County for years and his grandfather had been a deputy sheriff in Pensacola and part of the team that captured the notorious Texas desperado John Wesley Hardin at the train station there in the summer of 1877.

He was shrewd, this sheriff. He figured anybody riding the freightcars might think to jump off before the train pulled into the railyard. So he and a deputy, both of them in civilian dress, hiked a half-mile up the railway and hid themselves, one on either side of the tracks, on a sandy rise in the pines from which they could see along the rails a good long way.

When the train appeared far down the track they watched it closely but nobody jumped off as it came toward them. Then the train was rumbling by and they both saw the slatted stockcar flash past and if anyone was in it neither of them saw him. And then the train was past and no one had jumped off and just as the sheriff and his deputy were dusting themselves and about to step out of the pines, the deputy said "Look!" and pointed up the tracks and the sheriff looked just in time to see a man tumbling in the grass alongside the rails. The sheriff and deputy quickly got back into the cover of the trees and watched as the man rose stiffly and stepped about gingerly and tested his limbs and seemed to find himself hale. He was too far away for them to compare him to the description they'd been given but the sheriff was sure he was their man. The suspect looked up and down the tracks and peered hard at the woods flanking both sides of the rails and then set out at a quick pace along the tracks toward Jacksonville.

They followed at a distance but kept to the edge of the woods and faded into the cover of the trees every time the suspect turned to look over his shoulder. As they drew close to town the man veered from the tracks and took to a narrow dirt path through the pines and the sheriff and his deputy closed their distance from him now that they were better hidden in the shadowed woods. The suspect seemed less wary and but infrequently looked back anymore.

When they got into town they kept a couple of blocks back of him. Then he went into a drug store and they quickly closed the distance and the deputy took up a position on the opposite side of the street and from there watched the front door. The sheriff lit his pipe and casually strolled past the drug store and glanced in the window as he went by and he saw the suspect talking on the telephone and smiling and saw that he fit exactly the description he'd been given by the Palm Beach sheriff. A minute later the man was outside again. He looked at a piece of paper in his hand and looked around and got his bearings and set out toward the river. The sheriff and the deputy, one on either side of the street, followed at a block's distance.

Forty minutes later they were in a residential neighborhood near the river and the man stopped before a large Victorian house that had been converted to rooms to let. He checked the piece of paper in his hand once more and then went up the front steps and onto the porch and knocked on the door. The main door opened and he spoke to someone just the other side of the screen door. Now the door swung open and he went in and the screen door closed and then the main door behind it.

They waited ten minutes and then went around to the kitchen side door and knocked and the sheriff showed his badge to a shapeless woman who said she was the cook. She let them in and went to fetch the house manager. He was a bespectacled man of middle years and in answer to the sheriff's question said that the man who'd come in just ahead of them had been expected by one of the tenants, a young woman who'd received a telephone call from him a little earlier. Her room was on the second floor, number 222.

They ascended the stairs and moved softly down the hall and stopped at room 222 and drew their pistols. The sheriff put his ear to the door and listened for a moment and grinned at the deputy. He backed away from the door and mouthed the question "Ready?" and the deputy tugged his hat down and gripped his gun tightly in both hands and nodded. The sheriff raised his booted foot and delivered a powerful kick to the door that burst it off its lock and they rushed into the shrieking room.

"They say the Matthews boy went ten feet straight in the air when the door bust open," the day jailer said. He was a fat man named Glover who never stopped sweating. He was leaning on the cell bars and fanning himself with his hat. "They say he stood there with his hands stickin up in the air and his dick stickin out in front of him all shiny with pussy juice."

Hanford Mobley sat on his bunk smoking a cigarette and grinned. It galled him plenty that Matthews was the only one of them to escape being caught at Plant City, especially since it had been the bigmouth's fault that him and Clarence had been taken. If Matthews hadnt told that bitch in Sebring about Lakeland the cops never wouldve known where to hunt for them. Hanford couldnt help feeling a little lowdown for taking pleasure in a partner getting caught, but he didnt really mind the guilt. He was glad Roy Matthews had been caught while humping some whore and no use to deny it. The jailer had said Matthews would arrive at the Broward jail tomorrow. Hanford Mobley expected to be long gone by then.

"They say ever man in the house come into the hallway and all of em crowdin at the door and makin fun of the nekkid fella and gawkin at the girl in the bed with the sheet up to her chin and just cryin her eyes out," Glover said. "That sheriff up in Duval, he can be a good old boy or he can be one mean sumbitch, all depends, and this time he was feelin mean. Told the both of them to get their clothes on and never made a move to close the door to give them the least bit of privacy from all them old boys lookin on. They say the gal really got to cryin then and said would they turn they backs and the men all just laughed. The sheriff told her it was the price a person paid for a life of crime. She said she aint never led no life of crime and he said they'd see about that. Hell, he knew she wasnt no member of you all's gang, he was just blackassed about havin to foller Matthews over half of Duval County in the blazing sun and sweatin like a hog."

"Figured he'd make her blush some, hey?" Hanford Mobley said. He began to roll another cigarette.

"Made her damn good and mad too is what he did," Glover said. "At *ever*damnbody, includin the Matthews fella. When the sheriff asked him his name he said Reynolds, but the girl hollers no it's not, it's Matthews, Roy Matthews, and he's a no-good son of a bitch criminal who never brung her nothin but trouble is who he is. Whooo, she was hot! They say the Matthews fella looked like he wanted to kick her all the way to Georgia."

Mobley laughed. "That's the way it is with whores aint it—cant trust a one of them. I bet the sheriff made her get out of bed nekkid anyhow."

"Damn sure did. She tried to keep her arms crossed over her titties, but hell, she couldnt keep everthin covered all at once and get herself dressed too, could she now? Right goodlookin too, they say. Nice jugs on her. Real nice ass."

"You best quit tellin me such," Hanford Mobley said with a chuckle. "It aint polite to get a man all hot and bothered when he's in the can and cant do nothin about it."

"I wouldnt of minded seein that show my ownself," Glover said. "They say she was a *real* redhead that one, if you get my meanin and I reckon you do. Say she had a damn tattoo. A little turtle, like, right down here, just over her pussy."

Hanford Mobley sat with the cigarette to his mouth and a ready match in his hand and stared hard at something that was not there.

When Hicks the night jailer came on duty Hanford Mobley called him over to the bars and said he wanted to postpone things till the following night. His partner was being brought in tomorrow and he wanted to take him out with him.

"Whoa now, bubba," Hicks whispered, looking about and leaning against the bars. "That aint the deal. Old Joe paid me just for you. He didnt say nothin about nobody else."

"You'll get paid for it," Mobley said.

"How I know that?"

Hanford Mobley stared at him. Hicks licked his lips. "You'll tell Old Joe *you* asked for your partner too?"

Hanford Mobley turned and spat on the stone floor and then looked at him again.

"Goddamn, man, I just wanna be sure I get paid for it is all I'm sayin."

They brought Roy Matthews into the jail that afternoon and put him in a cell at the far end of the lockup. As Matthews went past Hanford Mobley's cell they looked at each other but neither said anything.

That evening W. W. Hicks came into the cell block with his heels clacking on the stone floor and a clipboard under his arm. Besides Hanford Mobley and Roy Matthews, there were but five other inmates in the lockup this night and some of them observed the proceedings with idle curiosity. Hicks went to Hanford Mobley's cell and called out loudly in his official jailer's voice, "All right, Mobley, you're on cleanup detail tonight and I dont want no fucken argument about it and no slackin on the job neither! You and . . ." He made a show of looking at his clipboard, of running his finger down a sheet of paper. "You and the fucken new fish . . . Matthews." He unlocked Hanford Mobley's cell and Mobley followed him down to the end of the block where Roy Matthews sat on his bunk and stared out at them. "Get on out here, new fish," Hicks said. "Dont nobody get free room and board, not in this jail. You gone earn you keep with a bucket and mop."

He led them to a closet just outside the barred door to the row and from it they took a broom and a mop and a bucket. "Now I want you boys to start out here in the store room where they was unpacking stuff this week and it's a real mess," Hicks said, still addressing them in his official voice as he guided them down the hall to a thick door he unlocked with his ring of keys. They went in and he closed the door behind them. The room was littered with broken boxes and small crates and baling wire and torn canvas tents.

"All right, you boys," Hicks said, "there it is." He pointed to a skylight nearly ten feet over the center of the room. The glass was thick and iron-framed and locked shut with a padlock through an eye-ring. A slim crowbar about two feet long lay on a box and Hicks took it up and said, "This oughta do for her." Roy Matthews took the crowbar from him and tested its heft.

"Now you got to tie me up good," Hicks said as he rummaged in the debris. "Make it look right." He came up with some thick strips of canvas. "This here'll work good as rope. Then you put a gag on me and get youselfs out that skylight and thats all she wrote. You just a coupla jailbirds got the jump on me and made away."

"Maybe that rope there be better for tying you," Roy Matthews said.

"What rope's that?" Hicks said, turning to look where Matthews pointed. Matthews swung the crowbar against the back of his head with a soft crack and Hicks fell as if his bones had gone to milk.

"God *damn,* man!" Hanford Mobley said. "What you do that for?" He stepped over Hicks so he could watch Matthews even as he squatted to check the fallen man.

"Make it look right, didnt he say?" Roy Matthews said. "Well, this'll look right and didnt take near as long. What the hell, he aint but a fucken jail hack."

"He's a friend of Grandaddy's, who he is," Mobley said. He probed for a pulse under Hicks' jaw and could not find it and was sure Hicks was dead and then he felt it. Mobley stood up. "He's alive, no thanks to you."

They both looked up at the skylight and then around the room. "Dont look like any these busted crates any good for standin on," Roy Matthew said.

"Give me that iron and make a stirrup with you hands," Hanford Mobley said.

Roy Matthews looked at him.

"I'm lighter than you," Mobley said. "You boost me up and I'll bust the lock. Then we'll make a rope of them pieces of canvas and I'll brace myself and haul you up."

"Real good plan, sonny," Roy Matthews said. "What's to keep you from going on without me once you make the roof?"

"You damn fool. You think I couldnt of got out of here before now? I been waitin on you. Not cause I give a shit about you—cause I dont. It's only cause Grandaddy wanted me to. Now we gone stand here arguin all fucken night or we gone get out of here?"

Matthews gave him the little prizing bar and interlaced the fingers of his hands to form a stirrup and Hanford Mobley stepped into it and Matthews heaved him up and braced Mobley's foot at belly level.

Mobley caught hold of the frame around the skylight with one hand to steady himself and worked the bar into the padlock yoke. On his third hard pull the yoke broke open. He took the lock out of the eye-ring and tossed it aside and pushed the skylight window up and it fell open onto the roof with a loud bang and it was a wonder the glass did not shatter.

"Shitfire!" Roy Matthews grunted under Hanford Mobley's weight on his hands. "Think you might can be a little noisier about it?"

Hanford Mobley laid the crowbar on the roof and called down, "Higher! Boost me higher."

"God *damn*," Roy Matthews said. He grit his teeth and raised Mobley's foot up almost to his chin, elevating him high enough so he could pull himself up onto the graveled roof by arm strength. Mobley took a moment to catch his breath and then slipped the crowbar into his belt and lay on his belly to look down at Roy Matthews who was quickly tying together some of the strips of canvas. Matthews then tied a loop in one end of the line and slipped it under his arms like a sling and tossed up the other end of the line to Mobley who took up the slack and wound it around his back for support and then sat at the edge of the skylight with his legs drawn up and his heels braced against the frame of it. He leaned forward into the opening and reached as far down on the line as he could and got a tight two-hand grip and then slowly straightened and leaned back and pushed himself away from the window frame with his legs and thus raised Roy Matthews up high enough so he could grab onto the skylight frame and work himself up on the roof.

They scurried to the corner of the building and shinned down the drainpipe there. They paused to listen for sounds of alarm but heard none and then raced across the moonbright stretch of grass to the woods beyond and plunged into the pines. They made their way to Turtle Creek and followed it eastward through the swamp where little light of the waning gibbous moon did penetrate. They came at last to the lagoon which formed a portion of the intracoastal waterway and they began searching for the skiff. The clouds of mosquitoes were so thick they could be clutched by the fistful and squeezed to bloody paste in the palm. They flailed at the maddening whine at their ears as they tramped through the brush and stumbled on mangrove roots along the lagoon bank and finally both of them dug dripping scoops of malodor-ous muck and coated their faces and arms with it against the rage of mosquitoes.

They found the skiff lashed to a mangrove in a small cleared portion of bank about twenty yards north of the creek. In it was a jug of water and a croker sack containing a dozen oranges, some smoked mullet and cornbread, a box of matches and a sheathed skinning knife. They gobbled down the food and Hanford Mobley put the knife on his belt. Then Roy Matthews set himself in the fore of the boat and Mobley pushed them off and took up the pole and stood near the stern and began poling north for Skeet Massey's fishcamp at Pompano.

Roy Matthews turned once and grinned palely in the moonlight and said, "We done er," and Hanford Mobley said, "Yeah we did."

They spoke no more as the skiff glided through the water with a barely visible green-yellow glow in its wake. The mosquitoes were not so severe out here on the water where there was at least a small breeze to help keep them at bay. From the dark pine came a deep hollow hooting of an owl. An enormous school of mullet broke the surface ahead of them in a great phosphorescent shimmer like a shattering of burning glass and both of them sucked their breath at the sight.

The moon rode high and made slow progress across the black heaven and its spangle of stars. After a time the mangroves drew in on them from both sides and shadows dappled the skiff and again mosquitoes closed on them in a densely humming mass.

Hanford Mobley put down the pole and slipped the skinning knife from its sheath. The blade was eight inches long and felt razorous to his thumb. He had intended to use the crowbar but a knife was so much better. An engine of keener intimacy. Used properly a knife allowed for at least a moment's mutual reflection between the principals and thus a truer sense of reckoning. He stepped forward lightly as a cat.

Roy Matthews noted the slowing of the boat and started to turn around as Mobley's shadow fell over him and he felt a sudden horrid pain at his neck and knew in the instant that his throat had been slashed to the neckbone.

His hands went to his wound in a desperate pawing and he tried to get up but Hanford Mobley kicked him in the chest and he sprawled in the rocking bow and felt the blood coursing hotly down his chest and sopping his shirt and his horror was such that he would have screamed but for windpipe and voice box having been severed as well. The sound from his mouth was the deep gurgle of a drain abruptly unplugged and blood rushed into his lungs and he choked and saw the dimming moon above and through his last loud try for breath he heard Hanford Mobley asking if she'd been worth it.

TWENTY-ONE

The Liars Club

THE RUMOR WAS EVERYWHERE THAT OLD JOE ASHLEY'D HAD A hand in Hanford Mobley and Roy Matthews slipping out of the Broward jail, and might could be he did or might could be he didnt. Only thing for sure about that rumor was the same as always: nobody had a lick of proof for it.

They say when Bob Baker heard about the escape him and Freddie Baker drove straight down to Fort Lauderdale and he went right into the high sheriff's office there and asked where that goddamn jailer Hicks was at. The sheriff said he was in the hospital with a skull fracture. Said he wished he's never accepted the two bank robbers into his jail because he sure as hell didnt need all this bad newspaper publicity. Bob Baker called the sheriff a dumb lazy peckerwood loud enough for everbody in the jailhouse to hear him. He stomped back out to his car and Freddie drove him over to the hospital and Bob Baker told the doctor he had to ask the injured jailer a few important questions. The doctor said all right, but the patient was in a bad way, so go easy on him. But Sheriff Bob wasn't in no go-easy mood, not with the fella responsible for his prisoners getting away laying right there in front of him. He grabbed Hicks by his hospital gown and shook him like a dog with a rabbit. Called him a lowdown shiteating son of a bitch and said he knew he'd helped the prisoners break out and he would by God prove it and send him to prison for the rest of his miserable life. They say Hicks's bandage was slipping down over his eyes and he was screaming for somebody to help him. It took the doc and Freddie both to pull Bob Baker offa him. That's the story we heard. Another thing we heard was that a couple of days later Heck Runyon was seen at side door of the county jail one evening and Freddie Baker let him in and they say Heck didnt come out of there again until late at night.

Hicks got fired sure enough. He told the newspaper he was being made a whipping boy. Said it was unfair to be blamed for being attacked from behind. He never really recovered from that whack on the head with a crowbar. It left him part-crippled and strange in the head for all his days after. He couldnt walk in a straight line but had to bear at a slight angle to the direction he really wanted to go, and one eye was always half-closing on him. He got to talking to himself, even when he was walking down the streets and there was people all around. He'd sit on a park bench sometimes and get into mean whispering arguments with himself. He took bad to drink. A coupla years after the jailbreak he killed a fella in a drunken fight or some such and got sent to prison for life. That's a true fact.

As for Mobley and Matthews, some said Old Joe sent them both out of Florida to lay low for a while. Others say it was only Mobley he sent away—sent him off to wherever John Ashley had hid out a dozen years before when there was a warrant on him for killing the Indian. Wherever it was Hanford Mobley went, he came back about a year later—which was the worst mistake of his life.

Most stories about Roy Matthews said he went off on his own, out to California or up to Tennessee or over to Mexico, depending on which story you wanted to believe. But nobody never saw hide nor hair of him again, not in South Florida. A Palm Beach County deputy who was visiting kin in Cleveland a few months after the jailbreak said he saw him working as a cook in a restaurant on Lake Erie. Said he got up from the table and headed for the kitchen to ask him a few questions but the fella saw him coming and ran out the back way and flat disappeared. Deputy *swore* it was him. Another story was that Matthews had gone up to Atlanta and took up with a gal who had a jealous boyfriend and the fella caught up to them one night and cut his dick off. Another rumor said he got killed in a bank holdup in Springfield, Missouri—him and some skinny Ozark gal he taken for a partner. Lord, there was some stories about him! Some even said he never left Florida at all, said he'd been hiding out with the Ashleys at Twin Oaks and got drunk one night and picked a fight with Joe Ashley and Old Joe brained him with a hatchet and killed him graveyard dead. Fed him to the gators to get rid of the evidence. It was ever kind of story about Roy Matthews and no telling which was true or if any of them was. The only thing we can say for a absolute fact is nobody we knew ever saw him again.

Clarence Middleton went to trial with his jaw still wired shut. When the judge read the charge against him and asked how he pled, guilty or not guilty, he said something through his clamped teeth and the judge said "What?" and his lawyer said "That means guilty, your honor." Middleton's lawyer was a Miami sharpie named Ira Goldman. The story was, Goldman made a deal with the state for Clarence to plead guilty in exchange for a fifteen-year sentence instead of the thirty years the state said it was gonna call for and the judge said he was gonna give him if they was put to the trouble of a trial. The whole thing didn't take twenty minutes. Two days later Clarence Middleton was on his way to Raiford. That was in October of nineteen and twenty-three.

There's a lot nobody's ever been able to figure out for sure about what exactly happened in the next few weeks after that, but there's no disputing the basic facts. It's a fact that when Clarence Middleton got to Raiford he was back together with John Ashley. And it's a fact that Ben Tracey—a convict friend of John's—finished his sentence and was set loose about a week or so after Clarence got there. Three days later Tracey was seen driving a brand new blue Chevrolet sedan on the streets of Tallahassee, about sixty miles southeast of Marianna, which is right near where the road camp was that Clarence Middleton got sent to after just a couple of weeks at Raiford. Ray Lynn, another prison pal of John Ashley's, got sent there with Clarence—thats a fact too. Finally, it's a fact that sometime in the first week of November and barely three weeks after he went to prison, Clarence Middleton and Ray Lynn escaped from the Marianna road gang. They did this just one day after John Ashley someway or other broke out of the penitentiary at Raiford.

All thats a fact. The rest is just stories. A lot of guessing and supposing and probly. What probly happened is Old Joe spread some money around to the right people at Raiford. That's what *probly* happened.

As time went by, the most popular story we heard about how Clarence Middleton and Ray Lynn escaped was they somehow picked the lock to their legchains just before the gang was lined up at the end of the workday to get put in the truck back to camp and next thing anybody knew, the two of them was gone into the pineywoods. The main highway wasnt but a few miles off and there wasnt no time to go get the dogs from back at the camp, so a couple of the guards with rifles took off after them. Said they damn near caught up to them. Said they saw them getting into a blue Chevy sedan and heading off down the road in the twilight and could hear them laughing. Said they fired at them but if they even hit the car they didnt do enough damage to stop it. That was the story we heard. Most times, whoever was telling it would wink when he said Clarence and Ray "picked" the lock to their chain, a wink meaning that like as not the "pick" used on the lock was a guard's key. There was lots of winks went with that story. Besides using their key, the guards might of been paid to run slow when they went after them, or to be sure to miss when they shot at them. In them days money could buy you a whole lot of cooperation from prison guards, who the state never did pay any bettern coolies. Everbody knew that. Old Joe had found out it was true the first time John went to prison.

It was money that got John Ashley out of Raiford too—leastways the way we heard it. One afternoon he told a rockpile guard he was feeling sick and so the guard took him over to the infirmary. The guard was spose to stay with his prisoner ever minute, even while the doc looked him over. But so happened the doctor wasnt in his office when they got there and the clerk didnt know where he was at. The guard told John Ashley to sit tight in the doctor's office where there wasnt even a window, and he told the clerk in the outer office to give a holler if the prisoner so much as stuck his head out the door. Then he went off to look for the doc. When they got back fifteen minutes later the clerk wasnt there and neither was John Ashley. The clerk told the investigators he'd forgot John Ashley was in the office and so he'd gone over to the guards' mess for a cup of coffee. The warden ordered an immediate lockdown and every foot of the prison got searched but they couldnt find him nowhere. They figured the only way he coulda got out of the walls was on one of the rockpile trucks that delivered boulders that afternoon. When the cops went out to the quarry company to talk to the drivers they couldnt round up but five of the six. They never found the other one, not then nor ever after, and so they were sure he'd been the one to help John Ashley to escape. It's as good an explanation as any, but that dont mean it's the true one. The only true thing anybody can say about that escape is that it was awful damn easy. The kind of easy you get only by paying for it.

Of course nobody could *prove* nothing, not even after they investigated everbody in the prison who might of had anything to do with

John's deliverance or with Ray Lynn and Clarence Middleton escaping
from the road gang. Nobody knew a damn thing—not the warden nor
his assistant nor the doctor nor the guards nor the truck drivers. No-
damn-body. The only thing to come of the investigation was three men
got fired—the assistant warden, for poor judgment in assigning two
dangerous felons to a road camp, and the guard and the medical clerk
who both left John Ashley alone in the doctor's office. They say that
less than a month later the assistant warden was hired as the jail
supervisor by some county up in the panhandle and the fired guard
and clerk were hired along with him.

You'd of thought that when he heard about three of the Ashley
Gang breaking out from prison within a day of each other and just six
weeks or so after Hanford Mobley and Roy Matthews escaped from
the Broward jail, Bob Baker would of let a holler you could hear to
Pensacola. But he didn't. They say when he got the news about John
getting away from Raiford for the second time in his life he was sitting
at his office desk and trimming a cigar. It was Slim Jackson who told
him the news and he said later that Bob Baker just looked at him with
no expression at all and then went right on trimming the cigar. Slim
sat down and waited to hear what Bob might have to say about it but
he never said a word. Just trimmed at the cigar till the leaf came apart
in his hands and he dropped the mess on the floor and brushed his
hands and took his pipe out of his shirt pocket and started cleaning
that. Slim sat there about ten minutes and then got up and left. They
say Bobby just sat there and fiddled with his pipe and smoked it some
and didnt say a word till some reporters came to ask what he thought
of the escapes. He said he expected all three fugitives to be recaptured
before long and he hoped that next time they were locked up in
stronger jails and looked after by more honest guards. They say the
reporters laughed but Bob Baker didnt smile when he said it.

Lots of folk was feelin sympathy for him. They saw him as a good
man and a good sheriff and had come to respect him plenty. His cousin
Freddie was probly the only lawman in all Palm Beach County who
was more popular. The Ashleys had always had friends and admirers
who appreciated their independent spirit but, little by little, more folk
were leanin to the Bakers' side of the matter. They could see how
things was changing. The Ashleys was the sort whose day was done.
The frontier life their kind had always lived was slipping away. More
and more of the Everglades was giving way to what they call develop-
ment—to more canals and landfills and roads, to a whole new world.

Whole regions of the Glades was little by little getting drained and burned clear and built on. You could see it happening from year to year. Some said a goodly portion of the Devil's Garden would one day mostly be the Devil's Parking Lot. You could say that Twin Oaks was a good example of the old ways and Miami was a good example of the new ones, and at the time we're talking about they was passing each other by in opposite directions. The old ways of the crackers was folks living apart and independent and making do on their own, settling troubles between themselfs. The new ways being forced on them and everbody else was people living close together and lots of them strangers and all of them having to depend on courtroom law. It was a world getting a whole lot unfriendlier to such as the Ashleys—and a whole lot more needful of such as Bob Baker.

They say Bob Baker seemed different for a time after he heard about John Ashley's escape. They say you could see it in his eyes, that even when he looked at you he seemed to be lookin at something somewhere else, something cold and mean and not all that far away. You never saw him with his wife and daughters anymore. Some said he didnt bring them out in public because he was certain the Ashley Gang was gonna try to kill him and he didn't want to put his family at risk. You never saw him now without some of his special gang of deputies around him. It was like he was waiting for something but wasnt quite sure what it was. Lots of folk had the same feeling. They said it was like a bad storm building just over the horizon but there wasnt any sign of it yet that you could point to. Like it was building without sound nor smell nor quiver but everbody seemed to know it was out there and headed this way.

One sunny morning in late November not even a month after he broke out of Raiford John Ashley and his gang robbed the bank at Pompano. Him and Clarence Middleton and Ray Lynn. They charged into the bank like Wild West outlaws whooping and waving their guns. Witnesses said Middleton and Lynn had a .45 in each hand and John Ashley carried an automatic rifle. They scared hell out of everbody. They none of them wore masks. They got nearly thirty thousand dollars in cash and securities and when they were ready to go Ray Lynn signaled from the door and here came a damn taxi driven by Ben Tracey, judging by the descriptions give of him by witnesses. He was blaring the klaxon and weaving down the street and scattering people ever which way. The gang tumbled into the taxi and they took off laughing. The people who saw it say it all happened so fast and loud it didnt hardly seem real.

Ten minutes later the Broward County Sheriff led a posse of police cars north on the Dixie Highway, hopin to pick up the trail of the robbers and they did. About a mile south of the Palm Beach County line they saw the taxi abandoned by the side of the road. They pulled over and examined the area and saw tire tracks leading off down a dirt and limerock road heading west into the pinewoods. They followed it and about a quarter-mile farther along they found a Nigra man tied to a pine tree. Turned out it was his taxi the gang had stolen for the bank robbery. The Nigra said they came tearing back down the pineywoods road in a truck they'd left parked alongside the highway and waved at him as they went by. One of them hollered to him that somebody would be right along and set him loose. The sheriff told the Nigra to get in the car with him and the posse moved on for another mile or so before it came to where the road ran out at the edge of a cypress swamp and they found the truck—which had also been stole of course—bogged in muck to the wheel wells. There wasnt nothing in front of them but the Everglades. Nothin but the Devil's Garden. The Ashley gang must of had dugouts waiting for them.

On the drive back out of the swamp the Nigra told the sheriff that John Ashley told him to deliver a message to Sheriff Bob Baker of Palm Beach County. The sheriff said the Nigra looked scared to say what it was and scared of what might happen to him if he didnt. Everbody knew the Broward sheriff couldnt stand Bob Baker, especially not after Bobby'd called him a dumb peckerwood right in his own office in front of his own men. But when he heard the message John Ashley was sending Bobby he personally drove the Nigra up to West Palm Beach to deliver it. He said he wanted to see Bob Baker's face when he got it.

A half-dozen witnesses saw the Broward sheriff stand in front of Bobby's desk and say to him, "Fella here's got somethin for you from John Ashley." The Nigra was scared shitless, naturally, being in a room fulla nothin but cops, but the Broward sheriff told him, "Go on, boy, give it to him."

Sheriff Bob put his hand out and the Nigra put a rifle cartridge in his palm. A Winchester .30–30 round.

"Mistah Ashley say give you that," the Nigra said. Bobby had a .30–30 of his own and always kept it in his car, but they say he looked at that round like it was the strangest thing he'd ever seen.

The Broward sheriff told the Nigra to go on and say the message that went with it, told him dont be afraid, he would only be repeating what Ashley had told him to say and the Palm Beach Sheriff wouldnt hold it against him personal. They say the Broward sheriff was just grinning and grinning.

And so the Nigra told Bob Baker that John Ashley said to come and get him if he was man enough. Told him he'd be waiting in the Devil's Garden with another bullet just like that one with his name on it. Said he wanted to deliver it to Bob Baker personal. Deliver it right in his heart.

TWENTY-TWO

October–December 1923

THEY TRIED HARD TO BELAY THEIR DESIRE UNTIL NIGHTFALL BUT shortly before supper they could stand it no longer and slipped away to the sidehouse so ravenous for each other they did not take time to remove their clothes except for her overalls so she could open herself to him. They tried to mute themselves with kisses but their concupiscent groans and outcries carried around to the porch where Old Joe sat in his rocker and sipped from his cup of shine and grinned. Ray Lynn and Ben Tracey sat in cane chairs facing him with their cups in hand. Ma Ashley and her two youngest daughters, twelve-year-old Jaybird and thirteen-year-old Scout, were setting the table and plying between the house and the kitchen out back and each yelp from the sidehouse tightened the mother's lips and widened the sisters' blushing smiles. Ray Lynn seemed undecided whether the caterwauling was funny. Ben Tracey looked becrazed by it. His glance kept going past Joe Ashley to the Scout girl whose breasts were already bloomed and filled her shirtfront snugly. Ray Lynn wanted to tell him to quit his gawping before Old Joe caught him at it but Joe Ashley was absorbed in the lovers' loud lickerish reunion and far enough in his cups to be unlikely to notice.

Earlier that day, after they'd hidden the blue Chevy in the pines well back of the kitchen building, John Ashley had introduced Ray Lynn and Ben Tracey to his family and Laura Upthegrove. He could tell that Old Joe liked Ray right off but was unsure about Ben. Yet he knew that any man who'd taken his side in a prison fight and maybe saved his life would receive the benefit of his daddy's doubt.

Clarence Middleton was not with them. He was staying with his girl Terrianne in St. Lucie. Bill Ashley had been here earlier to greet John and meet Lynn and Tracey but had then gone home to Salerno to tend his wife Bertha who was down with a fever. Hanford Mobley's parents, a polite but shy couple, had walked over from their shotgun house a quarter-mile from Twin Oaks to welcome John back. They smiled and nodded on being introduced to Ray and Ben and then took their leave and went home too. Joe Ashley had a half-dozen lookouts posted between the highway and the house with orders to come running the minute they saw anything that looked like it might be a posse. Every man at Twin Oaks went armed with a pistol. Their rifles and shotguns were stood all around the porch.

Now John and Laura came out of the sidehouse and around to the front porch and the men tried to restrain their smiles and then Old Joe laughed and Tracey and Lynn joined in. John Ashley grinned back at them. Laura blushed and put her fists on her hips and glared at them and said "*Well?* What of it? I aint seen this boy in about a lifetime is all! I'd say we're entitled, wouldn't *you* all?"

"You'd been in a fine fix if a posse'd come tearin in here when you all were in there foolin," Old Joe said. "You'd been what they call caught with ye pants down." He gave her a mock leer and waggled his brows. She stuck her tongue out at him and he chortled and slapped his knee. John Ashley hugged her around the neck and looked at her like the man in love he was.

It was a plentiful supper—the table laden with platters of fried ham and catfish filets and cornbread, with bowls of beans and greens and grits, roasted yams and molasses, rice and gravy. Old Joe told about paying off Hicks to effect Hanford Mobley's and Roy Matthews' escape from the Broward jail and they all laughed when he recounted how Bob Baker had been so hot about it he'd cussed out the Broward sheriff in his own jail and damn near beat the shit out of Hicks in the hospital. Albert Miller had waited most of the night at Massey's fishcamp for Hannie and Roy to show up before Hannie finally came poling out of the mangroves just before sunup and eaten raw by mosquitoes. Roy Matthews wasnt with him.

"Hannie said the Matthews boy done got out the boat back by Coconut Creek," Old Joe said. "Said he asked where he was goin but Matthews never said a word, just got out in the shallows there and waded ashore and got himself gone. I could see right off he was lyin."

He took a sip of shine to ease the passage of a mouthful of yam. "He was just too shamed to tell the truth of it."

"What's the truth of it?" John Ashley said.

"He got the horns put on him is the truth of it."

"Joseph," Ma Ashley said, and gave him a reproving stare which he fully ignored.

"How you know that?" John Ashley said. He gave his mother a sidelong look and saw her staring tight-lipped at Joe Ashley.

"When they caught the Matthews boy in Jacksonville, that's who he was with."

"Glenda?" John Ashley said.

"The very one," Old Joe said. "They was in what's called a compromisin position at the time."

John Ashley and Laura raised their eyebrows at each other. His mother shook her head in exasperation and bent to her supper.

Old Joe gestured for Scout to serve him another portion of ham. "I dont reckon we're like to see Roy anytime soon," he said. "But I'll tell you what. Hannie was wrong to blame him. Ye cant fault a fella for tryin a gal. It's natural as the rain for a feller to try. It's up to the gal to say yay or nay."

Nobody saw Ben Tracey wink at Scout except her sister and the girls looked at each other and blushed.

"You sayin he took his displeasure out on the wrong party?" John Ashley said.

"All I'm sayin is Hannie's young yet. Still got things to learn. Specially about women."

"*Joseph!* Now thats enough!"

Old Joe narrowed his eyes at Ma Ashley. "Talk a little blue for you, old woman? It's *you* said the women ought sit to the table with the men tonight since it's Johnny's homecoming and all." Ma Ashley glared. Old Joe smiled at his daughters and they looked down at their plates to hide their smiles from their momma.

He told John Ashley he had sent Hanford to Texas. He'd offered to send Clarence too, and Clarence asked his girl to go with him, but Texas sounded like the far end of the earth to Terrianne and she persuaded him to stay with her in St. Lucie. A friend of the Ashleys had driven Hanford Mobley in his truck to St. Marks where another of Old Joe's bubbas kept a fast sloop and in it carried Mobley to Pensacola. There the boy boarded a steamer to New Orleans and from there voyaged to Galveston.

"You sent him to Aunt July's?" John Ashley said with a wide grin.

"Said he'd long wanted to make his aunt's acquaintance," Old Joe said. He cut a sidelong glance at his wife. "I guess he'll be outa harm's way over there."

"I know whose acquaintance he wanted to make at Aunt July's," John Ashley said.

Ray Lynn and Ben Tracy chuckled lewdly. John Ashley had told them all about his Galveston days in his Aunt's establishment. The daughters had long heard whispers of their notorious Aunt July and they gave each other knowing smiles and giggled. Laura looked askant at John Ashley and said, "Who's Aunt July?"

Ma Ashley let her fork clank to her plate and her hip jarred the table as she abruptly stood and turned from the room and Old Joe just did manage to catch his jug before it toppled.

After supper the men and Laura Upthegrove repaired to the table outside and the talk turned to business. Old Joe said they were damn near broke. The payoffs to Hicks and Webb had nearly cleaned out the family treasury and there was little money coming in. A few months after Frank and Ed got killed he finally bought another rum-boat and Clarence and a young fella named Register made a couple of runs to West End in it before the Coast Guard happened on them one night. Clarence tried to run for it but the Guard shot up the boat and disabled it and killed the Register boy. They were a half-mile offshore and Clarence dove overboard and swam all the way in under a moonless sky without the cutter's light finding him. But neither Joe nor Clarence had wanted anything more to do with rumboats and that was the end of the Ashley smuggling business.

They'd lost other sources of income as well. When they settled accounts for Frank and Ed they of course put an end to the Bellamy payoffs. They'd expected the Chicago bosses to figure out who'd put the pick to Bellamy and send somebody to see them. But the weeks went by and nobody came. Either Chicago never figured out who did it or they knew who it was but didnt think it worthwhile to come after them in the Everglades. *Or* they knew who it was and didnt give a damn. Old Joe had heard that the Chicago bosses never much liked Bellamy and thats why they had sent him to Miami, which they saw as nothing but a sweaty swamptown. For whatever reason, Chicago let things lay. But they no longer drove loads through Palm Beach County or unloaded any boats off the county's shores. Hardly anybody else did either. And so hijack pickings had gone slim.

The whiskey camps had continued to bring in steady money until the gang hit the Stuart bank the month before. "Bobby musta took that robbery even more personal than I thought he would," Joe Ashley said. Since the robbery two of his whiskey camps had been found out and destroyed, one of them just ten days ago. Another camp had been leveled by a bad storm just a few days before that. "We down to two camps," Joe said. "A little one we set up just last year we call Gumbo, about a mile-and-a-half southwest of Hobe, that one and the Crossbone." The Crossbone camp was so-called because it was set near Crossbone Creek which ran into the south fork of the St. Lucie River. Though it was within three miles of Twin Oaks it had never been found out by searchers. It was their oldest camp and had long been their most productive.

"It's got right damn serious now," Old Joe said. "The sumbitches who busted up them camps didnt just scare way my help like Bobby done when you was in the jug the first time. No sir, they did in both my niggers at the little Loxahatchee camp. Sam and Rollo, remember them? Good boys the both. Killed stone dead. You could see they'd shot the Rollo boy from close up after he'd already been shot in the knee and couldnt run nowhere. When I found them they were half eat up by varmints and were startin to turn, so I buried them right there in the muck and weighted down the graves with big chunks of limestone. When I told Sambo's wife what happened to him and her boy she cried like she was gone die of sorrow."

The more recent attack was on the camp in the Hungryland Slough. "They killed another my niggermen and a good cracker boy name of Lee wasnt but fourteen-year-old and didnt have no livin kin. Jaybird seen him shiverin in the streets in Stuart one day last winter with no shoes nor even a long-sleeve shirt. She talked your ma into bringin him home with them and asked me would I do somethin for him, so I give him a roof and put him to work. It was another nigger workin that camp too, Mage Livermore, you know him. He got shot in the leg. Told me the men who did it was a breed and a fullblood Indian. Said the breed told him he was lettin him live so he could give me a message. Know what the message was? 'Your time has come.'"

John Ashley said it sounded like that breed called Heck Somebody who'd lived on the Baker place off and on and had been a county deputy for a time. "I never did meet him myself but everybody always said he's spose to be so damn scary. The one they say Bobby uses when he dont want to dirty his own hands."

"It's him for sure," Old Joe said. "I'd dearly like to make his acquaintance. He's cost me money and some damn good men."

"It's Bobby put him up to it," John Ashley said. "Listen Daddy, I been keepin off Bobby a long time cause you said to, but I got things to settle with that son of a bitch and I aim to settle them."

"Then goddamn *do* it, boy! I aint sayin keep off him, not no more. He sure aint keeping off *us,* is he? I swear I truly have had my fill of Bakers, by Jesus."

"All right then," John Ashley said. "Just wanted you to know where I stand on it."

"I *know* where you stand. I'm standin there too."

"All right then."

But before they did anything else, they needed to come up with some operating capital, on that they were agreed. Old Joe had been tipped that the bank in Pompano had lately grown fat with farm money. According to his source there stood at least twenty-five thousand in that bank every working day of the week, sometimes more. "We'll check is it true," Old Joe said, "and if it is, I'd say thats the place to start."

John Ashley nodded, and Laura said, "I'm drivin."

"No," John Ashley told her. "You're good, honeybunch, but you aint doin this one. You been lucky nobody recognized you with Hannie on them other jobs and they still aint got a thing on you. But they gone know me so easy it aint even worth wearin a disguise. If you with me they'll know you too for certain sure."

She argued about it for a while but he would not change his mind nor would Old Joe take her side. She finally heaved a huge sigh of frustration and sat back with her arms crossed and her face burning with anger and disappointment.

John Ashley said he only wished it was a Palm Beach County bank. "I want that goddamn Bobby to know the onlybody's time has come is his."

"Well then, leave him some kind a message when you do the Pompano, why dont you? A message he'll for certain sure understand."

Over the next weeks they moved cautiously and in pairs whenever they ventured from Twin Oaks into the towns. They drove most of the way to Pompano by backroad and scouted the bank. For a handsome recompense George Doster the Stuart banker made professional inquiries and reported to them that the Pompano bank's cash and securities holdings had indeed grown impressive in recent months due chiefly to the boom in local agricultural enterprise. Old Joe had apprised Bill Ashley of their intentions and Bill nodded more in resignation than accord. As they crafted their plan John Ashley decided on his message for Bob Baker. When he told his father what it was, Old Joe smiled and said, "I'd say it's clear enough."

They hit the bank and made away clean. And that night celebrated at Twin Oaks with bottles of bonded bourbon and jugs of Old Joe's shine while the lookouts kept watch in the woods for encroaching agents of the law. Old Joe got down his fiddle and despite his opposition to bank robbery Bill Ashley had come to the party with his wife Bertha and his banjo, and the music swirled through the house.

They danced and drank and told funny stories and it was a fine party until Ben Tracey got overly bold in his manner of holding Scout to him as they danced and then laughingly refused to release her when she tried to wrest herself free. Laura saw what was happening and slipped out of John Ashley's arms and kicked Ben in the leg and told him to let her go, goddammit. Tracey turned on her with a glare and John Ashley stepped up and said, "Do it, Ben. Raise your hand to her. See what happens."

Scout got between them and said it was all right, Ben hadnt *done* anything, for Pete's sake, she'd just been funning with him. Old Joe who was drunk asked what the hell was going on and why'd everybody quit dancing damn it. Ray Lynn pulled Ben aside and whispered in his ear and Ben nodded and looked hangdog and then told Laura he was sorry, he'd just been playing with the girl and hadnt meant any disrespect.

Ma Ashley entered the room as Ben made his apology and she gave Scout a hard stare and the girl shrugged as if to say *she* didnt know what was going on. Laura saw the girl's impish look and shook a finger at her and then told Ben she was sorry she'd kicked him. Ben Tracey showed a small smile and made a dismissive gesture. John Ashley punched his shoulder lightly and told him to get himself another drink. The party then resumed but it had lost its momentum, and a few minutes later Bill put up his banjo and he and Bertha took their leave and the celebration broke up shortly after.

In a still dark hour of that night, a lookout came to Old Joe's window and woke him with the whispered information that a pair of sheriff's cars had stopped out on the highway and let out a half-dozen men with rifles who were right now working their way through the woods toward the house.

By the time the sheriff's men, muck-caked and mosquito-ravaged, had positioned themselves in the surrounding brush and trees where they could keep the house under surveillance, the Ashley Gang was into the deeper swamp and making for the Crossbone camp.

He kept the rifle bullet in his pocket and throughout the day would take it out and finger it and roll it in his palm and then put it back. For more than a month now his anger had gripped hard inside his chest—squeezing heart and lungs so tightly he could feel his pulse behind his eyes and sometimes had to open his mouth to breathe. On the evening he'd arrived home after receiving John Ashley's message his wife had looked at him and paled and said not a word. His daughters too had gone wide-eyed at the sight of his face and it seemed they all three might cry and their mother had pulled them to her skirts and taken them to another room. But even behind the door mother and children could sense his fury quivering in the walls, could smell his hate drifting through the house like a caustic vapor.

The next day she read in the newspaper all about the Negro and the rifle bullet, read of John Ashley's arrogant challenge to her husband, of her husband's aplomb in the face of it. Read of his sneering dismissal of the Ashley Gang as worthless swamprats who belonged in a zoo cage or on a taxidermist's table more than in a jail cell. She read of his vow to bring them down. When she read of his promise to wear John Ashley's glass eye for a watch fob she felt she little knew this man she was wed to, the father of her children. He seemed unaware of the fear he was inspiring under his own roof.

After days of his oblivious and leaden silence she went to his den one evening and knocked lightly on the door and when she received no response knocked again and then entered. He sat at his desk and stared at her. "I just want you to know," she said softly, "that I'm *here*." He seemed not to recognize her nor care that he did not. He was rolling a bullet under his finger on the desktop. She retreated.

During the month that followed he came and went at all hours. Sometimes he slept at the jail. Sometimes he came home in the middle of the day and went to sleep and all the while there would be cops lolling in the parlor talking in whispers and laughing lowly. Cops in the front yard. His wife and daughters kept to other parts of the house. Christmas passed like a day of mourning. He would awaken and go back out after dark and not return until sometime the following day. He ate but little. And if at times there was whiskey on his breath he never seemed drunk, not to anyone.

*   *   *

"Guess who's *heeere!*" Laura trilled from the doorway, John Ashley smiling beside her and Wisteria's black face behind them showing a wide white grin. It was two weeks before Christmas and a wreath of fresh pine twigs hung on the open door.

"Well now, let me see . . ." Loretta May said. She was sitting in the middle of the bed and the room was bathed in bright morning sunshine. A marmalade cat sat tonguing itself on the bedside table and now looked up and John Ashley saw that it was one-eyed. Loretta's crossed legs were exposed under her parted robe as was most of one breast. He could smell her yellow hair freshly washed. Looking on her smiling face he realized how little she had changed in the eleven years or so he'd known her. She looked hardly older than the seventeen she'd been the first time he'd come to her bed and he believed he'd never seen anything so beautiful as she looked at this moment.

She drummed her fingers on her bare knee and held her chin in affected thought and said, "Who *could* it be?"

"Oh *you,*" Laura said. "You *know!* I bet you even knowed he was loose before I did, didnt you? I bet you . . . you know . . . *seen* us? In the sidehouse? In the *tent?*"

"Do you know this girl's blushin?" John Ashley said.

Loretta May smiled wide. "Sounds like she's braggin too. And you know what, mister? You sound a whole lot like a bad old gator hunter used to come see me ever now and then. Oh but he was bad about not payin, that one. I bet he owes me fifty thousand dollars for services unpaid."

"Well, from the looks of things I'd say he's bout to run that bill up some more," Laura said. "You oughta see—looks like he got a damn banana down his pocket."

Loretta laughed, and behind Laura, Wisteria giggled.

The cat sprang onto the bed and nuzzled her leg and John Ashley said, "Who's the one-eye?"

"Name's Johnny," Loretta May said with a smile, "just like all the one-eyed evil tomcats I know. But how you all *get* here anyway? I heard the bunch of you was hid out in the Devil's Garden and ever cop in the county's on the lookout for you."

"Hell girl, show me the cop who can make his way round the Glades good as us," John Ashley said.

"Well it sure took you long enough to make your way round to me," she said. "I only got one question other."

"What's that?" John Ashley said. His tongue felt thick with his desire for her.

"How much longer you gonna be about makin your way on over to this bed?"

John Ashley laughed and started shedding clothes as he went to her. The cat saw him coming and sprang to the beside table and almost upset the unlit oil lamp there and then leaped to the window sill and glared at John Ashley.

"I see dont *nobody* bother you all," Wisteria said to Laura as she closed the door on them. The girl's giggles faded down the hallway.

She stood with her back against the door and watched them come together. So avid was John Ashley that he climaxed almost immediately on joining with Loretta May. She held him close for a moment and then rolled him onto his side and sat up and said, "Hey boy."

"What?" John Ashley said, looking up at her.

"Where's your manners?" Her smiling sightless face turned toward Laura at the door.

He sat up grinning at Laura and said, "Hey girl, how much longer you gonna be about makin your way on over to—"

But she was already half out of her clothes and hurtling to the bed and tumbling into it and laughing and embracing them both and tasting the salt of her own happy tears.

On a cold afternoon in late December Bob and Fred Baker met with Heck Runyon at Springer's Restaurant in Salerno. They sat at a back table and drank coffee and Heck informed them he'd two days earlier busted up another of the Ashley camps. A small camp in a gumbo limbo hammock in the swamps west of Hobe. Bob Baker asked if any of the Ashley Gang had been there and Heck said no, only a nigger and his kid.

"Oh Jesus," Fred Baker said. "Did you—? How old was *this* kid?"

Heck Runyon shrugged. A man at another table casually glanced over and met his eye and instantly looked away.

"Shit," Fred Baker whispered.

Heck Runyon picked his teeth and stared at Fred Baker through half-closed eyes. Bob Baker reflected that he'd never seen Heck Runyon's eyes fully open nor ever to blink. It was as though he thought that to open his eyes too much would be to let others see into them and thereby know his secrets, that to blink would be to let down his guard. It was the look of a man at once mistrustful of the world's motives and bored with all possibilities of them. Now he turned to Bob Baker and leaned forward on his crossed arms and showed a smile that lacked everything most people associated with a smile. "*You* said get rid them camps."

"Yeah, but he didnt tell you—" Fred Baker started to say but Bob Baker made an abrupt hand gesture and said, "Never mind, Freddie."

"Aint but one camp left," Heck Runyon said.

"One?" Bob Baker said. "How you know?"

"I know."

"Who said so?" Fred Baker said sardonically. "That Miccosukee you run with—Roebuck?" Roebuck was a ropy renegade Indian, a known thief and reputed murderer who'd all his life moved like a shadow through the breadth and reach of the Devil's Garden. He'd been said to hijack the loads of plume hunters along the Shark River Slough and as far south as the Ten Thousand Islands, to have robbed gator skinners plying their trade on Lake Okeechobee's most desolate shores. He'd never been known to keep company with another human being until Heck Runyon took him as partner in manhunting for Bob Baker.

"Would Roebuck know?" Bob Baker said.

Heck Runyon turned his half-closed eyes on him and gave a slow nod and Bob Baker thumped his fist on the table. "That's where they're hidin—got to be. The men watchin the house aint seen a hair of any the men but Bill. The gang's off hid someplace and like as not it's that damn camp!"

He put his hand under the table and felt of the rifle cartridge in his pocket. "The National Guard outfit in West Palm's promised to lend us a couple of automatic rifles and all the ammunition we want. We got the men and the firepower. All we have to do is find that camp and we *got* their ass!"

Heck Runyon showed his teeth. "Done been found," he said.

John Ashley had been for killing him right after the Pompano job but Old Joe had argued against such haste. It was too risky yet, Joe Ashley said. Every cop in the county had an eye out for the Ashley Gang. Besides, Bob Baker wasnt showing his face in public without a half dozen of his best cops around him.

"You *might* can get up close and put him down," Old Joe said, "but you'll play hell getting away with it. And even if you somehow *was* able to get away, everybody'll know it was you and the cops wont never rest till they run you down. They dont hunt nobody like they hunt somebody who kills one their own. Course now, you could do for him at a distance with a rifle—but then he'd never know it was you done it and where's the pleasure in that? Best to let it lay awhile. He'll get tired of huntin somebody he cant find and then he'll let his guard down. You'll see. He'll get shut of them bodyguards after a time. *Then* you slip up on him. When he's alone. You want *him* to know it's you but nobody else to know. No witness, no murder warrant."

"Listen to him, Johnny," Laura said.

He looked from one to the other of them and spat to the side and flung up his hands in capitulation. "What the hell, I waited *this* long."

The Crossbone camp was set on a high dry range of ground marked by a heavy stand of live oaks ragged with Spanish moss. Crossbone Creek flowed in from the northwestern savannah and ran behind the oaks and into the heavy brush to the east and then made its secret way to the South Fork of the St. Lucie River a half-mile farther on. Only the Ashleys and their most trusted confederates knew of the boat route from Twin Oaks to Crossbone Creek, a route that followed a network of narrow waterways through a region called the Pits—a portion of swamp marked by cattailed sloughs and ponds, by cutgrass and tupelo and maidencane, a muckland where footing was more hope than substance and a man so luckless as to find himself there without a skiff might suddenly sink in mud to his ass or be swallowed entire by a quicksand bog in less time than it takes to tell and no mortal trace of him left behind. The route took them to the creekhead—where they kept mules and tack and muckshoes and wagons for carrying out cases of moonshine—and from there it was an easy skiff ride down to the camp.

Southeast of the camp lay a wide range of marl prairie too soft to bear the weight of a motor vehicle and marked by scatterings of saw palmetto and clusters of cabbage palms and myrtlebrush. The camp's high ground afforded a clear view across this prairie to the pinewoods a half-mile away. In those woods were a scattering of rugged trails on which motorcars might drive from the highway far to the east if they came slowly and carefully. Eastward to the South Fork lay impenetrable thickets of peppertree and buttonbush and black willows. To the west and southwest the grassy savannah ran flat and swift to the immensity of the sawgrass country.

Two of Old Joe's best Indian lookouts, Shirttail Charlie and Thomas High Hawk, alternated eight-hour watch shifts on a perch twenty-five feet aboveground in a pine strand a hundred yards south of the camp. While one kept watch the other took a meal in the camp and slept. A grayhaired Negro named Uncle Arthur James and his grown son Jefferson had operated this camp for Joe Ashley for years, maintaining the fire under the great copper kettle at just the right intensity and keeping the distillation box full of water, replacing the buckets under the tap as they filled, jugging the shine and packing the jugs into cases. Now and then father or son would pole a dugout to Salerno for supplies. On the gang's arrival at the camp the month before, Old Joe had dispatched Uncle Arthur to Twin Oaks to tend the property in his absence and make sure the Ashley women had whatever they needed by way of supplies or other necessities. Jefferson remained at the camp—and his dog, Paint, a one-eared mongrel raised from puphood in the swamp and considered magically charmed to have lived so long without falling prey to gator or snake or hunting cat.

Clarence Middleton would not be joining them, they knew that. Old Joe's lookouts had surely warned him of the police around the house and informed him that the gang had fled to the Crossbone. Clarence would have rightly decided there was no reason to risk capture by trying to slip out to the camp and would have returned to his girlfriend's place in St. Lucie.

During their first weeks at the Crossbone camp John and Laura taught Ray Lynn and Ben Tracey to navigate the channels of the sawgrass country to the south—and taught them more besides. John Ashley showed them how to cut open a cabbage palm and extract the succulent heart of it, a treat known to the local crackers as swamp cabbage and which could be eaten raw or prepared in a variety of ways. He showed them how to dig a scratch well in the hammock ground with a stick or just their hands. He and Laura smiled at the look on their faces the first time they dug a little well and the water came up sludgy and dark brown and they said they werent about to drink *that*. John Ashley told them to keep scooping and they did and then after a minute more the water began to clarify and then it was coming forth clear as glass and delighted them with its sweet freshness.

Joe Ashley continued to make whiskey and run it to the Indians. Ben Tracey, who'd always wanted to know the moonshine trade, was his eager apprentice. Joe showed him how to make his way to the cypress hammocks a full day's distance to the southwest where the Indian middlemen awaited the loads. Ray Lynn spent most his time with Albert Miller fishing for bass and bream, gigging frogs, netting turtles, snaring possums for the cookpot. They dared not shoot in case some trapper or posseman be sufficiently keen-eared to accurately fix the bearing of the gunshot even in the acoustical queerness of that vast and aqueous grassland where a report might carry for miles but seemed to whoever heard it to come from all points of the compass at once.

Laura Upthegrove and John Ashley would vanish for hours at a time. Ray Lynn asked of Albert Miller where they went and Albert smiled and winked. "Johnny and Laura are the king and queen of the Everglades," he said. "Them two know places in the Devil's Garden the rest of us aint even guessed is out here."

Now the dry season was on them and the mosquitoes were scant. The nights turned cool and clear and the stars did brighten. The dark sky seemed powdered with stellar swirls pale as talc. The moon in its fullness that month hung like a peeled blood orange. Frogs rang in the creeks and sloughs, owls hooted in the high pine. Sometimes came the deep rumbling growls and guttural barks of gators and now and then the high shriek of a panther near or far. John and Laura shared a tent but used it only to make love in private, after which they would come outside to sleep under the riotous stars on beds fashioned of Spanish moss.

Ray Lynn would like awake in the early nights and listen to the lovers in their passion and remember a time before he'd seen his first jail, a time when he was loved by a honey-haired girl with freckles like brown sugar on her breasts and a small chip in her front tooth. A girl he'd never seen again after going to jail for his first armed robbery and thereafter living the life of the itinerant holdup man from Pensacola to Key West. Thinking of her now he would ache with a loneliness he dared not admit for fear of weeping like a child.

TWENTY-THREE

January 1924

CHILL WINTER DAWN. THE EASTERN SKY SHOWING GRAY AT THE horizon. Pale mist rising in clouds off the wetland all about and dark trees ghostly in the fog. The air smelling of ripe muck. The world soundless.

Thomas High Hawk eased off his flatboard perch on the pine branch with his rifle slung around his chest and shinned down the trunk and lit softly on a carpet of pine needles. He was tired and his eyes burned. Last night's fog had cut his vision's range to a few feet but he had not heard anything unusual and the night had passed without hint of encroaching trouble. Nobody would have been out searching for their camp in such fog anyhow.

He yawned and stretched, hoping that either the black man or cousin Charlie had put a pot of coffee on the fire. Shirttail Charlie was his elder but he was lazy as a child and he often chose to sleep until Thomas shook him awake for his shift. He tightened his rifle sling and buttoned his jacket to the neck and headed into the fog, keeping his eyes to the ground in watch for mudholes and snakes.

A small stand of cabbage palms loomed darkly out of the mist and he held to the vague trail skirting around the trees. A dark figure emerged behind him and silently closed the short distance between them. An arm clamped around Thomas High Hawk's mouth and cut off his cry before it began and Thomas felt an instant's sickening pain at his backribs and then the blade was in his heart and he was dead even before Roebuck yanked away the knife and let him fall.

The sky showed now a long thin streak of pink at some distant point out over the Atlantic. The fog on the high ground was thinning fast but was yet dense as smoke under the trees and rose like steam clouds from the sloughs and flagponds and all along the length of Crossbone Creek as though the oaks were burning at their roots and all bodies of water in this swampland were on fire under their surface. A crow lit on a high branch of a scorched bony pine and his rasping squall was the day's first sound. The camp was absent two of its residents this dawn—Ben Tracey and Ray Lynn having departed a week ago, each armed with a Winchester 95 and a .45 automatic, and each trailing a dugout loaded with bush lightning for delivery to Indian buyers at the south end of Lake Okeechobee. They were not due back for a day or so.

The campfire had been revived by Jefferson James who sat beside it and now set a pot of coffee to boil on the firerocks. Rolled in his blanket near the fire Shirttail Charlie still slept. Joe Ashley emerged from his tent, his trousers unbuttoned and held by galluses over his undershirt. He unleashed his stream against an oak trunk and then buttoned up and stalked over to Shirttail Charlie and nudged him with his boot. The Indian grumbled and tried to squirm away and Joe Ashley cursed lowly and kicked him lightly on the leg.

"Aw right," Shirttail Charlie said, "I'm up, I'm up." He sat up and peered around at the misty morn. "Where's Thomas?"

"Aint come in yet," Old Joe said, squatting to pour a cup of coffee. "If he went to asleep out there I'll feed his ass to Jefferson's damn dog."

The dog was at that moment standing at the perimeter of the camp and peering intently into the thinning fog in the prairie beyond, its ears forward and its nape roaching. And then it bolted with a loud growl and fangs bared and the three men at the campfire all came fast to their feet as the dog sped toward a cluster of palmettos forty yards distant in the gray haze, its snarl rising as it closed on the brush. Then a shotgun blasted with an orange flare and knocked the dog in the air sideways in a burst of hide and blood.

A crackling salvo erupted from the prairie brush and Jefferson James grunted, staggered like a drunk and dropped. Joe Ashley ran at a crouch for his tent and his rifle that lay within as bullets kicked up dirt all around him. The coffeepot jumped away from the fire with a loud whang and rounds thucked through the sides of the tents. He lunged into his tent and snatched up his .44-40 and the canvas walls popped and shook with bullets and he was hit hard on the hipbone and dropped to his belly. He looked at his hip and saw blood and cursed. He levered a round and crawled forward to the doorflap. He fired several rounds into the expanse of prairie even though he had yet to see any of the attackers. A bullet hummed over his head. From his left came the hollow staccato popping of an automatic rifle and he looked over and saw Laura firing the Browning from behind an oak and giving John Ashley coverfire as John with a pistol in his hand ran out to the fallen Jefferson and knelt beside him and rolled him onto his back. A bullet snatched at John's sleeve and a chunk of limerock flew up beside him in a ricochet whine. At the forward edge of the camp Albert Miller lay behind a stump and levered and fired his Marlin. Now John Ashley turned and ran back for the trees as Laura stepped out in the open and fired the BAR from the hip as if she'd been born to it. Bullets chunked into the oak trunks around her. Then John was in the trees again and she side-hopped back behind cover. Shirttail Charlie was nowhere in sight.

Joe Ashley thought to follow John to the shelter of the trees but as he rose to one knee he was hit in the shoulder and he sat down hard. For a moment he was stunned and then tried his arm and found he could move it, but only awkwardly, and the pain was intense. He struggled to lever a round and felt bone grinding in his shoulder and even in the surrounding din of gunfire heard himself cry out. He crawled back to the tent flap and saw a man duck down in the myrtlebrush forty yards away. He fired into the brush and the man ran out from it and took cover behind a thick pine stump jutting from a clump of palmetto. Another man came running with a rifle in his hands and threw himself behind a low limestone outcrop not thirty yards away.

Laura was kneeling against a wide oak trunk and shooting now an Enfield rifle—working the bolt smoothly and firing steadily and now stripping a fresh clipload into the magazine and flinging away the empty clip and slapping the bolt home and firing again. One leg of her overalls was stained bright red. John Ashley had the Browning braced in the crotch of a large oak and was pouring fire into the open country and yelling, "Come *on*, Daddy! Come on, Al!"

Albert Miller jumped up and ran for the trees and he was almost to them when he was hit and went down. He was hit again as he got to his feet but he gimped ahead and now Laura had him and pulled him behind the cover of the tree. His shirtsleeve and pants leg were soaked with blood. A round had ripped through his hamstring muscle without hitting bone but his humerus was broken. Laura eased him to the ground and examined the wounds and said neither one would bleed him dead. She found a stick to serve for a splint and then tore the other sleeve off Miller's shirt and began to bind his arm. Albert bit his lip bloody against crying out.

John Ashley ducked down to replace the emptied magazine in the Browning. He said they were cut off from the west side of the camp where the dugouts were banked at the creek and they couldnt get away by water. The only way out was on foot through the Pits. "Like that goddamn Charlie—you see him? Took off in there like a spooked deer."

He was talking fast and kept glancing up over the crotch of the tree. He said they could make their way north through the Pits till they hit higher ground and then head east to the pineywoods and on to Twin Oaks where they had their vehicles hidden in the woods. He told Albert to go first. He and Laura would hold off the posse for a time so he could get a good head start and then they would follow after him.

"Watch yourself good when you get near the house," John Ashley said. "Cops bound to be watchin the place, so lay low. Get close enough to see what's goin on but stay put till you know for sure how things stand."

He peered up over the tree crotch and fired a long burst, then dropped down again and said, "All right, boy, go on. We be along directly." Dazed and bloody Albert Miller staggered away into the Pits.

Now John Ashley stood once more and called out, "Daddy, come on get up here!"

As Old Joe bolted from the tent the BAR quit firing and he knew it had jammed. A fierce clatter of gunfire rolled out from the prairie brush and he could hear that their attackers too had at least one automatic rifle and before he'd taken five strides he was hit in the foot and he fell. He turned and scrabbled back for the tent on all fours, his foot a numbed ruin but the pain in his shoulder making him yell. And now he was hit in the side and he screamed but kept on crawling and was hit in the ass and as he tumbled into the tent he was hit somewhere under his arm.

He lay facedown and gasped his pain into the dirt. He put a hand to his searing side and felt of a gaping pulsing wound and the hand came away coated bright and hotly red. He heard John yell, "Got one! I got the bastard!" and heard Laura yell something too but did not make it out. He sat up and looked out and saw a man lying on his side next to a palmetto clump and hugging himself as though he were napping in the cold.

It now occurred to him that if he went out through the back of the tent he would have at least a little cover as he made for the trees. He unsheathed his skinning knife and crawled through his pain and raised up on his knees and the rear canvas wall parted neatly before the slash of his blade. And then a bullet passed through his neck and Joseph Ashley felt nothing as he fell forward through the slashed tent but clearly recalled sitting on the bank of the Caloosahatchee at age seven while his daddy showed him the proper way to rig his line if he wanted to catch fish of a size to impress his mother.

John Ashley had thrown aside the jammed BAR and taken up his Winchester carbine. He saw his father hit several times as he scrabbled back into the tent and then saw a man peek out from behind a palmetto clump not twenty yards from the edge of the camp. He fired twice and the man cried out and fell clear of his cover and drew up on his side in pain, hugging his belly. John Ashley shot him again and saw his hair jump with the impact of the round. He hollered in exultation and Laura yelled, "Good, baby, *good*!" Then a man with a rifle peered over an outcrop and fired once and John Ashley saw his father spill out of the back of the tent with blood jetting from his neck and knew he was killed. The shooter ducked out of sight as John Ashley howled and fired three fast rounds at the outcrop and each glanced off the rock with a high whine.

Now Laura screamed. He whirled and saw her sitting with a hand to her head and blood rolling in thick rivulets from her hair. Her eyes were on him and now fluttered and closed and she fell back. He ran to her and shook her and shouted for her not to die goddammit. Blood ran into her ears and down her neck. Possemen were hollering one to the other and drawing closer and they sounded like a dozen or more. They continued to shoot as they came and bullets cracked through the branches and whacked against the tree boles and cut pale scars in the bark. He thought for a moment to run out to meet them and be done with it. And then heard Bobby Baker curse in a high wail, in a timbre of sorrow he'd never before heard in his voice, and he knew if he charged out there they would kill him before he got Bobby or even saw him. The only way to get Bob Baker was first to get clear of this killing ground. He loaded his pockets with ammunition and picked up his carbine. He put his fingers to his lips and then to Laura's and then was up and running for the deeper swamp.

*   *   *

Albert Miller slogged through the treacherous muck and struggled through the bracken and thorny brush and several times that long afternoon fell under the weight of his pain. His right boot was heavy with blood off his leg wound. His arm was a throbbing agony. He took his bearing from the sun, but even though Twin Oaks was a little less than three miles away as the crow flies, there was no route to it that did not cover at least twice that distance and all of it terrain so difficult he would do well to cover a mile in half a day. When he first heard the high excited yelping of the tracking dogs he guessed he'd been on the move about two hours. They were coming his way, but slowly, the swamp much rougher still on them than on a man. As the afternoon passed the hounds seemed to move off on a more easterly track into the deeper heart of the swamp and Albert guessed they were on someone else's trail, maybe John's and Laura's, or one of the other's if they'd split up. He almost walked into a quicksand bog but he threw himself back from it almost in the same motion of stepping forth and the action sent a streak of white pain through his wounds and he yelped despite himself. Some time later his heart lunged to his throat when a snorting redeyed boar all black and stinking and hung with ticks the size of grapes on his bristly hide crashed out of the button-brush and came for him with its yellow tusks forward and then veered away within a yard of him and vanished into the scrub. Why the brute didnt knock him down and gore out his guts would remain to Albert one of the mysteries of his life. He drank from a slough and was so tired and in such pain that he didn't care if it poisoned him. By late that afternoon he did not know where he was. He stripped moss from a dwarf cypress that evening well before dark and made a bed beside a small creek under a low overhang of elephant ears. He slept but fitfully for his pain and the onslaught of mosquitoes that throve even in winter in this soggy mire. He could feel small parasitic forms already feeding on his wounds. The next day he staggered through country so mean it reduced his clothes to rags before midmorning and when he came at last to the outskirts of the pinelands and its more solid ground he sat down to rest in the shade. The next thing he knew he was awakened by a kick and opened his eyes to a ring of grinning possemen all aiming cocked firearms at his head and recognized among them the Padgett brothers and Grover Pass. He tried to speak but his mouth was too dry to shape words. He wanted to tell them he surrendered, that he never was cut out for this outlaw life, that prison would by God come a blessed relief.

*   *   *

She regained consciousness to find herself sitting against a tree. Her skull felt cloven. She put her hand to her head and felt a makeshift bandage in place there, felt a shirt sleeve dangling alongside her right ear. Her fingers came away bloody. Her thigh bandaged too if only cursorily. Cops everywhere, probing every part of the camp. And now she saw, not ten feet to her right, the bloody and unmistakably dead forms of Joe Ashley and Fred Baker laid side by side. Their mouths and eyes were closed but ants were already filing into their noses and ears in attendance to timeless instinctual duty. Her breath caught and she looked everywhere but saw no other bodies, no sign of John— then heard the bark and bay of dogs across the open ground and knew he had made away.

Possemen were staring at her now, glaring with such raw hate she wanted to hug herself against it. Now a man stepped around from behind her and she saw boots with star facings and looked up past the gunbelt and the badged black vest to the tightly clenched face of Bob Baker, his eyes on her and brightly welled. He seemed to want to say something that could be expressed only in some language whose grammar he did not quite understand. He looked at Fred Baker and gestured awkwardly as though he must make her comprehend, but even the kinetics of grief seemed alien to him. He turned his face to the clouding sky for a moment and then squatted and looked at her and she saw nothing in his eyes but pain and rage beyond his powers of articulation. He cleared his throat and she thought he was going to spit on her but he didnt. He stared at her for a time and then took something from his vest pocket and held it up for her to see. She recognized the rifle cartridge. "He's . . ." He paused and looked about as if he might espy someone to speak for him, to translate accurately the lurch and shudder in his soul. Then looked at her again. "I'm . . ." Then he swiped at his eyes with the heel of his hand and rose and walked away.

By late forenoon the news of the battle had relayed all up and down the Dixie Highway from Fort Pierce to West Palm Beach. Local newspapers rushed to print fourth-hand reports of the attack and claimed a half-dozen outlaw dead. They lamented the death of good Fred Baker at the hand of John Ashley and alerted the populace that the desperado remained at large in the company of confederates. Aroused citizens from Fort Pierce to Jupiter converged at Gomez, the nearest hamlet to the Ashley place, every man of them outraged by the killing of Deputy Fred and each armed and avid for reprisal. Whiskey jugs now out of hiding and making the rounds and stoking the general fury. A clamor of calls to descend upon the Ashley property and search it every foot for members of the gang. Every such exhortation raising a chorus of ayes. In this party was a justice of the peace and mediocre bootmaker by trade who swore them all as deputies.

The sheriff's men heard them coming from a mile away. Whooping and rebel-yelling on rattling trucks slewing through the mud and jouncing over the corduroyed trail, calling for the blood of John Ashley. The deputy in charge of the surveillance team was a brave sergeant named Hazencamp who stood fast where the trail debouched into the cleared ground of Ashley property and within sight of Twin Oaks and he gave the mob no choice but to stop or run him over. He would permit no vigilante action without Sheriff Bob's sanction and ordered them to turn back. The vigilantes jeered him down and shoved the justice of the peace forward to apprise Hazencamp of their deputized status. Only now did Hazencamp and his men learn of the gunfight at the Ashley whiskey camp and of Fred Baker's death. In the face of this terrible revelation and on hearing of Sheriff Bob's open weeping over the body of his dead cousin the cops joined in the general cursing of John Ashley. Hazencamp was now unsure what to do—and in that moment of his indecision his men fell in with the mob and it surged toward the house.

The Ashley women stood back from the windows and watched them come. And here came Uncle Arthur James on the run from around the side of the house and his eyes wide and white in his frightened black face but his duty foremost. As he bore for the porch a rifle cracked and the round slammed the front wall and Arthur covered his head with his arms. He started up the steps as more gunshots sounded and his legs quit him and he tumbled to the ground. He rose to elbows and knees and began scaling the steps and was shot several times more—and still he kept crawling upwards. Then a bullet found the back of his head and blew away a portion of his forehead and he slumped dead.

The mob was shooting in force now and the windows burst and framed photographs along the mantel in the front room flew apart in shards and bullets whined through the room and the walls shed dust under the impact of the fusillade. The shooters laughing and yeehawing and having great sport. But now the women's screams from the house rose above the clatter of firearms and the clamor of the mob and Sergeant Hazencamp again and again hollered "Hold your fire—hold your goddamn fire!" The shooting slowly subsided and finally ceased altogether and Sergeant Hazencamp yelled out to know if John Ashley or any other man was in the house with the women.

Ma Ashley shouted back: "It's just us and you know it, you fool sonsofbitches!"

Hazencamp ordered them to come out with their hands up high and they did. When they looked upon Uncle Arthur James sprawled dead in his blood on the porch steps the girls began to cry. Hazencamp had the women taken aside and then led a party of men into the house to search it. In moments he smelled smoke and rushed out to the dogtrot to see the other side of the house in crackling flames. The men who'd done it stood together in front of the house and laughed and passed a jug. The fire fed on the resined pine so fast there was no hope of stopping it from spreading. The sidehouse was already burning as well. The blaze threw up great flaring sparks with cracks and pops like pistolshots and the mob cheered even as the heat drove them back. The fire filled the house and billowed red-yellow and lunged wildly from the windows and doors and leaped high off the rooftop shingles as if it would break free and run amok on the earth. They could hear glass breaking within, the loud crack and crash of the rooftimber coming asunder. Twenty feet back of the main house the kitchen roof suddenly sent up a roiling black cloud of smoke and then that building too was in flames. Ma Ashley looked on without expression nor sound as tears coursed down her face. Clutching fast to either side of their mother the Ashley girls wailed like witnesses to the end of the world.

Now the mob found the Ashley motor vehicles in the pines behind the house and quickly put the torch to them—to Ben Tracey's blue Chevrolet and Laura's Ford coupé and two of the gang's trucks. In minutes the vehicles were enveloped in rolling sheets of orange fire. The fuel tanks detonated each in turn with a deeply resonant *BOOOMMM!* and parts of the vehicles flew through the air and scattered the crowd even as each explosion raised great celebratory cries. A man standing too near the Chevy when its tank blew up was himself set afire and ran screaming and others pulled him down and stripped the smoking clothes from his blistered skin.

And now somebody shouted something about another house seen down the trail, and somebody else cried, "It's another damn Ashley place!" and the mob closed up again and made for the house in a great exultation of outrage and some among them carried flaming brands.

The Mobleys saw them coming and went out with their hands up and begged them not to burn their home. But someone shouted that the old man was Hanford Mobley's daddy and someone else informed loudly that the mother was an Ashley sister, and the mob's rage at all things Ashley would allow for no mercy. Torches smashed though the windows and in minutes the little residence was swallowed in fire.

The smoke of the Twin Oaks fires rose in towering black columns that could be seen all over the county. From where he squatted to drink from a swamp creek west of Twin Oaks, John Ashley saw the smoke pluming high above the pines and fixed its location and knew exactly what it meant.

Eight days and nights he stayed on the run in the swamps and pineywoods of the Devil's Garden with Bob Baker in relentless pursuit. The cry of the tracking dogs on the air and now and then gunshots— and God only knew who those peckerwoods were shooting in their fervor to shoot *some*thing. He slaked his thirst at creeks, ate birds' eggs raw, the bloody meat of turtles he caught at the creeks and broke apart on rocks, the fresh sweet heart of cabbage palms. Neither he nor the posse slept much. The dogs continued to come on after dark and he was obliged to stay on the move through the night. He sometimes slept for more than an hour and then woke to a louder baying of hounds and had to move faster all that day to open the distance between them again. Other times when he tried to sleep he would dream of his father lying in blood, of Laura's eyes fluttering closed, and he would wake up weeping furiously.

By his third day in flight he'd determined to take refuge with the only brother left to him in the world. He'd thought of making his way to Clarence Middleton at his girlfriend's house in St. Lucie but he did not know if Clarence was still in the clear or had been arrested or had fled for safer haven. Besides, he did not know Terrianne very well and so did not trust her, no matter that Clarence did. It had to be Bill. His big brother would likely not be happy to see him, not with every cop in five counties looking for him. But Bill was blood, and blood had to take your side.

He had first to lose his chasers. He slogged through muck and waded along the sloughs and wormed through the thorniest brush. He was a mass of bloody cuts caked with mud. He doubled back on his trail and set zigzag courses and was ever moving in a large circle so as to give no hint of his intention to head for Salerno. And still the dogs held his trail. It rained hard but briefly one morning and he heard the dogs' frustration when they lost his scent—but an hour later they were on him again. He could not but admire such animals and their handlers and thought Bobby must have some damned good trackers with him besides. He was weary to his bones and now had bad dreams the minute he fell asleep. His clothes were stinking bloody rags held together by sweat and muck.

On the sixth morning the dogs' yelping for the first time began to go faint and by that afternoon he heard them no more. He figured they had finally run themselves out or the posse had quit the chase. He had no way of knowing it was the third pack of dogs Bob Baker had used on this manhunt and all three packs had been run to exhaustion.

That midday he felt sure he'd lost them and at last turned toward the drier pineywoods perhaps a day's distance to the east and, a day beyond them, Salerno and Bill's place. He found a high-banked creek whose water came to his chest and he held the carbine up high and followed the creek through heavy black willows and buttonbrush until he arrived at a higher-ground stand of cabbage palm and wateroaks. He laid his rifle on the weedy slope of the bank and searched carefully along the creek and found a turtle nest and robbed it of its eggs. Then climbed to the bankrim and there sat to eat.

He was sucking the last egg dry when he suddenly sensed something behind him. He raised his arms defensively as he whirled around and a knifeblade cut through the back of his forearm like a lick of fire. He grabbed the attacker's legs as the blade slashed into the crown of his head and he pulled the man off balance and rolled sideways and they tumbled together down the bank and into the water. They came up gasping and spitting and John Ashley saw an Indian of blackfire eyes and brown teeth bared like a dog's. The Indian slashed at his neck and missed and John Ashley grabbed him in a bear hug that pinioned the Indian's knifehand between them and he drew a deep breath and plunged underwater with the man fast in his embrace. The water was murky and the color of tea and the Indian struggled and kicked in a wild desperation that raised thick clouds of mud off the creekbottom and still John Ashley clutched him with all his might, hugging himself to the Indian like a lover becrazed. And just as he thought his lungs would burst for lack of breath he felt the Indian abruptly go slack. He released him and thrust his head up out of the water, gagging and coughing and for a moment he could not gain his feet and everything remained blurred and he flailed against the water and thought he might yet go under and drown but then his feet found purchase and he stood upright and his lungs swelled and sucked huge draughts of air.

The Indian floated facedown in the sway of unsettled water, his long hair wavering about his head like swampweed, the back of his shirt bloated with trapped air. There was a stink of shit and John Ashley realized the man's bowels had let loose when he died. He stood gasping in the chest-high water and thought he would never again draw a deep enough breath. He tasted blood and wiped at his mouth and his fingers came away red and it took him a moment to comprehend that the blood was running from his head and he put a hand to his crown and felt the loose flap of scalp under his hair. And now was conscious of pain in his forearm and he saw the gash but it bled slowly and not very much.

He slowly pulled himself up the steep creekbank where his carbine still lay. And as he rose above the bankrim he saw the breed sitting crosslegged on the ground ten feet away and looking at him. On his knee was braced a .30-40 Krag pointed at John Ashley's face. The breed held it one-handed, finger on the trigger.

"Fucken Roebuck," Heck Runyon said placidly. "I was for shootin you from the trees while you was suckin eggs, but not him. Fancied himself a knifer. Thought a knife felt *sweet*. Dumbfuck Indian."

John Ashley could not recall if a round was chambered in the carbine lying before him and out of the breed's line of vision. He licked blood off his lips and hoped Heck Runyon was watching him more intently than it seemed under those half-closed eyes. He cut his eyes over the breed's shoulder and Heck Runyon instinctively flicked his own half-closed eyes in that direction and all in the same instant John Ashley snatched up the carbine and Runyon was startled and jerked rather than squeezed the trigger and the round batted John Ashley's collar as John Ashley thumbed the hammer and fired and shot him in the belly and knocked him on his back.

He jacked another round ready but the breed made no move to rise or take up the rifle fallen beside him. He climbed up the bank and stepped forward cautiously and kicked the Krag from the breed's reach. Heck Runyon was staring up at him without expression. "Damn quick," he said. The shirt over his belly showed a spreading stain brightly red. "Musta hit the spine," he said in a tone untimbred by plaint or bitterness. "Cant move."

"Damn thats sad," John Ashley said. And shot him through the Adam's apple.

Two miles away Bob Baker heard the almost simultaneous reports of two rifles and tried vainly to fix their direction. Beside him Henry Stubbs grinned and said, "Hear that Krag? I say the breed and the redskin got him, Bob. They got the advantage in this damned country. I say they did for him and we're shut of the sumbitch for once and all.''

Then came another report—a Winchester. And then nothing more. Bob Baker looked at Henry Stubbs who shrugged and spat.

Ray Lynn and Ben Tracey were poling along the sawgrass channel back to the Crossbone camp that early morning when they heard the sudden distant sounds of the gun battle. They sat in the dugouts and listened for a time and agreed that nothing good could be going on where so many guns were shooting. They turned around and headed back for Lake Okeechobee. The next day they hove up at an inlet of Pelican Bay, about four miles south of Pahokee. The bank was high and dry under tall willows and there they set up camp and stayed put for two days to let things settle. Then they cached their dugouts and rifles in the brush and pulled their shirts out of their pants to hide their pistols and walked up to Pahokee. They had a couple of beers at a fishcamp and two hours later cadged a ride on a catfisherman's truck bound for West Palm Beach.

In West Palm they heard all about the raid on the Ashley whiskey camp—and learned that Joe Ashley was dead. And that Albert Miller and Laura Upthegrove were under arrest and heavily guarded. And that Bill Ashley had driven down from Salerno and surrendered himself in exchange for the sheriff's posting of men at his house. Bill didnt want vigilantes showing up and terrifying his family and maybe torching his house too.

They learned that the Ashley home had been burned to the ground, and the Mobley house as well. That even Ma Ashley and her daughters and Hanford Mobley's parents had been jailed for a couple of days before being released to tend to Old Joe's funeral. Bill had been allowed to go with them. They'd buried Joe Ashley in the family graveyard next to the charred ruins of Twin Oaks. The only one present who wasnt a member of the family was the preacher, who later said everything about the Ashley place smelled of charcoal, Joe's grave most of all. He said Ma Ashley and her daughters keened like Indian women. After the funeral Sheriff Baker dropped all charges against Bill Ashley, his mother and sisters and the parents of Hanford Mobley. Bill had gone home to his wife. Ma Ashley and the girls were staying at the West Palm home of family friends with a larger house than Bill's.

They heard that Bob Baker was charging Laura Upthegrove with murder for helping John Ashley kill Deputy Fred Baker. John Ashley was still at large in the Everglades but Sheriff Bob told the newspapers he was confident the outlaw would be captured or killed any day now.

The bad tidings weighed hard on Tracey and Lynn. They repaired to a cafe and sat in a dim booth and toyed with the Blue Plate Special of pork chops and sweet potatoes. They drank coffee and smoked cigarettes. They told each other there wasnt a damn thing they could do now except watch out for their own asses. They still had the money from the hooch sale to the Indians—and with Joe Ashley dead and John Ashley likely to join him real soon, the money belonged to whoever had it in hand. They agreed the smart thing to do was lay low. An hour later they were on the bus to Miami.

Over the next two days he rested during daylight hours and listened to the possemen hunting for him in the swamp but they had no dogs with them and they sounded scattered and lost more than like hunters on a hot trail. He'd tended well to his wounds. A thick muckpack on his crown had finally stopped the bleeding and he'd bound his lacerated forearm with a sleeve ripped from his shirt. At night he moved fast and sure through the pineywoods and on the second night came at last to the highway and saw no traffic and he crossed and stayed to the deeper trees as he made his way to the Salerno town limits. The hour was late and the moon high and there was no one about the central streets but a stray drunk. Now came a lone police car moving without haste. John Ashley kept to the shadows of the eaves with his rifle cocked and watched the car pass and waited till it was gone from sight before he moved on. In the moonlit road his shadow stood so short under him it seemed itself to be trying to hide. Now he was on the dirt road east of town. As he went by a dark house set well back from the road a dog started barking at his passing and other dogs on the road ahead began to take up the alert. He stopped and faced the dark house and whistled as his daddy had long ago taught him and no human ear could hear the sound he made but the dog abruptly fell silent and then the others ahead did too.

A quarter-mile farther along he came to a side road and turned onto it and felt better for being now in the deep shadows of an oak hollow. Another two hundreds yards brought him to the narrow turn-in to his brother's house. He'd been on the alert for police all the while and now advanced slowly and looked and listened more keenly yet. The trail to his brother's house went through a dense wood of oak and pine and he could see the house just ahead and no cars in sight but Bill's Oldsmobile tourer in the dappled light of the moon. He stopped in the darkest shadows of the trees and listened hard and heard nothing but the sudden rush of an owl leaving its perch somewhere overhead and the splatter of a school of mullet jumping in the canal behind the house. No sounds other.

He went around to the back of the house and to the bedroom window and saw that it was open. He stood there and listened hard and after a time could make out Bill's steady heavy breathing and Bertha's light sporadic snores. He tapped lightly on the open shutter and Bill's breath altered and then held bated. Bertha snored once more and then she too fell silent. And then Bill said, evenly and very clearly: "I got a gun here. I'll blow your damn brains out without even thinking about it."

"Easy now, big brother," John Ashley whispered. "It aint but a wanderer lookin for shelter."

They raised no lights until they'd let him into the indoor kitchen and closed all the shutters. Then Bertha fired a lamp and at the sight of him she gasped.

"Sweet Jesus!" Bill said.

John Ashley tried to grin. "Probably dont smell a whole lot bettern I look neither, huh?"

They made him strip naked and Bill gave him a towel to wrap around his waist and Bertha stuffed his foul ragged clothes in an old croker sack and went out and disposed of them. When she came back she was lugging two full pails of water. She made John Ashley hold his head over the tin sink and she poured a bucket on his hair to wash out the dried muck. As the muck softened and fell away his scalp began to bleed again. While Bill set up a tin washtub in the middle of the kitchen floor and put in handfuls of soap shavings and then went out several times more for water, Bertha got a needle and thread and made John Ashley sit at the table and she stitched his scalp closed and then washed and sewed his forearm as well and applied a clean bandage to it. As he submitted to being tended to, John Ashley felt a tiredness greater than any he'd known before. He barely felt Bertha's needle. There was little talk among them until the tub was full of foamy water and Bill told him to get in it. Bertha excused herself to give John privacy while he bathed. Bill had brought in a quart bottle of beer he'd pulled up from the well and now poured two glasses and handed one to his brother, then lit two cigarettes and passed one of these to him also. They looked at each other a long moment. In a tight voice Bill Ashley said: "I thought they'd killed you too for sure."

He told John that Ma and their sisters were living with the Pattersons in West Palm Beach for now but it would be too risky for him to try to sneak over there to see them. Their mother had cursed Bob Baker publicly as the murderer of her husband and destroyer of her home and told the newspapers she hoped Bob Baker got paralyzed and had to be fed from a spoon for the rest of his life. She had sworn to build a new house on the ashes of Twin Oaks. "She can afford to do it, too," Bill said. "Daddy buried money all over the place and she knows where a good bit of it is."

What about their daddy's grave, John Ashley wanted to know. Could he go to it? He wanted to say goodbye to him.

Bill told him to forget it. Bob Baker still had the posse on duty and had deputized what seemed like half the men in the county. Cops were everywhere. Thinking John might try to visit his daddy's grave, Bobby was keeping it under close watch by deputies armed to the teeth.

He told John of the rumor that Ray Lynn and Ben Tracy were in Miami, but nobody knew it to be true for sure. Clarence Middleton hadnt shown a hair of himself since the news of the raid and was likely still in St. Lucie. Bertha had written a note to Hanford Mobley telling him what happened and to stay put right where he was. She'd mailed it by way of a friend in Pensacola who relayed the letter to Galveston—just in case the cops were checking the mail going out through the local post offices. As for Laura, Bill said, Bobby'd given up trying to stick even an attempted murder charge on her and wouldnt be able to convict her for anything more than a misdemeanor or two and she wasnt likely to serve more than a few months at the most.

John Ashley stared at him and the stub of his cigarette fell from his mouth into the tub water now thickly purpled with dirt and old blood. He put his head in his hands and sobbed so loudly Bertha came running with face afright.

He slept all the next day and despite his exhaustion he came awake on the instant that afternoon when he heard a car pull up in front of the house. He peeked from behind the curtain and saw two cops in the car, the driver talking to Bill Ashley who was wearing a straw hat and had gardening tools in his hand. Bertha knelt at her nearby flower bed and trimmed weeds. Bill was talking amiably and one of the cops smiled and shook a finger at him. Then both cops grinned and waved so long and the car wheeled around and left. John Ashley once more checked the .45 under the pillow to ensure a round in the chamber. He lay back and thought to himself, *She's alive, oh yes she is,* and smiled so wide it hurt his mouth and he happily drifted back to sleep.

That evening Bertha served a supper of fried chicken and corn-bread, rice and greens, and John Ashley had second helpings of every-thing and then two huge wedges of pineapple pie for dessert. Over coffee and cigarettes Bill told him the best thing to do was go away to Texas. He would make all the arrangements for him.

"The law's on you for killing a policeman now," he said. "They figure they got a score to settle and they wont never let it lay and you know it. You stay round here and sooner or later they'll catch up to you and if they dont shoot you dead on the spot they'll sure's hell see you hang."

"Well goddamn, Billy, I figure *we* got a few scores to settle our ownselfs, dont you?" John Ashley said. "What about Daddy? Dont you figure thats a score needs settlin? Hell, man, it's *lots* of damn scores I still got to settle with that fucken Bobby, scores nobody even knows about but me and him. Scuse my language, Berty."

Bill Ashley heaved an enormous sigh. "All this"—he gestured vaguely—"this *shit* about settlin scores. It's too damn many people with too damn many scores to settle in this world, Johnny. If we dont start lettin go of some of these damn *scores,* thats all we'll be doin the rest of our days, tryin to settle em. That aint no goddamn way to live. It's just a way to not live long."

John Ashley set down his cup and stared hard at him. "What the hell you talkin about? The son of a bitch killed my daddy."

"*Our* daddy."

"Well you damn sure dont act like he's any daddy of yours. I seen you out there talking to them cops today, jokin with them like they was just a coupla old boys."

"They *are* just a coupla old boys. Christ, Johnny, *they* didnt shoot Daddy. They didnt have a thing in the world to do with it."

"It was cops killed him and they're *cops,* aint they? Anybody who can smile at cops thataway aint no son of—"

"Goddammit, dont talk to me like that! He was as much my daddy as—"

"Billy, you stop now!" Bertha said. "The both you—stop!"

Bill Ashley glared at John and looked at Bertha and then made a half-growl in his throat and looked off to the window.

Bertha turned to John Ashley who lit a cigarette and angrily ex-haled. She said softly, "Can I say somethin? I promise I'll only say it once and then I'll keep my trap shut and go back to mindin my own business."

He looked at her. "You can always say anything you want, Berty, you know that."

"Just last night you thought Laura was dead, didnt you? You'd thought it for days. You felt like there wasnt a reason in the world to go on living except to get even with Bobby Baker for her and your daddy. Then you found out she was alive and it made you so happy you cried—yes, you did, John Ashley, I saw it and you know I did, and there's nothin in the world wrong with that. Knowin she was alive made the world a whole lot better in a hurry, didnt it? But *now* just listen to you. Here you are all over again talkin about gettin even with Bob Baker for your daddy and you know it wasn't even him that killed him, you said so yourself—no, wait, let me finish . . . You figure Bobby's responsible no matter who did the shootin, but what difference does it make anymore, Johnny? I swear, you and that damned Bobby Baker sound exactly the same. He's sayin in the newspaper he wants to even things with *you* for killing his cousin Freddie. How two men who already suffered and caused as much pain as you two can talk about nothin but causin *more* pain is something I'll never understand. How I pity that man's poor wife and children. But *you*! Even if you cant think of yourself or of your own brother here, cant you at least think of what you'd be doin to Laura? That girl loves you *so much*. Why in the world do you want to take a chance on getting killed or goin back to prison and makin the rest of her life so miserable? Why do that when you and her can just go away somewhere and be happy together? Why cant you just *quit* all this awful business? I'm sorry to sound like Little Miss Know-it-all, because I surely aint any such a thing, but if I was you I'd just want to get away from all this meanness and sadness and trouble and go someplace where I could live a peaceable life and wake up happy ever day because I'm with somebody I love and who loves me back and I'd try and remember how damn lucky that makes me."

She was crying as she rushed from the table into the bedroom and shut the door behind her.

The brothers sat in silence for a moment without meeting each other's eyes. Then Bill looked at him and showed a small crooked smile and said: "Now look what you done. She'll be at least a week blamin me for any pain any man's ever caused a woman."

John Ashley chuckled softly. "Sometimes just havin a dick means we're guilty, dont it?"

They fell quiet again. After a time John Ashley said, "You say she'll do about three months in the lockup?"

"Three, four, wont be much. He aint got much on her."

"They mistreatin her?"

"Hell no. I know that for a fact. I talked to her before I got let go. She's lookin fine, I swear. Luckiern hell that bullet only scraped her skull. And the leg wound wasnt much. She was already gimpin around in the cell a coupla days after. Bobby told them to treat her right, she heard him say it herself."

John Ashley looked at him. "Why would he do that? I thought he wanted to hang her?"

Bill Ashley shrugged. "He wanted *somebody* hung for Freddie. Anyway just cause he wanted to hang her dont mean he cant be a gentleman to her. Hell, *I* dont know. I quit tryin to figure why people do any the things they do. It only tired my mind to try."

He stayed with Bill and Bertha two days more and then was sufficiently rested to slip out in the late darkness of the following night. He made his way through town and into the pineland swamps and on to a creekside waycamp where they'd long before cached a skiff and ammunition and a few supplies. By sunrise the next day he was headed for the Devil's Garden.

Three days later he was forty miles away at Laura's house deep in the sawgrass country and the Thousand Hammocks where nothing did abide but the ever untamed.

TWENTY-FOUR

The Liars Club

BOBBY BAKER'S RAID ON THE ASHLEY CAMP MADE HEADLINES THAT stood higher than a whiskey glass. We couldnt hardly believe Old Joe Ashley'd been shot dead. Lots of people didnt believe it till they went to the funeral parlor and saw the body for themselfs. And young Fred Baker shot dead too. He was chock full of piss and vinegar and damn near everybody liked him. It's hardly any wonder the Ashley and Mobley places got burnt down and all their cars and trucks set afire. Lord, it was wildness for a time—it was like the Old West. Men with guns were everywhere and just aching to shoot somebody, to burn something. Albert Miller tried to get away in the swamp but was too bad hurt to make it very far and a posse run him down quick. And Laura Upthegrove! The woman got shot in the *head* and lived to tell of it. The "Queen of the Everglades" the newspapers was calling her.

Sheriff Baker told the newspapers he'd by God bring John Ashley in dead or alive and do it any day now. The bullet John Ashley sent him by way of the Nigra had angered Bobby in a way nobody'd seen before. He said he'd be damned if some outlaw could make threat on his life and get away with it. He'd said he'd wear John Ashley's glass eye for a fob on his pocketwatch and nobody thought he was fooling.

Over the next few months John Ashley was a major topic of conversation in cafes and barbershops and fishcamps and speakeasies from Jacksonville to the Keys. Some believed he'd been shot up so bad in

the whiskey camp fight he'd bled to death out in the Devil's Garden
and his bones never would be found. Others said he was healing up
out in the Everglades and just waiting for the chance to get even with
Bob Baker for the killing of Old Joe. Others thought he'd left the state
and was smart enough to stay gone forever.

Reports of John Ashley sightings started making the rounds. Stories
of his fate. He'd been seen in a gambling joint in Jacksonville and
he'd been winning big. He'd been spotted in a fancy Atlanta nightclub,
dressed to the nines and drinking champagne from the shoe of a beautiful blonde. He'd been arrested for armed robbery in Memphis and was
in the Brushy Mountain penitentiary under a false name but nobody
was sure what it was. He'd lost both legs trying to board a freight train
out of New Orleans and was in a wheelchair and pimping for a nigger
whore in the French Quarter. He'd had his other eye cut out in a
barfight in Pascagoula and was in a home for the blind under the name
Bruno Traven. He'd been stabbed to death by a whore in Birmingham
and some said the whore was none other than Julie Morrell who Bobby
Baker had wanted to marry till John Ashley had his way with her.
There was a story he'd been beat to death by a bootlegger in the
Blue Ridge Mountains. There was another he'd been shot dead by the
Knoxville cops during a robbery and been buried nameless in a pau-
per's grave. It was all the usual kinda stories about him that get told
about most dangerous men who vanish.

And then Laura Upthegrove got out of jail and she disappeared
too. Some said she wanted to get away from a place that had so many
bad memories for her. They said she'd gone to live with kin up in
Georgia someplace. Some said she'd been too full of grief to live without him and had killed herself with poison. But them who believed
John Ashley yet lived were sure she'd gone straight to him, wherever
he was. And a lot of folk figured if that was true—if John was really
alive—then we hadn't heard the last of him, not yet. Not with his
daddy shot dead and the man responsible for it still walking the earth.

TWENTY-FIVE

February–October 1924

HE FISHED AND HUNTED AND HE TOOK HIDES OF ALL SORTS SIMPLY
to keep his hand in. He fashioned a small still to provide himself
with sipping whiskey. Laura's daddy had long ago inserted
wooden-peg footholds into a high thick-boled pine for easy climbing,
and twice a day John Ashley ascended to the top of the tree and
peered with binoculars through its branches out to the vast viridity of
the sawgrass country under the endless Everglades sky of everchanging
blues. He never saw another soul except for Henry Quickshoes, an
Indian devoted to Bill Ashley these last two years. Bill had one day
come upon him carrying his eight-year-old son along the shoulder of
the highway and he had stopped the car on seeing that the boy's foot
was wrapped in a white shirt sopped with blood. They got in the car
and as Bill sped them to the hospital in Stuart he learned that the boy
had been setting otter traps along Gomez Creek and somehow one of
them snapped shut on his foot. The man came running and pried the
trap off the boy's crushed foot but bones were jutting out top and
bottom and the wound was streaming blood. When the clerk at the
admissions desk showed reluctance at checking in an Indian who anyway didnt have the money to pay, Bill Ashley leaned across the counter
into his face and in a razorous whisper threatened to break his neck
in three places if the boy didnt get into surgery immediately. The boy's
foot was saved, though he'd walk with a limp evermore, and Bill
Ashley settled the bills with surgeon and hospital. Since then Henry

Quickshoes was ever ready to do for Bill Ashley any service he asked. He was now poling out to John Ashley's hideaway every ten days or so, bearing supplies and news from Bill.

In this way was John Ashley informed that their mother had rejoiced on learning he was alive and well. And that Laura had been convicted of illegal production and possession of distilled spirits and sentenced to 120 days in the county lockup. She was serving her time with little discomfort. Bertha visited her several times a week with rations of food, magazines, cigarettes. In a note brought by Henry Quickshoes, Bertha said that when she whispered to Laura that John was all right and would await her at the Everglades house, she had wept and laughed at the same time and given herself such a bad case of hiccups it took her the rest of the day to get rid of them.

Bill reported that Clarence Middleton and Terrianne had abandoned St. Lucie for Vero where a friend of Clarence's from Miami had started a charter boat business. Clarence had taken the name Calvin Walker and was growing a beard and working as mate on the boat.

Ben Tracey was in the Dade County Jail under the name Harry Brown serving ninety days for battery and indecent commission. "What's 'indecent commission' anyhow?" Henry Quickshoes asked John Ashley. "Bill says he dont know." John Ashley said he didnt know either but it sounded like something fun. Whatever the specific transgression was, Ben committed it with a woman on the Elser Pier dancefloor after cutting in on her partner. When the woman let a shriek in response to Ben's indecent commission, the partner came rushing to her defense and thats when Ben committed the battery.

Ray Lynn was said to be crewing on a rum schooner plying the Caribbean out of Key West.

He tried not to think about things. In the first few nights in the Everglades house he had terrible dreams. He'd several times seen his father lying in his own blood and staring up at him with a look of accusation. And he'd several times dreamt of Old Joe wandering pale and ghostly in a distant twilit mist of the Devil's Garden. His father would turn and look at him as if waiting to hear what he had to say. His neck wound ran blood. John Ashley wanted to tell him he would avenge him, that he'd even the score with Bob Baker—but each time he opened his mouth he could make no sound. And then he'd suddenly be seated at Bill's table and Bertha would be telling him yet again how much he sounded just like Bobby Baker and how she pitied Bobby's wife and how awful damn lucky John was to have somebody who loved him as much as Laura, how only a damn fool would risk losing that for some dumb-ass notion of getting even.

Then he got the still set up and working and he found that if he drank enough every night he would dream not at all—or if he did dream, he would not remember it clearly, which was just as good. And so he spent his days trapping and hunting and thinking of nothing but the beauty of the surrounding sawgrass world. At night he gave himself to drinking and dwelling on Laura and sometimes taking himself in hand in his yearning for her and then falling into a fitful sleep. One night he had a vague dream of fire and heard a woman's single scream that carried in it as much of loneliness as of terror and he started awake half-drunk with his heart lunging hard but he could recall no details of the nightmare. When he went back to sleep he began to dream of his father and so woke again and took several more deep swallows of shine and once more fell asleep and dreamt no more that night.

She was released in the early days of June. Bill and Bertha Ashley met her at the jailyard gate. They drove her to a West Palm Beach restaurant and bought her a huge steak for dinner. During the meal Bill passed her an envelope holding five thousand dollars. Bertha had brought a change of clothes for her and she went into the women's restroom and put on her overalls and laced on her boots and slipped the money into her bib pocket and buttoned the flap. Then came out and said she was ready to go.

A pair of cops had followed them in a county car and sat waiting outside. Bill wasnt surprised. "Bobby's bound to figure you'll head for Johnny if he's anywhere around," he said. "He knows damn well he aint gonna be able to follow you once you get in the Devil's Garden but he's gotta try, dont he?"

He drove her to a friend's fishcamp out on the canal road on the rim of the sawgrass country. Waiting there for her was a skiff loaded with supplies. She hugged Bill and Bertha and kissed them goodbye and then got in the skiff and started poling north along a sawgrass channel. Even if Bob Baker had assigned someone to follow her, once she got into the Loxahatchee Slough she'd be able to lose anybody on her trail. Not until two days later when she was absolutely sure she was not being followed did she turn westward, and not until a day after that did she turn again and bear for the south of Lake Okeechobee and home.

*   *   *

Henry Quickshoes had brought to him the news of her release and every day thereafter he spent most of the daylight hours in his high pine lookout. And then one cloudless midmorning of pale sunshine there she was, poling around a distant palm island. His heart jumped at the sight of her. He skimmed down the tree and raced around to the far side of the hammock to the boat landing hidden in the brush and the wide overhang of the oaks. Here in the deep shadows the grass and thorny weeds were shin-high and the air humid and the smells rank and ripe. He paced and twirled and smoked one cigarette after another and finally heard the soft plash of her pole in the water and he hid behind a thick myrtlebush. He soon heard the dugout's prow slide up onto the sloped bank and heard her feet hit the ground and heard her grunt as she pulled the boat the rest of the way up onto dry ground. The sound of her laboring breath made him hard for her.

He gingerly pushed aside the myrtle branches and saw her sling her rucksack onto her shoulder and start for the path toward the house. Then she stopped and lifted her face to the air and sniffed at it and he knew she'd smelled him or the cigarettes he'd been smoking. She was a wilderness child, no question. She smiled and eased the rucksack to the ground and looked around and then fixed on a wide-trunked oak. She went into a crouch and began to sneak up on it as quiet as a thought. John Ashley slipped out from behind the bush and moved after her in a quick silent scuttle. She darted up to the oak and looked behind it and her face fell to see he was not there—and then she let a shriek as he grabbed her from behind and they tumbled and rolled in the grass and thorny weeds, both of them laughing now and hugging each other tightly and kissing and kissing, faces, necks, eyes, mouths. Then their clothes lofted in every direction and caught on bushes and tree limbs and her shirt sailed beyond the bank and into the water. They coupled as if they would break each other's bones, bucking and tossing and howling until they came—and then kept right on at it and he lapped at her breasts and she clasped him tight with her legs and they rolled over and now she was on top and gripping his shoulders and they humped hard and fast and cried out and came again and she flexed into a single quivering muscle in her orgasm, her sex locked tight around him, and she stayed that way for a long moment and then let a deep sigh and relaxed and folded down beside him and he rolled with her to keep from slipping out. They lay gasping and looking at each other and he grinned at the small gold quarter-moon in one of her eyes. "Hey, girl," he said, "how you keepin?" And kissed her golden eye and then the other. Then her mouth. Her breasts. Her belly.

And then he was at her vulva and she arched herself against his tongue and made sweet moan.

After a time they gathered up their clothes and her rucksack and they saw and felt now the scratches they'd gotten in the thorny grass and they joked about looking like they'd been in a catfight. Up in the house they applied moonshine to the cuts on their elbows and knees and legs and she giggled when she saw that he had a scratch on his pecker and he made fun of the cuts on her ass and they ministered to them with the moonshine and then kissed each other's wounds to make them all better.

Some time later they lay in bed and smoked cigarettes under the open window with no light but that of the pale moon upon their nakedness. He'd told her all that he'd been thinking. That there wasnt any need to go after Bobby Baker. That revenge was a silly notion anymore. Maybe if Bobby's daddy was still alive he could even things up by killing him, but George Baker was long dead. Besides, he'd killed Fred Baker who was Bobby's best kin, so that made it all even, didnt it? In a way?

He told her what Bertha had said about him and Bobby Baker seeming alike and how much that chafed him. He wasnt *nothing* like that son of a bitch. She'd made sense about some other things, though, Berty had. She could be pretty smart. She was damn sure right about him being awful lucky to be loved like he was.

He asked if he was making any sense. Did she think he was right?

She held his face between her hands and kissed him deeply. Yes, she told him, he was making all the sense in the world.

"Well all right then, it's all settled," he said, grinning big and slapping her hip. "Galveston, here we come."

He sat up and lit another cigarette and cleared his throat and said, "Listen honeybunch, there's just one thing. I dont know what you'll think of this, but hear me out, okay? I been thinking that, well, Loretta May, you know, she aint got nobody. Now, you know she loves you to death, you know that, and it's always seemed to me you care a whole lot for her too, and so I was thinking, well, why dont we just take her with—"

Laura howled and buried her face in his lap. He sat stunned, so suddenly had she burst into tears and so wrenching were her sobs.

And then he knew. And said, "Damn."

She tried to talk but could not, she was crying so hard. He stroked her hair and made soothing sounds and let her cry it out. And he thought of the bobbed blonde hair and the skin that always smelled of peaches and the sightless eyes that could see so much.

"I thought you knew," she said in choking sobs. "I thought you just . . . you didnt want to say nothin because . . . because it's just so terrible and sad."

She'd been in jail a month when she heard about it. Miss Lillian's maid Wisteria had come to visit her several times by then to give her messages from Loretta May in a blushing whisper through the bars. "Loretta had her say just the boldest things to me. They'd make me blush too and me and Wisteria would both of us bust out laughin and the matron would look over at us like we'd lost out minds," Laura said. She heard about the fire from the matron the morning after it happened and only then did she realize the bells that had awakened her with their wild clanging the night before were of fire engines going to Miss Lillian's. But it wasnt till the tearful Wisteria came to see her later that morning that she found out about Loretta May. "I'd cussed them bells up and down for wakin me up," Laura said. She sobbed into her hands and he stroked her shoulder. "I was cussin them damn fire bells . . . and all the while poor Loretta was . . . oh *God*, Johnny!"

The place was so old, the wood so dry, it had burned down in less than twenty minutes. Everybody got out but one. According to Wisteria, the man who'd been with Loretta May in her room told the firemen the whole thing started when Miss Loretta's one-eyed cat sprang up on the bedside table and knocked over the oil lamp. He said the fire just jumped up the wall. Said it shot across the floor like some circus trick. He said he'd had to run through fire to get out the door.

"He ran out of there in his underpants—just run out and left her there in her darkness and all that fire," Laura said. Her voice was different now. Hard. "If God gave me just one wish, Johnny, just one, I'd ask Him to please let me find that man."

She looked at him and saw his face streaked with tears. She sat up and held him to her.

"The firemen thought everybody'd got out. Wisteria was right there and she said the girls was all screaming when they come running out the house and they all stood out in the street and watched the fire. Wisteria said didnt none of them hear nobody screamin inside and so they thought everybody was out. She went all through the crowd lookin for Loretta May but couldnt find her and then Miss Lillian come up to her and asked where's Loretta May and thats when they both realized she must still been inside and they screamed to the firemen to do something but it was way too late. They couldnt nobody get near the house by then the fire was so bad. She said that ole place burnt up like it was made of newspaper. But she said she never did hear her scream, Johnny, she *swears* she didnt. And if Loretta didnt scream she musta been unconscious, aint that right? And if she was unconscious she wouldnt of felt nothin, would she?"

John Ashley shook his head.

They sat silent for a long minute.

"She sure did love us, didnt she, Johnny?"

He nodded and dug at his eyes with the heels of his hands.

"Oh God *damn* it, Johnny!" She wailed into her hands.

They held each other close all through the night and wept together for her whom they both loved, she who had loved them both. They whispered of her and after a time could not help but smile at some of their shared memories. And after a while longer they were chuckling at recollections of the wonderful times they'd all three had together. And in the red light of the rising sun they made love once again and kissed each other goodbye for their lost Loretta May.

They poled up the sawgrass channels and adjoining creeks to Lake Okeechobee and then up along its coast to Pahokee and were met there by Henry Quickshoes. He drove them over the rugged backroads all the way up to Fort Pierce. John had wanted to see his mother one more time but the house where she was staying in West Palm Beach was still too closely watched by Bob Baker's men. She sent word through Bill for him not to try to see her, to just get clear of the region and be safe. Bill had arranged for a new Model T to be waiting for them at a filling station owned by a family friend. They thanked Billy Quickshoes and said so long and then drove up to Vero to visit with Clarence Middleton and Terrianne at their rented cottage overlooking the Indian River Lagoon.

Clarence was overjoyed to see them but Terrianne was terse and little more than polite. She was lean and honeyhaired and had pouty lips and quick dark eyes and she had always thought Clarence's troubles with the law would be over if only he would break away from the Ashley bunch—though she'd never said so to anyone but Clarence and said so only once. It was the only time he'd ever been openly angry with her. Her argument that they would be so much safer and in better position to start a family had carried little weight against his loyalty to the Ashleys, and she'd not mentioned the matter again. When they first heard the news of the Crossbones camp raid, both Joe and John Ashley were supposed to have been killed, and Clarence went into a deep gloom. She tried to comfort him—but in truth she'd felt that they were at last free from the dangers attached to that criminal bunch. Then Bill Ashley sent word that John was alive and safely hidout in the Devil's Garden and Clarence showed his first smile in nearly two weeks and Terrianne cursed under her breath. Now here John Ashley was, right in her house, laughing and carrying on as though he had not a care in the world—and every cop in South Florida ready to shoot him dead and anybody they found with him.

They had a fish-fry that evening and were joined by Clarence's charter boat friend Wayne Lillis and his wife Marie. Near midnight they were all a little drunk and Terrianne grew more sullen and Clarence upbraided her for it and she stalked away into the house. Clarence said for them to ignore her, she'd been out of sorts lately. But he seemed distracted and Wayne and Marie took their leave shortly after.

John and Laura had a nightcap with Clarence and told him he and Terrianne were always welcome to come visit or even to live with them after they got settled in Texas. Clarence said he couldnt speak for Terrianne but he just might take them up on the offer. Then again he might see about going to work for his brother Jack in Jacksonville Beach. John and Laura looked at each other. Neither had known Clarence had a brother.

"Jack's never much cared for me livin on the wrong side of the law," Clarence said. He'd recently trimmed his beard to a close goatee and was now in the habit of stroking it when he mulled. "Owns a damn nightclub but he aint crooked, if you can believe that. He's long been after me to quit the criminal life and go to work with him. I got so tired of hearin it I pretty much kept my distance from him these last few years. Now I just dont know. He's all the kin I got. Maybe I'll go see him."

Laura put an arm around his shoulder and kissed his cheek and said not to be too hard on Terrianne. "Dont matter what she thinks of me and Johnny," she said. "Whatever you do decide to do, I think you'd be wise to take her with you." She hugged him tight and then he showed her and John to the spare room where a bed had been made up.

When the sun broke over the mangroves across the narrows in the morning they were already on their way to Jacksonville.

Daisy and her husband Butch were doing well—he had been a foreman at the shipyard for nearly three years now—and John's nephew Jeb was grown to a husky nine-year-old who loved to fish and to shoot his daddy's shotgun. There had been two new additions to the family since John's last visit—four-year-old redhaired Janie, pretty and shy, and two-year-old Eddie Frank, who loved to gnaw things with his new teeth. They barbecued ribs on the backyard pit that evening under a blazing bone-white moon and drank beer and later on danced to the radio in the living room.

Daisy was glad to hear they were leaving South Florida for good, although she wished they would settle in Jacksonville rather than move all the way out to Texas. "I dont like to say I tole you so, Johnny, but way back when you were last here I tole you there wouldnt be nothin but trouble if you went back to Twin Oaks. Last time it was three others with you and now all of em dead. My heart just broke when I heard about Frank and Eddie three years ago and I dont know if it was an accident like they say or not but I still cry most ever time I think about them. But I aint grieved about Daddy for a minute and I never will. The only thing I'm sorry about him dead is Momma— though why she ever loved that son of a bitch is a mystery I will never understand." She and Old Joe had never made their peace. Ma Ashley had told her that Joe always regretted not being able to see young Jeb, but her mother could not deny that he'd had no interest whatever in the next two of his grandchildren by her.

Butch asked what John intended to do for a living in Texas and John said he didnt know yet but he was thinking of going into some kind of business for himself. Maybe a gun shop or a fishcamp. He didnt see the look Daisy gave him, as though she thought he had to be joking. She then turned to Laura who just smiled slightly and shrugged.

They all went to the beach next day and got sunburned and half-drunk on beer. The following night they went to a moviehouse in town and laughed all through a swell Chaplain double-feature and when they came out of the theater they all tried to outdo each other at walking like the Little Tramp and they agreed that Laura could do it the best. The next day Daisy left the kids in a neighbor's care and the four of them went canoeing on the St. Johns. Butch took his throw net and they caught a mess of mullet and filleted them and baked them in palm fronds in a firepit in the sand. Afterward while Daisy and Butch napped John and Laura went into the pines and found a soft bed of needles and there made love with hordes of dragonflies bobbing in the still air.

The next morning they said goodbye. John shook young Jeb's hand as manfully as he did Butch's and he picked Janie up and swung her around and Laura cuddled Eddie Frank one more time and there were hugs and kisses all around. Butch reminded John that he and Laura and any of their friends always had a place to stay when they needed it, and John thanked him but said he didnt think he'd be back this way again. Then they got into the Model T and set off for Pensacola.

They took their time about getting there and after their arrival they passed a few days playing in the gentle Gulf waves on beaches with sand as fine and white as talcum powder. They sold the car and bought passage to New Orleans and there they stayed a week. They every night dined on Cajun or Creole cooking and they walked all about the exotic French Quarter and drank pitchers of beer as they tapped their feet to the music of Dixieland bands. They rode a sidewheeler up the Mississippi to Baton Rouge and back. Just before they departed New Orleans John sent a telegram to Aunt July notifying her of their arrival date.

Their ship docked in Galveston on a sweltering late afternoon of heavy humidity. Hanford Mobley was there to greet them. He looked fit and was sportily dressed in blue-striped seersucker and a white boater with a black band. When he grinned he showed a new gold canine. He was accompanied by a pretty and sweet-natured brunette named Ella whom he introduced as his fiancée. John whooped his congratulations and hugged Ella tight and patted her behind and kissed her on the forehead, then grabbed Hanford in a bear hug and swung him around. Debarking passengers passing by smiled at the happy sight of them. Hanford kissed Laura's hand in greeting and she blushed and said, "Declare, *somebody's* sure picked up some fancy manners in Texas." The girl Ella smiled and took Hanford's arm and he beamed upon her. They all got into a cab and repaired to Aunt July's.

On the way there Hanford Mobley asked about the police raid on the Crossbones camp. John Ashley said they could talk about it another time but assured Hanford that his parents were well and living comfortably in a new cottage Bill Ashley had bought for them just down the road from his own house in Salerno. As the cab turned onto Aunt July's street John Ashley asked Hanford what happened with Roy Matthews. Hanford smiled and said, "Roy who?" and laughed and said no more.

They had not seen each other in ten years, John Ashley and his aunt. She'd gone to corpulence but seemed at ease with her fleshiness and less given to general fret. She was thrilled to see him and remarked that he was even handsomer then he'd been a decade ago. When he introduced Laura, Aunt July said, "So *this* is the girl who won the heart that couldnt be won," and hugged her to her copious bosom. She could not stop smiling at John Ashley and made him sit beside her on the parlor sofa so she could pet him as they talked. Laura took immediate liking to her as she had to Ella, and the three women were as easy with each other as longtime friends.

When Aunt July questioned him about her brother's death John Ashley recounted how Old Joe had been killed. Aunt July began to cry and Laura hastened to her side and put her arm around her and told of the dignified funeral Ma and Bill Ashley had arranged for him. "They told me there was just a whole *hill* of pretty flowers on his grave," Laura said. Aunt July apologized for her tears, saying she had sworn she would not cry about it anymore, not in front of them, and now she meant it, by God. She dried her eyes with a lace hanky and called for one of the maids to turn on the radio to a music program.

That evening the five of them went to supper at a bayside restaurant and caught each other up on things still further. Aunt July said that none of the girls who'd worked in the house at the time John had lived there were with her any longer—a revelation prompting Laura to give John Ashley a smiling sidelong look. Some of the girls had married, some had gone to bigger towns in chase of bigger money. Some had gotten mixed up with criminals and were likely now in jail. Some had simply disappeared and none knew whereto or why. Roan-haired Sally who'd been one of John's favorites had developed a cancer in her breast and died within six months of its discovery.

"Nineteen years old," Aunt July said sadly. "So many old people doing nothing but meanness in the world and such a sweet pretty thing has to die so young. If there's a God in heaven He sure aint much of a one for fairness."

John Ashley said he was surprised to hear such a commonplace sentiment from someone so experienced with the world as his aunt. "Well," she said, "I expect it's exactly because of people's experience with the world that such notions get to be so common."

Cindy Jean, whose sweetness on the eve of his departure from Galveston John Ashley well recalled, had married a wildcatter and gone with him to Texas where he struck oil six months later. "She wrote me a letter," Aunt July said. "She said, 'Maylon struck oil so I guess I for damn sure struck gold.'" She laughed along with the others and said, "I just love a story about hard work paying off, dont you all?"

They all laughed too at Hanford's account of wanting to be the man of the house just as his Uncle John had been when he'd lived in

Galveston. On his arrival at Aunt July's Hanford had followed John Ashley's example and challenged the resident houseman to a fistfight for rights to the job. But Hanford lacked both the size and the fistic talent of his uncle, and the houseman, a big quick man named Mack, had in short order beaten him insensible. Hanford claimed to hold no hard feelings. In truth Mack was a pleasant man who was always ready with a joke and the two had become friends. Hanford had since been earning his keep as Aunt July's general handyman, tending to small repairs around the house and keeping up the yard and garden. This position did not, however, carry the houseman's perquisites, and whatever pleasures Hanford desired from the girls in residence he'd been required to pay for like everybody but Mack, albeit he got a discount price of a dollar and a half.

Ella had been the only one not to charge him. "I cant even say what, but it's *something* about this boy," she said. He sat next to her and she patted his arm. She said she had fallen in love with him the minute they met but it had taken him a while longer to reciprocate. "I guess because of havin so many pretty girls under the same roof," she said. "I guess being a man he had to try everything in the candy store before he could settle for just one kinda treat." Aunt July and Laura smiled knowingly at John Ashley but he affected to be engrossed in the condition of his fingernails. Once Hanford realized the prize he had in Ella they started spending most of their free time together, going to the beach and sailing on Hanford's dinghy and watching movies in the coolness of the local moviehouse. Three months later he proposed marriage on the condition that she give up the whoring life and she said it was the easiest deal she ever made. They'd since been living together in the small gardner's cottage behind the main house. They planned to wed on Thanksgiving Day.

Laura said that was just the sweetest story. She shook a finger at Hanford Mobley across the table and said, "You best treat her right, you hear?" Hanford grinned and said, "Yes, mam, I aim to."

Aunt July asked about John's plans and he told of his intention to go into business though he hadnt yet decided what sort. If he caught any of the looks of doubt that exchanged around the table he did not give sign of it. Aunt July then expounded on her growing boredom with the whoring business and recited a litany of complaints—the greedy policemen, the extortionist politicians, the ever-higher taxes, and the ever-lower quality of whores come looking for a house to work. "Present company excepted," she said to Ella, who smiled and blushed and said, "Oh, I know."

They stayed at Aunt July's for more than a week before they found a rental house they liked just a block from the beach. She had insisted they should save their money and continue living under her roof, but they as vigorously insisted they would not impose upon her hospitality any more than they already had. They signed a lease on the house, paid the first month's rent and moved in.

Nearly every morning they packed a picnic basket and went to the beach to swim in the Gulf, nap on the sand under an umbrella, fish for snapper from the jetties. The rainy season was on them and every afternoon raised huge indigo thunderheads off the Gulf that blackened the entire sky and then the storm came crashing down. They'd sit on their little porch with cold beer in hand and watched the play of pale lightning over the sea while thunder crackled and rain hammered the roof and poured off the gutters and the wind blew cool and fresh. Sometimes they'd lie in bed under a partly open window and let the rain spatter them as they made love.

Bertha sent letters with news. Ma Ashley and the girls had recently moved into the new house she had contracted to have built at Twin Oaks. It was a little smaller than the old house but spacious enough for the three of them. It had a little sidehouse for guests and Clarence Middleton was now living there. Terrianne had left him, just up and run off—some said to Miami, but no telling if that was true. If Clarence knew where she'd gone he wasnt saying. He'd gone to see Ma Ashley and asked if he could pitch a tent at Twin Oaks till he decided what to do. She said she'd be proud to have him there but she insisted he make himself at home in the sidehouse.

A good bit of the news in the paper lately, Bertha informed them, was about Bobby Baker. He'd finally called off the search for Johnny and publicly proclaimed that John Ashley was either dead in the Everglades or run off to somewhere else for good. He'd also announced he was running for reelection. The newspapers were backing him all the way and praising him as the lawman who busted up the Ashley Gang. They were calling him the best sheriff in South Florida, maybe the best in the state. For the first time in ages he was showing his family in public. At recent official ceremonies his wife had been at his side, and every Saturday afternoon he was spotted with her and his daughters at some restaurant or moviehouse somewhere in the county. "The man seems pretty well satisfied with himself," Bertha wrote.

They took long walks around town and admired the ornate architecture. He took her to the theater to see her first play ever and she was enrapt and insisted they thereafter go at least twice a week and they did. On Sunday afternoons they went to a park frequented chiefly by Germans and from a vendor they bought grilled sausages on bread with mustard and ate them while they listened to the polka bands. Galveston had changed but little in the ten years John Ashley had been gone. The main difference was in the greater volume of auto traffic. Cars were now everywhere. Laura noted that the weather was much like back home but she admitted she sometimes missed having the wildness of the Everglades hard by. "Back home you could always run into the Glades if there was need to get hid," she said. On a little island like this there was nowhere to hide. John laughed at her comparison and said she had a naturalborn criminal mind. She punched his arm and said she certainly was not a naturalborn criminal, she'd had to learn every bit about being an outlaw from him.

For all their larking and carefree living, she sensed that he was restless. Not that he didnt laugh or smile very often, because he did. Not that he lacked his usual robust appetite, because he didnt. Not that his enthusiasm for lovemaking had fallen off, because it certainly had not. But more and more often now—sometimes for long minutes at a time, while they were having supper, while they were waiting for the curtain to rise at the theater, while they were lying in bed and smoking after making love—his gaze would turn inward and fix on some private vision that gave him no rest. And each time he returned from that far place in his mind his eyes would be quick and uneasy, his movements nervous. She somehow knew it was Bob Baker on his mind, but sensed also that he could not explain these thoughts to her. She suspected he could not explain them very well even to himself. She wanted to say to him that he could tell her anything, that maybe she would understand and maybe she wouldnt but she would by God *try*. She wanted to tell him she was *there*. But she knew he already knew that.

They'd been in Galveston about two months when he started having nightmares so bad he'd suddenly shout in his sleep and bolt upright and she'd wake to find him sitting wide-eyed and dripping sweat and gasping as though he'd been running far and hard. She'd hold him close and croon soothingly and tell him it was all right, it was just a bad dream and his quivering would slowly subside and his breathing ease to normal. The first few times it happened she asked what he'd dreamt but he'd only mumbled that he wasnt sure, he couldnt remember. At first the nightmares came but once or twice a week but in another month they were a nightly visitation. One late-summer night she heard him cry out the name of Bobby Baker just before he came awake. When she told him what she'd heard he sighed and held her close and told of his father coming to him every night now for months, half-rotted and dirt-smeared as though he'd dug out from the grave, his voice a horrible rasp for the black bullet hole in his neck and asking why he hadnt settled things, asking how he could live with himself while Bobby Baker yet breathed and walked on the earth and bragged of how he'd killed Joe Ashley and set John Ashley running like a kicked dog.

She stroked his head and kissed him and whispered fiercely that he was just feeling guilty for something that wasnt his fault, that they were free now of all that meanness back there, that they didnt have to do anything anymore except live their life. But her heart was careering as she spoke because she could sense that he'd already made up his mind what to do.

A week later she woke in the middle of the night to find him gone. Her breath seized in her throat. She ran out wearing but a shirt and saw only the empty street. She hurried for the beach lit pale under the bright half-moon, toward the dark sea spangled silver, and there she found him, sitting in the sand and staring at the Gulf. She wanted to slap him for scaring her so, but could only hug him tight and cry and ask why he couldnt let the damn thing go, why couldnt he.

"If I knew that," he said, "I'd know everything."

Back at the house they had a terrible row about his refusal to let her accompany him. "I wont be gone but long enough to settle things and I'll be right back," he told her. "If I have to run for it I'll be able to move faster if you aint with me. Now thats the end of it, girl."

"It aint the end of a damn thing! I can move fast as you, fast as anybody."

"Hannie and Clarence is all the help I need for this. Probly get Ray Lynn on it if I can find him, and maybe even Ben Tracey if he aint in jail. They'd be good backup, but I can do it with just Hannie if I have to."

"I can shoot better than them and almost good as you! It's not a thing any them can do I cant and you *know* it!" She was almost in tears and hated herself for it.

John Ashley looked at her a long moment and then grinned and said, "Can you piss out a window in the rain without getting your ass wet?"

She gaped at him. *"What?* Oh, God *damn* you!" She flew at him with fists swinging and he fended her wild flailings until she tired and fell weeping into his arms. And then they were both laughing and by and by were naked and in bed and she had the hiccups and they laughed about that even as they undulated in each other's embrace.

When Hanford Mobley answered his knock on the cottage door the next day, John Ashley said, "It's somethin I didnt take care of in Florida that I shoulda. I might could use a hand."

Hanford Mobley grinned and said, "Well hell, uncle, I just been waitin for the word."

Three days later they stood on a steamer deck in a gray morning of October chill, both of them armed with a pair of army .45's in holsters under each arm, and waved to Laura and Ella standing on the deck and looking like bereaved women beyond their years.

TWENTY-SIX

October 1924

THEY DISEMBARKED IN KEY WEST AND MADE INQUIRIES AND found Ray Lynn in a place on Duval Street that called itself Kate's Cafe but otherwise didnt even try to disguise its true function as barroom. In this free-spirited town of piratical heritage Prohibition seemed but vague rumor. Booze was sold and consumed openly and even the cops now and then stopped in for a short one.

"Well I'll be a sad son of a bitch," Ray Lynn said on spying John Ashley come through the door. They pounded each other on the shoulders and neither one could stop grinning. "Man, I thought you were dead!" Ray Lynn said.

"If I was, I'd still look a sight better than you," John Ashley said. Ray Lynn's eyes were ringed with purple bruises and one ear was swollen and discolored and he bore a large scab on his chin.

"Hell, you oughta see the other guy," he said. "Big old honker was in the lockup with me last week. Said he'd have my supper rations or know the reason why."

John introduced Ray and Hanford and the three of them took a jug to a back table to talk. Ray Lynn said he had been working on a rum schooner named *The Pearl* until two weeks ago when he drew ten days in the Key West jail for beating up a navy sailor for some reason he couldnt afterward recall. *The Pearl* had sailed without him and eight days later was sunk by a Coast Guard gunboat two miles off the Dry Tortugas and all hands lost. "I tell you, boys," he said with a wild grin, "it aint nothin in the world worth more than good luck."

"Could be you're luck's still runnin good," John Ashley said. He told him in low voice that he was going to kill Bob Baker and he wanted some backup in case there was need of it. If Ray threw in he could forget about turning over the money from the moonshine sale to the Indians.

Ray Lynn smiled sadly and said, "Truth to tell, that money was the first thing come to my mind when I seen you at the door. I didn't reckon you'd let me ride on it. Ben spent some of it too, you know."

John Ashley said he intended to discuss the matter with Ben. He said if Ray wanted to come to Galveston and be business partners with him and Laura after the job here was done, he was welcome.

Ray Lynn said it was the best offer he'd had in a good while. He'd never been to Texas but at least they didnt have any warrants on him there. He was in.

John inquired after Ben Tracey and Lynn said he was but a month out of the Dade County Jail and tending bar in the backroom speak of the Blue Heaven Dance Club in the old Hardieville section of Miami. "I saw him up there a coupla days before I come back here and got that ten-day jolt," Ray Lynn said. "I offered to get him a spot on *The Pearl* but he'd just met a Cuban gal was workin at the Blue Heaven and he wanted to stick around and see could he get anywhere with her. She espicks like thees, but he dont care—he says he likes her accent. She warned him she's got a big ole jealous boyfriend works a dredge out in the Glades and comes to see her once a week, but you know Ben. He takes a shine to a gal he loses every bit of what little common sense he got. But you see what I mean about luck? If he'd taken me up on the *Pearl* job he'd been on her when she went down last week."

The next day dawned hot and muggy and the three of them took the train on Flager's overseas railroad to Miami. They marveled at the feeling of flying over the water. Nothing to see on either side of the coach but sparkling green sea under an infinite blue sky bright with sunlight. The air rushing through the windows smelled of salt and seaweed. Great squalling flocks of gulls fed on baitfish running in the shallows. A flock of pelicans in low V formation glided over the water with hardly a wingbeat. Billowing cumulus clouds shone white in the distance and a speck of a ship rode the horizon under a thin black plume of smoke.

By the time the track made the mainland just north of Key Largo the wind had roused and was swaying the trees. The clouds had gone dark and swelled to thunderheads and swiftly closed landward and now rain came sweeping over them in great blown sheets and clattered against the coach windows like flung gravel. It fell for ten minutes and then abruptly abated to a sprinkle.

From the depot they took a taxi through congested streets and a continuing gray drizzle to the Ford dealership and there had a long wait before anyone could attend them. The receptionist smiled wearily and told them they were in luck—a new shipment of autos had just that morning arrived by flatcar from Detroit. The Boom was bringing in so much business they could hardly keep up.

It was that way all over town. Miami had seen booms before but nothing like this. Half the men in town dealt in real estate. They wore white boaters and seersucker suits, rolled toothpicks in their mouths and extolled the wonders of South Florida like evangelists describing Eden. South Florida real estate was being hawked in newspapers and magazines all over the country and every day's mail brought fresh money from people avid to buy their portion of earthly paradise. The sharpies were pulling in profits like croupiers. Contract binders on property lots changed hands a dozen times a month and each time sold at higher price. Once again they were selling swampwater lots to the fools—and every wised-up sap was a newborn con foisting his folly onto the next sucker in line. The town abounded with hustlers of every stripe. The streets were an incessant cacaphony of klaxons and traffic-cop whistles and corner newshawks. Cargo ships crammed the bay. A skyscraper courthouse was going up next to the Florida East Coast depot where hundreds of newcomers stepped down daily. The population had tripled in the last five years and stood close to 100,000. The city was a clamor of construction projects. The air smelled of dredged muck and limerock dust and ready money.

"I'll tell you what," Hanford Mobley said, staring out the dealership window at the heavy traffic on the rain-sheened streets. "I bet they's deals being made in this damn town like you wouldnt believe."

John Ashley nodded and said, "Likely so—just like always."

A harried salesman finally took them in their turn and twenty minutes later they drove away in a new sedan.

They bought two pump-action shotguns at a gun store and then went to a Miami Avenue jewelry store they'd heard about in Key West. John Ashley told the manager they'd been sent by General Lee and the man smiled at the code phrase and led them into a backroom. A few minutes later they emerged and Ray Lynn now had a .45 automatic under his shirt and John Ashley carried under his arm a paper package containing a brand new Browning Automatic Rifle and three full magazines.

They drove over to the Blue Heaven Dance Club. It was late afternoon and the place had just opened its doors for the evening and the parking lot held but three cars. The sun had come out again but was down almost to the trees. The long low clouds in the west looked on fire at their core. Roosting birds clamored in the high branches. The ground yet steamed from the rain. They entered the coolness of a large dim room about half of which was given over to a polished dance floor fronted by a bandstand. Tables with white cloths and already set for dinner were arrayed along the walls. They were approached by a man in a tuxedo who introduced himself as the manager and asked if they wanted a table. John Ashley said he wanted to see Ben Tracey.

In that moment—as if the action had been cued by mention of Ben's name—the door at the rear of the room banged open and Ben Tracey came backpedaling through it and ran into a table and upset it with a crash of dishware and fell hard on his ass and slid on the slick floor. His mouth was bloody. A huge man in overalls and a sleeveless shirt came stalking through the door after him and a young woman right behind him and yelling in Spanish. As Tracey scrabbled to his feet the man grabbed him by the collar with one big fist and drove the other hard into his stomach and the breath blew out of Tracey and he sagged in the man's grip. The woman jumped on the big man's back and clawed his face and the man cursed and bucked her off onto the floor. He still held Ben Tracey breathless in his grasp as he wiped at his scratched face and the woman scrambled to her feet and came at him once more. He hooked her in the jaw and sent her tumbling unconscious on the floor, her skirt riding up high and exposing much of her fetching legs.

Hanford Mobley laughed and cried out, *"Whoooo!"*

John Ashley pressed the muzzle of his pistol to the back of the big man's head and cocked the piece and said, "That'll do, bubba."

The big man went still and let Ben Tracey fall. Tracey braced himself on all fours and vomited loudly. The man in the tuxedo muttered, "Oh, for pity's sake." Ray Lynn went to Ben and helped him to his feet and led him away toward the front door. Ben was still struggling for breath.

The big man slowly turned and John Ashley had to look up to meet his eyes. "You best get that thing out my face before I make you eat it," the big man said.

John Ashley brought his knee up hard into the man's balls and the man grunted and lunged forward at the waist with his eyes wide and John Ashley held his thumb tight over the hammer and hit the man across the nose with the pistol barrel. The man's legs gave way and he dropped to his knees with a great moan and both hands clapped to his nose and blood running through his fingers. John Ashley kicked him in the chest and he fell over on his side and curled up protectively, still clutching his face.

Hanford Mobley went to the woman and knelt beside her and checked her pulse at her neck. He looked at John Ashley and said, "She's all right." He looked on her legs for a moment and then lifted the hem of her skirt to peek at her white panties and the little black hairs curling out from the underwear's edges at her pubic mound. He looked up at John Ashley and grinned.

"Oh man—you're bad as that damn Tracey," John Ashley said. "Let's go." He turned and headed for the door.

Hanford Mobley hastened outside after him and got behind the wheel of the car and John cranked up the motor. In the backseat Ray Lynn said to Ben Tracey, "Didnt I *tell* you not to fuck around with a woman with a dredge operator for a boyfriend? Didnt I? She's a looker, I'll admit it—but those fucken dredgers are some mean-ass mothersons."

Ben Tracey wiped with his shirttail at the vomit and blood on his mouth. "That wasnt him," he said. Hanford wheeled the Ford out of the lot and headed for the boulevard.

"That wasnt the dredger fella the gal warned you about?" Ray Lynn said.

"Nuh-uh," Ben said. "He's with a crew over to Fort Myers right now and wont be back for a coupla weeks yet." He nodded at John Ashley and said, "Good seein you, Johnny," then gestured at Hanford Mobley and said, "Who's the youngster?"

"My nephew Hannie," John Ashley said. "So who the hell was *that* peckerwood thumpin on you?"

Ben Tracey shrugged. "Big honker come tearing in through the kitchen door just as I had her up against the bar and was kissing on her and copping me some tit. Hollerin he was gonna break my neck for snakin his girl. You know what? I believe the bitch got her a few more boyfriends than she let on."

John Ashley laughed. "You think so, hey? You really dont know who the fella was?"

"Beats the shit out of me," Ben Tracey said.

"He damn near did," Ray Lynn said, "if that gal you called a bitch hadnt lent you a hand. Her and Johnny here."

Ben Tracey laughed along with them.

The deskman of the McAllister Hotel told them he was sorry but the hotel was completely booked. John Ashley slid a fifty-dollar bill across the counter and asked him to check his book again and the clerk found that, oh yes, there *were* two rooms available after all. They checked in and got cleaned up and then went downstairs and treated themselves to a steak dinner in the hotel restaurant. John Ashley said the town wasnt as much fun anymore. "It's bigger and faster and louder," he said, "but just *look* at em." He swept his fork through the air in a gesture that took in the crowded restaurant and the thronged sidewalk just beyond the large plate glass windows. "They strainin so hard to have a good time they aint havin no fun at all, you can see it in their face."

They repaired to the Elser Pier dancehall but it now had a bouncer at the door and he recognized Ben Tracey for trouble he'd caused in the past and would not permit him to enter. Hard words ensued but Ray Lynn pulled Ben away before a fight broke out. "Who's that son of a bitch think he's callin a troublemaker?" Ben said. They went out to the sidewalk and stood there smoking cigarettes and Ray Lynn suggested they go to Old Hardieville and get laid. Ben seconded the idea. Hanford looked at John and shrugged and said, "Why the hell not? I'm engaged but I ain't gelded."

So they went to The Palmetto House Inn, and even though the others made fun of him and said Laura had him damn well pussy-whipped, John Ashley just grinned and remained in the parlor to smoke and talk with some of the girls while his friends had their lark upstairs.

Quite early the next morning they drove north out of town on the Dixie Highway. They pulled in at a Fort Lauderdale roadhouse for a breakfast of eggs and pork chops and grits. Their plan thus far was vague. They would first of all have to find out when Bob Baker would be home. That much John Ashley had decided: he would kill him at home and then burn down his house as Bobby had burned his. He had not dreamt again of his daddy since deciding on his course of action.

Late in the forenoon they came to West Palm Beach and all pulled their hats low and tried to keep their faces averted from the street and any who might recognize them. John Ashley pointed down a dirt road

branching off the highway into a woodland and said, "That's the way
to Bobby's house. Bout five miles yonderway."

Hanford Mobley slowed the car. "You wanna go on over there
and see if he's home? He might be sitting in his easy chair this minute
and reading the newspaper and smokin his pipe and feelin on top of
the damn world. We can hide the car in the trees a ways from the
house and sneak up on him. If he's there you can settle the thing right
goddamn now."

John Ashley hesitated. Then said: "No. If he aint there his wife'll
tell him about the strange car that come up to the house today. I dont
want him on his guard. Besides, when I do him we're gonna have to
haul ass. Best we go see Ma and the girls now, while everything's nice
and quiet. We'll see does Clarence want in on it and we'll plan the
thing out and see about when Bobby's gonna be home."

"What if he's home tonight?" Hanford said.

"Then tonight's it," John Ashley said.

Hanford Mobley thumped his fist on the steering wheel and
grinned.

So they drove on. And five miles away Bob Baker—who'd been
up late the night before investigating an abandoned rum truck his deputies had discovered by the side of the highway with half its load missing
and blood on the cab seat—napped soundly in his front porch hammock and without dreams and with no firearm to hand while his wife
and daughters tended the flower garden in the backyard.

Ma Ashley had rarely been demonstrative in her affections but she
wept happily to see her son John whom she thought she might never
behold again and she hugged him hard to her breast. His sisters held
to him one on either arm and petted him and laughed delightedly at
every wisecrack he made. Clarence Middleton came up and clapped
him on the shoulder and said, "I guess I know why you come back."

Ma and the girls got busy preparing dinner while the men sat out
on the little front porch and formed a plan. They had earlier stopped
at a filling station near the Olympia depot and John Ashley used the
telephone there to call the sheriff's office in Stuart and ask for deputy
Abner Franks, long a friend and a valued informant to the family. He
told Abner what he wanted to know and Abner said to call back in
twenty minutes. They bought bottles of beer from the filling station's
backroom and sipped them slowly and remarked on the prettiness of
the day. When John Ashley called Abner again the deputy was craftily
circumspect in his end of the conversation, surrounded as he was by

other cops in the office, but in his careful way he was able to tell John Ashley that, yes, it seemed the sheriff would be at home this evening and, no, there was no likelihood that any other policemen would be there. John thanked him for the information and told him to forget this conversation had taken place. Abner Franks said, "What conversation?" and rang off.

Now John Ashley told Clarence Middleton what he had in mind and Clarence said he was in. "Your daddy was never nothin but good to me and I'll be proud to help you see that Baker sumbitch dead for killin him. Truth to tell, Johnny, I was sore disappointed the last time I saw you and you were off to Texas without settlin accounts with that damn sheriff."

"I was sore disappointed too, Clarence," John Ashley said. "I just didnt know it yet."

But Clarence declined John's invitation to go back to Texas with him. He'd recently spoken to his brother Jack by telephone, their first exchange in years, and Jack's offer of a partnership in the nightclub still held if Clarence gave up his life of crime. "I believe I'll take him up on it," Clarence said. "I'll go with you boys on this one out of respect for Old Joe, and then I'm out of it."

Their plan was simple. They'd wait until late that night and then drive out to Bob Baker's house and park the car a ways from the house and John Ashley would sneak up and slip inside and kill him. Ben and Ray would stay with the car and keep an eye out for anyone coming down the road. Clarence would keep watch outside the house. Hanford would go in with John to guard his back. As soon as Bob Baker was dead they'd set the place afire and get out of there before the flames lit up the night and drew notice.

"What about his family?" Clarence wanted to know.

"We'll put em outside and leave em to watch the place burn down like Ma and the girls had to watch Twin Oaks burn," John Ashley said. Besides, Bobby's family would be a help to them in their getaway. "We'll drop a coupla loud hints about goin to Key West," John said. "The cops'll be two weeks findin out we aint there. By then we'll be long gone and forever."

They would take a rest in Vero, at Wayne Lillis's piling house at the marina where he kept his charter boat. Then they would push on to Jacksonville and take Clarence to his brother's club. John and Hanford and Ray would visit with Daisy and Butch for the night and the next day head for Pensacola and a steamer to Texas.

"And then what?" Hanford Mobley said.

"And then we live happily ever after," John Ashley said with a grin. "What else?"

"Sounds pretty fucken fine to me," Ray Lynn said.

They told the plan to Ma Ashley over dinner and she got wet-eyed with gratitude that she would not go to her grave with her husband unavenged.

After dinner there was naught to do but pass the time until dark. Around midafternoon Ray put down for a nap on the front porch. Hanford and Clarence stretched out under one of the big oaks shading the house. Ben hiked down to Yellow Creek with a cane pole and a can of nightcrawlers. John Ashley watered and fed the milkcow in the makeshift stable Bill had put up and then he wrung the necks on three chickens for his mother to fry for supper.

Ma sent Scout and Jaybird to the creek to check the trotline and bring back any fish or cooters they found on it. She told them to pull a pailful of sweet potatoes from the garden on their way back. When John Ashley came into the kitchen fifteen minutes later with the three plucked hens she said his rattlebrained sisters had forgotten to take a bucket for the sweet potatoes and asked him to take one to them.

He found Jaybird on the path coming back from the creek. She was carrying a string of three catfish in one hand and held a headless snapping turtle by the tail in the other. She was looking back over her shoulder as she came and did not see him until he was almost to her and then she gave a startled gasp and stopped short.

"You best watch where you goin, girl," John Ashley said, "before you step on somethin you wish you hadnt. Give me them and take this." He took the fish and turtle from her and handed her the pail. "How'd you expect to bring back any sweet taters with no bucket?"

Only now did he notice her nervousness. She glanced back down the path again and then looked at him and everything in her manner bespoke unease. He looked along the narrow sun-dappled path flanked by moss-hung oaks and pines and dense palmetto shrubs. "What is it, girl?" he said.

Her eyes on him were large and fearful. He looked down the empty path again. "Where's Scout?"

She shook her had and shrugged and glanced down the path and then said, "She'll be along."

John Ashley put the fish and turtle into the pail she held and started down the path and Jay came after him, saying with low-voice vehemence, "Leave her be, Johnny! She said she'd be along and to leave her be!" He turned and pointed at her and said, "Get on up to the house, Jay. And dont forget the sweet potatoes. Go on now."

Jaybird watched him go off and then turned and hurried for the house.

He went along the path without footfall nor rustle of brush, halting every few yards to listen intently. As he neared the creek he heard them in the woods to his right. Half-smothered laughter. He eased through the palmettos and wove through the tightly clustered pines toward where the trees opened up in a clearing beside the creek. He advanced in a crouch to a dense growth of bushes at the edge of the clearing and peered through the shrubbery and saw them sitting together on a fallen pine.

She sat with her knees drawn up and he was astraddle the trunk and had one hand around her waist and one at her breast and was kissing her cheek and neck and whispering in her ear. She was smiling and blushing furiously and she had hold of his hand at her breast but John Ashley could see that she was not trying to push it away. Now Ben removed his hand to fumble at the fly of his trousers and then took her hand and put it to himself and her eyes went huge and she looked sidelong at the thing in her grip as though she were afraid to look at it directly and yet she permitted him to move her hand on him in a stroking motion and thats when John Ashley came charging out of the bushes.

Scout shrieked and leaped away from Ben and yelled, "*No, Johnny!*" Ben was up and shoving his penis back in his pants and saying something but John Ashley wasnt listening. His punch caught Ben on the nose and broke it and sent him tripping backward over the log. As he scrambled to hands and knees Ben yelled "She didnt mind, man!" and John Ashley kicked him in the ribs with enough force to lift him partway off the ground. Ben fell over on his back and could not catch his breath and John Ashley stepped up to him and brought the heel of his brogan down squarely in his face and felt bone and teeth give way.

Now Scout had him by an arm and was pulling at him and crying, "Stop! *Stop* it!" He grabbed her by the shoulders and pitched her aside and turned back to Ben who again was risen to all fours and pouring blood from his mouth and nose. He kicked him in the side of the head and blood slung as Ben fell over and tried to scrabble away and John Ashley followed after and kicked him in the face and Ben fell on his side and curled up tight with his arms around his head.

A pistolshot cracked and Scout's wails cut short and John Ashley whirled in a crouch to see Ray Lynn at the edge of the clearing with a revolver cocked and pointed at him.

"No more, Johnny, you'll kill him," Ray Lynn said. Jaybird stood back of him and partly behind a pine with her hands to her mouth and tears running down her face.

John Ashley straightened up and stared at Ray Lynn. Ben Tracey lay on his side gasping wetly and unevenly. And now here came Clarence and Hanford with guns in their hands and they took in the scene at a glance and Hanford aimed his pistol at Ray Lynn's head and said, "Get that off him, bubba."

"Hannie," John Ashley said. He gestured for him to put his gun down.

"Him first," Hanford said.

Ray Lynn sighed softly and put his pistol in his pants pocket. Hanford stepped back from him and lowered his own gun but kept it in hand. Scout shouted, "Damn you, Johnny!" and ran off toward the house with Jaybird right behind her.

Ben Tracey coughed and choked and turned onto his stomach with a loud groan and braced himself on his elbows and spewed blood. Clarence squatted beside him to examine his injuries. One side of his face was already enpurpled and grossly swollen and he lacked most of his top row of teeth. Each time he coughed he grimaced and expelled a mist of blood a little brighter than that running off his broken mouth. "I'd say his ribs're all busted up and could be one nicked a lung," Clarence said. "I knew a fella one time got a rib through his lung and drowned in his own blood."

John Ashley looked on Ben Tracey with disgust. "She's but barely fourteen, you son of a bitch." Ben Tracey did not even try to look up at him.

"Let me get him to the hospital, Johnny," Ray Lynn said. "It's no need to let him die."

"That dick of yours gone get you killed," John Ashley said, still glowering at Ben Tracey. "I *ever* see you again—anywhere—I'm like to rip it off and shove it down your throat. You understand?"

Ben Tracey nodded awkwardly.

"Get his worthless ass out of here," John Ashley said, and started back for the house with Hanford right behind.

Clarence helped Ray to get Ben Tracey back to a car, Ben crying out at every misstep or sudden jolt. As they drove him to the hospital at Stuart, Ben kept fading in and out of consciousness. The woods along the highway were already in deep twilight. They parked at the emergency entrance door and left the motor running while they supported him on either side and walked him inside and turned him over to a pair of nurses. Clarence told them he'd fallen off a scaffolding. One of the nurses said they'd have to fill out a form at the admitting desk and Clarence said, "Sure, just let me move my car from blockin the emergency entrance." Then he and Ray Lynn went out and got in the car and drove away.

But they had not thought to relieve Ben Tracey of the pistol tucked snugly in his waistband under his loose shirt, and when the nurse undressing him found it she did not even touch it but hastened big-eyed to her supervisor who returned with her to the ward and took the pistol from unconscious Ben and then telephoned the police.

Sheriff Bob Baker arrived home a little after dark in a sporadically gusting wind and under a roiling sky of gathering stormclouds. His wife and daughters met him at the door and after receiving her kiss he bent to the girls so they could kiss him in their turn. The girls then repaired to their room and Annie went into the kitchen to fetch for him a glass of iced tea. He hung up his gunbelt in the den and took off his boots then went to the dining room where Annie had set the tea on the table. He laced the drink strongly with some of the dark Jamaican rum from the jug he kept in the sideboard, then went to the parlor and settled into his rocker with the latest issue of the *American Mercury*. He was glad to be indoors and out of the bad weather bunching up. He lit his pipe and added the roasted-nut smell of its smoke to the redolence of a pot roast nearly ready.

He was the picture of contentment, but in truth he had in recent months been visited by a chronic and awful dream—a vague vision of John Ashley looming over him with one eyesocket dark and empty, and sometimes at his side his brother Bob, naked and ghostly pale. He would come awake in a gasping lurch that would wake his wife as well. She would hold him close until he recovered his breath and his tremors eased. But she never asked to know the dream and he never offered to tell it.

Sometimes he'd sit at his desk in the den and take out the bullet John Ashley had sent him. He'd hold it in his palm and roll it under his finger and a great smothering rage would close upon him so tightly he could barely draw breath. But those moments—like the unsettling dream—had of late become less frequent, and he was confident they soon would cease altogether. There had not been a single reliable sighting of John Ashley anywhere in Florida in more than three months. According to some of Bob Baker's informants, John Ashley had been badly wounded in the whiskey camp fight and his arm had since been amputated. He was gone to Georgia or Texas, maybe to California. And the rumor was, he was sworn not to return.

Bob Baker was eating his supper when the telephone rang. Annie got up to answer it in the parlor. He heard her soft muted voice and then she was back to tell him it was Deputy Elmer Padgett on the line. Elmer apologized for interrupting his supper but just a few minutes ago there had been a head-on collision on the Dixie Highway about four miles north of town. Two carloads of kids. Three dead, four injured— two of them in awful bad condition. Both cars reeking of hooch.

"Slim called it in from Riviera," Elmer Padgett said. "He's back at the scene waitin for an ambulance. He thought you'd want to know one of the criticals is Commissioner Jensen's daughter. Slim says she was in the backseat of one of the cars and, ah, her skirt was up around her waist and she wasnt wearin no underpants is what he said. The boy back there with her, his pants was wrapped around his ankles. He's dead with a broke neck. Slim says it sure enough looks like they was goin at it when the cars hit." Elmer chortled. "Hell, man, I can think of worse ways to go."

"Quit," Sheriff Bob said. "It aint funny."

"No sir, I'm sorry."

Bob Baker sighed. Damn cars. Kids could go off to who knew where and do every kind of wickedness in them. The automobile was the ruination of morality in the young, no question about it. And now Commissioner Jensen's daughter—a situation as much political as tragic. Elmer had been right to call him about it. He'd have to do it all himself, write up the accident report and go to the commissioner's house to break the news to him in person and then visit the newspaper office and make sure that the business about drinking and nakedness and who knew what else did not get into print. It looked to be a long night ahead—and a nasty one, judging by the sound of the wind in the trees and the flicker of sheet lightning at the window.

Elmer said he was calling from headquarters and could stop by for him unless he wanted to take his own car. Sheriff Bob said to come get him, then hung up and went to the den to put on his boots and gun and get a rain slicker. Annie took his half-finished supper off the table and covered it and set it in the oven. She asked him to call home before he started back so she could warm it up by the time he arrived.

"Probably be awful late before I get this wrapped up," he said. "You're like to be sleepin."

"I dont mind," she said.

Then Elmer arrived and Bob Baker went out and got in the car and they left.

Two hours later the telephone shrilled again. It was Deputy Grover Pass calling from the hospital in Stuart. She had to press the receiver to her ear tightly to hear him clearly above the rain drumming on the roof. He asked Annie Baker to please tell Sheriff Bob to call him there as soon as she saw him or heard from him. It was awful important. Of course, she said in her soft pleasant accent, of course she would.

It's *all* so awful important, she thought, as she hung the receiver back in its cradle.

By the time they arrived at West Palm Beach the wind was whipping the trees and lightning was branching brightly and thunderclaps shook the air. Hanford Mobley turned off onto the dirt lane leading through the pinewoods to Bob Baker's house and switched off the Ford's headlamps. Clarence Middleton kept watch through the rear window but there was no one behind them. As they approached a bend in the road they suddenly made out a faint light through the trees and Hanford stopped the car. Through a series of back-and-forth wheelings he turned the vehicle around on the narrow road to face back toward the highway and then carefully backed off the road and into the deeper shadows of the pines. They checked their weapons once again and then John Ashley and Hanford Mobley, each armed with a pump-action shotgun and a .45, got out of the car into the blowing rain. Hanford took the one-gallon can of gasoline Clarence handed him and they started walking toward the house, keeping to the shadows of the roadside trees. Clarence Middleton and Ray Lynn remained in the car to keep watch for anyone who might come down the road.

The rain was hard and cold and rattled through the hardwood leaves and pocked the muddy road. In seconds their clothes were stuck to their skins. They saw Bob Baker's green Ford runabout parked in front of the house. A large front window of the house showed bright yellow. They came across the yard at an angle to avoid its misty cast of light. The room at the front corner was unlighted and they edged past it and moved along the front of the house and past the stonework of the chimney and stopped at the lighted window. They peeked in through slightly-parted curtains and saw a parlor with plush furniture. One of Bob Baker's cob pipes was propped in an ashtray on a table beside an armchair. They went up onto the porch, stepping lightly, and moved to the front door. John Ashley tried the knob and it turned.

He slipped into a foyer and Hanford Mobley stepped lightly after him and gingerly set down the can of gasoline. A gust of wind came in behind them and fluttered the pages of a wall calendar. Hanford eased the door to and they stood motionless and listened for voice or footfall but heard only the falling rain and the water running off their sopping clothes onto the wooden floor. With his shotgun at port arms John Ashley moved ahead into the parlor and again stopped. The room was well-lighted by table lamps at opposite walls. He looked down at the carpet muting the water dripping off their sopping clothes. He'd known no one who lived in houses with carpeting except whores. The rain was falling even harder now and the crashes of thunder came more loudly and more closely together and quivered the floor under his feet.

The parlor gave onto a dining room just ahead and it too was bright with lamplight. A hallway led off to their right between the parlor and dining room, and to their left, across the parlor, was another open hallway. The house was spacious and warm and seemed to John Ashley a comfortable place to live. He knew bob Baker had lived here since before his daddy died and he became the sheriff. John Ashley suddenly felt strange in some way he couldn't define—and then his uncertainty became anger. Just do it, he told himself. Find the bastard and do it.

He went forward and paused before the hallway to the right and craned his neck to see into it. There was a closed door on either side of the hall but no light showed under either door. He peered into the dining room and saw another door, this one ajar, to the left, and from beyond it now heard the muted sound of voices. He looked back at Hanford Mobley and gestured and Hanford looked into the dining room and saw the door and now heard the murmuring voices and nodded and tightened his grip on the shotgun.

They moved silently to the dining room door and paused there and John Ashley listened hard for Bob Baker's voice but heard only those of children and that of a woman: "All right now, we need to beat four eggs." He looked at Hanford Mobley behind him and gestured for him to back out into the parlor and he followed after.

"I dont think he's in there," John whispered at Hanford's ear. "Could be he's sleepin." He nodded toward the near hallway and led the way into it. Standing to the side so he would not be framed by the doorway, he eased open the door on the left and listened for sound in the darkness within and heard none. He crouched and peered into the room and after a moment made out in the dimness that it was the children's bedroom and the two beds were empty. He pulled the door to and moved across the hall and opened the other door in the same way, again crouching before peeking inside. Another bedroom, the window curtains open. In a quivering blue flash of lightning he saw a large neatly made bed and that no one was in the room.

They crossed back through the parlor to the other hallway and the door to their right opened into a bathroom and John Ashley and Hanford Mobley looked at each other with raised brows at this luxury Bob Baker had added to the house. The other door opened into Bobby's den. John Ashley waited for lightning to illuminate the room and reveal that no one was inside, then went to the lamp on the desk and lifted the glass and lit the wick with a match. A rack of guns on one wall held shotguns both pump and breech-break, carbines both bolt and lever. On another wall was a row of animal heads—a ten-point and a twelve-point buck, and two wild boars, their little red eyes looking almost alive, their tusks shining whitely in the lamplight against their black bristly hides. One of them wore a St. Louis Browns baseball cap at a jaunty sideward tilt and had a cigarette in its mouth. Several fishing rods stood clustered in a corner, and on a table beside them was a litter of tackle and reels and lures. Over the roll-shaded window was mounted a largemouth that looked to scale at least fifteen pounds.

"I bet he really likes it in here—in this whole damn house," Hanford Mobley whispered. "It's gonna be a pure-dee pleasure to burn it down."

The window shade went blue-white with lightning, and the almost simultaneous blast of thunder rattled the window. John Ashley opened the righthand desk drawer and saw within a gunbelt with a holstered .38 revolver, and a bottle of dark rum. He let the gun alone but took out the rum and uncapped the bottle and took a drink and passed the rum to Hanford Mobley whose deep swallow bubbled the bottle. Now John Ashley opened the shallow middle drawer. It held a few pencils and pens and gum erasers and blank sheets of paper. And a bullet. He recognized it at once and grinned and took it out and set in on its base on the desktop.

"He's not home," Annie Baker said.

They whirled around with shotguns up and Annie Baker gasped and lunged back from the door with her hands up to her mouth.

"Dont move," John Ashley said. "Not a muscle." He hollered,

"*Bobby!* I'll blow her damn head off, you dont show yourself with your hands up."

"He isnt home, I told—"

There was a brilliant white flash at the window and an enormous ripping sound and an explosive blast of thunder that shook the house. And then a wailing of children and a loud call of "Momma!"

Annie Baker looked down the hallway and called, "It's all right, girls, I'm—" and then squatted with open arms to receive her two daughters rushing to her. "I *told* you to stay put," she said, but her rebuke was without temper. The girls held tight to her, crying with their faces against her breasts.

"We tole *you* dont move, goddammit!" Hanford Mobley said. He was aiming his shotgun at her as though at some distant target.

The woman stood and held her whimpering daughters to her skirt. "You're scaring the children," she said. "Arent you ashamed, the both of you?"

"God damn it, woman, I'm—"

"Please dont use profanity in front of my daughters."

"Shit, lady, you dont—"

"Hush up, Hannie," John Ashley said. "Take that gun off her." He held his own shotgun with the muzzle toward the floor. He had seen occasional photographs of Bobby's wife in the newspapers over the years and now reflected that the pictures had not done her justice. "Miz Baker? You tellin me true he aint home?"

"It's the truth. See for yourselves if you like and then please go away."

"I know thats his car out there."

"He was called away to a highway accident," she said. "A deputy came for him." The rain clattered hard on the roof and lightning flickered and flared almost without pause and one thunderclap followed on another.

"Well hell, we'll just wait for him," Hanford Mobley said. "We'll lay for him right here and give him a big surprise when he gets back."

The look on Annie Baker's face reminded John Ashley of the way Bertha looked that night at Bill's just before she'd run tearfully from the room—and the way Laura looked as she waved goodbye from the dock. He suddenly had a feeling they all three understood something important he did not. In that moment he somehow knew that this woman truly loved Bobby Baker and likely always would. And in some way as inexplicable he knew too—though he knew it only as a feeling, as an understanding beyond language—that Bobby did not know she

loved him, that he *could* not know it, not if she told him so every day
for the rest of his life, no matter how she might try to show him that
she did. The realization came to him that nothing he might do to Bob
Baker could be as bad as having to live in such a circumstance, in
such . . . what? Emptiness. In such emptiness of the heart.

He sensed all this in the span of a heartbeat. And then wished he
were with Laura right that minute, wished they were in their bed in
Galveston with moonshine or rain either one falling over them through
the window.

Well hell, boy, all you got to do is to do it.

He put the shotgun barrel up on his shoulder and smiled at Annie
Baker. The woman's eyes were intent upon him and now they suddenly filled and she showed a small uncertain smile.

"Let's go, Hannie," he said. "I cant wait to get shut of this place
and get down to Key West."

Hanford Mobley looked at him like he'd spoken in a foreign
tongue. "Say *what*? How come? We can lay for him right here and—"

John Ashley was still looking at Annie Baker and now his grin
widened. "And from Key West a boat to Mexico, where the arm of
the law dont reach too good." He glanced at Hanford and said, "Let's
go," and started from the room.

Hanford came rushing after him. "Goddamn, John, what's going
on? The son of a bitch killed Granddaddy. It aint right we—"

"He didnt do any such a thing," John Ashley said tiredly as he
crossed the parlor to the front door where he stopped and looked back
at Hanford. "Daddy always done exactly what he wanted and he died
the same way."

Hanford Mobley snatched up the gasoline can and said, "Well we
damn sure ought to burn down his fucken house! He burned down
my momma and daddy's house and I aim to pay him in kind."

John Ashley grabbed the can from him. "We aint burnin nothin.
It aint just Bobby's house, Hannie, it's them's." He gestured at Annie
Baker and her daughters, standing on the other side of the room and
watching them. "Hell, it's more them's than Bobby's. What we got
against *them*?" He put a hand on Hanford's shoulder. "Listen. Let's
just go, all right?"

Hanford Mobley shook his head and cursed under his breath and
followed his uncle into the tempestuous night.

And Annie Baker hurried to the door and shut it hard against the
buffeting storm.

* * *

A year earlier, following Clarence Middleton's and Ray Lynn's getaway from a road gang the day after John Ashley escaped from Raiford, Sheriff Bob Baker had requested and received from the state penitentiary the prison records of all three men and of all convicts who'd been known to associate with them. Each convict's folder included a photograph. After studying the material, Bob Baker had put it all in his Ashley Gang file. He had since made it policy for his officers to check any strangers arrested in Palm Beach County against the photos and descriptions in the Raiford records. And so, when Deputy Grover Pass received a telephone call from the station in Stuart informing him that the local hospital had reported a battered patient armed with a pistol when he was admitted, he took the Ashley Gang file and drove up to Stuart in a furious thunderstorm and went to the hospital ward to have a look at this patient who said his name was Walter Jones.

Deputy Pass had a good eye for features, and despite the man's battered aspect, he recognized him as the same man in one of the prison photographs in the file. The file report said the man's name was Ben Tracey and that he had been in the same cell block and work gang as John Ashley and Ray Lynn. He had served out his sentence only a short time before their escapes.

The battered man had watched Deputy Pass carefully as he looked back and forth from his face to each photograph in turn. When he looked twice at the same photo and then grinned, the man had said, "Shut," through his mutilated mouth and broken nose. Deputy Pass cuffed Ben Tracey's wrist to the bed and went to the desk to call Sheriff Baker. Several of the other ward patients had been looking on and fell to murmured speculation among themselves. In a neighboring bed a man with two broken legs grinned at Ben Tracey and said, "Sometimes it aint no end of trouble, is it?" Ben Tracey glared at him and said, "Uck you."

It was dawn when the sheriff arrived at the hospital. After visiting with the commissioner whose daughter had been injured in the car crash and then stopping by the newspaper office in West Palm Beach to have a talk with the night editor, he had called the station to check in and the desk clerk had relayed Grover Pass's message to call him at the Stuart hospital. When Grover told him he had arrested a patient who might be in the Ashley Gang, Bob Baker ordered the suspect moved to a private room and a pair of deputies placed on guard at his door. He then had Elmer Padgett drive him directly to Stuart. The wind had fallen off and the thunder and lightning had ceased their action, but the rain yet fell.

The interrogation did not take long. When Bob Baker asked Ben Tracey where John Ashley might be found, Ben said, "Uck you wid a arden hose." Bob Baker said he had him for bank robbery but would drop all charges against him in exchange for information on John Ashley and his gang. "Aint no rat," Ben Tracey said. Bob Baker stood over him and gently laid a hand on his bandaged chest and repeated his question. Tracey cursed him once more and Bob Baker leaned hard on his chest.

Tracey's quavering scream brought nurses on the run but the two cops outside the closed door would not permit them to enter the room. One of the nurses ran off to find a doctor but she was ten minutes in returning with one in tow and by then Ben Tracey had come to see the wisdom in accepting Bob Baker's deal and had hastily confided all he knew about John Ashley's immediate intentions. The sheriff was already on his way out of the hospital when the doctor arrived.

Bob Baker told Elmer Padgett to round up his brother Joel and deputies L. B. Thomas and Henry Stubbs and get up to Fort Pierce as quick as they could and call on St. Lucie County Sheriff J. R. Merritt. "I'm puttin you boys in his charge. Tell him exactly what this Tracey shitbird told us," Bob Baker said. "If he aint lyin and the Ashley bunch stopped to see their bubba in Vero tonight, J.R. can maybe catch up to them there, or maybe further along the road. They got no reason to think we know their plan, so they got no call to be in a hurry. I'm gonna go check on Annie and the girls back at the house. Keep me posted."

He took the car they'd come in and Elmer took the guard deputies' car and followed him out to the Dixie Highway. There Bob Baker turned south for West Palm Beach and Elmer wheeled north to the county sheriff's station in Stuart where he would telephone his brother and the other two and tell them to get up to Stuart right now and he would explain things to them on the way to Fort Pierce.

Bob Baker did not telephone his wife before heading home. It had occurred to him that on finding he was not at home John Ashley might have decided to wait at the house in ambush for him. If so, he did not want to tip him off that he was coming.

The morning was darkly gray with lingering storm clouds. He turned onto the muddy road to his house and slowed to hardly more than walking speed. He studied the wooded sides of the road carefully in search of a waiting car but did not see one. He stopped at the bend in the road and regarded the house, some forty yards distant. There was a light in the parlor window but nothing looked out of the ordinary. He jacked a round in the chamber of his pump action and got out and headed for the porch. Before he got halfway there the door swung open and he raised the shotgun and had his finger on the trigger before he saw it was Annie silhouetted in the light from inside.

He looked in on the sleeping girls from their door and then softly shut it again. He made Annie sit on the couch in the parlor and tell him everything, and she did—all of it, including John Ashley's remark about going to Key West to catch a boat to Mexico. She told him everything except about the smile John Ashley had given her. A smile that had given her ease, though she could not have explained why.

Bob Baker looked off to the hallway leading to his daughters' room and looked at the muddy tracks across the carpet from one hallway to the other. She felt the heat of his raging eyes and said, "They didnt scare the girls, Robert. The girls were scared of the storm more than anything."

"They brought *gasoline* in the house?" Bob Baker said. "And they didnt use it?"

"The little one, Hannie, he wanted to, but John wouldnt let him."

"John?" His look was as accusatory as his tone. *"Hannie?"*

"Those are their names, arent they?" She reached out to put her hand on his arm but he abruptly stood up and began pacing. She watched him for a moment and then said softly, "I had the feeling he didnt really want to be here. Whatever it was he had against you . . . well, I dont think it matters to him anymore. I had the feeling he was going away. He wont come back here again, Robert, I know he wont."

Bob Baker turned to glare at her. "Since when did you get to know so awful much about him?"

She looked at him a moment, her aspect unfathomable to him, and then got up and walked down the hall and into the bedroom and gently closed the door.

He went to the kitchen and poured a tall glass of cold tea and sugar and then added rum from the sideboard jug. Then he returned to the parlor and turned off the lamp and sat in the gray gloom of the morning and of his own thoughts and drank slowly.

Sneak up and shoot you dead while you were sleeping is what he meant to do. When he saw you werent here he run off because he's too cowardly to try to shoot you any way but in your sleep.

That wasnt true and he knew it. The man was a sonofabitch but he wasnt a coward nor a backshooter.

Why'd he leave? Why not lay an ambush for when he got home? How come he didnt burn the house? He'd come ready to.

He drank and thought. Annie was right, the man was leaving. Not to Key West and Mexico. That was a bullshit story meant to distract him from looking for them along the upper coast until they were long gone. Jesus. How damn stupid did they think he was?

Well, he thought, he would either get away from J.R. and the boys or he wouldnt. In either case it would finally be done with.

He fell asleep in the chair and when next he woke it was the middle of the afternoon. His neck was sore. He could hear Annie and the girls laughing faintly in the kitchen. The parlor window was softly bright with sunlight. He got up and went to the kitchen and the girls rushed to him for a hug and Annie smiled and said she hadnt had the heart to wake him from the chair, he'd been so deeply asleep. He asked if anyone had telephoned and no one had. He assumed Sheriff Merritt and the deputies had not found Ashley and his gang in Vero or anywhere else. The man was gone, he was sure of it. He couldnt help smiling, and Annie herself seemed to brighten in the light of his good cheer.

He sat and sipped coffee and chatted with his daughters while Annie fried a steak and potatoes for him and sliced bread to toast in the pan with the steak juice. He cleaned his plate and then had a large serving of peach pie for dessert. Then his daughters took turns showing off for him by reading aloud long passages from their schoolbooks. He had not enjoyed himself this way in longer than he could recall.

Evening came on. While Annie fixed a fresh pot of coffee he called the station to see if his deputies had returned from St. Lucie County yet or filed a report. The desk officer said he had been just about to call him. Elmer Padgett had telephoned not five minutes ago with a message.

"He said tell you they're at the Sebastian River Bridge," the desk officer said. "Said to tell you, 'We're on em,' in exactly them words. I asked what that meant and he said you'd know. What the hell's Elmer and them doing way up in St. Lucie, Sheriff?"

Bob Baker hung up and stared at the parlor window gone dark with nightfall.

It wasnt done with.

"We're on them" wasnt the same as "We got them." What if he was to get away? Maybe Tracey was bullshitting about Johnny wanting to go to Texas for good. Maybe Tracey was trying to put him off his guard. Maybe Johnny had been bullshitting Tracey.

Even if he did go away, who was to say he wouldnt be back? He'd gone twice now and come back both times. Tracey said he'd come back this time just to kill him. He had no trouble believing that.

Bob Baker could not have explained what he felt at that moment but its similarity to fear was enraging.

"Here you are, sir," Annie said brightly at his side, holding out to him a steaming mug of coffee. He turned to her and she saw his face and her smile vanished.

He mumbled something about paperwork and turned away without taking the coffee and went to the den. He lit the lamp in his room and saw the rifle bullet set upright on the desk.

His chest went so tight he could hardly breathe. A sudden red pressure swelled behind his eyes.

Son of a bitch.

He heard John Ashley's laughter as plainly as when he'd run off in the rain after busting his head against the jailhouse wall, as plainly as when he took his leg and gun.

He could see him grinning as big as when he came out of the pineywoods behind Julie.

Julie. He could in this moment smell her hair and remember the feel of her breath on his face. Could see her eyes and how they shone for him. And then shone for him no more after she'd been to the woods with John Ashley.

He picked up the bullet and closed his hand so tightly around it his fist trembled.

And then howled and drove the fist into the desktop and his knuckles left their imprint in the heavy wood.

And then spun and snatched up his gunbelt and stalked out to his runabout and roared away through the night toward the highway.

TWENTY-SEVEN

November 1, 1924

BY THE TIME ELMER PADGETT, SLEEPLESS AND HAGGARD, HAD tracked down his brother and the other two deputies and they all came together in Stuart it was almost noon. It was past two o'clock when St. Lucie County Sheriff J. R. Merritt and two deputies he introduced as Wiggins and Jones met with them at the Bluebird Café on Orange Avenue in Fort Pierce.

As Elmer Padgett explained the situation the St. Lucie cops listened intently. J. R. Merritt had a reputation as a tough sheriff. There were rumors of rumrunners who had driven their loads into St. Lucie County and never been seen again. He'd been appointed sheriff by the governor two years ago and was facing his first election to the office in just three days. He was known to have political ambitions, and the public recognition to be had from busting up the Ashley Gang could be invaluable to his future. Listening to Elmer repeat what Ben Tracey had told Bob Baker, Merritt could not restrain a smile. He told the Palm Beach officers he was deeply grateful to Sheriff Baker for the opportunity to bring to justice such a bad bunch as John Ashley's. "The question is," he said, "was this Tracey fella telling Sheriff Bob the truth?"

He turned to a deputy and said, "Jonesy, why dont you go see if this bad-ass really is at Lillis's place. We'll be waitin for you at Rhonda's." Deputy Jones nodded and went.

Wiggins led the way in the St. Lucie police car and Sheriff Merritt rode with the Palm Beach deputies. He sat in the backseat with Elmer Padgett to one side of him and Henry Stubbs on the other, each one holding one side of a fluttering regional map he'd opened up. He tapped his finger on Vero where it lay about fifteen miles north of Fort Pierce. He knew Wayne Lillis and knew the marina where he lived in a piling house and docked his charter boat. He said it was not a good place to try to take a tough bunch. The house and boat were both at the far end of the marina and anybody approaching along the piers would be spotted in plenty of time to allow for a getaway. With his finger on the map he showed Padgett and Stubbs how the bandits could flee downriver to the Fort Pierce Inlet or upriver into the serpentine channels of the mangrove narrows—or go straight across to the barrier island and run north or south under cover of the high brush and then cross back to the mainland at some safer point.

"What about if *we* get us a boat?" Elmer said. "Come up on em by way of the river?"

"*You* can do that if you want," Merritt said. "I aint about to go out there in the river and make myself a wide-open target."

"All right then, what?" Henry Stubbs said.

Sheriff J.R. Merritt studied the map for a moment and said. "Oh, I maybe got an idea." He looked up and grinned from one to the other of them. "But it aint worth spit if they already gone, is it? Let's wait and see are they still around."

Rhonda's was a small cafe off the Dixie Highway a half-mile north of Vero. They sat at a large corner table and ordered coffee and two buckets of fried oysters. They ate without conversation until Merritt said, "You know, boys, grateful as I am to Sheriff Baker for the chance to nab this bunch myself, I cant help but wonder how come he didnt come along with you all. I always heard he had a special dislike for that whole Ashley family and for John in particular. I mean, you'd think he'd make special sure to be in on this."

The Palm Beach deputies looked sidelong at each other as if each would have one of the others answer the question. Though they had not spoken of it among themselves they had all wondered the same thing. Then Elmer Padgett said, "He had to go see about his family. Tracey said Ashley was goin out to his house. He had to go see if they all right. It's only natural."

"Well you right about that," Merritt said. He scratched his ear contemplatively. "I guess if he sees his wife and kids are all right, he'll be along, wont he? I mean, he aint about to miss out on takin down about the worst bandit we ever had in this part of the state, is he?

Especially one that sends him a bullet and says he's got another one with his name on it."

The Palm Beach deputies looked at him.

"Oh yeah, I heard that story," Merritt said. He blew on his coffee and took a sip. "You know, it's somethin else I've long heard. I aint never believed it for a minute, you understand, but still, I always heard Bobby Baker's always been just a little, well . . . scared of John Ashley. They say it's been that way since they was pups. Now boys, just between us, why you figure anybody'd say such a thing about Sheriff Bob?"

"Well, sheriff, all I can tell you for certain sure is Bob Baker aint afraid of any man alive," Henry Stubbs said. "I can tell you that sure as I'm sittin here." The other Palm Beach deputies nodded.

"Some people seem to just naturally prefer a lie to the truth of a thing," Elmer Padgett said. "Who can say why? Lie's just more excitin for em, I guess."

Merritt chuckled in the manner of one responding politely to a awkwardly told joke. "I guess," he said.

And then Deputy Jones was coming through the front door and spied them and came over and took a chair at the table. He looked at their expectant faces each in turn and without expression said, "They aint at Lillis's."

The Palm Beach cops muttered curses and sagged in their chairs. Jones grinned to see their disappointment and then said, "They aint at Lillis's but they still in town. They're at Mel's shootin pool."

The Palm Beach deputies sat up and exchanged excited looks.

"You boys described them pretty good," Jones said. "But I tell you what—they dont look the least bit worried somebody might be on their tail."

Elmer looked at Merritt. "Can we take them there?"

Merritt shook his head. "Not unless I wanna risk shootin bystanders—and I dont." He pulled out his map and spread it open on the table. "Here," he said, pointing. "If they're going north they have to cross here."

The others leaned forward to see his finger at the mouth of the Sebastian River—where they all knew there was a bridge.

"Let's get out there before they do," Merritt said as he stood up.

Except for Hanford Mobley who was still a little sulky because John Ashley had prevented him from burning down Bob Baker's house, they were in high spirits. John Ashley felt like a fresh new life was opening up to him.

They had gone out on Wayne's boat early that morning and taken several dolphin just outside the Fort Pierce Inlet and then reeled in some trout on light tackle as they chugged back up the lagoon to the marina under a bright noon sun. They fileted the fish and took them to Lucy's Kitchen up the street and lingered over a leisurely meal of fried filets and scrambled eggs, fried potatoes, grits and gravy, biscuits and coffee. They had then taken haircuts at Shorty O'Malley's shop across the street and passed some time chatting with a few of the oldtimers in the local Liars Club who came together there every day to argue politics and tell stories of the old days and shake their heads over the abject state of the modern world. One of them made bold to ask John Ashley how he had managed to break out of state prison twice in one lifetime and John Ashley told him and they all listened raptly to his story. In days to come most of them would at first retell the tale almost exactly the way he told it, but after a time each man of them would begin to embroider it in his own fashion.

The gang had then repaired to Mel's for a few games of pool and bottles of beer. The first games sparked such a fierce competition for the title of King of the Table that they set up an elaborate six-man playoff system. By the time Marie Lillis banked the cue ball off the side rail to sink the eight in an opposite corner pocket and beat Ray Lynn for the championship, the windows of the hall had been dark for hours and they were all a little buzzed on beer. Marie beamed with delight as the men happily chided each other for having lost to a woman.

They took their leave of Wayne and Marie on the street in front of Mel's and got into the Ford. Hanford Mobley, his spirits improved, tooted the klaxon and they drove off up the highway.

Twelve miles north of Vero was the hamlet of Sebastian and three miles farther on was the Saint Sebastian River and the flat wooden bridge that traversed it. The region was isolated and smelled of tidal marshes and rarely sounded of other than wind hissing in the cattails and seabirds squalling at their feed. The south end of the bridge rested on the tip of a long and narrow spit of land where the highway was flanked to either side by high shrubs and clusters of pines.

The sun was still well above the horizon when the two police cars arrived at the bridge and crossed over it and turned around and parked on either side of the road to face any traffic coming off the bridge from the south. For the rest of the afternoon they waited with guns out of sight but at the ready. A few cars came over the bridge but none conveyed the Ashley Gang. After a time Sheriff Merritt wondered aloud if John Ashley was simply taking his time about getting underway for Jacksonville or if he had decided to turn back south for some reason.

At sundown the sheriff told Elmer to move the Palm Beach car onto the bridge and he then positioned his own car across the foot of the bridge to block all passage at this end of it. He removed a heavy length of chain and two large flashlights from his car and handed them to Henry Stubbs and L.B. Thomas in the other vehicle and told Deputy Jones to stay with the St. Lucie car and tell any motorists who approached from the north that they would have to wait until morning to cross or they could press on by some inland route. He then got in the Palm Beach car with the others and they returned to the south end of the bridge and all got out except Elmer Padgett who was driving. They removed the chain and flashlights from the car and Merritt told Elmer to drive back to Vero and borrow a red lantern from the train depot. "Another few minutes it'll be dark enough so nobody'll see it's a cop car unless their lights shine on you," the sheriff said. "Could be our boy's gone back, but keep an eye open for him anyhow."

Forty minutes later Elmer had the lantern and he followed the depot agent's directions to Mel's and as he went chugging by on the darkened street he saw them still in there shooting pool and drinking beer and laughing. He wheeled around and headed back for the river and then thought Sheriff Bob must be wondering what they were up to and so stopped at Rhonda's Cafe and asked the use of the telephone to call his headquarters in Palm Beach County. When the desk clerk said the sheriff was at home, Elmer gave him a message to relay to him, couching it in sufficiently cryptic terms to keep the cafe eavesdroppers from knowing what was going on. Then he went back to rejoin the others at the bridge.

As they drove past the few scattered buildings that composed Sebastian, Clarence Middleton was telling about a duck who went into a speakeasy and asked the bartender if he had any fudge. "Barkeep says, '*No*, I aint got no fudge. Cant you see this is a barroom? Get the hell outa here!' Duck leaves, comes back the next day. 'Got any fudge?' Barkeep says, 'I tole you yesterday I aint got no fudge. Now get the hell outa here!' Duck leaves, comes back the next day. 'Got any fudge?' Barkeep said, 'You little feathery son of a bitch! You come in here one more time and ask me that I'm gonna nail your goddamn beak to the bar.' Duck leaves, comes back next day, says to the bartender, 'Got any nails?' Barkeep says, '*What?* No, I aint got no nails!' Duck says, 'Got any fudge?' "

A Dodge sedan turned onto the highway directly in front of them from an intersecting dirt road and Hanford Mobley applied the brakes hard and the Ford stalled. Beside him John Ashley bumped his head hard on the windshield and behind him Clarence Middleton and Ray Lynn were thrown against the front seats.

"Bastard!" Hanford Mobley shouted and the only two people on the street looked at him. The Dodge sped away without even slowing. "Let's catch him and whip his ass!" The Dodge went out of sight around a bend in the road ahead.

Clarence rummaged under the seats till he found the crank and then got out with it. He had to twirl the balky motor three times before it fired up.

"Hurry up, dammit!" Hanford said as Clarence held his hand to a headlamp light and examined a callus he'd ripped open with the crank.

Clarence got in and Hanford Mobley gunned the Model T ahead, smoothly and swiftly working levers and pedals. The motor rapped sweetly and the car swayed as it picked up speed.

John Ashley laughed. "Whooo! Lookit this boy go! I hope you catch em, Hannie, but I hope they're little fellas, cause you're the one's gonna brace em, you being the one who's so hot to whip their ass and all."

Hanford gave him a look. "I aint scared of em and I dont need you all's help. I'll brace their asses, you watch."

"I got a dollar says old Hannie dont catch em before we hit the bridge," Clarence Middleton said.

There were no takers and Hanford muttered, "You bastards, *I'll* take the bet," and the others laughed.

The road wound through the darkness and a heavy stand of pine and they had gone more than two miles before they caught sight of the single red taillight of the car ahead.

"There the sumbitches are!" Hanford said, and leaned forward on the steering wheel as if to lend more speed to the Ford.

"Damn if they aint movin right smartly their ownselfs," Ray Lynn said. "They probably know Hardtime Hannie here's after their ass."

And now they saw a red light shining up ahead on the spit of land where the bridge began. The Dodge slowed as it went out onto the spit and its lights closed in to illuminate a red lantern fixed to a chain hung across the foot of the bridge. The car rolled up to within a few feet of the lantern and stopped.

Hanford Mobley was laughing as they reached the spit and he slowed the Ford. "You mulletheads sure missed the chance of a easy dollar," he said. "Pay up, Ray!" He brought the car to a halt a few feet behind the Dodge. A pale pair of faces looked back at them through the car's rear window.

"Whoever the hell closed off the bridge," Ray Lynn said as he handed a dollar over the front seat to Hanford Mobley, "you oughta give em half this for the help."

"Well now you caught em, let's see you whip their ass," John Ashley said. "They just sittin there waitin on you."

The driver of the Dodge was a young man named Ted Miller and the friend with him was S.O. Davis, whom some called So-So despite his hatred of the nickname. They had been to a dance in Fort Pierce earlier that Saturday evening but were disappointed by the paucity of pretty girls and so decided to drive around and sip from their shine jug and see what adventures the night might bring. After an hour of aimless driving and talking about girls, they headed for home in Sebastian. They were almost to Davis's house when So-So said maybe they ought pay Angie Cambone a visit. Angie Cambone lived in a shack across the river and was reputed to do the trick for a dollar. Neither of them had ever even seen her but they'd heard of her since early adolescence—and long heard the old joke that she was so ugly she had to sneak up on a glass to get a drink of water. Miller gave Davis a thin look and said a man had to be hornier than a billygoat to go to Angie Cambone. Davis said he didnt know about Miller but he himself was about as horny as a damn *herd* of billygoats. They looked at each other and laughed and Miller admitted that *he* was so horny he didnt care if Angie did look like her momma'd sat on her face at birth, he was going to need a wheelbarrow to get his hard-on from the car to Angie's door. He goosed the Dodge down the dirt road and made a tight turn onto the Dixie Highway and neither of them even took notice of the Ford that had to brake sharply to avoid hitting them.

They were arguing about which of them would go first with Angie when they saw the red light ahead. "What the hell's this?" Miller said. He slowed the Dodge and as they drew closer they saw it was a red lantern hooked to a chain hung across the entrance to the bridge.

Davis groaned. "Of all the damn times to close the bridge."

Miller braked the car a few feet from the chain. The headlamps cast their yellow beams onto the empty bridge planks beyond. "Shoot, I dont see nothin wrong with it, do you?" Miller said. "How come they closed it I wonder."

Headlights fell over them from the rear and only now did they become aware of the car closing up behind them. "I want you to look here at this sumbuck who's gonna have to back around before we can," Miller said.

Davis looked back at the car coming to a stop directly behind them and said, "Might could be some ole boy even hornier'n us on his way to see Angie. Boy, is *he* gonna be chafed to find out he cant get across."

The driver's door of the car behind them swung open and a small vaguely silhouetted man stepped out.

Flashlight beams suddenly blazed from the shrubbery on both sides of the road and lit up the interior of the car behind them and Miller and Davis saw three men yet in the car and the small man outside— he looked hardly more than a boy—was wide-eyed and starkly illuminated and immobile as a jacklit deer.

"STAND FAST YOU SONOFABITCH OR WE'LL BLOW YOUR DAMN HEAD OFF!"

"Oh Jesus, *what*?" Davis said.

"PUT YOUR HANDS UP NOW! *NOW!*—OR WE'LL BLAST YOU TO HELL!"

The man outside the car raised his hands up high, his eyes still fixed hugely into the bright flashlight beam.

"OUT OF THE CAR—ALL YOU—*OUT*—NOW! HANDS OUT WHERE WE CAN SEE THEM. *MOVE*, GODDAMNIT!"

"It's a damn *holdup*," Miller said, his voice high and tight. He quickly stripped off his watch and put it under the car seat, then dug into his pocket for the few dollars he had and tucked them under the seat too. Davis immediately did likewise, saying, "Oh sweet Jesus, oh lord."

Behind them the other three men in the car all got out on the driver's side and put their hands up. Men emerged from the dark foliage on both sides of the road and two of them held a flashlight in one hand and a pistol in the other and the rest were armed with rifles and they formed a loose semicircle around the surrendered men who stood squinting into the blinding glare of the flashlights.

"STAND FAST!"

Two of the armed men hastened into the blaze of light and quickly relieved the surrendered men of their pistols and then backed out of the lights again. And now another moved in with a fistful of handcuffs and began to manacle the prisoners' hands behind them.

Miller opened his door and stepped out into the glare of headlights and raised his hands. One of the armed men came toward him and in the peripheral cast of the Ford's headlights he saw that it was the St. Lucie high sheriff.

"Is your name Miller?" Merritt said. "Dont I know your daddy?"

Miller nodded jerkily. "Yessir, it's—you do—I mean, thats my name, and Daddy fixed your boat—your outboard—a coupla months ago."

The sheriff smiled. "Why your hands up, boy? Is it somethin I ought arrest you for?"

Miller dropped his hands. "No sir, no. I—we—didnt know what's happenin. We thought we was bein held up."

The sheriff laughed. "We just nabbed the goddamn Ashley Gang is what we done." He pulled a .45 automatic out of his waistband and looked on it as though it were a special gift. "This here's John Ashley's gun." He looked back at the men holding their hands up and laughed again. "That's him on the right. See how the light shines on that glass eye?"

With his good eye narrowed against the flashlight beam John Ashley appeared to be holding a wink. He looked to Miller to be irritated but not at all afraid. So did the others.

"My car's at the other end of the bridge," Merritt said. "How bout a ride over?"

Davis hurried around to the backseat of the Dodge so the sheriff could sit up front and then Miller drove over the river. His headlights came up on a St. Lucie County police car blocking the end of the bridge. Leaning on a front fender was a St. Lucie deputy.

Merritt asked where they were headed and Miller said they'd just been taking a ride and would go on back home now. Merritt and the other officer got in the police car, Merritt behind the wheel, and the sheriff backed out of the way so Miller could pass him by and turn his car around, and then Merritt led the way back across the bridge. Miller and Davis kept looking at each other and grinning. "The Ashley Gang!" Davis said. *"Hot damn!"*

The bandits' car yet stood in the road and Merritt called for one of the deputies to move it out of the way. He parked his car on the grassy shoulder opposite the side of the road where the bandits were bunched with their hands cuffed behind them. A line of four deputies held them at gunpoint in full glare of the flashlights. As the Ford was backed off the road, Merritt waved Miller on by and Davis said, "Go, man!" and Miller gunned the Dodge and they went.

They sped back toward Sebastian in high excitement, both of them jabbering at once and eager to tell everyone about their witness to the capture of the Ashley Gang. So enrapt were they with their adventure that neither paid the least notice to the green runabout that hurtled past them in the opposite direction.

The instant the flashlights hit them from both sides of the car they knew they had no chance to make a fight of it. They were in a car and in bright lights and could not see the men who had them under the gun. Even the BAR on the floor was of no help under such conditions. Clarence cursed and Ray Lynn sighed and John Ashley's first thought was that it was going to be godawful hard to break out of prison this time without Daddy's help. But he had Laura out there. He'd find a way.

As he got out of the car and put up his hands and squinted his eye against the glaring lights he decided the first thing he would ask of her was to find Ben Tracey and kill him. The bastard ratted. That was how this trap got set.

And now they stood cuffed and under gunpoint in the blaze of the flashlights and the Dodge was heading off back toward Sebastian and the leader of this bunch came across the road and said, "Mister Ashley, I'm pleased to meet you. My name's Merritt."

John Ashley knew him by reputation. "Pleasure's mine, Sheriff," John Ashley said. "This was a nice piece of work."

Beside him Hanford Mobley snorted and spat.

Merritt grinned. "Thank you, I believe it was. Now what I'd like for you to do is to step on over to my car and—" They heard the high raspy flutter of a Model T motor working hard and both of them looked up the road and saw a pair of headlamps closing in.

The runabout slowed and its brakes screeched and the car halted and then lurched against the sudden application of its hand break. Bob Baker stepped down from the car without cutting off the motor. He held a Winchester carbine in one hand.

J. R. Merritt said, "Well *hey* now, Bob, I'm damn glad you made it. Your boys here were—"

Bob Baker stepped past him without a glance, his eyes on John Ashley. He looked like a man in a bad waking dream. He stood before John Ashley and held a hand up in front of him and said, "Remember this?"

John Ashley saw that he was holding a rifle cartridge. He grinned. "Got my message, hey? But damn, Bobby, I sent that thing—when?— a year ago? I like to died of old age waitin for you to come out to the Glades for the other one."

Without taking his eyes off him Bob Baker slipped the round into the Winchester and levered it home and held the carbine pointed at him from the hip.

The deputies backed away from John Ashley and glanced at J. R. Merritt, who looked on and said nothing. In the sideglow of headlamps and flashlights Bob Baker's face looked as hard and bloodless as barked pine. His eyes seemed fixed on something more than John Ashley, something no man else could see but which John Ashley believed he could smell. A faint odor of rage undercut by fear. It was the smell of one more victory over this man who could never beat him.

He grinned. "You gonna shoot me, Bobby? In front of all these witnesses and with my hands locked behind my back? I dont reckon. But tell you what: you just wait for me. I'll break out soon enough and come see you. You know I will. Maybe by then you'll find you a pair of balls. Your wife told me she'll be glad of it when you do." He laughed in Bob Baker's face.

And got the surprise of his life when Bob Baker shot him in the heart.

As John Ashley went sprawling back Hanford Mobley screamed and kicked at Baker and Deputy Wiggins shot him in the throat and blood jumped off Hanford's neck as Clarence and Ray Lynn stood agape and then the darkness detonated into sparking blasts of gunfire and every prisoner went down in the fusillade and the shooters stepped up to the fallen men and shot them repeatedly and then ceased.

They stood for a time in deep silence and the rising haze of gun-smoke. Then Bob Baker went to John Ashley and squatted beside him and none saw what he did but every man of them knew. Then he stood and his hand went to his pocket and he looked around at them all and they looked back at him mutely.

He went to his car and got in and turned it around and drove away into the darkness.

And behind him seven policemen drew together and even though no living soul could overhear they conversed in whispers.

TWENTY-EIGHT

The Liars Club

THE FIRST ANYBODY HEARD ABOUT WHAT HAPPENED WAS WHEN A
coupla Sebastian boys named Miller and Davis come tearing into
town in their car late one Saturday night hollering that the cops
had captured the Ashley Gang out at Sebastian Bridge. Folk was standing out in the street jabbering about the news when here come the
High Sheriff J.R. Merritt to tell them his deputies had killed John
Ashley and three of his gang when they tried to resist arrest. Some
people cussed at the news and some cheered and said it was about
time somebody killed that whole bunch of lowdown outlaws. Sheriff
Merritt picked out six men to serve as a coroner's jury and they got
in cars and all went out to the bridge. The way we heard the story,
when the jury got there the dead men were all neatly laid out next to
the road. The jury had their official look at them and then the bodies
were stacked in a car and driven to the Fee Hardware and Mortuary
in Fort Pierce. It was the middle of the night when they got there but
the news had traveled ahead by telephone and they say it was a good-
sized crowd waiting on them. The cops laid the bodies on the sidewalk
so everybody could have a good look. The undertaker, W.I. Fee,
showed up early that Sunday morning and had the bodies taken inside
and by that afternoon he'd embalmed all four.

The news just flew up and down the coast. That afternoon Jack
Middleton came into Fort Pierce on the train from Jacksonville and
claimed the body of his brother Clarence. Ma and Bill Ashley came

with the elder Mobleys to take home the bodies of John and Hanford. When they were told Ray Lynn had no known kin and would go in a pauper's grave Ma Ashley said no he would not, he could be buried in the graveyard at Twin Oaks. Some who were there and saw her said she looked to be a hundred years old.

The bodies were in the ground by the time of the inquest three days later. The day before the inquest J.R. Merritt was elected to remain sheriff of St. Lucie County for another two years—despite the rumor going around that the Miller and Davis boys had seen John Ashley and his men under arrest and handcuffed at the Sebastian Bridge and it might be the police had executed them in cold blood. The lawmen who'd been at the scene refused to talk to reporters about the rumor and they hired lawyers to represent them at the inquest. They say when Ma Ashley heard the rumor she cussed the cops for murderers with badges and hired a lawyer named Alto L. Adams to attend the inquest and make sure some important questions got asked.

The presiding judge was Angus Sumner and the first witness was undertaker W.I. Fee. One of the first questions Adams asked him was if he had seen any marks on the dead men's wrists, especially marks that might of been made by handcuffs. Fee said he hadnt seen any such a thing. They say the undertaker was sweating bullets and kept licking his lips and looking over at the seven cops who never took their eyes off him the whole time he was testifying. They say the judge didnt seem too pleased with Adams' line of questioning but the jury looked mighty interested.

Then the Miller and Davis boys took their turns on the stand and both of them testified under oath that they'd seen the four bandits under arrest and with their hands cuffed. No amount of badgering by either of the two lawyers for the cops could make either one change a word of their story. The coroner's jurymen looked to be hanging on every word of the boys' testimony. None of them had seen any marks on the men's wrists when they went to the bridge, but like one of them said later, it had been dark and none of them had had reason to look very closely at the men's wrists anyway. When Adams made a motion to have the bodies exhumed so they could be examined for handcuff marks, several of the jurymen nodded like they thought that was a fine idea.

The judge didnt think so. He said the question of whether the jurymen had seen marks on the dead men's wrists when they went to the bridge to view the bodies now made them material witnesses and so they couldnt serve as impartial jurors. He disbanded the jury and said he would impanel a new one and hold another inquest in three days.

And thats exactly what he did. The new inquest took place on the following Saturday and this time the cops took the stand, all seven of them in their turn, and every one of them said he had shot in self-defense when the prisoners—who were not handcuffed and probably acting on a secret signal from John Ashley—all made a try for their guns at the same time. After all the testimony had been given, the coroner's jury reached a unanimous decision of justifiable homicide.

Some folk couldnt believe it. Some still dont. The suspicions about what happened on the Sebastian River Bridge that night of November first, nineteen and twenty-four, will probably never go away. Hell, our own Liars Club been arguing about it all our lives, and some of us side with the cops' version and some with the Ashleys'. Ever few years one local newspaper or another will bring up the story of the Ashley Gang but they dont say anything we aint heard a hundred times before.

One more thing. Before John Ashley's body was in the ground a week there were stories going around that when his body got to the undertaker's it was missing its glass eye. Everybody knew somebody who claimed to know somebody who'd seen the body laying in front of the undertaker's and seen that the eye was missing, but nobody ever said they'd seen so with their own two eyes. The undertaker said the eye was in place when he did the embalming, but some say he was too scared to tell the truth, which is that one of the cops took it and gave it to Bobby Baker, who'd always said he meant to have it. But Bobby always denied that anybody'd given him the eye and said the only way he ever wanted to have it was if he could of taken off John Ashley himself. The Ashley family—what was left of it, Ma and Bill and the sisters—they all said the eye was buried with John, but how would they know unless they opened his eye to check and nobody saw them do it when they came for the body at the undertaker's. Maybe they checked for it before they buried him and it really was there. Or maybe, like some say, they were just trying to save face by not admitting that somebody got the best of John Ashley at the end by making off with his eye.

It's just one more thing the Liars Club been arguin about for years and years.

TWENTY-NINE

December 1924

A GUSTY GRAY EVENING OF UNSEASONABLE RAIN A FEW DAYS BE-
fore Christmas. He arrived home and parked the car under the
wide live oak to one side of the house and cut off the motor. The
rain pattered on the car roof as he buttoned his yellow rainslicker and
tugged down his hat.

He was just about to get out of the car when the passenger-side
door opened and a figure in sopping clothes and a black hat with a
wide downturned brim streaming with rainwater stood there holding
an army .45 pointed at him.

"Give me it." She coughed wetly several times—hacking so hard
the veins stood out on her neck.

It took him a moment to recognize her. He'd not seen her since
the raid on the Ashley whiskey camp when she sat against a tree with
blood staining her pantleg and running from her hair. That had been
not quite a year ago but she looked to have aged far beyond that. She
was obviously sick—perhaps with only a bad cold, although the cough
sounded bad enough to be consumptive. Her eyes were redly swollen.

"*Give* me it!" she said, and again fell to hacking, her eyes straining
on him, flooding with tears.

"Give you *what?*" he said. "And you best get that gun off me right
goddamn now." The tightness in his voice surprised and angered him.

She coughed wetly and leaned into the car and cocked the pistol.
"I didnt come all this way to listen to your bullshit," she said in a

strained rasp. "Give me it or I'll put one in your brainpan and you best fucken believe I mean it."

"Now just hold on," he said, raising his hands slightly, palms out. He shifted his weight imperceptibly, readying himself. "What makes you think *I* got it? I wasnt even there. Everybody knows that."

"*You* got it," she said. "I *know* you do." She leaned closer and put the muzzle within inches of his eye. "Now give—"

Another hacking fit befell her and she sagged under its force and her eyes lost focus and in that instant he snatched and twisted her wrist and took the gun from her and grabbed her by the shirtfront and the shirt ripped as he pulled her forward onto the car seat and off her feet and her hat fell away and her hair spilled onto the car seat as he wrestled her around onto her back. She kicked and struggled to right herself but he pinned her under his weight with one hand and pressed the pistol muzzle to her cheekbone just under her eye.

"You sorry bitch!" he said. "Point a gun at me! I ought blow your brains out."

"Give me . . . it," she said, sickly breathless, coughing and half-choking, mucus coursing from her nose, her hands weakly pushing at his flexed arm pinioning her. "*Give* me."

"I aint *got* it!" His voice sounded made of tin.

"*Liar!*" she rasped. "Black liar! I *know* they gave it to you, I *know* it! You dont—" She gagged on mucus, her face darkening, and for a moment he thought she might strangle to death. But she managed a deep rattling breath and said, "Give me it or kill me, you son of a bitch—or I'll kill you, I swear I will. I'll kill you if I got to"—she hacked, choked, rasped on—"if I got to crawl on my hands and knees through hell." She seemed entirely indifferent to the pistol muzzle against her face.

Her breasts were heaving and one was almost wholly exposed where her shirt had torn. Fixed on his face, her eyes burned redly in their dark hollows. "It's all of him left in the world, you low bastard. It belongs to *me*. Give . . . me . . . *it*."

She struggled in his grip with a sudden rush of strength and it was all he could do to hold her down.

"God damn, woman, you wanna get shot?" he said. She craned her head forward and tried to bite his arm. He cursed and hit her in the mouth with the gun butt and split her lip against her teeth and her strength swelled in her fury and she tried to spit blood up in his face and then she was choking again and fell back and turned her head aside and hacked up bile and mucus onto the car seat. She gasped as someone drowning. "Give . . . me . . . it," she managed. "Give me it. . . ."

She looked up at him with her burning eyes and he saw that she was not even a little bit afraid, not of anything. Not of him, not of pain, not of dying. Not of any truth or trial in the world.

And he knew that was not true of himself. And felt his chest tighten with an awful familiarity. Felt his own breath hard to draw.

"You're crazy," he said. "You're crazy as he was."

But he knew it was as she'd said: he would have to give it to her or he would have to kill her.

Oh hell, he thought. *Oh hell.*

He drew away from her and she scrabbled to her knees on the car seat and turned her wild face to him as he probed under his slicker and into his vest pocket and took out the watch and fob. He had never shown it to anyone for fear of the questions it would raise—and so had not derived the pleasure from its possession he thought he would, the pleasure he thought was his due.

She looked on it and her face fell. She was crying softly and could not take her eyes off it as he removed it from the chain and gave it to her. She cupped it in her hand and smiled on it through her tears.

And then closed her hand tightly around it and lashed the fist into Bob Baker's mouth with all her weight behind it.

The punch snapped his head back and he felt a top tooth give and before he could recover she was out of the car and running hatless into the ghostly twilit rain and he saw her vanish into the pines.

An hour later the world was gone dark and the rain was falling hard again. The windows of Bob Baker's house showed warmly yellow and his wife and daughters were within and waiting for him to come home.

And all the while he yet sat in the car and stared into the rainy blackness as though he might descry some wild thing lying in wait, watching him and grinning at the hard beating of his heart.

▓ Perennial

Books by James C. Blake:

WILDWOOD BOYS
ISBN 0-388-097749-4 (hardcover)

From the raw clay of historical fact, Blake has sculpted a powerful novel telling the heroic and unsettling saga of "Bloody Bill" Anderson, a fearsome guerilla captain of a band of Kansas "redlegs."

"Blake's prose is a coarse, gritty, and seamless poetry that fistfights and breaks the law and takes no prisoners." —*Milwaukee Journal Sentinel*

RED GRASS RIVER
ISBN 0-380-79242-7 (paperback)

The legend of two men: one a criminal, a fold hero, a man of intense passions and his family's brightest star; the other a lawman born of lawmen, a husband and father, a symbol of a community thriving. As youths, they were close companions. As men, they were most bitter adversaries.

"A strikingly noir historical western and an inventive addition to Blake's work." —*Publishers Weekly*

BORDERLANDS
ISBN 0-380-79485-3 (paperback)

In this extraordinary collection of short fiction we journey from the nineteenth century Mexican frontier to the borderlands of the present day in eight unforgettable tales of love, vengeance, and violence.

"A wonderful story, brutal and thought-provoking, the work of a master story-teller and a master writer not afraid to take chances with his material." —*El Paso Herald-Post*

Available wherever books are sold, or call 1-800-331-3761 to order.